Marshall's Law

all the best,
Denise A. Agnew

Other Books by Denise A. Agnew

Midnight Rose

Dangerous Intentions

Treacherous Wishes

Love From the Ashes

All I Want for Christmas

Forevermore

Bridge through the Mist

Treble Heart Books
1284 Overlook Dr.
Sierra Vista, AZ 85635-5512
http://www.trebleheartbooks.com

ISBN:

Acknowledgements

To Dick Rosengreen, Joe Yarina, and Terrance Agnew for weapons information.

Marshall's Law

Denise A. Agnew

Treble Heart Books

Dedication

To my own "Brennan," Terrance Brennan Agnew.

Chapter 1

Thunder roared overhead and startled Dana Cummings as she drove her Taurus into the long driveway of Aunt Lucille's old Victorian home.

Sheet lightning arched through the clouds surrounding the mountain town of Macon, Wyoming. Dana held back a vehement curse as a hard gust slammed against the car. Trepidation tightened her arm and leg muscles. Wind had buffeted her vehicle for the last few miles. Towering thunderheads gathered overhead, deepening to purple and black mixed with green.

"Not exactly an appetizing sight."

Good thing no one had accompanied her on this road trip. They would think she'd lost every brain cell in her possession. Whenever something unpleasant threatened, like a tooth extraction or an impending visit to the Motor Vehicle Department, Dana broke into self-chatter that had others looking askance at her.

She took a firmer grip on the steering wheel as wind tried to shove the car to one side of the dirt driveway. Muttering another choice obscenity, she snail-crawled the car up to the house.

Tall ponderosa pines surrounded the home, guarding the building like towering sentinels. "Perfect atmosphere for a haunting."

Static sizzled over the radio. "Well, folks," the announcer said, "This is Charlie at WKNR and the big one seems to be hitting us right now. Conditions are ripe for a tornado. Please stay tuned to this station for more information. Keep your eyes on the skies with WKNR."

"Lovely." Dana sighed. "Figures. Perfect. Just perfect."

Lightning illuminated the darkening sky, and thunder crashed.

Dana winced. "Whoa."

Her reaction seemed to introduce the storm's opening fury. Clouds burst, sending horizontal rain slashing across the windshield. Nothing like a good old fashioned frog-strangler storm in August.

The DJ came on again. "Received a—"

Static broke his voice.

"Too many calls at present. Just keep tuned for updates. If you hear—"

Static obscured the man's voice.

Turning the dial, she looked for another radio station and received nothing but white noise.

"Probably isn't another station in this itsy bitsy town." She glanced at the house and noted the windows were dark. Aunt Lucille had said she'd be home, but there was no sign of her station wagon.

Instead, the place looked scary and empty. Like something she'd write about.

Think you could settle in Macon long enough to find more inspiration for another horror novel? Like Stephen King, you could start writing most of your novels set in a particular state like Wyoming. The Macon Horror. Yeah, that's it. No. The Macon Demon. The Macon Menace. Ugh. How completely unoriginal and banal.

"Fat chance in hell."

So much for vacation optimism.

Aunt Lucille had moved into the Victorian house three months ago and had heard strange noises emanating from the basement. Weird and crazy sounds.

Dana hadn't known whether to believe her aunt or not, and that had precipitated this trip as much as other annoying factors.

Of course, if Aunt Lucille did have a ghost in her house, it might spark some intriguing ideas for the novel Dana had started a couple months back. Maybe. Hopefully.

What more could she ask for?

A good tumble with a gorgeous man.

"Shut up," she said to her subconscious.

Dana turned off the ignition and the Taurus sputtered, then died.

Patting the dashboard, she smiled grimly. "I hope to you were just coughing bugs out of the grill, Bertha."

As the unrelenting storm pounded the car, Dana decided she would make a mad dash for the front door. She scrambled out of the car. Rain soaked through her short denim jacket and T-shirt. Lightning rammed across the sky. She flinched as thunder rattled her nerves.

Good. She'd made it to the porch intact. Sighing in relief, she grasped the gold ring suspended on a chain around her neck. She fingered her father's gold college ring and looked into the dull blue glass facets. How many times had she touched this jewelry and polished it for luck like a superstitious person rubbed a bald man's head?

As she shook water out of her hair, she rang the doorbell. Several moments passed. Lucille didn't answer. Dana tried knocking on the door and ringing the doorbell again. Nothing. She shivered. Right now a hot tub and a steaming cup of green tea sounded great.

"A hot tub, a cup of tea, and a sizzling man."

Now wouldn't that be a nice combination? She smiled.

Thunder cracked overhead. She put her hands over her ears and squeezed her eyes shut. Rain slanted onto the porch, splattering her shoes. She let her hands drop from her ears.

"Oh, God." Funnel clouds, ripe to create havoc, lowered over Macon. "This is not good."

Dana knew what she had to do. Get inside to the basement. She remembered Aunt Lucille kept a spare key hidden inside the garden shed.

More rain landed on her legs and shoes. She had to take shelter. If a tornado came, she couldn't afford to be caught in the open.

"It's now or never."

She ran down the steps and rounded the left side of the house to the detached garage. To her surprise, Aunt Lucille's garage door was open about three inches. Yanking it up, Dana rushed inside the dim interior. Her aunt's station wagon sat inside.

"What on earth?" Mild panic, supplied by the storm lashing outside, surged into Dana's system. "If Lucille's car is here—"

A burst of light and slashing thunder heralded a close hit that almost vaulted her out of her shoes. She gave a startled shriek. Leaving the garage, she ran toward the shed just behind the garage.

She'd gone three steps when a branch ripped from a pine near her and sailed through the air.

Dana had a few seconds to react. She lunged sideways. Not good enough. The limb caught her across the top of the shoulders and the back of her head. Pain slammed through her and as she fell face first onto the wet pine needles, her breath whooshing out of her in a rush. She gasped for air and blackness threatened. Struggling for oxygen, she managed to suck air into her lungs. She groaned, reaching for consciousness and the awareness of rough ground beneath her cheek. Dana's fingers dug into the earth as she pulled herself up on her hands and knees and shook her head to clear the fuzziness. Stumbling to her feet, she staggered toward the garden shed. She couldn't afford to pass out now.

She yanked open the door and reached inside where the light toggle should be. Flicking the switch up she got—nothing. Electricity out. Another terrific crash of thunder made her start. She fumbled around trying to prop the door open. If she couldn't see, how would she find the little metal key holder Aunt Lucille promised to leave inside the door? Touching a metal garden shed while lightning streaked overhead wasn't exactly a good idea.

Seconds later, she found the key holder and let out a hoot. "Hot damn!"

She left the shed, slammed the door, then ran toward the back of the house. Aunt Lucille had said the key opened the back door only. Not only did Dana need to take shelter, but if something had happened to Aunt Lucille, she had to get inside and help her. Dana knew she'd never forgive herself if she didn't check on her aunt.

Shaking off dire thoughts, she pulled open the screen door and jammed the key in the lock. For a moment it wouldn't go all the way in and she made an impatient noise. "Come on, come on, come on." She twisted the handle. It wouldn't budge. She tried pulling the key out of the doorknob. It came out halfway then stuck. She gave the key another yank and it slid from the doorknob, and took a healthy chunk of the skin on her index finger along with it. "Ow!"

Pain lanced through her right hand. Blood seeped from the side of the offended digit.

"Sheriff's Department! Hold it right there!"

Another yelp erupted from Dana as her heart slammed into her throat. She whirled around. "What the…."

A large, mean-looking dude stood several feet away, leveling a gun at her. He held the weapon in his right hand, his left hand supporting his right wrist. His stance, slightly bent at the knees, suggested law enforcement. His attire did not.

Water dripped off the man's tan baseball cap and straight into his just-below-the-collar length dark hair. His red-checkered flannel shirt over a tight, dark T-shirt said lumberjack, and so did his slim-fitting jeans and brown boots. With a week's worth of beard and mustache on his face and a don't-mess-with-me scowl, he looked ready for anything. Including shooting her where she stood.

Now that she thought about it, she'd been A-number-one stupid for whirling around like that. He could have gotten trigger-happy and shot her butt off.

Her hands went up. "Hey, wait a minute—"

"Don't move." His words came like bullets fired without mercy. "What do you think you're doing, breaking into this house?"

Fear slid into instant hacked-off and ready to rumble. She'd about had enough of today. She glared at him. "Trying to get inside before I drown. What does it look like? In case you haven't noticed, it's raining like Beelzebub, and it looks like a tornado—"

The warning siren went off, wailing over her words. Fright rocketed through her. Any minute now she'd either be sucked up by a tornado or arrested by this weird-looking lawman. She could see the headlines now. Best-selling horror novelist inhaled by tornado. The body has yet to be found. Or best-selling horror novelist's fame cut short by out-of-control policeman in little Wyoming town.

The so-called lawman uttered a curse and ran toward her. "Get in the house now!"

"But—"

"Don't have time to argue!" He ran onto the small porch and stuffed the gun back into a shoulder holster under his lumberjack flannel. "Get inside!"

"It won't open. That's what I was trying to do when you showed up and scared me half to death."

Sending her a searing, I-don't-give-flying-flip look, he jiggled the doorknob, then grabbed the key out of her hand when she held it out to him. He tried jamming the key in the lock. "This isn't the right key. Stand back."

He growled as he took a swift kick at the door and it flew open, sailing with a tremendous bang against the wall. Before she could protest, he grabbed her right arm and shoved her inside. He latched onto her arm again. "Gotta take shelter."

"The basement?"

"The basement."

He tugged her through the utility room and into the living room. One set of stairs led upstairs, the other down. She went down the steps ahead of him. On the carpeted stairs she almost lost her footing and overcorrected as she leaned back.

He caught her arms to steady her. "Watch out! Hurry up!"

"I am hurrying!" Dana plunged down the steps and almost fell forward into the basement.

"The bathroom!" He grabbed her hand and raced passed the pool table, the ping-pong table, and the bar.

As they passed a king size, heart-shaped bed, Dana rammed her toe into one of the legs, and as pain zipped through her she let out a howl. She hopped on one foot. "Damn it all to hell!"

Law Man pulled her into the tiny bathroom and shoved her toward the bathtub. "Get in."

She held back. "We need the mattress as a shield."

"No time and its too big. Won't fit through the door."

A roaring sound echoed overhead and Dana let out a gasp. "Oh, God. It's coming. It's coming." For a few seconds stark terror arched through her, and she linked gazes with the man. His dark, chocolate eyes registered that same fear, then cleared into determination.

She hopped into the bathtub.

Before she could say a word, he climbed into the tub and stretched over her, his weight smashing her. She wanted to protest, but she knew he had a good reason for plastering himself to her like moss on a log.

Along her length Dana felt nothing but rock solid man. He covered her head with his arms and buried his face in her neck. As the roar above them increased, she felt a shudder ripple through his body and into hers. She thought she might suffocate.

His voice came harsh and rough. "Keep your eyes closed! Hang on to me!"

She followed the stranger's command, wound her arms around his trim waist, and held on with all her strength. Above them, the roar increased and Dana's heart hammered. Her ears popped and she couldn't get her breath.

Darkness swirled in front of her vision. Oh, damn. As the earth seemed to tremble all around them, she let the blessed blackness envelop her.

Chapter 2

Heat. Hardness. Warmth. Protection. A gentle touch along her cheek.

The weight pressing down on Dana lifted somewhat. She inhaled and caught blessed oxygen and a musk scent that teased her senses. Her arms remained wrapped around his waist. Convulsively, her fingers dug into hard muscle. It felt good to have an anchor in the swirling world. Her temples throbbed, and her neck ached. His rapid breath puffed against her ear. Something unyielding pressed against her side. His gun.

Someone cupped her face and Dana thought she felt a callused thumb caress her cheek.

"Hey, you all right?" A husky, rumbling voice prodded her into consciousness. "Come on, talk to me."

"Yeah," she croaked.

Anxiety mixed with her dazed state. Shudders rolled through her body. She held back a moan as she opened her eyes to semi-darkness. An amalgamation of anger and worry mingled in the depths of his eyes. His hair, still soaked, dripped water onto her face. She swiped at the tickling liquid and his penetrating gaze narrowed again. He brushed his fingers over the other side of her neck and held up fingers smeared with blood.

"You're bleeding. Where are you hurt?" he asked sharply, and levered himself away from her. He climbed out of the tub and knelt next to it as she sat up.

"I'm fine."

He tore off some toilet paper and wiped his hands.

Then she remembered. "Aunt Lucille!"

"Easy. Take it easy."

Mortification.

She'd wanted to be brave, and, instead she'd wimped out under the strain. Very heroine like. *Put that in a book, why don'tcha?*

"We're alive." Dana looked around the bathroom and realized it remained intact. "We've got to look for my aunt."

She vaulted over the side of the tub and ran for the door, the big man following close behind. She rushed up the stairs, calling her aunt's name. As they searched the house looking in each room, Dana's stomach tumbled. If anything had happened to Aunt Lucille, she didn't know what she'd do.

"I don't think she's here," the man said as they checked the bedrooms.

"And how do you know my aunt isn't here? Her station wagon is in the garage. And she was expecting me this afternoon."

"I don't know. I came to check on Lucille and warn her to watch out for the weather. That's when I saw your car."

"And you automatically assumed a burglar was trying to get into the house?"

One corner of his mouth lifted in a half smile. "No ma'am. Not until I saw the shed door open and heard someone cursing and rattling the back door. Besides, she doesn't use that kind of language."

She wanted to make another scathing comment, but realized she didn't have one in her ammunition right now. Not only that, this man may have saved her life. There was no reason to get snippy with him. Fear made her agitated and uneasy.

Dana looked around the formal living room with Lucille's collection of never-sat-in Chippendale furniture. A red brick, double-sided fireplace resided between the formal area and the family room. The family room sported a cozy, sagging chintz sofa and loveseat. Two cracked windows graced the area and the carpet was a tad wet under the windows.

Once they'd surveyed the entire house and found no sign of Lucille, Dana felt a wild rush of relief barrel through her system that she hadn't found her aunt injured or worse. A tight, odd trembling in her body overcame her, and she couldn't remember feeling this weak in a long time. Not since Daddy had died all those years ago.

The man's gaze assessed her. "You're shaking." He put his hand on the side of her neck and held his fingers there. "Fast pulse. Are you going to pass out on me again?"

"Of course not."

"I think you're in shock and don't realize it. You're off to the hospital for an examination."

"I don't need a hospital. I'm perfectly fine."

"Then where is all the blood coming from? It sure isn't me." He reached for her hand and looked at the index finger she'd gouged with the key. His tight, warm grip and stern expression said no nonsense. "You've cut your finger."

An irrational wave of anger went through her. "No? You think?"

He caught and held her gaze with an intense, overwhelming attention. She took in his features and everything about him she'd missed before. He looked about thirty-five or thirty-six. Maybe six feet tall and one hundred ninety pounds of muscle. His long hair waved high off his forehead and back from his face. His beard and mustache was trimmed close to his face.

"Something wrong?" he asked.

"You sure don't look like a man of the law."

"Yeah? And what exactly do you think the law should look like?"

Embarrassed that she'd stared at him for so long, she shrugged. "Sorry. Forget I said anything."

Mister tall, dark, and silent led her past the huge gourmet kitchen toward the back of the house. Rain had seeped under the door and soaked the rug at the utility room back door, and their shoes made squelching noises as they walked.

His cynical frown remained. "You have identification on you, ma'am?"

"It's in the car."

"You usually leave your purse in the car?"

"No. My fanny pack is—what are you looking at?"

"You're not wearing your fanny pack on your fanny." His gaze centered on her jean-clad butt for longer than necessary, and to her complete surprise a grin about three miles wide stretched his mouth. A completely unrepentant male grin.

She gave him a dirty look. "I'm Dana Cummings and Lucille Maxine Metcalf is my aunt. My mother is Ethena Cummings, her sister."

His 'yeah right' expression didn't ease one iota. "As soon as we get to your car, you can prove it to me."

As they stepped onto the porch, Dana realized the rain had stopped and the sky had started to clear. A dramatic rainbow arched over innocent-looking clouds. The storm had moved away. Pine tree limbs littered the ground and deep puddles of water attested to the furious soaking.

She took a deep breath and a tickling in the back of her throat threatened a cough. Determined not to be a weakling, she straightened. "Looks like the place is pretty unscathed for a tornado."

"Might have passed overhead without touching down." He glanced around. "Or it might have plowed through some houses and forest farther down the road. Let's hope not."

Thunder rolled low in the west, reminding her of the noise the tornado had made. "It really did sound like a train."

The lawman paused and looked down at her. "You've never been in a tornado before?"

Dana shook her head. "Never. Bad storms, of course, but nothing like this. I saw the green clouds, and I knew something was up."

As she stared back at him, caught in the concentration in his eyes, the darkness seemed to ease.

Despite his unbreakable grip on her arm, his touch gentled and so did his gaze. "You're trembling."

Deep inside her a sensation unfurled, like a sweet, plucking, swirling delight in her stomach. She shoved it back, afraid of what the odd sensation meant. What she feared it meant. "Yeah, well, it isn't everyday I get waterlogged, attacked by a madman claiming to be a police officer, crammed into a tub, and almost eaten by a tornado."

One of his dark brows twitched. "The madman has a name. Brennan Marshall."

She smiled uncontrollably. "Marshall, eh? Isn't that convenient? Howdy, Marshall." The ridiculousness of the situation hit her. "It's not every day I get to snuggle up to a lumberjack in a bathtub."

She knew the words sounded flirtatious, but they'd slipped from her lips before she could stop them. *Way to go. Your irreverent tongue will get you arrested for sure.*

They headed back toward Bertha.

"Thank you, Lord," she said when she saw only a couple a fallen branches lying over the hood of her car. Next to Bertha sat a white Grande Cherokee, emblazoned on the side with a gold star declaring it Cedar County Sheriff's Department.

Suddenly, she felt exhausted. The tension of the storm and the thought of what had almost happened caught up to her. To her chagrin, the tickle in the back of her throat changed to an unstoppable cough. She cleared her throat, but it came on without remorse, settling in to a hollow, hacking sound that vibrated her lungs and made her gasp for air.

"What the—" Marshall put his arm around her as she bent over slightly and let the cough have its way with her. "Are you all right?"

"Recovering from—" she gasped. "Pneumonia. Four weeks back."

Something that looked almost like regret covered his face, and a muscle twitched in his jaw. "No wonder you're shaky. Come on, you're going to the hospital."

She cleared her throat. "I'm not. This is silly. I thought you were ready to throw me in the clink for breaking and entering."

"Not until after a doctor says you aren't going to drop dead in my custody."

"Gee, thanks." She rubbed the back of her aching neck and her hand came away tinged with blood. "Oh, man. I think I know now where that blood was coming from. I guess that branch did some damage."

"What branch?"

"The one that clobbered me on the way to the garden shed."

Marshall's expression hardened. "Lean against the Taurus while I get the first aid kit and call for an ambulance."

"No ambulance. I've got to find my aunt."

He stopped on the way to the SUV and glowered.

She licked her dry lips. "Please. If anything's happened to her, it'll be my fault. Look, if I fall over dead in the next few minutes, I won't blame you."

Then he did something she didn't expect. It started with a twinkle that lit his eyes and transfused his face for a nanosecond with something that looked like humor. Mister poker face actually grinned.

He turned toward his Cherokee before the full impact of that devastating smile materialized. Had she imagined it? Had the whack on the head pulverized her brain? He'd looked—dare she think it—endearing? Human. Sorta cute. No. Sorta handsome.

That bizarre little fluttering went off in her stomach again, and ignoring it did no good.

She heard him talking on his police radio, but he didn't ask for an ambulance, thank God. Dana stared in fascination at the way the T-shirt and flannel covered his impressive, wide shoulders. His slim hips and sculpted tight butt encased in jeans caught her attention next.

She wiped the blood off on her jeans. "Face it, you've lost it, Dana. You're actually lying in a coma in the hospital hallucinating."

He rummaged in the SUV. "What?"

"Never mind."

As he marched toward her, she saw his pooh face had returned. Dana had the almost uncontrollable urge to stick her tongue out and mist him with a huge raspberry. Instead, she wrinkled her nose. "So are you arresting me or what? Because if you aren't, I'd like to find my aunt."

He put the first aid kit on the hood of her car and searched inside. "Please turn around and lift your hair."

"What's this? A new search procedure?"

Marshall's deep sigh told her she'd pushed the edge, so she turned as commanded. "Anyone ever tell you that you've got a smart mouth?"

Amused rather than angry, she held up her hair. "My agent." She paused as he used gauze to clean the wound. "And my mother." He touched something that stung like mad. She sucked in a breath. "And my friends." A few seconds later she said, "Maybe the mailman…once."

"Humph." He dabbed at her wound. "Doesn't look too bad. A small cut right at the back of your neck." She felt him apply gauze and tape. "That'll hold you for now. You're still going to the hospital."

Dana swung around. "I'm finding out what happened to my aunt first."

The stubborn set of his jaw told her she'd pressed him as far as he'd go on the issue.

She put her hands on her hips. "I haven't seen your identification, either and you expect me to just roll over and accept your—"

"I'm off duty right now." He held up a hand to stop her tirade, reached inside his back pocket and pulled out a badge and I.D. card.

After scrutinizing the evidence, she handed it back to him.

"Satisfied?" he asked.

"No. I won't be satisfied until I know where Aunt Lucille is."

"Agreed. We have to find her." His gaze narrowed. He snapped the first aid kit shut and started toward his car. "Please get that identification I asked for, ma'am."

She opened her car and fumbled in her fanny pack for her wallet while he spoke on the radio. When he came back she handed him her driver's license.

After perusing the license, he called the dispatcher again. While he waited to see if she qualified as an escaped convict, bank robber or a serial killer, Dana crossed her arms and tapped her foot on the wet ground. Maybe she'd give Aunt Lucille that raspberry when she found her safe and sound. The fact that Marshall knew Aunt Lucille didn't mean much. In a town as small as this, everyone probably knew the sheriff's deputies.

She decided she'd check Bertha for damage and when she tried to start the Taurus it wouldn't even sputter. "Oh, great."

Marshall gestured at her to come to him, his expression worried. "A boy has fallen into a swollen river down the road."

As he started to turn away, she trotted toward him, fanny pack in hand. "My car won't start. Can I come with you?"

He hesitated a second, then nodded. "All right. Hurry."

She'd barely buckled her seatbelt when he sent the car flying down the driveway. He slammed on the brakes at the end of the driveway, checked both ways, and then roared down the street. He snapped on the lights and siren.

Dana grabbed at the dashboard as the car bounced over a huge dip in the road. She forgot the throb in her finger, the ache at the back of her neck and her pounding head. A boy's life was in jeopardy.

As they sailed down the road, she took covert glances at Marshall's profile. When she'd first seen him, he'd looked mean. Of course, now that he didn't have a gun pointed at her, it made him less threatening.

She realized he'd lost his baseball cap somewhere during the tornado and she hadn't seen it since. His hair had almost dried into luxurious, shiny dark brown waves that curled over the collar of his shirt. His long lashes gave new meaning to the word sinful, turning his eyes from scare-me-silly to gorgeous-beyond-belief.

No! She couldn't afford to find anything about him intriguing, least of all thinking he had to-die-for eyes. *Nope. Nada. I don't even like him. He's a bit arrogant. Not even good looking. Okay, sort of good looking. Mildly attractive.*

Enough!

She realized she'd popped her lid. Everyone knew that during a crisis or near disaster heightened emotions could do funny things to perceptions. So she chalked up her pseudo attraction to this big cop as just that—heightened emotions.

Seconds later, they came to a turnoff where the trees thinned and she could see two women standing at the river bank. Marshall swung the vehicle off the road and careened over bushes and ruts as he went to the edge of the rampaging river.

He jammed on the brakes so hard the back wheels fishtailed in the mud. "Stay in the car."

He slammed the vehicle into park, opened his door and jumped out. The young blonde at the side of the road grabbed his arm, babbling and gesturing all the while. Marshall peeled the woman's hands away and ran toward the river.

Dana left the SUV and trotted along in his wake. Then she saw the boy and her heart made a sickening jolt. "Oh, no."

The boy clung to the rock in the middle the river, his face ashen with shock or fear. He couldn't have been more than ten. How much longer could the child hold onto the rock? Dana's entire body stiffened with apprehension.

A woman of about forty-five, her hair matted and her clothes covered in mud, slumped down near the river bank. The blonde woman sobbed non-stop.

Marshall flung off his flannel shirt, boots, and holster and with a quick leap, dove into the rushing water.

"He'll never get him in time. Tommy is already losing his grip," the older woman said.

The blonde choked back a strangled sound.

"No. He'll get him," Dana said. He'd get the boy to safety if it were the last thing he'd ever do. How she knew this, she couldn't say. "He'll save him."

The older woman shivered. "He's got to." She swallowed hard. "I warned Tommy to stay away from the river. We stopped during the storm and took shelter in the ditch. When the storm was over the car wouldn't start. He wandered to the river edge while we called for a tow."

Dana nodded. "It'll be all right."

Dana's breath snagged in her throat as Marshall swam with powerful strokes toward the boy. Then, just as Marshall reached the rock, the boy slipped and the water swallowed him up.

The blonde screamed. "Tommy!"

ment, he stopped next to the SUV and flung his flannel shirt into the back seat.

Throwing her a glance that burned right through her, he stripped off the T-shirt and tossed it in the back seat. In one glance he conveyed cocky sureness with something that looked like…nah…couldn't be. Yep, there it was. Flirtatiousness and frankness. Her jaw dropped for a second, then she clamped her mouth shut.

"Hop in the car," he said.

Just before she moved around to the passenger side of the car, she saw amazing muscles. Hard, carved arms. The kind of brute force that spoke of working the land rather than using a weight set. A generous amount of dark hair sprinkled around his pectorals and down his flat stomach.

"Heaven help me," she said.

"What?"

"Nothing."

Okay. So he's got a great bod. Big deal.

One hundred percent satisfied with that assessment, she sat back in her seat and tried not to wonder when he'd become heroic, intriguing and too mouth-watering for his own good.

Marshall Street, named after Brennan's great grandfather, had flooded almost up to the middle of the tires on the SUV. As Marshall eased the vehicle back into the minimal traffic on Main Street, he gave his temporary companion a thorough look-see through stealthy glances.

Marshall had never met a more irritating woman than Dana Cummings. Well, okay, maybe two other women. But he didn't have time or inclination to think about them right now.

Dana Sue Cummings according to her New Mexico driver's

license. Somehow, he knew if he started calling her Dana Sue, she'd hit him with that enormous, black leather fanny pack she'd strapped to her waist.

On second thought, Dana's jump-straight-into-the-fire attitude reminded him of Tabitha. Tabitha, the precocious nine-year-old daughter of his friend, Eric Dawes, almost drove Marshall nuts with her antics.

No, the craziness he felt around Dana came from a different source. He was highly annoyed with himself for feeling so attracted to a woman he'd just met.

The woman had infuriating written in every inch of her carrot top, shoulder-length hair, wispy bangs and hazel eyes. It didn't help that she possessed a killer body in a five-foot six-inch frame. He allowed a quick glance at her jean-clad form. Yeah, she might not be model beautiful, but that suited him fine.

Marshall had had it with bone-thin women with all the personality of a cucumber. This woman possessed curves in places a woman should have curves. From the first moment he'd been close enough to smell her delicate, fresh perfume, he'd found her irksome. *Irksome and driving me straight out of my ever lovin' mind.* A tight sensation centered in his gut.

Marshall slammed back the attraction. He couldn't let down either his guard or open his heart. Besides, his heart had disappeared long ago.

As the Grand Cherokee dipped into a huge puddle of water, his cab companion grabbed at the dashboard like a lifeline. He glanced at her disheveled state and worried look. Worried about what? The storm? Did she believe that he still considered her a breaking and entering suspect? Her license and other identification indicated no known priors or outstanding warrants. She hadn't tried to escape.

Yeah, Marshall. She just tried to argue you to death.

He understood her worry about her aunt, but he had a hunch

Lucille was fine, and there was a perfectly reasonable explanation for why she hadn't been at the house.

Marshall thought back to the strange things that had been happening at Lucille's house and wondered about the woman next to him. Deep inside, he didn't want to believe this doe-eyed, quick-tongued woman could be part of a plan to drive Lucille insane and away from her house.

When he'd first seen Dana Cummings trying to get into Lucille's house, he'd thought she had to be the prettiest burglar he'd ever seen. The tornado took away other thoughts when the siren had blasted a warning. Run now. Wonder later.

When she'd lain in the tub, and he knew she'd fainted, he'd seen everything about her in a heartbeat. He'd seen a little mole just under her right ear, high on her neck. Her nose had a small scar over the bridge, like a permanent line from glasses. Eyes that snapped with curiosity, fear, and anger in less than a minute had added a weird charm he'd never encountered in a woman. Uh-huh. Now he knew he'd lost it. Maybe he'd lost a brain cell or two when his favorite baseball cap had been sucked away by the wind.

Now that really pisses me off. Tabitha had given it to him last year for his birthday.

As he headed for the sheriff's department, he savored the unscathed area around them. "Doesn't look like the tornado touched down here."

Dana glanced over at him. "Are we going to the park to check out the damage?"

"No." He shifted his hands on the steering wheel and the SUV rolled to a stop at a traffic signal. "We're going to the sheriff's office first. It's either that or the hospital."

Dana straightened like someone had rammed a stick up her spine. "What kind of hospital? Are you having me committed?"

Marshall fought the urge to laugh. "Don't tempt me."

Dana sighed. "Has anyone ever told you that you have a rotten sense of humor, Marshall?"

"Probably at least two people. My sister and my brother." He paused for effect. "Maybe my dad on a bad day when he's feeling stubborn."

She made a soft noise. "Only when he's feeling stubborn?"

Marshall knew what she implied and chose to say nothing. He'd found silence drove many people insane. Instead, he grunted. She folded her arms, uttered another elaborate sigh, and shook her head.

The light turned green and he proceeded through the intersection. Marshall drove to Decatur Street, which ran alongside the sheriff's department. This small avenue hadn't seen pavement yet. Mud clung to the wheels of the vehicle as he inched down the narrow road.

After they turned into the parking lot, they exited the vehicle and headed for the double glass doors into the main lobby. Once inside he saw that several ceiling tiles lay in the empty reception area, including a large one that had landed on a small row of chairs against one wall.

Marshall moved farther into the room, his eyes widening as he surveyed the plaster that littered everything. A couple of deputies worked at cleaning up the mess. They paused long enough to greet Marshall.

Marshall led her back to his office. After they entered the office, she slumped into a chair in front of his desk. He grabbed a Pittsburgh Steelers cap from a table and plopped it on his head.

Dana wondered what town in its right mind allowed a police officer to wear a get up like this? Absurd. The whole situation reminded her of a madcap spoof of Mayberry mixed with L.A. Confidential.

As she looked at him, a strange tugging sensation moved inside her. An awakening. A curiosity. Something animal moved through him, and she sensed it like prey evading predator. His personality had a hold on her thoughts like a tenacious tiger devouring a meal. Tension grew between her shoulder blades and she shifted in her chair. Her movement didn't attract his attention.

Dana watched him shuffle papers and rearrange desk items, a black pencil cup with a pink desk blotter. You have to be kidding. A girly girl blotter. What was that all about?

Now that she thought about it, who would ask him? He could be wearing clown pants and Groucho Marx glasses, mustache, and nose, and no one would squeak in his general direction. A man like this one, with a defiant tilt to the head and scorching eyes, would smash them like a maniacal monster from a B-movie. No, not a B-movie. A harmless looking critter that metamorphosed into a serious, in-your-face beast. They'd be terrified. Ready to pee their pants.

She, on the other hand, refused to frighten.

Right, Dana. Well, at least she wouldn't give him the satisfaction of knowing he made her uncomfortable. She inhaled, gathering courage. Without his presence near, she took a cleansing breath. This man had turned to her with gun drawn, a bite-me scowl that would eat through acid. Then he'd saved her life.

He left the desk to reach for the coffee carafe, not even looking in her direction. He filled a gargantuan cream-colored mug that held about three cups worth of liquid. Seconds later, the double-wide coffee mug came to rest on the desk in front of her, attached to a broad, huge hand with thick fingers. A bruiser's hand.

He leaned near. Dana started when his voice, deep and sonorous, said close to her ear, "Black's all we've got."

She dared to look up as he retreated. His gaze seared her, tangible and authoritative. Inside her something trembled, and she sucked in a stabilizing breath.

"I didn't say I wanted coffee."

"You need a good shot of caffeine. You look about ready to collapse."

As he returned to the chair behind his desk, she pulled herself together. No sense in acting like a dazed cow. She stared at the steaming mug as if he'd offered her poison.

"Something wrong with the coffee?" he asked.

Reaching for the mug, she dared to meet his gaze as she took a tentative sip. Big mistake. His gaze skimmed her face, then cruised down to her breasts and back up to her eyes. It was a quick, relentless assessment, but that flaming look packed more repressed tension than a harnessed pit bull. She nearly choked.

His eyes narrowed on her. "You okay?"

She took another mouthful of ancient brew. "It's not only black, it's thick as sludge."

The intensity that always lingered around the edge of him reared to life. "This isn't the Ritz. We don't get much call for whole bean, gourmet, triple-French-roast crap."

"No, I don't suppose you would."

She wanted to toss the blistering liquid in his face. Instead, she reined in the outrageous impulse as she stared him down. Marshall's unwavering gaze made her quiver in places she'd never known existed.

She couldn't understand it. She'd never been this mesmerized by a man's eyes. In fact, she couldn't remember the last time she'd stared so rudely at someone. Dragging away her gaze, she looked around the small office, taking in everything with a bored air. Despite her expectations, the rest of his office looked ordinary. In fact, it seemed sterile. A few certificates lined the sidewalls, and she didn't take time to read them. One framed document caught her attention, a diploma from the University of Wyoming.

Her mouth dropped open. "English lit? A bachelors in English lit?" She peeled her gaze away from the certificate long enough to catch his glare. She folded her hands in her lap. "I have a Bachelors in Business and a Masters in Humanities."

"Humanities."

Without thinking why, she decided to take offense. "Something wrong with Humanities?"

"I didn't say that."

"You didn't have to. It was in your tone."

"I don't have anything against Humanities. Does overreaction run in the family, too?"

Dana almost left right then, but the challenge in his voice kept her riveted to the chair. "Aunt Lucille is a painter so she has to have a good imagination." She sniffed. "Does being a man of the law take any imagination, Mr. Marshall?"

"Just Marshall."

"Not Deputy Marshall? Or maybe Officer Marshall—"

"I'm the Under sheriff, not a deputy." He leaned forward in his chair, his attention glued to her.

She'd seen the sign on his office door, but had chosen to ignore it. An uncomfortable feeling crept over her, as if he could see inside her to the deepest parts of her soul.

His scrutiny came hot, penetrating like bullets. "Tell me why you're in Macon."

"My mother and I are worried about Aunt Lucille. We wanted to check up on her and make sure she isn't flying south permanently."

Dana hoped he might smile, but his concrete expression remained. "Flying south? As in going nuts?"

"Exactly. Mom's a little paranoid, and so is Aunt Lucille."

He sat back in his chair, swiveled to the side, and plunked his booted feet onto the desk. "Does it run in the family?"

Despite the insinuation, she decided not to rise to the occasion with an insult of her own. *Besides, I can't even think of a good insult when I need one.* "Yeah, it goes way back. One of my great uncles was a paranoid schizophrenic."

How do you like them apples, Marshall?

He took his feet off the table and they landed on the floor with a thump. He didn't say anything.

A steady throbbing took up residence in her skull and she longed for aspirin. Sliding down in the padded metal chair, she clasped her hands over her stomach and sprawled with her legs open. Not ladylike, but she didn't care.

Marshall sighed, closed his eyes for a moment, then rubbed one finger under his nose. When he opened his eyes, he snatched a pencil from his desk and jotted on a stenographer's pad. Did anyone even use shorthand any more?

"Crazy thoughts, Dana," she said out loud before she could stop herself.

He glanced up, his brows drawing down. "What?"

Embarrassed, she reached for her coffee and took another sip of the disgusting liquid. "Nothing."

He scribbled on the pad again. "She talks to herself."

"Don't worry, Marshall. Last I heard it's not contagious."

The scribbling continued, and he didn't look up. "But it's hereditary. Lucille has full blown conversations with herself all the time."

"Are you stuck on this genetic craziness thing or what?"

His pencil stopped its relentless movement. He looked up and sighed. "I'm sorry. It's been a long day."

The weariness in his tone and the genuine regret on his face made her soften. "So you don't believe her when she says her house is haunted?"

Running a hand over his beard, he contemplated Dana for a few unnerving moments. "I don't believe in haunted houses, but I do believe in criminal mischief and harassment."

Ready to respond, she opened her mouth. Before she could speak, he asked, "What do you do, Miss Cummings? Or is it Mrs.?

She tried not to bristle at his change of direction or his insistence on giving her a title. "Ms."

"Ms. Cummings." His pencil skipped over the steno pad again. "What is your career field?"

She looked at the fat mug in her hands and gazed into the contents as if fishing for answers. "I'm a writer."

"What do you write?"

"Horror."

When he didn't speak, she looked up and caught his curious expression. She didn't see a hint of reproach, disbelief or condescension. Often, she expected one or all three when she told people about her career.

The scratching of the pencil sounded loud in the room. "I see. Anything I'd know?"

She tried smiling, but the caffeine hadn't perked her up much. "Shades of Darkness. It's about a woman who comes back to a town she used to live in and finds out her old home is infested with evil spirits."

He shook his head, his face devoid of expression. "Can't say I've heard of it."

"It was on the New York Times best seller list for ten weeks. Hit number eight."

Leaning back in his chair again, he scrutinized her.

She wanted to twitch. The old adage about being a bug under a microscope fit her situation.

"I never pay much attention to best seller lists," he said.

"Good. Neither do I. Except in the sense that it means I did really, really well."

A smile teased his lips, then jumped to his eyes for a nanosecond. "Do you think Lucille has been reading too much horror fiction lately?"

Dana couldn't be insulted by his insinuation. She had plenty of doubts about the source of Aunt Lucille's problems. "I don't know."

"I'm asking because I hope you've got answers to why these things are happening to her."

Brennan Marshall could have pooh-poohed Lucille's case, but he appeared concerned.

Dana didn't want to like him for that, but she couldn't help it. She placed the cup of sludge on his desk with a thump. "She's a dear woman, and I don't want anything to happen to her."

"Tell me what you think is happening with your aunt, and I'll take you out for a fresh cup of coffee later tonight."

His soft voice held a hoarseness that reminded her of evenings by a fire. Naked. On a bearskin rug. She shoved away the intimate vision. "Sorry. Can't. I have a date."

"A date? You just got here." His incredulous tone surprised her.

"With a friend. Maybe you know her. Kerrie Di Mecio."

He sat up straighter. "Stuart Di Mecio's widow?"

"She's the one."

She thought of Stuart. Strong, handsome, fearless and invincible. Invincible, that is, until he made a mistake on a hike one day and plunged into a ravine to his death. She shuddered as she remembered receiving the phone call from Kerrie's mother telling of Stuart's demise.

Marshall pitched his writing instrument back in the pencil cup, and the clank startled her. He reached for a pen; his eyes took on a grimness she'd seen when he'd rescued the boy. "I found his body. I'm on the county volunteer search and rescue team."

Silence gathered in the room. She didn't feel like responding, and he apparently didn't care to elaborate about finding Stuart.

"What did Lucille tell you about these strange occurrences plaguing her?" he asked, leaning his arms on the desk.

"She called my mother a few weeks back. Mom said Aunt Lucille had this trembling voice, like she was scared. That's not normal for Aunt Lucille. She bends under pressure but never gives in. She's one tough lady. Anyway, Aunt Lucille said that she'd heard noises in the attic and in the basement. Especially the basement."

"What kind of noises?"

Dana wished she hadn't opened her mouth and mentioned

the basement. "Uh…well…." She glanced up and saw he waited, twiddling his thumbs like he had all day. "You're not going to believe this but—"

"Trust me, I've heard just about everything at least once."

"Not this you haven't."

He tossed her a smile. "Humor me."

"Okay. You asked for it. You know that big…uh…heart-shaped bed downstairs?"

"Yeah."

"Well, she started hearing people having…" She squirmed in her chair and made a face.

"Go ahead. People what?"

"People having sex. She heard people having sex on the bed. But when she went downstairs there was no one there."

Chapter 4

Marshall never twitched. Yet Dana saw the suspicious twinkle in his eyes before he managed to smother it. Instead, he did something much more disturbing.

Rising from his chair, he came around the side of the desk and paced the broad area behind her chair. She craned around to watch him.

"What kind of sounds exactly?" he asked.

Her chair made an obnoxious protest as she turned it so she could observe his purposeful stride. Eight big steps one way, eight big steps back. Eight big steps one way, eight big steps back.

"I'm going to get hypnotized watching you do that. Would you mind taking a seat?"

He increased his pace. "I think better this way." He came to an abrupt halt, leaned against the wall, cocked one booted foot across his ankle and hooked his thumbs in his belt loops.

She gulped. Good thing he wore that flannel shirt. If he'd stood there in that tight T-shirt—

"What kinds of sounds?" he asked, jerking her back to the real world.

She couldn't say it. *Come on, Dana. You aren't a blushing teen talking to a boy in high school. Spit it out.*

When she didn't answer fast enough, he walked toward her and rested his hands on the arms of her chair. She leaned back, inhaling a quick, startled breath.

"What are you trying to hide from me? Maybe you know something about the sounds?" The query came filled with subtle, sensual nuances that caused his voice to vibrate in his chest and made her tingle in places that shouldn't be tingling.

In defense she crossed her arms. "Of course I'm not hiding anything." When he glared, she took the plunge and elaborated. "You have heard people having sex before, haven't you, Marshall? Gasps. Sighs." She shrugged. "Grunts. Moans. She said it's like people having sex and they never get to…you know."

A thunderstorm seemed to build in his eyes, but not the kind that promised rage. The type that guaranteed sinful, daring pleasures. She'd never seen a man look at her this way. Predatory and intense all at once, ready to eat her alive. No mistaking that look.

His lips parted and she stared at his mouth.

"No, I don't know," he said. "Why don't you tell me?"

A tiny, rebellious corner of her almost refused to speak. What could he do to her anyway? Spank her?

A hot blush swept into her face. Oh, boy, oh boy, oh boy. Marshall's devouring gaze cruised over her face. His attention landed on her lips.

Crazy arousal spiraled through her, and she leaned forward until they almost touched noses. Dana couldn't remember the last time she'd felt so out of control and so turned on all at once. Hell, she'd never felt this way before. "These….these horny ghosts or whoever they are never get to finish—"

"Coming?"

Her entire body felt like it might go up in flames. Oh man!

Why couldn't he have said something like 'climaxing?' Did he have to use a word that described the nitty gritty?

"Yeah. That's it," she said, licking her lips and swallowing hard. She slumped in the chair.

He backed up so fast, it was like someone had poked him with a live power line. Returning to his desk, he settled down. "What else?"

Glad he'd moved on to another subject, she turned her chair around. When she glanced at him she wanted to curse. The damned man looked as cool as a glacier. No sign at all that he'd appeared less than two minutes ago like he might go thermonuclear.

"Apparently a day or two later she heard noises outside the house. Rustling bushes, thuds, thumps. Things like that."

"Could have been the wind."

"That's what I thought. Then she heard my uncle, my long dead Uncle Brent, talking to her after she went to bed."

"Dreams?"

"Maybe."

After a lengthy pause he asked, "That's all she told you and your mother?"

"She said things moved around the house. She'd get up in the morning and things weren't where she'd left the night before. Nothing major, just items she always left in a certain place."

"Like a toothbrush?"

"Her dental floss, actually."

"Whatever."

His gruff tone didn't surprise her, but she hadn't recovered from the melt down she'd experienced a few minutes ago. Her brain felt like oatmeal processed through a blender. Frustration, excitement and fear all made grits out of her thought processes. At least when she let them. *All you gotta do is imagine him ugly. He has a huge wart on his nose and—*

She forced herself to focus. "It isn't much to go on, and from what Mom has described to me, all of these things could be the wind, hallucinations, loneliness. Who knows what? Anyway, I needed a vacation, so I said I'd visit Aunt Lucille and see if I could figure out what is going on."

He snatched a pen from the holder again and started an annoying tap on the blotter. Her head throbbed, and she wondered if she should have gone to the doctor. At least she wouldn't be here now with this pain-in-the-patootee, flannel-wearing, boot-stomping, hairy beast of a man.

"There is one thing that has me worried, though. I'm wondering if maybe all her troubles are my fault," she said.

He scowled. "Why would you think that?"

"There's a scene in my book that corresponds to the occurrences she's described." Dana winced, wondering if she could regurgitate the words without turning another shade of crimson. "The heroine in Shades of Darkness hears people having sex in her basement."

This time he really did look disbelieving. "Let me guess. On a heart-shaped bed."

She pointed at him with an affirmative index finger. "You got it."

Seconds passed while he contemplated the top of the desk. When he looked up she didn't see amusement, but inquisitiveness. So she continued.

"She's had the bed forever. Actually my uncle and aunt had the bed in their old house until he died last year. She's only been in the new house awhile and decided that she wanted to move the monstrosity into the basement. Said the thing reminded her too much of him."

"Then you wrote the scene where the heroine hears people having sex, and then after Lucille reads your book she hears the same thing in her basement."

"Why would she hear it months and months after she read the book?"

Marshall's big shoulders rose and then dropped. "Never can tell how people's minds work."

"So has Aunt Lucille called the cops out to her house?"

"Three times. I investigated once, two other cops investigated the other times."

"I'd have thought an under sheriff had far more important things to do than go out on prowler calls."

"Generally I do. But I like Lucille and we're friends."

Dana didn't want to like his answer, but she did. "I'm impressed, Marshall."

She wanted to find Aunt Lucille, alive and in one piece, call her friend Kerrie and collapse on a bed and sleep. Preferably not a heart-shaped bed. She'd have dreams all night.

A small smile escaped to her lips, and then she stood. "I've got to go. It's been one long day, my head is killing me, and your coffee tastes like motor oil."

She didn't get far. A wave of sickening dizziness assaulted her, and she gasped. As she reached for the chair back, she closed her eyes.

"What the—" Marshall came around the desk in a rush.

Before he could reach her, the lights went out.

Dana Cummings will probably sue me. And Sheriff Pizer will have my ass for lunch. The thought ran through Marshall's head as he paced the waiting room. He jammed his hands into his pockets and stalked behind a row of chairs. Several people in the waiting room threw him curious glances.

CNN played on the small television tucked high into a corner. A reporter squawked about some social injustice in a land most people hadn't heard of.

Marshall didn't care. In his world one person mattered right this moment. Worry made him wonder if he'd lost his mind during his dip in the river.

A flash of Dana, running along as he dragged her through Lucille's house, came into his mind. She'd had a strange courage all wrapped up in her fear. Timid but brave. Soft but resilient. He shook his head and stared out of the windshield. Way to go, Marshall. Trying to get in trouble again? Isn't two broken hearts enough?

"Brennan?" The soft query issued from the end the hall, and he spun around.

Jenny Pizer. Sheriff Pizer's twenty-two-year-old daughter would make most men pause on a street corner, then walk right in front of a speeding car. Most men. Not him. Spirals of long, blonde hair flowed down her back and touched her hips. Her green cat eyes sparkled with interest, but not with warmth. Her smile always looked seductive and promised pleasures untapped. He'd never entertained the idea of asking her out; her youth and immaturity had hit him square between the eyes.

Marshall didn't say anything, and she strode toward him. He noticed her long, black wool tunic and matching leggings that curved along her long legs. At almost six feet tall, she could practically look him in the eye. Yeah, a nice piece of work, but not for him.

He'd tried two lithe, succulent blondes like Jenny before and both experiments had almost ripped out his heart. As she strode toward him, he assumed she'd been on volunteer status in the executive director's office. She wouldn't work a position requiring that she get her hands dirty, but hobnobbing with big wigs appealed to her.

"Evening, Jenny."

"Good evening."

Jenny's murmur of greeting drifted like soft snow, and he knew more than one man had probably heard that purr against his ear. Gossip said half the males in town had touched, tasted and taken her. He didn't need to listen to talk to know what people said rang true. Marshall had seen her in action trying to seduce men at parties.

Not that you've been to many parties lately, old boy. No, he hadn't in the last few months, feeling himself close up in ways he didn't understand. Time went by and he didn't see light breaking over the horizon anytime soon.

"Brennan?"

He realized she'd been talking to him and he'd missed what she'd said. "Sorry. I drifted off."

Her mouth twitched. "Thanks."

"Sorry." He hated saying it again.

"I heard you saved a life today." She pushed back a wide swath of curls from the side of her face. "Two lives. A boy and a woman. A burglar, no less."

"I didn't save the woman. She just happened to be in the wrong place at the wrong time when the tornado hit and I was there, too."

"Lucille Metcalf's house?"

Tension seeped along his shoulders, and he felt a deep ache start in one muscle. He rolled his shoulders to relieve the tightness, but it didn't work. "Your father tell you that?"

A tiny smile curved her full mouth. "Word gets around quick at our house." She reached up and brushed her fingers over his shoulder. "Were you hurt? Is that why you're here?"

Impatience drew his mouth into a hard line. "The woman passed out in my office. She's in the examining room right now."

"So?"

So? He felt the cold blast like refrigerated air. "I feel responsible."

"Oh? So she's a suspect? I mean, Dad said something about her trying to break into Lucille's house."

"She's Lucille's niece."

"Lucille's niece tried to break into her house?" The incredulous tone added to her cool façade, an icy beauty that he knew would freeze a man if he got close. "That's despicable."

"Guess your father didn't tell you the whole story." He wondered if she'd run to the gossips in town and spill the information. "She's just visiting her aunt and the key her aunt left for her didn't work. No burglary involved."

"Oh."

Jenny's habit of tagging 'oh' onto many of her sentences grated on his nerves. He didn't have the inclination or the desire to have nice-nice conversation with her.

"We haven't seen you around the house much lately," she said.

What could he say? "I've been busy."

"You're always busy."

Jenny's words sounded hard and final. He'd known from the moment she came into view a few years back as a teenager that she wanted something from him. He'd seen it coming for a long time and tried to ignore it. Her subtle smiles and touches, designed to seem casual, held a blatant message. Marshall didn't want her or want her to like him. After all these years she hadn't taken the hint.

"Yeah, I am. And I'm always going to be busy, Jenny."

"I'm just trying to be friendly. I admire a man who saves lives." She attempted a smile and it looked more like a leer before she dipped her head. A cascade of curls covered her expression for a moment. "I've always admired you."

When Jenny looked up, her shy grin had transformed to pure seduction. Her gaze devoured his face, shoulders and down until her message came through like a bullhorn. She liked his body. She wanted his body.

He said nothing, aware of their location. He filled his mind with the realization that Dana Cummings had looked at him like that when he'd stripped off his shirt. A quicker look, but there, nonetheless. *No way, Marshall. Dana Cummings doesn't want you anymore than you want Jenny. You imagined it all.*

Jenny started to turn, then looked back. "You're a hard man, Brennan. I hope someday you learn to soften up. If you don't, you might regret it."

With that parting shot she left. Relief made its way through his body like a sinuous snake, traversing his veins and relaxing him. Marshall glanced at his watch and impatience renewed. Too long. If he didn't hear news about Dana soon, he'd march into the examining room and find out for himself.

"Did you scare the ever loving stuffing out of that girl, Brennan Marshall?"

Dana heard her aunt's strident voice before she saw her. Not quite awake, not quite unconscious, she listened to the conversation.

"Lucille—"

"Don't give me any flack, young man."

"She's a lot tougher than that. I doubt she scares easily."

"You don't know the kind of effect you can have on people when you get all puffed up like one of those...those...those puffer fishes."

"What?"

Marshall's baffled question made Dana smile. Ah, yes. That's Aunt Lucille. So urbane. So witty.

"If you guys are going to argue, can you keep it down?" Dana asked, opening her eyes and glancing around her hospital room. "I seem to have some sort of hangover."

The small, private room, painted an unusual soothing blue, surprised her. Fancy that. This place was almost better than her hotel in Casper, by golly by George.

Lucille squealed and grabbed Dana's left arm so hard, Dana echoed her aunt's exclamation with another noise. "Ow!"

Tall, well-proportioned, and youthful looking for a seventy-year-old woman, Aunt Lucille pressed Dana's arm again and gave her a teary-eyed smile. Lucille's bright lime pants suit hurt Dana's eyes. Marshall stood at the foot of the bed, wary observation and concern in his gaze.

"Hi, Aunt Lucille. Where were you hiding during the storm? I came to the house, your car was in the garage, I couldn't get inside the house, and..." She took a quick look at Marshall. "This guy showed up."

"Oh, darling, I wasn't hiding. My friend Linda had picked me up earlier for shopping and we were on the way home. We'd stopped at Mr. Kramer's camera shop because I know he has a basement. When the tornado was over I came home and saw Bertha sitting there alone and then the back door was broken open and you weren't there. I was never so frightened in all my life."

"I know. I mean, sorry about the door. Marshall here had to do some quick thinking."

Aunt Lucille gave him a bleary smile. "Thank goodness for Marshall."

Amazing. Minutes ago Aunt Lucille reamed him for scaring the daylights out of me, and now she grinned at him like a schoolgirl. Ohmagosh. Aunt Lucille isn't falling for the big doofus, is she?

Marshall approached the other side of the bed at a crawl, almost as if he expected Dana to bite. *Come to think of it, I just might nip him if he gives me any more flack.*

Dana smiled instead, deciding to lure him into a false sense of security. "So sheriff, what brings you here?"

His worry appeared to dissipate and transform into annoyed. When he didn't speak, Dana glanced at Lucille. "He never shuts up."

Marshall glared. "Is she delirious? Maybe I should have Eric come back in here."

Aunt Lucille's face creased into wrinkles as she smiled. She patted Dana's hand. "She's going to be fine." She touched Dana's brow with warm fingers, then closed her eyes. "Oh, yes. She's getting better already. She's just had a humdinger of a day and needs rest."

Dana had seen her aunt do this before, and glanced over at Marshall. He didn't look surprised. "She's doing a scan."

Marshall started pacing. He put his hands on his hips.

Lucille's eyes popped open and she took her hand away. "Hmm. I think I know what's wrong. It's more than exhaustion and injury. You're having trouble with your writing. Of course, I knew that already. This is something else."

Marshall stopped his infernal pacing. "She has a concussion, that's what's wrong." He crossed to the side of the bed. "When you fainted you collapsed so fast, I almost didn't catch you in time."

Even with a leftover headache, the idea of him holding her sent unwelcome bolts of pleasure through Dana's stomach. Oops. Can't have that, now can we? "Don't worry, Marshall. I'm not going to sue."

He plowed onward. "You could have cracked your skull wide open. Now you understand why I wanted you to see a doctor."

Dana gave him her best nonchalant face. "Jeez, I'll bet you're fun to wake up to in the morning."

Silence covered the room, and Dana had the distinct pleasure of seeing his face turn red. Somehow, she didn't think embarrassment could be the cause. Nope. This time he looked ready to string her up and fry her over a pit of hot coals.

"Brennan is a dear, but he can be scary sometimes." Aunt Lucille squeezed her arm again. Dana thought she might have a bruise there if she kept it up.

"Oh, give me a break." Marshall made that male rumbling sound that women recognize as universal. "I wanted her to go to the hospital, but no. She blew it off. Now she's lying in this bed."

He jammed both hands through his hair and looked like he might let out a Tarzan-inspired yell of frustration. When he waved a dismissing hand and stomped out, Dana didn't experience the satisfaction she'd expected.

Dana sniffed. "He's a weird bird." She paused. "And mad as hell. Again. Have you given him a scan to see if he has high blood pressure? He looked about ready to bust a cork. He must have health problems with saving people from tornados, rescuing drowning boys, and interrogating suspected and obviously dangerous burglars."

Lucille grinned, her big smile warm and comforting. Most people might consider Aunt Lucille unusual, but Dana figured that's why she understood her so well. They both ran into strange looks and uncomprehending stares on a regular basis.

Aunt Lucille nodded. "I heard all about it." She moved away to the window and glanced outside. "At least twice."

Dana sighed and shifted, groaning when her muscles protested. "This has been one long day." Shadows encroached on the room. "What time is it?"

"Five o'clock."

"Oh, man! I've been unconscious for that long?"

"Now don't get worked up. If Marshall comes back in here and sees you riled, he might worry."

"Come back here? Worry about me?" An alien concept like this made no sense to Dana. She made a grunting noise that sounded similar to Marshall's trademark noise. "Hardly. He hates my guts."

Aunt Lucille turned away from the window and pursed her lips in thought. Multi-colored bracelets on each wrist jangled. "Drivel. You misinterpreted his mood, darling. Yes, he suspected you at first, as any good man of the law would have under the circumstances."

Dana had to give him that. "I suppose so. It doesn't explain why he's so cranky all the time."

Aunt Lucille gazed outside as if she'd decided to contemplate the heavens. "He gets like that when he's mad. Or perplexed. Frustrated. Or in your case, all of the above."

"Great." Dana sighed. "How did you find out I was in the hospital?"

Lucille turned toward her again. "I called the police station when I realized your car was at the house, but you weren't. Frankly, my dear, I thought the tornado might have sucked you up."

Rather than think about what had almost happened, Dana said, "It almost did. But it's ludicrous to think Marshall is worried about me. " She glanced at the clock. "I've barely known him a day."

"I knew your uncle less than a week and I decided he was the one for me."

The insinuation made Dana twitch. "I hope you're not thinking what I think you're thinking."

The door swung open and in walked a man about thirty years old with startling silver-blond hair, and a smile that made him look like he'd escaped from a male beauty pageant.

"Dr. Dawes." Aunt Lucille beamed. "Thank goodness. Will you tell this girl to pipe down and relax? She's going to give me an aneurysm."

Reaching for her wrist, the doctor winked at Dana. "Giving Aunt Lucille trouble?"

If the man hadn't been so incredibly good looking, Dana might have growled at him. "I'm not any trouble. Except when I've had a very bad day."

Dr. Dawes had a wicked twinkle in his blue eyes, one that probably sent women into heart failure on a regular basis. "That's what Marshall tells me."

Aunt Lucille let her hands fly up again, and Dana wondered when one of those jangling bracelets would fly off and sail across the room. "She won't listen. She's jumpy as a rabbit in a cage."

"You would be, too, if a tornado had almost peeled your skin off," Dana said. "Can I leave now, doctor?"

"Afraid not. Besides the fact that Marshall would peel my skin off if I let you go, I don't think it's wise. You've already passed out twice today. I also understand you're still recovering from pneumonia?"

"Yeah."

"How long ago did the pneumonia start?"

"About four weeks ago. Maybe five. That's why I'm on this vacation. My agent suggested I take leave or else."

She admitted to no one, least of all her worrywart mother, that she didn't feel one hundred percent. Occasionally a nasty cough would rattle her frame, taking her breath and turning her a sickly shade of olive. Sometimes the spasms sent her running into the bathroom and she had to fight not to lose her last meal.

The illness made it easy to explain why she couldn't write more than Chapter One of her new, as yet untitled horror novel. People might nod and say they understood, but she knew deep inside unless they'd had the same experience, they couldn't comprehend her frustration. She had to take charge of her problem and she hoped a change in setting would do the trick.

Dr. Dawes looked pensive. "You're staying put until we make sure there aren't complications."

"Where is Deputy Do Right anyway?" Dana asked.

"I sent him to the cafeteria to get something to eat. I could hear his stomach growling clear across the hospital." He chuckled. "He was wearing a hole in the floor and driving the nurses batty."

She could believe that.

As he finished her examination, she noted several things about the man. Taller and thinner than Marshall, with the lanky build of a runner, Dr. Dawes possessed no animal magnetism whatsoever. Why she noticed this, she couldn't say. Maybe she realized it because Marshall stirred hot, daring, and knee-buckling reactions deep inside her. That didn't mean, of course, that she couldn't force down dangerous impulses and keep away from Marshall. No need to complicate her already busy and screwed-up life with an incomprehensible interest in the man.

After Dr. Dawes left, Aunt Lucille stayed until visiting hours ended. Kerrie also visited as soon as she heard Dana was in the hospital. Marshall, though, didn't show his face again that evening.

Dana didn't like that. Not one bit.

Chapter 5

Dana couldn't sleep. The hour grew late, and yet her mind sped along like she participated in a grand prix. Cozy under the blankets and quilt, she inhaled and commanded her body to relax from the toes up. She imagined a soft, green pasture with frolicking horses, floating butterflies, and the cheery music of birds.

Fifteen minutes later she lay wide-awake.

She'd had one day of recuperation at Aunt Lucille's home. She'd tried working on a chapter of her book, but to no avail.

Earlier that day a couple of older men from town, friends of Lucille's, arrived to board up broken windows until they could be replaced. Dana didn't overdo, but she helped a little. Dr. Dawes had told her that if she overworked he'd hear about it and send Marshall in to give her a difficult time. He'd said it with a teasing smile, and for that reason alone she didn't believe him.

"Besides, it's not like Brennan Marshall gives a rat's butt," she said to the dark room.

He hadn't stopped by to see her at the hospital again, nor had she expected him to come to the house. *Problem is, you kept hoping to see him all day yesterday and all day today. Didn't you? Huh? Huh? Huh?*

"Yes, damn it."

But why?

Wind fluttered through the closed drapes, and Dana realized the bedroom was chilled. Rather than huddle under the covers, she slipped out of bed and pushed back the curtains. Before she could close the window, she saw something move below and that jerked her into total awareness. Every hair on her body seemed to prickle and she froze. All her senses went on alert. Moisture-laden air floated by in foggy tendrils, and the breeze stayed so gentle she felt the slightest touch on her cheek. Moonbeams peeking between clouds gave the ground below an ethereal, eerie radiance. Dana held her breath as she looked out the open portion of the window. Scanning, she searched for any sign of human or animal. Then she saw it.

A man scampered into the trees from the bushes alongside the house. Heart hammering, she called out. "Hey, you!"

That's it. Scare the bastard.

She slammed the window, wondering if her screech had awakened her aunt. She hurried to the bedside table and picked up the phone. Her aunt had installed fancy cordless extensions all around the house that worked off a single telephone line. As she dialed 911 she wondered if all the doors and windows were closed. The 911 operator kept her on the line as she reported the prowler.

Dana put on soft slippers, then scampered out her bedroom door. As she crept along, Dana realized her heart rate had propelled into overdrive. *I'm freaking crazy. What if he's down here? No, he can't be. I saw him outside and heading for the woods.* She turned on the hall light and then the light high above the stairs.

A bang echoed somewhere in the house and she let out a gasp. "Jeez!"

Scanning the staircase and what she could see of the foyer below, she started down.

She reached the bottom of the steps when the operator came on the line again. "The sheriff's office is being dispatched to your area, Miss Cummings."

Although the woman's voice had a soothing cadence, Dana's heart didn't care; it banged against her ribcage in a panic she'd never experienced before.

A few seconds later, Dana heard another peculiar sound coming from the basement. A groan? A soft moan? A gasp? Were the ghosts trying to have sex again? She went still as deadwood listening for a telltale sound. Another noise, like a woman in the throes of sweet passion, came to Dana's ears. The next sound was louder, like a man striving to reach the finish line. The noises grew in volume until they were unmistakable.

She blushed. Not that she'd never heard other people having sex before. In her first apartment, the people in the unit above her had done the nasty at least three times a week at full wail. She'd felt downright annoyed when the noise had escalated to bull elephant status. It perturbed her no end when people didn't consider the racket they made.

Especially when it seemed everyone was having sex except for her.

"Oh, boy." Cold air rippled over her, and she jerked around, wondering where the breeze came from. She tiptoed toward the kitchen, turning on lights as she went.

The 911 operator said, "Are you still there, ma'am?"

Dana kept her voice at a whisper. "I heard something in the house." She stopped at the kitchen entrance and scanned the area. She heard nothing but her own breathing. Zilch moved inside the room, though she speculated if someone hid behind the kitchen island.

Determined not to succumb to total heebie-jeebies, she left

the kitchen and went toward the front door. Her heart did a hop skip as she moved along slower than a snail.

A shadow crossed the window coverings near the right side of the front door, and she let out a startled gasp.

"Ma'am?" The operator asked.

"I'm here."

"What's happening?"

"I saw a shadow move across the window."

Thump!

"Oh-oh."

"What's going on? Are you all right?"

"There was a thump against the door."

"Don't open it unless it's the police."

No shaving cream, Sherlock. Dana wanted to tell the operator she had more brains than a bag of cashews. Then again, the operator couldn't know that. Crime programs on television regurgitated shows featuring dunce heads doing stupid things.

Another bang hit the door, this time a steady knock, and Dana's heart did a Roger Ramjet imitation. She stepped toward the door, the phone gripped tight and her throat as dry as sandpaper. Why hadn't Aunt Lucille bought a door with a peephole in it? She snapped on the porch light.

"Who is it?" she asked.

"Marshall. Are you all right?"

Relief slid through her like sweet honey and she let out a thankful sigh. "Thank God." Though she recognized his rough, husky voice, she had to double check. "How do I know it's really you?"

"Don't you recognize my voice?"

"Of course, but tell me something that only you and I could know."

"What?" The incredulous note in his voice amused her.

"Miss, are you all right?" the woman's voice on the telephone asked.

"Yeah, I'm good. I think. Just let me make sure the guy outside is really Brennan Marshall."

"Dana, are you talking to someone in there?" Marshall's voice sounded suspicious.

She'd better open the door before he broke it down. Still....

"Yeah, the 911 operator. Now what's the password?"

A couple of Marshall curses issued through the door. "All right. You've got a mole just under your right ear."

Warmth spread through her in waves of unexpected pleasure. He'd noticed that? *Don't get too excited, Dana.* He might think it's repulsive. One boyfriend she'd had asked her why she didn't have it removed.

No doubt about it. No other man in town knew she had a mole there. She slipped the chain loose, the deadbolt, and the lock on the knob. "It's the law, operator. Thanks for everything."

Dana clicked off the phone before the woman could make a sound. She opened the door.

Marshall stood there dressed in all black. Stocking cap, turtleneck, jeans and boots. In one hand he held a slim flashlight, in the other a weapon.

She allowed a sigh to escape and stepped back for him to come inside. As usual, his trademark scowl made him appear ready for a fight and fierce. He shut the door behind him, shoved the weapon in his holster, and gripped her shoulders.

Undeniable concern hardened his features. "Are you all right?"

"I'm fine. You got the call?"

His forehead wrinkled a tad as he frowned. He released her. "What call?"

"I called 911."

"I'm off duty. Is Lucille all right?"

"She's great so far as I know. I can't believe this didn't wake her up." She explained what she'd seen and heard. "If 911 didn't send you out, what are you doing here?"

Before he could speak, a sheriff's car rolled up with lights on but no siren.

"What in goodness name is going on here?" Aunt Lucille's voice came from the top of the stairs. "Marshall?"

Aunt Lucille came downstairs clad in a blue chenille robe and fuzzy pink slippers.

Dana explained about the figure she'd seen in the woods and Marshall said it was him.

The sheriff's deputy, a rookie with the wide-eyed enthusiasm of a teen boy on his first date, took copious notes. He seemed to cringe under Marshall's everlasting glare.

Dana wouldn't admit it, but she'd rather have Marshall investigating the prowler than the rookie.

"What are you doing here, sir?" the rookie asked when Dana had finished giving details.

Marshall pinned his no nonsense frown on the younger man, and remained quiet for so long she thought he'd never answer. He cleared his throat. "I was on a stake-out in the woods around the house and saw some movement around the area."

"Oh, my," Lucille said.

"What did you see?" Dana asked, apprehension running through her.

"I'm not sure. It might have been a deer. Maybe a bear."

"Oh, come on." Dana crossed her arms and giving him her best cynical gaze. "You can't tell me that a man who has lived in the woods as long as you doesn't know the difference between a deer and a bear."

Tilting his head, he pinned her with a half weary, half surprised gaze. "Yeah, well, this time I didn't see it clearly enough to be sure. And if it was a bear I sure wasn't going after it."

With a nervous smile, she said, "Can't say I blame you."

For a nanosecond his dark, penetrating gaze swept over her Big Bird T-shirt, down over her bare legs, and landed on her yellow ballet slippers. She thought she saw amusement, interest, and maybe a little lust ignite in his eyes. To her mortification she stared him down, knowing that he had to see how much she liked the idea. *Damn and double damn and triple damn. I can't let him think I want to jump his bones.* I can't. She jerked her gaze away.

Marshall removed his stocking cap and his hair emerged in messy waves. One toss of his head and the miraculous strands went back into place. Figures. She put money into a good cut and hair products to achieve an effortless look. He probably washed his hair, ran a comb through it, and grinned at the mirror. He cleared his throat, and Dana realized he'd caught her staring.

"If you two are done, I think I'll put a pot of coffee on," Aunt Lucille said, a smile as wide as the Colorado River creasing her face.

"Finished, Closky?" Marshall asked the young deputy.

The deputy tipped his hat. "I'll be patrolling the area."

"That's comforting," Dana said before she could stop herself.

Deputy Dog smiled, his youthful appearance nothing next to Marshall's clear, masculine authority. The rookie left, closing the door behind him.

Marshall put his hands on his hips. "Will you ladies be all right?"

Aunt Lucille patted his arm. "We'll be fine. Thank you so much for looking out for us. Are you sure you don't want coffee?"

Marshall shook his head. "It'll keep me up all night."

Aunt Lucille shrugged. "I won't be able to sleep after this anyway."

His gaze traveled to Dana. "I need to speak to Dana. Alone."

Aunt Lucille headed to the kitchen, humming a happy tune like nothing unusual had happened.

"What if something is out there?" Dana asked, hating to think about it. She shifted closer to him, as if his big, warm body could keep her safe.

His gaze warmed, landing on her mouth and staying there for a lingering moment. "You'll be all right." He swallowed hard, and she watched his Adam's apple move up and down. He inhaled deeply. "And I'll be watching."

Intense and hot, his evaluation made her nerves feel raw. She couldn't tear her gaze away from him. He moved a step closer, and Dana enjoyed that nearness all the way through her body. "Why did you come here in the first place?"

"I was…worried."

"So you do believe Aunt Lucille."

He lowered his voice. "She might be an eccentric, but she's not crazy. And neither are you."

Gratification swept though her. She hadn't expected him to give her the benefit of the doubt, even if he did believe her aunt. "I heard those, uh, sounds tonight."

"People having sex?"

His matter-of-fact statement, laced with a husky undertone, sent ripples of reaction over her skin. "Full blown and with extra volume. Not as noisy as a Fourth of July fireworks display, but easy to hear. I'm really surprised Aunt Lucille didn't hear it this time."

"Did she say she heard it every night?"

Dana shook her head. "No."

His face turned speculative and he looked around the huge foyer and up at the crystal chandelier sparkling with light. Pinpoints of color seemed to flicker through his eyes. "Did you flip on all the lights as you went through the house?"

"Yes."

"And you still heard the noises when you turned on the lights?"

"Yes. Where are all these questions leading?"

Instead of answering her, he poured on more queries. "Did the noises of people having sex get louder in any particular part of the house?"

She considered it. "Just at the bottom of the stairs. As if they were going at it in the basement. Just like it would if real people were down there."

Nodding, he headed for the stairs. "Come on."

Shivering, she descended the basement stairs, walking behind him. She recalled the last time they'd barreled downstairs, rushing to avoid inhalation by tornado. The mad scramble and almost falling backwards into his arms. What a strange time to think about this. *Get with the program and attend to business, Dana.*

At the bottom of the steps, Marshall opened the door, flipped on the light and stepped into the large room. When he stopped she almost ran into him.

"What is it?" she asked.

He moved ahead, not bothering to answer her. One of these days she would brain him for that nasty habit. She followed and when they reached the heart-shaped bed, she saw why he'd stopped earlier. Red satin sheets and lace-trimmed pillows spilled across the surface like someone had slept here or perhaps made torrid love.

"Oh, boy," she said.

He placed his hand on the center of the rumpled sheets. When he glanced up his gaze showed a cross between cynicism and amazement. "Put your hand here and tell me what you notice."

As ordered, she laid her hand almost in the same spot he'd touched. In surprise, she snatched her hand back from the sheets. "It's actually hot."

"Like someone has been lying here."

When he looked at her as if she might know something about the condition of the bed, she decided on a swift retort. "Don't look at me. I haven't been down here in quite awhile." Dana's mouth twisted into a sardonic smile. "Gives new meaning to the saying, 'burning up the sheets.'"

"Do you think Lucille would have a reason to sleep down here?"

"If you're implying what I think you're implying—"

"Don't get defensive. Just answer the question."

She swallowed another hot reply and continued. "She was upstairs in her room when I heard the noises. You saw her appear at the top of the stairs."

He seemed to consider the information carefully. "When was the last time you saw this bed made up?"

Dana shrugged. "I don't know. I haven't looked down here in at least two days." She added an accusing tone. "I've been recovering from the concussion and staying in bed."

Right then, a cough caught hold of her, air rasping through her dry throat. She covered her mouth and released a few bone-rattling, wheezing coughs.

Marshall's eyes narrowed. "You all right?"

"Never been better." She gave him a weak smile. "These coughs aren't as bad as they sound."

After a long pause, he nodded. His expression turned solemn. "You're sure? Eric said you'd be okay."

Her heart softened. "Yes, thank you."

He switched his attention to the bed and the moment disappeared. "Something fishy is going on here."

"Tell me about it." A chill swept through her at the idea someone might have slept down here while she and Aunt Lucille had snoozed upstairs without a clue.

Marshall grabbed a knitted throw hanging over a chair near the bed and walked toward her. "You're cold."

She didn't know what to say to the truth. When he swirled the throw around her shoulders, then tucked it close, she shook with a different feeling. How could she read his mood when he switched from brusque to sweet in five seconds flat?

Dana huddled into the fabric. "Thank you." Instead of replying, he continued that unnerving assessment that she couldn't interpret. "What are you staring at?"

"You."

"All right. Me. Why are you staring at me?"

"I was thinking you and Lucille should pack some things and stay at your friend Kerrie's house."

Startled, she gaped at Marshall like he'd told her the sky had turned purple and that scientists had confirmed life on Mars. He moved toward the stairs, but she caught up with him and grabbed his arm. He swung around and she stepped back to keep distance.

"Why do you think Aunt Lucille and I should stay at Kerrie's? Do you think there's something seriously wrong?"

"I don't want to worry about you all the time, that's why."

Warmth flowed into her, and it sure didn't come from the cover bunched around her shoulders. "You're concerned about my safety?"

He made a noise on a higher note than his usual grunt. "Damn, but you ask a lot of questions."

Exasperation made her reach for his forearm again. "I only ask questions when people act like a stubborn ox and don't tell me the whole story. Come clean. You wouldn't tell me to leave here unless..." A new possibility came to her, and it made her release him. "Wait a minute. You don't think I have anything to do with this?" When he looked down and said nothing, she received an ugly feeling. "Why you...you...how could you believe that?"

That purposeful, stolid blaze entered his look. "I don't know you from Eve, Miss Cummings." Marshall's expression turned speculative. "Call Kerrie tomorrow morning and see if she'll let you bunk at her house."

"I'm not going." Planting her hands on her hips, she allowed the throw to slip from her shoulders and land at her feet. Screw it anyway.

He leaned in closer, his stance threatening, his eyes dark with demand. "You will if your aunt asks you to."

She gasped, and poked him in the chest with her index finger. "You wouldn't dare."

"I would."

Exasperated, she made a disgusted sound. "God, you're unbelievable."

Once again he turned and headed up the stairs. "Just do it."

Dana chose to make a sound of protest, one that probably came out childish. But the man made her so mad she didn't give two hoots. She stomped her foot and clenched her fists. "Ooooooo!"

Chapter 6

"Dana, I think Marshall is right," Aunt Lucille said. "If you stay with Kerrie, maybe you'll be safe from whatever is haunting my home."

Dana huffed. "He wanted both of us to go to Kerrie's. I'm not leaving you here alone." Dana settled into a chair in the big kitchen nook. She took a sip of hot orange spice tea. "Now, are you going to tell me what you think is going on here, or am I going to have to hurt you?"

The evening after Marshall had ordered Dana to leave, she still hadn't called Kerrie about staying with her. And she didn't plan to.

Lucille wore an eggplant-purple fleece turtleneck and matching pants. Comfortable, yes. Ugly, yes. Totally Lucille, yes. Lucille grinned like a little girl and poured water into her cup over a peppermint tea bag. She moved to the antique Eastlake table and sank into a chair. "Ghosts are taking things, moving them around. My goodness, I'm lucky they haven't taken my teeth." Her gleaming grin took on new proportions. "They make the most peculiar racket, you know."

"Your teeth or the ghosts?"

Lucille laughed, then lifted her cup. "The ghosts."

"So, do you have any idea who the ghosts are? You must have heard something about this old place before you bought it."

"Well, yes. I didn't say anything to you or your mother because I didn't really believe the gossip." She waved a hand to encompass the area. "I've got an open mind, but I'm not totally gullible, you know."

"Of course not."

"Apparently, back in 1900, a young couple fell in love in this house. You know, a well-to-do young lady, pauper-boy story. The young man was a stable hand and he fell in love with the only daughter of J. P. Nicholson."

"Wait a minute. I've heard about Nicholson. Didn't he own several businesses in town for years? Didn't he murder his daughter and the stablehand?"

Aunt Lucille nodded. "That's the one." She leaned forward and lowered her voice, as if afraid the ghosts might hear. "The daughter and the stable hand had a tryst in the house while her father was away. The father came home and caught the daughter and the stable hand making love. Then he shot them both."

Dana shuddered, imagining a tragedy staining the house with its vibrations. "Wasn't there a messy trial and Nicholson lost everything?"

"That's right. He committed suicide in his prison cell about a year later. The house had scads of owners over the years. When I decided I wanted to move out of my other house and I took a look at this one…well, I fell in love with the place. Didn't even think about spooks. That's one of the reasons the price was right. No one else wanted it, even though it's in good shape." Aunt Lucille turned her mug around and around, then heaved a sigh. "The noises and the hot sheets you encountered last night certainly give credence to the idea of randy ghosts on the prowl. Someone or something was having sex on that heart-shaped bed last night and it certainly wasn't me."

Dana wanted to cringe. Talking with her aunt like this felt too much like chatting with her mother about sex. "We don't know the sounds I heard or the bed sheets being messed up had anything to do with ghosts doing the horizontal tango."

Aunt Lucille leaned forward and the steam from her cup rose around her face. "Darling, I've been around enough years to know what it sounds like when people are making love. Sex wasn't invented last year, you know."

Heat rose into Dana's face, and she wondered if her nose glowed like Rudolf the Red-Nosed Reindeer. "Marshall probably thinks we're both Loony Tunes."

"Surely not." Lucille put let her hands up in her trademark dismissal. "He felt the sheets and saw the bed was messed up. If anything he thinks I'm the one with walnuts for brains."

Indignation rose in Dana. "He told you that?"

Lucille shook her head, an indulgent, warm expression on her face. "Now don't get all worked up again. The stress isn't healthy. You and Marshall need to take a chill pill."

Dana almost choked on her tea. "Chill pill?"

"Cool expression, eh? I learned it from Tabitha."

"Tabitha?"

"She's Dr. Dawes' nine-year-old girl. A real pistol." A lock of gray hair fell over her forehead, and she pushed it back as if annoyed. "A pain in the kisser sometimes, but she's a good girl at heart. Just has too much of her mother in her."

"Dr. Dawes is married?"

Lucille shook her head. "No, she died about a year ago. Sad business. She took Tabitha out for some shopping in Casper. A really bad snowstorm came over Aspen Pass. Really bad." Lucille's face clouded like the storm she described. She tapped the side of the mug with one well-manicured, shell-pink fingernail.

"Fool woman came back over the pass when she should have stayed in Casper. They slid off the cliff."

"Oh, God." Dana's stomach lurched, a sick feeling engulfing her.

"Exactly." Lucille grimaced. "Tabitha's mother, Eva, died instantly. Somehow, by a miracle only, Tabitha survived. She had a broken arms and broken ribs."

Goosebumps rippled over Dana's arms as she imagined the little girl trapped in the car, injured, with her dead mother beside her. "It's hard to believe she made it."

"Eric was frantic to find them when they didn't come home on time. Marshall went with the rescue team. He's a part of the volunteer group. He rappelled down the cliff and found Tabitha first."

Dana again imagined what it would be like to come upon the horrible scene. "At least the girl lived. Dr. Dawes had to find that a blessing." She knew she spoke the words to comfort herself, too. "Losing both of them…"

"Yes."

Dana felt Lucille didn't want to speak of it anymore, and right now she didn't either. How could Eva have been so careless with her daughter's life? Dana's writer's brain spoke too much and showed too much. Horror might be her trademark, but she only enjoyed the wild imaginings when they came from fictitious experiences she created. Real life horror meant disaster and unimaginable human suffering.

"Sounds like Marshall makes a habit of rescuing people," Dana said.

"Oh, yes. He's quite the man." Aunt Lucille cleared her throat. "Enough talk about ghosts and Marshall. When are you going to finish that new novel?"

Dana knew she couldn't avoid talking about it. "I'm hoping that bed-bouncing ghosts won't get in the way of my inspiration."

"Yes, but why do you have a block in the first place?"

Dana shrugged, then took a sip of her cooling tea. "If I knew, I'd get rid of the problem. Maybe I wouldn't even be here." She knew she'd said the wrong thing when her aunt's face grew sad. "I didn't mean that like it sounded. I want to help you discover what's happening in this house. You know that."

Aunt Lucille's expression lightened. "I know the last month or so has been hard for you. You've got so much to look forward to, even if it doesn't feel like it right now."

"Maybe I'm just a one-hit wonder. You know. Margaret Mitchell. Harper Lee. Not that I think anyone will think of me on the level with those writers." She took the last sip of her drink, then headed to the kitchen sink. She methodically washed the cup. "Only one book written. Pfft! Kaplooy!"

"No, darling. You're more talented than you know. I've read your work and while I was never a fan of horror, your book is so well written. The characters are fresh, lively, inspiring. Scary as all get out. I see you with hundreds of books over the years."

Dana returned to the table, leaning forward and propping her elbows on the gleaming wood surface and listening to the chatter of birds outside through the open window. A soft breeze filtered through the butter-yellow curtains. Dana reached over and patted her aunt's hand. She marveled at how frail Lucille appeared, yet she knew strength lay in her bones, muscles, and heart.

"You're the best, Aunt Lucille." She smiled. "And don't you forget it."

"Thank you." Aunt Lucille seemed to brighten with the praise, and then she rose from the chair. "Now, I say we head out for some serious shopping."

Happy to see her aunt enthusiastic again, Dana liked her proposal. "Sounds great. For what?"

Aunt Lucille started walking toward the living room. "You need a new party dress."

Dana paused in the kitchen doorway. "Why?"

"Because, my dear, you're going to a party tomorrow night."

As Dana and Aunt Lucille strode across the grass toward the community building close to the center of town, Dana noticed a bush half obscured a 'do not walk on the grass' sign.

"Crud," Dana said.

"What dear?" Aunt Lucille came to a stop under a streetlight. Fog drifted across them with a cool mist that dampened the skin.

Dana shook her head. "Nothing. Let's get this party over with."

Earlier that day, Aunt Lucille announced that Gregory and Neal, her stepsons, had arrived in town. Dana didn't like Gregory one iota, but Neal was good to Aunt Lucille.

Taking her niece's arm, Aunt Lucille guided her toward the wood double doors on the old log building. "I've never seen you so negative. Are you certain something isn't wrong?"

"Other than the fact this hemline creeps up like thong underwear and the neckline dips lower than the Royal Gorge?"

Aunt Lucille stopped again before they reached the door. Her frown said Dana had pushed over the line. "Now Dana. Really! If you didn't like the dress, you could have said no."

"Right. You would have nagged me until I bought this…." She looked down at the velour. "This dress is for twenty-year-olds with x-rated bodies."

Dana reached for the door and held it open.

As Aunt Lucille went through the door she said, "Darling, you're not serious. You're just nervous. Besides, you have a stunning figure." They moved into the entrance hall. "Slim, long legs—"

"Fantastic!" The deep voice made Dana jump about a mile.

A tall, sandy-haired man in his late thirties stepped up and engulfed Aunt Lucille in his arms for a hug.

"Gregory!" Aunt Lucille hugged her stepson.

He wore brand new jeans and an expensive, startling gold silk sweater. *Huh. Probably matches his new Lexus.*

She had nothing against luxury cars. Except when jerks drove them.

Dana had never liked her stepcousin. His closely-spaced eyes ruined his classic cut nose and rugged jawline. Of course, she didn't dislike him because of his looks, but for the things he'd said and done in his life. He gave her what she'd call an 'icky feeling'. Gregory's new position as CEO of a computer firm in Casper had inflated his already watermelon-sized ego. His brother, Neal, a lawyer in New York, was much nicer and easier to get along with.

Gregory turned toward Dana and swaggered a couple of steps. She wanted to gag. Every movement of his powerful body spelled arrogance. His false charm and pretences slid into a person's space like a lethal virus on the hunt.

"Dana, you look fantastic. What a dress."

Smarmy. Dana managed to stretch her lips into a smile. She shook his hand to discourage him from hugging her. "Hello, Gregory. Haven't seen you in a long time."

One tawny brow quirked, and his tall, lean body seemed to tense. "You're so far away in New Mexico. But now that you're finally a success, I'm sure you don't have time for a small place like Macon too often."

Dana wanted to spit, but said nothing.

Amazing how the man could take a compliment and still make it sound like an insult. Dana wanted to make a rude noise. "Undoubtedly."

"Is Neal here?" Aunt Lucille asked, patting Gregory's arm in that eternal mother gesture.

Gregory gestured behind her and Neal strode across the room as if he'd heard his stepmother's call.

Smiling, Dana watched Neal approach with more pleasure. At thirty he was nine years younger than Gregory, yet his outlook seemed more mature. At five feet, eight inches tall and with a wiry runner's build, Neal didn't stand out. His tan slacks and light blue sweater went well with his silver blonde coloring. He walked up to the small group with an engaging grin in place.

"Hey." Neal waved. "I was almost late."

He gave Gregory a smack on the shoulder that made his older brother grunt, and then he wrapped Aunt Lucille in a huge hug.

Neal gave Dana a genuinely affectionate kiss on the cheek. "Hey, Dana. I heard from some people in town, you had an adventure your first day here."

"Adventures. Plural."

"Multiple barrels of fun," Neal said.

"You could say that."

"Not eager to tell us about it?" Gregory asked.

Not you. Jerk. She wanted to smack him with the tiny, beaded black purse she'd left in the trunk of the car. No, that wouldn't do. For a head as thick as his she'd need her trusty fanny pack.

Dana had learned from experience that if she told him about her encounter with the tornado, he'd find some way of ridiculing her. "I think there's probably enough gossip flying about what happened that day."

"Did you hear some?" Aunt Lucille asked.

"Not yet, but give it time. I'm sure I'll be hearing the fish was this big." Dana held her hands out so that fourteen inches filled the space between her hands.

Gregory shifted and crossed his arms. "I don't know how Mom stands it here."

His booming voice carried well, and several people heard him. Dana saw their expressions of consternation and didn't blame them. Annoyed with his boorish behavior, she couldn't resist asking, "Why are you in town, Gregory? Other than a nice little, boring vacation."

"I was ready for a little time off. Plus, I'm helping a business in town update their computer system. Place is about a decade behind."

Dana put her hands on her hips, and Gregory's gaze shifted to the velour encasing her body. She wanted to tell him to keep his squinty gaze away. "That must be a chore. I'm surprised you subjected yourself to it."

She knew her voice sounded sarcastic, yet she didn't care. Gregory's expression said he couldn't tell if she teased him or meant each word.

Before he could retort, several townspeople strode forward to meet Dana. Sheriff Pizer, skinny as dental floss and dressed in Western wear, tipped his Stetson in an old-world gesture. In a deep voice he introduced his equally thin wife.

"Mrs. Pizer is the chair for the committee that put together this gala," Aunt Lucille said, grinning as wide and strong as if she'd won the prize at an auction. "She's also heading up the end-of-summer picnic this week."

"Will you be staying in town long?" Mrs. Pizer asked Dana, voice starchy. "We still need volunteers for several of the booths at the picnic."

Dana wanted to grimace, but managed to hold back. She didn't volunteer when working on a book, but since she was here investigating her aunt's house…what the hell?

"Are you chairing that committee as well?" Dana asked, injecting sweetness into her tone to eliminate her apprehension.

Mrs. Pizer sniffed. "No. Kerrie Di Mecio is coordinating that project."

Dana nodded in relief and satisfaction. "I'll be seeing her sometime tonight."

A young woman of about twenty-two strode up to the group. Her attire included a western-style shirt, bolo tie, broomstick skirt, crap-kicker boots, and a beautiful smile.

Dana didn't trust the smile, for it came with a gaze that passed over her, stopped, and assessed. Analyzed, Dana decided, as if she saw an enemy. The young woman had thick curls that cascaded down her back in a porno-queen style. Her pale, clear skin and dark brows made a striking contrast with her hair.

"Jenny," Aunt Lucille said. "How are you? Dana, this is Jenny Pizer."

Jenny's fingers felt hot against Dana's and her grip verged on painful. Dana slipped her hand from the other woman's with urgency. Dana almost looked down at the Black Hills gold ring on her right hand to see if she had permanent indentations in her fingers.

Sheriff Pizer slipped his arm around the woman. "My daughter."

"I hear you're going back to college this fall to complete your degree," Aunt Lucille said.

Jenny's gaze zipped around the room and settled on Lucille. "Stanford. University of Wyoming just wasn't the place for me."

Mrs. Pizer's smile took on self-assured proportions. "We were delighted when Jenny learned she'd been accepted. Of course, we'd love it if she stayed in Macon, found a nice man and settled down."

Jenny leveled a somewhat aggravated gaze on her mother, then hid it under a smile.

"Good God, no," Gregory said. "There aren't any eligible men in Macon for a woman with the brains to attend Stanford."

Pig. Dana imagined braining him with the nearest chair.

"Oh, I wouldn't say that," Jenny said, drawling her answer.

Curious, Dana watched Gregory and Jenny's gazes catch and hold. A prickling warning stirred through Dana. She didn't understand where the feeling came from and shoved it aside as an aberration.

"Want to dance, Jenny?" Neal asked.

Jenny seemed to hesitate, her gaze skimming Gregory's form once before nodding. "Sure."

Mrs. Pizer's nose seemed to wiggle like a rabbit's for a second before settling back into its thin, hawk like demeanor.

Soon the little gathering broke up, and Gregory traveled the room in search of conversation and no doubt female company.

Dr. Eric Dawes came by and appeared almost edible in a blue flannel shirt tucked into slender-fitting jeans.

"You look great," Eric said to Dana after kissing Aunt Lucille on the cheek and then shaking Dana's hand.

"Thank you, but I feel overdressed." She scanned the room and saw an abundance of women dressed in denim, suede; you name it. Anything but velour.

Eric looked bemused, and she knew she'd hit a topic women understood all too well and most men tried to ignore.

Aunt Lucille rescued him. "She stands out in the crowd. I think it's a lovely dress."

Dana wanted to say conspicuous wasn't always a good thing. She directed the conversation another way. "Better watch that flannel, Dr. Dawes. Everyone will think you're in competition with Marshall."

Eric laughed and his eyes held inner warmth. "I don't even see him here tonight."

Dana tried not to feel disappointment at the news, but it arrowed through her anyway. She kept a tight hold on her expression.

"Come to think of it, he does wear a shocking amount of flannel, doesn't he?" Aunt Lucille asked, tapping her chin with her index finger. "Let's see, Christmas is in a few months. We're going to have to do something about that boy's wardrobe, Dana."

"We?" Dana almost squeaked.

Aunt Lucille winked, then took Eric's forearm. "Come on, dear, let's have a dance. The music seems to have slowed to my pace."

Standing against the rough, log wall, Dana stared at the vast room. Wallflower for the evening. Dana didn't care; she'd rather hang near the door and hope for an easy escape. She sighed. Despite everything she'd heard about welcoming small towns, she felt the stranger through and through. Nothing fatal, of course. Just boring and—

"May I have this dance?" The deep voice rolled over her like silk and honey.

She hadn't noticed the stranger's approach from the side, and when she gazed at him her mouth almost dropped open. Holy Toledo. Incredible broad shoulders filled his navy and red flannel shirt. The rest of him had been poured into new blue jeans and cowboy boots.

The devil on her shoulder asked, 'What is it with the men of Macon? Did they own stock in the flannel industry?' The angel on her other shoulder asked, 'Who cares? At least they know how to wear their jeans.'

His wild black hair, shiny and wavy, tossed about his shoulders like he'd arrived in a windstorm. His angular face defined rugged, utter masculinity. Dark chocolate eyes sparkled with a fire that made her breath hitch for a moment.

"Um…yes," Dana managed to croak. "I'd love to dance."

As he led her onto the dance floor, she liked the way he kept a respectful distance. Like he'd wait to know a woman before trying any funny business. His warm, big hand cradled her fingers and his other hand cupped her waist.

"I'm Logan Reece. I'm a good friend of Brennan Marshall's. He's told me all about you."

Alarm bells pealed in Dana's head. "Hmm. That's interesting considering he doesn't know all about me."

Logan's mouth moved into a small smile that disappeared in a flash. "Let me rephrase that. He said you're in town for awhile, living at your Aunt's house."

"Ah, I see. How long have you known him?"

"Since high school."

Yeah. When you were both gawky, pimply, awkward sorts? As if! She doubted either man had experienced an awkward childhood. Dana's curiosity flamed. As they turned about the crowded floor, she glanced around. No sign of Marshall.

"He's not here." Logan grinned, a sinful concoction that no doubt drove women within inches of lunacy. To her surprise, his handsome face didn't fire either her imagination or her libido the way—

Oh, no, Dana. Don't go there. You will not think of Marshall that way now or in the future if you know what's good for you. Nada. Nein. Nope.

"Is he on duty?" she asked before she could stop herself.

Logan's big shoulders lifted, then fell. "I'm not sure. For all I know he might have a hot date."

His grin teased, but her stomach did an elevator drop into the basement. "Oh." Several moments went by before she spoke again. "So Marshall mentioned me to you?"

"Yeah. Once. Then Aunt Lucille said you'd be at this party. I ran into her in the grocery store the other day."

Oh, man! Aunt Lucille had already planned for her to attend this dance days ago. "Oh, oh. She's not trying to set you and I up, is she?"

His thick brows went up. "Maybe. She did say she hoped you wouldn't be lonely while you were here. You looked pretty unhappy standing against the wall."

Nothing like being direct. "I was bored."

The dance ended, but another slow tune started and he kept a grip on her hand. She went along, deciding his good humor and pleasant personality far outweighed her stepcousin, Gregory. She glanced at the sidelines and saw Gregory eyeballing her and Logan with a strange glare in his eyes.

"Do you live in Macon?" she asked.

"I grew up on a ranch outside of Macon. Now I'm parked in Atlanta for the time being. Marshall asked me to help him with a case."

Dana's suspicion-o-meter rose several degrees. "Don't tell me you're a cop, too?"

For the first time he appeared uncertain, and the doubt flickered in his eyes for a second before vanishing. "Not exactly. Not anymore."

"That case wouldn't happen to involve Aunt Lucille and a haunted bed, would it?"

He nodded, surprising her that he'd admit it so fast. Niggling alarm went through her. "Wait a minute. He must think something is drastically wrong if he's asking for outside help."

Logan's face went as stiff and immobile as a log. "You'll have to ask him."

"But he's not here, and I'm not that patient. Now you tell me what's up or I might have to hurt you."

He laughed, a rich sound that rippled and flowed. "He said you might tell me that. And you know, I think you probably could hurt me."

"I will if you don't tell me what's going on."

"I can't do that. Not unless Marshall gives me the go ahead or tells you himself. It's confidential." He leaned in closer, and his warm breath touched her ear. "I'm not going to say anything in a room full of people."

"He's right, Dana."

Dana jumped, startled by Marshall's sudden appearance behind her.

Logan released her, and they stood in the middle of the dance floor while other people boogied around them to a faster tune.

Marshall turned his attention to his friend. "Thanks for keeping her out of trouble."

Logan gave Marshall an irreverent grin and salute. "My pleasure."

Dana planted her hands on her hips. "Keeping me out of trouble? You make me sound like a toddler in need of corralling."

Marshall shrugged as if to say, 'if the shoe fits'. Dana stood, open mouthed, as the dancing, noise, and partying went on around her. Logan, like a dark phantom, faded into the crowd.

Marshall stepped forward and without preliminaries tugged her close. Dana's hands found purchase at his powerful shoulders. His arms slid around her waist, and before she knew it he had her plastered closer to him than peel on a banana. Taking a chance, she gazed into his eyes. Warm, sinful flutters entered her stomach and made her want to shift closer to him.

She licked her lips. "I thought you had to work."

"Just got off."

"Did you really send Logan to keep an eye on me?" She wanted to feel indignation, but couldn't.

"Not exactly. He said he'd be here, and because of your case, he's keeping a close watch for strange activity. You qualify as strange activity."

"Thanks, Marshall. Remind me to write you out of my will."

He nodded toward Aunt Lucille, who did a slow waltz with an older man. "I really want him to keep tabs on Lucille, but he'll also keep a watch on you."

He snuggled her against him, and it forced her arms to slip around his neck. Moments ago she'd appreciated Logan keeping his distance. Now she allowed Marshall to press tight against her from chest, to groin, to thighs, to knees. Dana shivered, but not with cold or distaste. She stifled a groan of pleasure. Maybe she could give in, for a while, to the overwhelming physical attraction churning in her gut. Perhaps one night of—

No!

Her excruciating relationship with Frank Bevans all those years ago had served to spoil her on men for the last several years.

Besides, a one-time bed session wouldn't solve the intermittent craving she had for male companionship. She hadn't known a man's lovemaking in almost ten years, but her body hadn't forgotten what it felt like. Something deep inside always reminded her of her sexuality and that she hadn't lost her human needs along with her broken heart. Dana eased away from old memories. Her broken heart mixed with the shame and guilt she experienced when she thought of Frank.

Not a good time to reminisce.

Marshall's gaze slid down to her low neckline and warmth filled her face. He swept a heated glance over her that almost melted her knees. Her feelings jumped from amazed to excited. Inhaling deeply, she caught his warm, spicy scent. *How can I think about a man's crazy-making sensuality at a time like this?* But she did. His eyes held a thousand mysteries and made her want his protective embrace. Brennan Marshall inspired fantasies of satin and velvet pillows piled high by a roaring fireplace, popcorn and hot cider. She didn't dare go further than that. Venturing deeper into fantasy meant visions of him naked in bed. With her.

No. That went way over the top.

He nodded toward her neckline. "That's an interesting piece of jewelry. I haven't seen too many women wear a ring on a necklace."

She almost touched her Dad's ring. "Thanks."

"Old boyfriend's college ring?"

Dana let out a tiny laugh. "No. Not hardly."

She half expected him to probe for answers like a good cop would. Instead, he kept his mouth clamped shut.

When Clint Black and Lisa Hartman sang about love forever more, Marshall moved her a little faster, drawing her into a sinuous, sensual tempo. The man danced with a sexual rhythm that sent her libido into trip-hammer overdrive. Continual heat washed through her as his body slid against her in ways that made her want him.

Stop, Dana. Don't give in to some odd hormone rush. It doesn't make any sense.

"Are you going to stare at me like that all night?" she asked in defense. "Or do I have to drag that information out of you, too?"

"Don't try driving a hard bargain with me, Dana. Logan's here as a consultant. That's all you need to know."

"What is he? A psychic?"

Marshall closed his eyes for a moment as if he might lose patience. When he opened his eyes, he slipped his right hand a little lower on the material covering her hips. Any lower and he'd cup her butt.

She doubted he'd do that in public, but the hint of the forbidden made her want to squirm. She made a tiny, uncontrollable shimmy with her hips.

His hand moved back to her waist. Damn! Damn!

"I don't think he's got a psychic bone in his body," Marshall said.

"A sex therapist?"

He jerked his head back almost as if she'd slapped him. "What?"

Dana's hands slid down to his shoulders. "A sex therapist. You know, they—"

"I know what a sex therapist is." His eyes narrowed, his brows lowered. "Why would you think Logan is a sex therapist, for God's sake?"

She shrugged. "Well, maybe we need someone to decipher the noises coming from the heart-shaped bed." She dragged her gaze back to his and observed his heightened color. "Are you embarrassed, Marshall?"

"Why would I be embarrassed?"

"You never know. A man your age might find the topic—"

"My age? How old do you think I am?"

"Forty?"

He cursed softly. "Thirty-six."

"Keep your voice down. Someone will hear you."

Marshall tightened his grip around her waist and she felt nothing but a powerful chest and the unmistakable hint of his…arousal. Oh, my lord. This time her face flamed.

"What's the matter?" he asked.

"Uh, nothing."

"Huh."

"You know, I think 'huh' is universal man language. Guess we haven't progressed that far from the cave."

"Huh."

"See what I mean?" Once on a roll, though, she found she couldn't stop baiting him. She shifted gears. "Logan is a striking man."

He grunted. "I'll let him know you said that."

"Don't you dare."

"How are you going to stop me?"

"I…." She didn't have a clue, and she almost whacked his shoulder with her fist. "Don't tell him."

"All right." Something challenging, angry, and yet excited flew through his gaze. She saw it all and it made her stomach tingle with equal urgency. "But it's going to cost you."

Wary, she leaned back a tad and glared. "What?"

"Don't worry. I'll think of something." His nice, carved mouth moved, intriguing her far too much as her gaze settled on his lips.

His suggestive tone took her off guard, and she performed her automatic defense mechanism. Sarcasm. "Chinese water torture? Spending time at another community center dance? Being locked in the clink at the sheriff's department? Hand cuffed?"

"Hand cuffing sounds like a good idea," he said huskily.

Dana had already blushed about twenty times since he'd pulled her into his arms. When she realized what he implied, heat washed over her. She almost gasped. She realized they'd fallen head first into a sexual dance that involved more than their bodies.

"You're a very naughty boy, Marshall."

Marshall's whiskered face took on that lumberjack expression she'd seen the day she'd met him. "Are you always so flippant?"

His hard tone cut through to the bone, and she flinched. She knew she deserved it. "Yes."

"I don't believe that."

She shrugged. "That's not my problem."

Anger prickled in his gaze and Dana knew she'd fallen into deep quiche. He took her arm and before she knew it, he'd drawn her into a back room adjacent to a kitchen area. She had two seconds to realize it was a huge pantry. The light flicked on and then he closed the door.

Oh, boy, Dana. You're gonna get it now.

Chapter 7

"Hey, what are you doing?" Dana asked with a squawk. "You seem to have this thing for hauling women around by the—"

"Dana, be quiet, please," Marshall said with a soft, raspy tone that rippled over her skin and through her body. "Listen to me for once. I'm not going to hurt you."

Her pulse triple timed and her heart pounded with anticipation. What did he have in mind? Suddenly, she noticed the pantry held an inordinate amount of peanut butter jars and tomato soup. She inhaled various scents: spices, honey, flour. She could almost taste each on her tongue and her stomach growled in response. *Stop it! This is ridiculous. Now isn't the time to think about food, especially when almost two hundred pounds of pure male has me cornered in a pantry.*

"All right. I'm listening," she said softly.

When he stepped forward, she moved back and bumped the wall behind her.

His brow furrowed. "Are you afraid of me?"

"Well, let's see. It's not every day a man marches me off the dance floor and flings me into a pantry and closes the door. Wouldn't you expect me to be afraid?"

When he put his hands down on either side of her head, she almost jumped out of her skin. His hot gaze did a foray over her dress, then back up to land with maddening precision on her mouth. "I didn't fling you. I guided you. I never fling women anywhere. But you should be frightened."

A tingle of apprehension made its way up her spine. "What are you going to do? Frisk me?"

His gaze hardened. Mistake! Mistake! Her mind shrieked. Maybe she'd gone too far this time. She shivered, the cold wall soaking through the velour like she was naked.

"If I was your Wile E. Coyote stepcousin out there, I just might," he said.

"Neal or Gregory?"

"You know which one I'm talking about. Gregory. Now I have a few questions for you, and I want some straight answers."

She pressed her palms against the cool wall. The bumpy logs behind her felt uncomfortable. But she'd endure it, even if it meant getting a splinter in her can. "Fire away."

"Tell me more about Gregory."

"You probably know as much about him as I do."

"Does he have financial problems? Does he think Lucille has money stashed in her house? A large bank account that he could inherit if she suddenly died?"

The implications set her back, her heart taking a plunge at the thought. "I don't know. What are you saying? That you think Gregory would…would murder her?"

"Anything is possible."

"Well, I don't know. I haven't got access to his bank account. How should I know if he's got problem? You can be very sure I have nothing to do with him most of the time."

"Most of the time."

She sighed, exasperated. "Is there an echo in here? That's what I said."

"So you've never had a thing for Gregory?"

The wild idea that Marshall could be jealous ran through Dana and gave her an odd jolt of pleasure. She smiled. "You're kidding, right? A worm like him?"

"Doesn't matter. Some people are turned on when someone doesn't like them. Maybe he thinks you're playing hard to get."

Dana couldn't believe the direction of the conversation. "I don't know what he thinks."

Marshall's well-carved mouth tightened, and she could have sworn she saw something different enter his eyes. "Are you afraid of him? Has he ever hurt you or threatened you?"

Startled, she answered quickly. "No. He's never hurt me." She realized Marshall had hit on something disturbing. "In the past, when I was younger, he did scare me a couple of times. He can be pushy and intimidating. He's greedy and amoral. Aunt Lucille doesn't always see it, but I do."

His entire body seemed to tighten, his muscles bunching and his face going cold with restrained anger. He looked like he wanted to hit something.

When he didn't speak, her unquenchable desire to exasperate him arose again. "Is this the way you usually interrogate suspects?"

One corner of his mouth dared to twitch. His jaw tightened. "You're not a suspect, Dana."

"Okay, then, do you usually sequester women in pantries and trap them between your arms?"

"No."

"Then why am I so different? Some women might charge you with harassment for something like this."

"Would you tell Sheriff Pizer I'm harassing you?"

She contemplated the idea, but it didn't sit well in her stomach. No need for him to know that. "Maybe."

"I don't believe you. One, you know I'd never hurt a woman. Two, you know I have Lucille's best interests at heart. Three, you know none of the other officers in the sheriff's department would believe that heart-shaped bed story." Soft and sincere, Marshall's voice made her believe. "And I want you to remember how easily a man could harm you. I've got you trapped in this pantry, and I'm between you and the door. Don't ever let a man get you in this position again."

His warning made her blood chill. A ripple of fear made her shrink back.

Remorse altered his expression, and he brushed her cheek with gentle fingertips. "Cold?"

"A little."

His gaze coasted over her dress, and an appreciative smile flitted over his lips. "I can see why."

Dana shivered again, her palms still flat against the wall. "The dress was Aunt Lucille's idea, not mine."

He took in her neckline, her breasts, hips and legs in a way that trailed pure fire. His obvious interest reheated her blood. "I like her taste."

Time seemed to hang like a bird riding a thermal, lingering, floating. She could hear the sexy wail of a saxophone through the walls, and wondered if she'd entered la-la land where anything can and did happen. If Dana thought she'd felt heat before, nothing compared to the undeniable tension she experienced whenever she came near him. Dangerous, very dangerous. Her mind screamed a warning while her heart slammed in her chest. Why else could one burly, tough-as-cowhide cop make her want to hold him all night long?

A sweet languor spilled through every sinew as she took in his rapt expression. *No. I have to be imagining it. The man looks like he wants to eat me up with a spoon.* Wild, uninhibited tenderness made her lean a fraction closer. Was his mouth closer? *Oh, man. He looks like he wants to kiss me.* Her lips tingled.

Suddenly he moved back a little, cupping her shoulders. "I'm sorry I was a little rough on you just now."

Dana had never seen a man so capable of playing the hard-nosed cop one minute, then turning into a concerned teddy bear. "No sweat. It's not every day a cop pins me to a wall in a...." She looked around. "A pantry fully of peanut butter and tomato soup, by golly."

He grinned, then reached in his rear jeans pocket and retrieved his wallet. He extracted a business card and held it out to her. "Here. My office, home and cell phone numbers are on it. You hear or see anything suspicious at Lucille's house, you call me. If you think there's immediate danger, call 911 instead. All right?"

Dana gazed at the card like it had a disease. Finally, she snatched it from his hand. With a grin and a wink she tucked it into the neckline of her dress and into her bra.

Marshall's gaze snagged on her breasts until she cleared her throat. She saw heat crawl up his neck and into his face and had the perverse pleasure of knowing she'd rattled his cage.

He swallowed hard, then opened the door. Dana stepped through, almost running into Kerrie.

"Hey, there you are." Kerrie grinned and hugged Dana. She tossed Marshall a teasing grin. "Hi, big lug."

To Dana's complete surprise, Marshall cracked a face-splitting grin and wrapped Kerrie in a close hug. Curiosity and another emotion Dana refused to acknowledge jumped up and bit her. Maybe Kerrie hadn't told her the whole story about her relationship with Marshall. The idea her friend might have the hots for Marshall and vice versa burned a hole straight through her gut.

"How's things?" Kerrie asked them as Marshall let her go.

Marshall glanced from Kerrie to Dana with a sardonic expression. "As well as can be expected."

Kerrie didn't look convinced. "Uh-huh. I heard you guys came back here."

Dana felt the heat of embarrassment, certain that Kerrie and others thought she'd come in here to rendezvous with Marshall. "We were talking about Aunt Lucille's haunted bed."

"Did you come to any conclusions?" Kerrie asked.

Marshall brushed by Dana and Kerrie. "Nothing we can agree upon. I've got things to do, ladies. I'll see you."

"Oh, before you go out there, Tommy is here. His mom and dad wanted to thank you again for saving his life," Kerrie said.

Marshall's relaxed expression went back to stony. "He doesn't need to thank me. I was doing my job."

"Tommy has a present for you," Kerrie said. "And I think he'd be very disappointed if you didn't talk to him. He might not understand."

Marshall's shoulders tensed, as if she'd hit him with something. "I can't help it if he doesn't understand."

Shocked at his insensitive behavior, Dana glared at him. "He's just a boy, Marshall."

He seemed to sag under a great weight, his demeanor changing to doubt. "Of course. I wasn't thinking. I'll see you later." He turned away and went for the door, but stopped with his hand on the doorknob. "Remember what I said, Dana."

Kerrie peered at her once he'd left. "What was that all about?"

Dana started for the door. "It's a long story. Come on. I'll buy you a drink."

Back in the thick of the party, though, Dana saw something that made her stop.

Kerrie almost bumped into the back of her. "What is it?"

Dana nodded toward one corner of the room where Marshall stood with Tommy and his parents. While Marshall shook the parent's hands, the boy gazed up at Marshall with clear hero-worship. The boy spoke, and Marshall's stern expression dissolved into a genuine warm grin.

Dana's breath caught in her throat as Tommy handed Marshall a wood carving of an animal. It was too far away for Dana to see what type of animal. Marshall turned the object over in his hand, inspecting it, his grin widening. Then he got down on his haunches, bringing himself down to the boy's level. When he drew the boy into his arms for a hug, Dana saw something that looked like genuine happiness mixed with unbelievable pain cross Marshall's face.

Sympathetic tears stung Dana's eyes as she absorbed the implications of the little scene before her. So Marshall did have a soft side. This fact made Dana glow deep inside, filling her with a feeling of admiration she didn't want to acknowledge.

"Wow," Kerrie said.

"Yeah," Dana whispered around the hard lump forming in her throat.

Dana watched as Kerrie cruised her living room, straightening things with the age-old habit installed in her by her neat-freak mother. They waited for the kettle in the kitchen to scream. A hot cup of tea would go a long way to curing what ailed Dana. At least she hoped it would.

She'd told her aunt she needed some quality time with her good friend. Aunt Lucille said she'd ride home by way of Gregory or Neal, because she had no intention of leaving the party yet. Anxiety had crept through Dana about her aunt's welfare, but Kerrie insisted the older woman would be fine.

As a punctuation mark to her bizarre evening, Dana noted before she left the revelry that Marshall and his sidekick Logan had already disappeared from the party.

Dana felt at ease for the first time tonight. Nothing like a good old-fashioned girl talk session to clear the brain. The kettle wailed and Kerrie ran to make tea. She came back a few moments later with steaming, huge mugs. As she glided into the room, Dana couldn't help but admire her friend.

Kerrie's commanding presence, all six-feet of her, always made Dana feel like a midget. Not that five feet, six inches came close to short. Dana tried to stop comparing herself to others, but she hadn't reached the mark yet.

Dana self-consciously tugged down the dress, something she'd been doing all evening. Now Marshall's business card seemed to burn her breast and itch at the same time. But she sure wasn't going to reach in her bra and pull out the card.

Kerrie stopped bustling a moment, sagged into a recliner, and took a sip of tea. She pushed a strand of her long, straight blonde hair away from her face. "If you watch over this place when I head off to Jamaica soon, it'll be great knowing you're here."

"Oh, yeah. Watching over this beautiful house would be such a hardship."

Kerrie laughed. "No wild parties while I'm gone, eh?"

Kerrie's laugh cheered Dana to the core. Maybe Kerrie could heal while she traveled. She tried to imagine the tremendous pain Kerrie had experienced when her husband had been killed last year.

Tears welled in Dana's eyes, but she forced them back. "No wild anything. I'm looking forward to quiet and quieter. Just what I need to get rid of this block."

"I think you'll find plenty around town to rejuvenate your muse. Any ideas why you're stuck?"

"I'm dried up. R and R is in definite order."

"So you don't plan on doing actual writing while you're here? Just absorbing?"

Dana shrugged. "I might just soak up atmosphere. If the writing comes, it comes."

Kerrie scratched her long nose with a carnation-pink polished nail. "I thought you said discipline is important?"

"It is. But this is more a vacation, vacation rather than a working. You know what I mean?"

"Your way with words is incredible. Vacation, vacation."

Puffing up like a proud hen, a silly grin curving her lips, Dana said, "That's what I'm paid to do. Entertain with words."

"Well, I don't think you'll be disappointed in Macon for inspiration. It's got enough character for a whole library."

Dana snickered. "Don't I know it? If the last few days are any indication, I'd say I've done well to survive the hospitality."

Frowning, Kerrie took another sip of her tea, then put the mug down on a cork coaster on the side table next to her chair. "So what do you think?"

Dana uttered a weary sigh. She leaned her head back. "About what?"

"Him."

"Nothing like being clear. Who?"

"Brennan Marshall. Intriguing man, no?"

Dana's insides did a double flip. Tonight's close encounter had escalated her libido into Indianapolis Five Hundred status. She reached for her Dad's ring and rubbed the precious metal with nervous fingers.

Kerrie waved a hand. "Earth to Mars, is anyone home?"

Flipping Kerrie an irritated look, Dana said, "He's arrogant, opinionated, and he dislikes me as much as I dislike him."

Kerrie's eyes narrowed to slits. "That's rather strong."

Dana shrugged. "Well, he disliked me first."

A sigh parted Kerrie's lips. "That was a misunderstanding."

"Hah!"

"You know your Aunt Lucille wouldn't like him if he didn't have a good heart and neither would I. You've seen how good he is with her. And that little boy Tommy? He saved his life and was so modest about it."

Dana understood all right. The way he'd taken care of the little boy had filled her admiration. She'd only experienced that kind of excitement around a man one other time. That situation had ended in disaster. A thousand pieces of her heart had littered the ground like confetti when Frank had left.

Still, Dana couldn't stop visualizing the worry on Marshall's face when he'd pulled the boy to shore. Top that off with the idea that Marshall might have died saving him, and Dana's gut clenched in reaction. No. She wouldn't think about it. Not now, not ever.

Kerrie blew an errant piece of hair off her forehead, then leaned forward. "You haven't known him long enough. Dana, I've never seen you this judgmental."

Before she could stop herself, Dana said softly, "I've never met a man like him before."

"Oh." One blond brow twitched. "I see."

"You see nothing."

Kerrie laughed. "He's pretty intense, isn't he?"

Crossing her legs, Dana pursed her lips and put an index finger to her chin in a thinking pose. "Gee, I dunno. I'd say growling about once an hour might qualify as intense."

Another set of giggles escaped Kerrie. "You've caught him during some bad times. You don't know the whole story."

"And I suppose you're going to tell me?"

"You want to see me live through next week? Marshall will kill me if I tell you."

"See, that's what I mean. Why would he treat a friend like that if he were so freaking nice?"

"You've seen how he treats me."

"Yeah, I've seen. Like you're a Faberge egg."

Kerrie propped her sandaled feet on the coffee table. "Jealous?"

"I thought you said there was nothing going on—"

"No, no." Kerrie flapped her hands in dismissal. "But I saw your reaction when he was hugging me. You shot not only daggers my way, but I think if you'd had a sword you would have cut off my head and his uh…you know." Kerrie's golden laugh trickled free again and one lock of her hair flopped across her eyes. She pushed the strand away, holding her hair back in a bunch for a moment before letting it cascade back to her shoulders. "Granted, he's not easy to know. He's deadly serious with his work. Not a man to cross."

"You're telling me."

"You're a writer. Maybe you should take notes about his personality. Could make a great character in a novel someday."

"I'm not curious enough to take notes."

Dana stood, ready to run from the conversation, frightened of how easily Kerrie read her. Instead, Dana reached for the nut bowl and grabbed a handful of cashews. As she snacked, she paced behind her chair.

Kerrie reached for her tea, shifted to the couch, and put her legs up.

Dana wished she could relax. Her nerves were stretched to the bursting point.

"I've known him since we were kids. So I've had a lot of time to see his million sides," Kerrie said.

"Sounds a little multiple personality to me."

"Maybe two personalities. People either hate him or love him. Doesn't seem to be any in between. I happen to be in the love camp. He just cuts the meat and doesn't stop to dribble steak sauce. Not everyone can handle that. His job requires quick action, and I think he is a wise-ass when he believes a person is being stupid."

Rubbing her temples again, Dana sighed. "So if he's so all fired wonderful, how come you didn't bag him a zillion years ago?"

"We're not about that." Kerrie plunged onward, her eyes alive with amusement. "He's like my brother. He's wicked and funny and cares about things so deeply I think he teeters on the edge of caring too much. I'm not a match for him, and he's not for me."

"Humph."

Kerrie's grin turned conspiratorial. "You might be the first woman I've known who didn't get an almost immediate crush on him once they'd met him."

Dana made a disgusted sound. "You've got to be kidding."

"Haven't you noticed what a hunk he is?" Kerrie made a sweeping gesture with one hand.

Dana shrugged. "He's kinda plain, actually. Ordinary even."

"Plain? Ordinary? Girlfriend, where are your eyes? He's built with a bod to die for."

Unwilling to admit that she thought he looked beyond good, Dana sneered. "His face is sort of…I dunno…almost baby cute. No, that doesn't quite explain it."

Kerrie threw her head back and laughed. "In his own way he's striking, Dana. Women I've talked to say he's got this…this palpable heavy-duty masculinity. A sort of raw animal magnetism that reels them in."

"For the kill, yeah."

"That's not it. Maybe it's his passion. He lives each moment and gives everything he can to something he believes in. How many people do you know who can say that about themselves?"

Dana winced. She was all too aware of her own shortcomings. "Practically no one."

Silence enveloped the room while Dana stewed. A niggling thought entered her consciousness, prickling like an irritating feather applied to the bottom of her foot. *What if I don't like him because he turns me on? Because my hormones don't give a flip what I think of his personality. Bah!*

"Are you sure you don't want to move in here with Lucille while I'm in Jamaica?" Kerrie asked after a lengthy silence. "Think of all the peace and quiet."

"I didn't even bring my lap top." Dana took a few steps toward the foyer.

"So write in the sunlight with pen and paper. Haven't you ever done that?"

Dana nodded. "I prefer my keyboard. If I write it out, I have to type it all into the computer later."

Kerrie gave her a 'aren't you a lazy wench' look. "So? Wouldn't you rather have good writing you could use? Aren't you afraid the muse will hit and if you don't write it down you'll miss it?"

Dana stopped at the hall tree and retrieved her light jacket. "Are you sure you're not a writer?"

Kerrie pushed back her hair again. "No, but I know you well enough to realize this writer's block won't last forever. You just need time to discover what is blocking you. I think if you spend time with pen, paper, and nature, you'll write again."

A strong upwelling of emotion made Dana's eyes water, and her throat tightened. Not being able to write was damned hard work. She knew all she had to do was sit down and write and somehow the right words would evolve. Dana looked at the floor, not wanting her friend to see how she felt.

She shrugged into her jacket. "Thanks for the advice, Kerrie. You're a good friend. I'd better hit the road before it gets too late."

As Dana opened the door, Kerrie turned on the porch light. "Ten o'clock sharp tomorrow. Booth twenty. You forget and your butt is mine."

Dana laughed and waved as she unlocked her car door. "I'll be there."

The car ate up the road as Dana headed down Kerrie's long driveway and into the night.

Sighing to rid her body of tension, she peered into the darkness. Kerrie lived out in the country past Aunt Lucille, on the same road, and the lonely night seemed to swallow everything in blackness. Dirt road ran beneath her wheels, dust flying into the headlights like particles of snow. She hadn't gone far when she saw headlights approaching from the rear. She ignored them.

She thought forward to tomorrow's town fair and the booth she'd promised to man. Good old Kerrie had refused to give details, saying that any money produced by the booth went to charity. Dana knew the fair needed help, and if Kerrie said she needed assistance, Dana wouldn't deny her. Still, Kerrie wouldn't be above mischief.

Suddenly, lights blinked in the rear view mirror, blinding in intensity. She glanced into the mirror and saw the car behind her barreling like crazy toward her.

"Shit!" Her heart leapt upward and jammed somewhere around her throat. "What the hell does this guy think he's doing? Fine, moron, go around me. I'm already going over the speed limit. I hope Marshall pops out of the woodwork and nails your ass."

Before she had a chance to become frightened, the car rammed the rear bumper with incredible force.

Chapter 8

Dana cursed as the impact snapped her head back and Bertha swerved. Fighting the wheel, she ignored the twinge in her neck. Dana's car lurched again as the crazy person behind her smacked the vehicle with a powerful blow.

Another bone-rattling crunch sent Berta into a sidewise twist. Dana's heart slammed as she wrestled her car into a straight form on the narrow dirt road. Tires crunched rock and bounced over the washboard surface. Dana poured on the speed, cramming down the urge to scream. Her throat tightened until she rasped, shivers of terror threatening to overrule her ability to cope. Struggling with overwhelming fear, she reached for courage.

With a last, murderous push, the car behind her sent Bertha into a spin. Dana's car careened to the left, fishtailing. The steering wheel wrenched from her fingers and the car bounced like a demented Mexican jumping bean off the road and down the long embankment toward the trees.

Dana didn't scream. Instead she cursed and cursed as Bertha bucked like a wild horse and plunged over rocks.

That's it. Bertha's had it. I've had it.

The car hit a tree near the bottom of the steep embankment, wrenching her body like a rag doll.

Lucille's house looked calm tonight, but Marshall didn't want to leave. Closky parked a ways down the road to intercept any cars that approached. Although off duty, Marshall had decided he'd check around the house before he left. Now he sat in the Grand Cherokee in front of the house and wondered if he'd lost his mind. He'd gotten Sheriff Pizer to put Closky on Lucille's house full time for a couple of nights. It took some finagling. Marshall had explained he suspected prowlers were menacing Lucille, and he'd never mentioned the bed that made noises. He didn't want anyone thinking Lucille had flown the chicken coop without all her feathers.

He gritted his teeth as he remembered the rest of the evening.

He couldn't believe he'd danced with Dana. Number one, being anywhere near her caused his heart to beat in ways that threatened his sanity. Second, he couldn't believe he'd pulled her into the pantry. He wouldn't have been surprised if Pizer called him into his office and told him to turn in his badge and gun pending an investigation into sexual harassment charges.

No. He hadn't sexually harassed Dana.

Yet, when he'd stood near her, had her in his arms, he'd almost lost control. Almost dipped down to taste her lips. *Face it, sport. You wanted her in that pantry so you could get her alone.*

God, but he'd been tempted to gather her closer. But this time not to dance.

And the idea of Gregory touching her made his gut clench in anger. He held the steering wheel tight, staring into the night. He wished he could stop the unsettled feeling gripping him tonight after he left Dana and Kerrie at the party.

Seeing Kerrie had been a relief. With Kerrie he felt companionable and safe. Nothing sparked between them like a firestorm. When he got within a few feet of Dana Cummings, the world seemed to light up with an earth-shattering energy he couldn't escape.

He'd tried to understand, other than pure animal attraction, what he felt for her. He liked her intelligence, wit, and fortitude under pressure. She also drove him nuts with her demands, her barbs, and her mistrust of him.

His suspicions were raised when he saw Gregory and Neal at the party. Both men didn't make it into Macon often. He'd wondered right away if Gregory had a plot going to drive sweet Lucille insane. Not that it made sense for Neal. The man didn't seem to possess a greedy bone in his body. He would question both men and discover if they had any part in the odd happenings at Lucille's house.

Thoughts of Dana intruded again. She might drive him bonkers with sexual urges, but long ago Marshall realized he couldn't trust his instincts when it came to women. As he simmered in thoughts of Dana's flaming red hair and taunting eyes, he paid little attention to the squawking radio. Wrenching his traitorous mind back to business, he stared into the night.

Dana groaned as an ache passed through her body, the sinking and settling of the car trembling into her skin, her bones, her innards. She heard the rat-tat-tat of the engine as it sputtered to an end. Creaks and groans coursed through Bertha like a dying person.

Dana cursed. "Fifthly, stinking, ass, creep, jerk! The bastard has killed my car!"

Get over it. You're still alive, aren't you?

She hadn't blacked out, but her entire system felt shocked by the impact. She opened her eyes and gave herself a moment to assess damage. From the splintered windshield, slight upward tilt of the dash, and the crooked way the front doors hung on the car, she knew the vehicle was totaled.

An odd calm swept over her, as if she had nothing to worry about but the anger bubbling through her. She shifted her arms and legs slowly. Nothing seemed broken. Full realization she survived the crash sent relief washing through her. Then a new fear stabbed her. What if that butthead is out there watching?

She tried to smile around her trepidation. "This is a fine mess you've gotten yourself into, Cummings."

Dana inched her body around to gaze into the darkness and groaned as a muscle in her back protested. She didn't see any headlights. Good. Still, she didn't feel safe. Should she play dead and stay in the car until help could reach her? Someone had meant to either hurt her or kill her, and if they watched nearby, they may already realize she'd survived the crash.

She couldn't see much in the darkness, but she unbuckled her seatbelt, fumbled through the glove compartment and found her cell phone. Marshall. She needed him now. She slipped the business card from her bra and squinted into the darkness, trying to see the tiny letters. Lucky for her the moon rose high and almost full, affording enough light for her to read. She dialed his cell phone, hoping she'd picked the right number to reach him. He could be anywhere. Her fingers trembled as she put the phone to her ear and waited one ring. Two rings. Three rings. Four. *Please, please. Answer.*

"Marshall." He barked the word out, startling her.

"It's Dana." Her voice cracked. "I need your help."

"What? Where are you?"

She gave him the location. "There's been an accident. I've been run off the road, and I hit a tree. I'm not sure the bastard who ran me off the road isn't still lurking around."

Marshall spilled a couple of vehement expletives. "Are you hurt?"

"No. No—"

"Don't move, don't get out of the car and stay quiet. Do you see anybody around?"

She looked around and nothing but moonlight and darkness greeted her. "No. Maybe he's not here." Dana thought she heard noises in the background, then the roaring of an engine. "Where are you?"

"In the Cherokee. Don't hang up. I'll be right there. I'm putting the phone down while I radio this in. Don't hang up."

"Yes, sir," she said feebly as she heard noises in the background.

Less than a half minute later, though, the cell phone let out a beep, almost vaulting her off the seat in fright. Trembling, she looked at the display on the phone.

"Oh, great." Low battery. "Of course! Of course!"

Then, as she watched, the phone blinked out. Served her right for not remembering to charge the thing. A full range of expletives, minus editing, spewed from her lips. When she felt somewhat better, she stopped.

Minutes passed as she waited for Marshall. She didn't like feeling this helpless, and decided if the maggot who'd run her off the road came near her, she'd break his neck. As the seconds passed claustrophobia entered her and she fought to hold it back. Trapped like a rabbit in a cage, she imagined eyes watching her from the woods, waiting…waiting….

The predator would spring out and—

"Stop!" She couldn't let her imagination turn her into a weenie. Fear remained high, trickling into her system with a flight or fight response. Could her intuition be trying to tell her something?

Maybe leaving the car wouldn't hurt. Dana tried the driver's side door and found it wouldn't budge. She grunted as she pushed with everything she had. Nope. Crawling over the middle console, she attempted to open the passenger side door.

"Bertha, I swear if you don't open—" The door protested with a wretched squeak, and she pushed it wide open. "Thank you, thank you, thank you."

From the direction of town, lights bounced down the road, and she stiffened in apprehension. It could be the person who'd wanted to make road pizza out of her. Better to stay near the car in case she had to lock herself inside. No. If they came near she could run, not be trapped in the car. Wait. What if they caught her when she ran?

Indecision played serious games with her mind as the headlights came nearer. *Well, at least I have two choices. Barricade or run.*

Dana waited, strung on a high-wire tension she thought would make her scream. Quivers raced across her body in the cold mountain air. She rubbed her arms.

Marshall's car roared to a stop at the top of the embankment, and she heaved a sigh of relief. She'd never been so happy to see anyone.

Marshall jumped from the vehicle, first-aid kit and flashlight in hand. At a speed that looked dangerous, he slid down the embankment. When he reached the bottom, Dana wanted to run to him. Instead, she stayed with her butt propped against the passenger door.

His chest heaved a little from the exertion of careening down the hill. He marched straight toward her, and then she saw a look she never thought she'd see in a man's eyes more than once in her life. When he'd gazed down at her in the bathtub after the tornado, concern had filled his expression. That same look reappeared, overlaid with a deeper worry. Seconds later, it transformed to angry.

All ideas about rushing into her rescuer's arms vanished as he stomped up to her. "I thought I told you to stay in the car!" He dumped the first aid kit on the ground. "Stubborn, pain in the—"

"Well, excuse me! I felt trapped in there."

"I should have known you wouldn't listen to me." He grasped her shoulders gently, but irritation etched his face. "Are you hurt anywhere? That's one of the reasons I asked you not to move."

Dana sensed the plug in the volcano giving way, and the fright and adrenaline pushed her over the edge. A huge shudder overtook the small tremors racing through her body.

"I told you I'm fine! In fact, now I'm sorry I even called you! I…I…" Tears sprang into her eyes and she couldn't stop their flow as they hit her eyelids and spilled. "I would appreciate a little more kindness, thank you very much! I just got the crap scared out of me and all you can do is yell!"

A sob escaped her and then her vision blurred. She heard rather than saw him come closer, and then his warm hands drifted from her shoulders to her face. He'd ditched the flashlight somewhere. Marshall cupped her face gently, and when another sob issued from her lips, he kissed her forehead softly. More surprise rippled through her.

"God, I'm sorry," he whispered. "Are you sure you're not hurt anywhere? An ambulance is on the way."

She nodded, afraid if she opened her mouth all that would issue forth would be gibberish. Another incredible shudder went through her. He released her, then took off his jacket. He slipped the coat around her shoulders and engulfed her in his heat and masculine scent.

Then, to her utter amazement, his drew her into his arms. He cupped the back of her head, pressing her into his shoulder. With his other hand he caressed her back with reassuring strokes, then gripped her tight. "Shhh. It's all right. You're all right."

His tender tone undid her, and the sobs came in earnest. Man alive. Where was all this fear and angst coming from? Dana didn't know, and right now didn't care. She felt too good wrapped in his care.

He made more reassuring noises, all the while caressing her back. "Easy. Easy."

She could have sworn she felt him kiss her head again, so tender that it made tears come harder. "I…I'm sorry."

"Why?" he asked softly.

Dana looked up, gazing into the warmest eyes she'd ever seen. Sweet comfort eased into her. "I yelled. I was just scared."

A small smile curved his mouth. "The lady admits she's scared. That surprises me."

"Was scared. I'm not anymore."

The grin turned broad. "Good." He reverted to the old Marshall, easing her back but keeping his arms around her. "Did you see anyone lurking around after the crash?"

"No."

"What is going on around here?"

"You're asking me? I've decided Macon has it out for me. This is scarier than a Stephen King novel." She gripped his shirtfront with both hands, mortified at the spot she'd made on his shoulder.

"Did you turn off your cell phone?"

"The battery went dead."

He released her. As he looked around the area, his expression became grim. He retrieved the flashlight and surveyed the area. "What a mess."

Tears threatened again, and she stifled them. "The jerk killed Bertha."

Marshall turned and stared at her. "Who?"

"My car. Bertha."

"Oh, yeah. Right." Sounding distracted, he peered into the tree line that created a wall along the embankment. "Did you see who was driving? What kind of car was it?"

She shook her head. "I think it was a sedan."

"Make and model?"

The cold seemed to get worse, clinging to her like mud on a pig. She couldn't remember the last time she'd felt this vulnerable and this useless. "I don't think…I don't remember."

Marshall reached for her, brushing his fingers over her forehead in a comforting gesture. "Did you hit your head again?"

"I wish I could use that as an excuse. I was just so rattled and it's dark. This butthead was trying to kill me, so I spent a lot more time trying to survive than worry about little details like the jerk's car."

To her surprise, he nodded. "It's all right. Don't worry about it right now."

Sirens wailed in the distance, and she pined him with a defiant look. "I'm not going to the hospital."

"Damn it Dana." He switched to other tactics, slipping his warm hand behind her neck, careful not to touch the spot where the branch had clobbered her. "You're going to the hospital if I have to hog tie you to the stretcher."

She almost didn't say it, but the thought came at the same time it escaped her lips. "That could be fun."

Instead of releasing her, he drew her a little closer. Dana thought she'd go up in flames as his gaze caressed her with a hot, welcome need. *Jeez, Louise. The man is looking at me like that again. As if he wants to take me up on the idea.* Everything around her dissolved. Fear, anger, and aches and pains.

Before he could speak, the ambulance and another sheriff's car roared to a stop next to Marshall's vehicle. As he released her, the link broke, but not before he gave her a last searching look that asked more questions than it answered.

Marshall knocked and announced his presence, then waited for Neal to answer his hotel room door. The Sleepy Side Hotel boasted the only semi-luxury accommodations in Macon, and Marshall guessed Neal made enough money to stay for as long as he liked.

One thought powered into his mind above all others. *If Neal had anything to do with Dana's accident, I'll grind the bastard into powder.*

Marshall had sent a deputy out to locate Gregory. He'd grill him to a crisp if he'd caused Dana's accident. Thoughts of what could have happened to her churned the acid in Marshall's stomach.

Marshall restrained the urge to pound on the door again, well aware he'd wake half the area if he did.

Screw it. He pounded on the door again. "Metcalf, open up!"

The door sprang open and Neal appeared at the doorway, a pair of silk blue boxers clinging to his skinny frame. Neal's blurry-eyed expression said he'd been in a deep sleep. "What's going on? It's almost oh dark thirty."

"Past that. I need to speak with you. We can either talk here or you can come down to the station."

Neal's open expression changed to indignation. Marshall knew he was rubbing over people like sandpaper right now, but he didn't care. Dana had almost lost her life tonight.

"Are you arresting me?"

"I'm asking you to answer my questions."

"So ask." Marshall brushed past Neal and Neal turned to glare at him as he closed the door. "What's going on?"

Marshall surveyed the room as he scanned for a weapon. Nothing in plain sight. The room held two queen-size beds. An open suitcase resided on the bed nearest the door, and Marshall caught a glimpse of a girly magazine peeking out from behind a pair of pants. The room smelled like stale cigarettes. He didn't remember ever seeing Neal smoke.

"Where were you tonight about midnight?" Marshall asked.

Neal's eyebrows pinched together and wrinkles covered his forehead. "Why?"

Marshall propped his butt against the mirrored bureau and crossed his arms. "Just answer the question."

"Hey, just let me get some clothes on."

"Sit."

"What?"

"Sit."

Like an obedient dog, the man sat on the bed next to the suitcase, his expression tangling between irritation and bewilderment. "Just ask the damn questions already."

"Where were you last night about twelve o'clock?"

"Sleeping. What the hell else would I be doing?"

"You could have been out driving."

Neal's eyes narrowed. "I was in bed. Sleeping. Just like I was a few minutes ago until you banged on the door." Neal's edge of defiance eased, but didn't disappear. He stood. "Hey, this isn't something about my Mom is it? Is she all right?"

The panic in the man's voice half convinced Marshall that Neal hadn't changed from the cheerful, mild-mannered Clark Kent his image projected. "She's fine. It's Dana."

Neal's mouth opened, then closed. "What? What's happened to her?"

"She was in a car accident tonight around midnight."

Neal planted his rear back on the bed. "Is she all right?"

Marshall nodded, then kept silent, hoping the quiet treatment would yield more results than wringing the man's neck for answers. He felt calmer now, but no less interested in finding the truth.

Neal's hair looked like it had been twisted through a food blender, and when he jammed a hand through it, the mess increased. "Thank God, she's okay. What happened exactly?"

"She was run off the road by a person or persons." As Marshall explained minor details about the accident, he watched Neal's expression and eyes for signs of deceit. He detected none.

Neal looked shaken, but Marshall had seen men lie and smile and never break a sweat.

"Mom said things have happened at the house, and to tell the truth that's part of the reason I wanted to come back to Macon for a visit. I wanted to see if she was...you know...imagining things."

"And you believe she is?"

He shook his head. "I don't know. I mean, it's freaking bizarre. Now Dana's accident." Comprehension dawned over his face.

"You don't think I ran Dana off the road—" He swore. "You do. You wouldn't be here otherwise."

"I'm investigating." Marshall's voice edged upward, turning it raw and harsh. "And if you know anything, anything at all, you'd better tell me now. If you don't, it'll be more than hell to pay. It'll be Armageddon."

Neal's face went chalky white and he stood. "Look, I don't know crap about this. I can't help you. I'll go over to the hospital and see Dana."

Marshall straightened to his full height, aware the smaller man would be intimidated. "It's past visiting hours and she's protected. You won't get near her."

"Protected?" Neal's eyebrows hitched up in a cartoon fashion. "Has she had death threats?"

"Yeah, I'd say getting run off the road qualifies as a death threat, wouldn't you?"

Neal's hands went up in a helpless gesture. "It could've been kids on a lark."

Disgusted with his reasoning, Marshall made a sound of disbelief. "I doubt it. There aren't that many murderous teens running around this town and you know it."

Neal fumbled for words, his mouth opening and closing like a dying fish. "Gregory wouldn't do something like that. He's a bastard sometimes, but he'd never kill anyone. A crazy drunk probably ran into her and then got scared and took off." When Marshall played stare down with Neal, the younger man's nervousness showed plainly on his face. "I'd never hurt Dana or anyone. It's not in me. You've known me long enough to realize that, Marshall."

His hands went up again, palms out, as if he would say something profound. Then his mouth closed and he said nothing.

"What were you going to tell me?" Marshall edged closer, moving away from the dresser.

Neal shook his head. "Just a thought. Nothing important."

"Tell me." Marshall bit out the words for emphasis.

Neal's eyes widened, a smidgen of fear and maybe sadness showing in his depths. "I dunno. I mean, I don't think Gregory would try to murder her for God's sake, but—"

"Spill it now, or I can promise you'll regret the day you met me."

Neal's eyes shot proverbial daggers and lightning bolts. "Did Dana ever tell you what a bastard he's been to her?"

A deep, icy cold sensation entered Marshall's stomach. He wanted to hunt down Gregory right now. "No. What did he do?"

Neal slid both hands through his hair, looking ridiculous and uncomfortable. "He's always been after Dana."

"Let's cut the obtuse crap, Metcalf. After Dana? What does that mean?"

Neal shrugged. "He's always thought she was hot. So he's been trying to get in her pants since she was a teenager."

"You mean when she was jail bait?"

"Exactly." Neal gave a nervous laugh. "We may not be related to Dana by blood, but the thought of cousins…I dunno. Makes my stomach lurch."

The bonfire burned higher within Marshall, and anger almost overruled his restraint. He clenched his fists at his sides and took two deep breaths. *Don't lose it now. You need a clear head to see what's happening here.*

He stalked to the door. "Thanks for the information, Metcalf." Yanking the door open, Marshall headed outside. "And if I hear you even breathed in Dana's general direction, I'll kick the shit out of you."

Chapter 9

Morning light spilled in Marshall's office, striking his face. He'd drifted in and out of sleep, stretched out in his chair with his feet on the desk. His mind felt like a marshmallow burned on a stick, his eyes gritty and his mouth dry. Peeling his eyes open, he stared at the single light in the office. A lamp illuminated a small circle on his desk. A report on last night's incidents awaited his attention. His computer needed booting up so he could dig through files.

Instead of starting to work on the report, he reached for the coffee pot and flipped the switch. He'd filled it with fresh water and coffee a few hours ago, but had never started it. It sputtered and coughed before doing its duty. He slumped back into his chair and closed his eyes again.

A door slammed somewhere in the outer office, then a voice, sharp and strident bellowed. "I'll sue the whole sheriff's department!"

Marshall groaned. Great. Freaking great. He'd recognize that whiny-assed voice anywhere. Gregory the "pissant" Metcalf.

Amazing how the man's suave and debonair façade cracked under a little pressure. His eyes popped open and he straightened in his chair. No more sleep for him today. Might as well pour a cup of sludge and prepare to roast Gregory Metcalf on a spit.

Skeeter knocked on the door and entered, announcing the obvious. "Gregory Metcalf is here. Do you want me to bring him in?"

Marshall stood. "Put him in the interrogation room."

Skeeter nodded and then started to close the door. Then he produced a strained look. "Oh, yeah, the Sheriff wants to talk with you. He got in ten minutes ago." Skeeter's expression eased into a tentative smile. "I think he'd be in here chewing your ass. But he got a call."

"Great. Looking forward to it," Marshall said, adding a sarcastic tinge to his words. "Where did you find Metcalf?"

"At the The Billiards Motel outside town. Way outside town."

"Uh-huh." Anyone who'd lived in town longer then six seconds knew The Billiards hosted a variety of prostitutes on a weekly basis. Gregory had probably been indulging in a little slap and tickle overnight. "Nobody with him?"

Skeeter shook his head. "Nope. Alone and naked as a newborn's butt. He opened the door that way."

Marshall laughed. "You're kidding, right?"

"Nope." Skeeter chuckled and closed the door.

As Skeeter left Marshall wondered if Sheriff Pizer wanted his butt because Dana had called him, or because Neal wanted to complain about police brutality or some other nonsense. No, Dana hadn't acted angry once he'd held her in his arms and comforted her. She'd clung to him like a child, and her sobs had torn at his heart. Dug into him and opened up places inside he thought closed forever.

Concern for her ate at him, as it had when she'd first fallen into his arms in this very office. No, it went back further than that. He remembered how she'd felt under him in the bathtub. He'd felt the kick way down in his gut and lost his breath in the same instant.

He reached for the phone and started to dial, but he hung up. No, Dana didn't need him waking her up. She needed rest after what had happened to her. Besides, Marshall had arranged for another protective measure. Logan kept watch on the house through the rest of the night after Closky left for the evening. Logan phoned last night when Dana had returned home from the hospital, and he'd reported in on a regular basis throughout the night. She'd be safe for now.

For now. He knew, in a visceral way, that he couldn't count on her safety forever. Security, like a mirage, was an illusion. Accidents happened, illnesses occurred. Most of the time he didn't clutter his mind with gloomy thoughts, but the last few days hadn't made for easy thinking or sleeping. He'd lost his appetite and his stomach churned. Taking a deep breath to shove away the tight feeling in his gut, he poured a fresh cup of coffee and headed for the cross-examination room. Grill 'em and spill 'em. That's what Sheriff Pizer called it, and the name fit right.

When he first saw Gregory, he noted a fine sheen of sweat covered the man's face. Features women drooled over looked strained and harried. Good. Served the bastard right. He hoped the guilt leaked out of the creep right here. There'd be no one to mop him up.

The prominent businessman, used to cool-as-a-polar bear's-ass-on-ice negotiations, didn't come across calm or collected. Gregory's right eyelid twitched, and his hair looked almost as messy as his brother's had earlier. His long sleeved white dress shirt appeared rumpled, and he lacked a tie. Amazing. This man never went out of the house without a tie, or so Lucille had told him long ago.

Marshall let Metcalf stew as he took a long, slow sip of coffee. He looked at Gregory over the brim of the gargantuan mug. Then he sighed with satisfaction. Nothing like a good caffeine jolt. "Coffee, Metcalf?"

When Gregory's jaw clenched Marshall knew his deliberate casualness grated on the toad's nerves.

"What I want is some answers!" Gregory's face twisted into a mask of hate. His gaze shifted to the two-way mirror on the wall to his right. "Is the sheriff out there watching this fiasco? I hope so, because when you're done I'm going to sue you and the department to kingdom come."

Marshall kept his temper under control and eyed the other man with a weary, unconcerned gaze. "I heard you earlier." He took another sip of hot, black java. "Certain you don't want some coffee this morning? It's hot, and today it tastes pretty good. That's not a sure thing every day."

Without a doubt the big prick sitting behind the table looked about ready to blow like Mount St. Helens. "I want to know what I've been brought here for."

"Brought here?" Marshall lifted one eyebrow, then looked at the deputy leaning against the wall with casual disinterest. "Jackson, did you give Mr. Metcalf the impression he was under arrest?"

Jackson smiled. "Of course not. I told him you'd come down to see him if he didn't come along with me."

"Intimidation will get you nowhere." Gregory's gravel-loaded voice irritated Marshall to within an inch of screaming.

Instead, in a flash, Marshall watched Gregory's expression turn from pissed to worried. Mr. Business Tie yanked on his collar.

Marshall laid on a casual smile. "I needed you to come down here for my convenience, actually. It seems I've been too busy to come out and accommodate your schedule."

"Either tell me what this about, or I'll call my lawyer right now."

Marshall sat his cup down on the table and a little coffee sloshed over the edge. "You haven't called him yet? I'm surprised. But you see, when you say things like that it makes you look guilty. You don't want that, do you? A friendly chat doesn't amount to a suing offense, does it?"

Taking a deep breath, Gregory showed blinding white teeth in a parody of a smile. "Of course not."

Marshall let Gregory simmer in his own juice a little longer.

"So are you going to ask me questions or stare at me all day?" Gregory asked after excruciating long minutes.

Deputy Jackson suppressed a smile, and Marshall decided Gregory had marinated long enough. "Where were you last night at about midnight?"

"I was with a friend," Gregory said.

"Who and where?"

"A woman friend."

Marshall retrieved his mug and took a slow sip of coffee. "Okay, so now we've established you like women rather than men."

Gregory shot up from the chair as if he'd vaulted out of a canon. The deputy reached for him, clamping a restraining hand on Gregory's shoulder.

Marshall didn't flinch a millimeter. "Sit down."

When the deputy applied pressure to Gregory's shoulder, he sank into the chair with a thud. "This is outrageous!"

The pleasure that came from watching this big, arrogant man humbled and surprised Marshall. He'd never felt this much antagonism for either Metcalf brother before. He'd never liked them, but now his suspicion and distaste rose to new heights. Part of his brain screamed that he'd pushed too far.

Marshall nodded to Jackson. "That'll be all for now, Jackson. Mr. Metcalf and I are going to have nice little talk."

"What's this?" Gregory sneered and placed his hands flat on the table as if he might launch upward again. "Playing bad cop Marshall?"

Marshall remembered Dana had asked him the same thing last night. "Good guess." After the deputy left, Marshall decided the time for playing cat and mouse stopped now. "Who did you visit last night at midnight?"

Gregory glanced at the mirror again. "I can't tell you."

"You can't or you won't?"

"Won't." Gregory's jaw kept a defiant angle as he leaned back in the chair and folded his arms.

Marshall had to concede he couldn't hold Gregory for not telling where he'd been loitering at midnight. Still.... "If you're innocent, you have nothing to hide."

"You haven't told me what crime I've committed."

"Did I say you committed a crime?" When his adversary didn't blink, Marshall took a deep breath. "Don't tell me you don't know what happened last night?"

"No, I don't know." Gregory threw a full force glare at Marshall.

"Dana was in an accident last night. A very bad accident."

Gregory's face turned pale and pasty in two seconds. "What?"

"She's alive. She's one very lucky lady."

Gregory unfolded his arms and leaned forward, his eyes wide with a good impression of innocence and concern. "Is she hurt?"

"Last I heard she's fine and resting at home. Someone ran her off the road." Marshall planted both hands on the table and pinned the other man with a stare. "And if you had anything to do with it, I swear I will hunt you down and see you're prosecuted."

Gregory's eyes widened, but he leaned back in the chair and rearranged his face into a calm, almost bored look. "I had nothing to do with it. And if you know what's good for you, you'll leave it at that." A speculative gleam entered Gregory's eyes. "I see what the real problem is here."

Marshall didn't move. "The real problem is you. If you lay a hand on her—"

"You've got the hots for her, don't you?"

Anger and a touch of reality seeped into Marshall, but he kept his aggressive stance. "We're talking about you. I don't want you within a mile of her. That means you're going to stay away from Lucille's house. I don't care where you stay. You can go back to that roach motel for all I care. Or you can make me real happy and get out of Macon all together."

"This is rich." Gregory's mouth went up at the corners but didn't form a complete smile. "Looks like the boy's in love. Or is it lust? I can understand. So did you ever get your money's worth?"

A burn started in Marshall's gut. He looked at his coffee for a moment in case he could blame the liquid for the pain. He wouldn't admit love or lust because neither applied. Dana might be more than attractive, but he didn't plan on doing anything about it. Instead, he straightened and gave Gregory the silent treatment again.

"So?" Gregory said after a full minute. "Have you kissed her yet?"

It spilled from Marshall before he could hold back. "Yeah, I've kissed her. Good and long and hard." Marshall immediately felt like a heel for lying, but he relished seeing Gregory's face go flat and mad. "Now, let's get back to the real issue. Who were you with last night?"

Again Gregory's gaze flashed to the two-way mirror. "Unlike you, I don't kiss and tell."

Another burn roasted Marshall's gut. He shrugged. "Like I said before, if you don't tell me, it makes you look guilty. No alibi."

"So arrest me."

Marshall knew he couldn't throw Gregory in the slammer any more than he could Neal. Not yet. "We'll have information very soon on the identity of the car that pushed her off the road."

"So? One of your deputy's already looked at my car and you bastards took a sample of paint. You're not going to find a scratch on it. It's a brand new car and sure as hell wasn't used to push anyone off the road."

After a long pause, Marshall said, "You may think we're a hick town with no resources, Metcalf. But I can guarantee if you had anything to do with Dana's accident you will be arrested and prosecuted to the full extent of the law. I'll make sure of it."

Gregory plastered a bored rigid look onto his face. "Am I free to go now?"

Marshall backed away from the table and gestured toward the door. "Get out of here."

Dana walked with Aunt Lucille along the grassy lane that led into the park in the center of town. People had started filing into the park even though most of the booths hadn't opened yet.

Dana noted that despite the tornado destroying the gazebo and tearing out some of the grass, the park looked good. The day had dawned sparkling clear with a forecast in the upper seventies. She'd dressed in a short-sleeved copper micro fiber blouse and stone washed jeans. Aunt Lucille wore a multicolored caftan over jeans. The cowboy boots didn't exactly go with the picture, but oh, well.

Makes her look like a fortune teller.

Dana looked back and saw that one of the deputies assigned to their protection trailed behind several yards. Although he wore plain clothes, everyone in town no doubt knew him. Dana shoved her hands in her pockets. "Looks like Skeeter's still shadowing us."

Aunt Lucille chuckled. "He's kinda cute, don't you think, dear?"

Dana gazed in disbelief at her aunt. Whatever blows her skirt up. "You're not serious? Do I detect some interest there?"

The older woman batted her eyelashes. "I may be old, but I'm not dead. I recognize a hunk when I see one."

Dana issued a bark of laughter. "Aunt Lucille, should I have locked you in your room?"

"What? Can't an old woman have fun?"

"Stop answering a question with a question."

"Okay, I just don't feel that old. I've got lots of great ideas, youthful feelings, and a zest for life. What can I say? I don't plan on slowing down, haunted house or no haunted house."

A kid on a bike whizzed passed, zooming along at a perilous speed. Dana hunched over and imitated an old lady walking with a cane. "Young whipper snapper."

Aunt Lucille giggled. "Dana, you're a hoot. I'm so glad you're here."

Dana slipped her arm around her aunt's shoulders and gave her a brief hug. "Me, too. I mean, I'm glad I'm with you. I'm not so sure about here." She glanced around at the growing masses and grimaced a little. "I think I like my mayhem securely captured on my TV screen. This might be a little too much."

"Are you sure you want to do this?" Aunt Lucille asked as she stopped. Her collection of bangle bracelets jangled. "If you're not feeling up to it..."

"Are you kidding? And leave you all alone with Skeeter?" They dissolved into giggles and they had to stop walking. Dana gasped for breath and her sides ached from mirth. "By the way, is his name honestly Skeeter Buffit? Sounds like a country music singer."

"Actually, I think his mother had a crush on a country music artist one time. She insisted they name him after two famous singers." She tapped her finger on her chin as she thought. "That's right. Dwight Skeeter Buffit, I think."

Dana laughed but didn't say a word.

"I didn't think you'd be up to this. Last night was a horrible ordeal," Aunt Lucille said.

Dana shrugged and started walking again. "I'm good. No reason to back out of a little fun because someone tried to kill me." Aunt Lucille's frown said she didn't think Dana's comment amusing. Dana hadn't seen her Aunt look this grave in a long time. "I'm fine, Aunt Lucille."

The last assurance seemed to help her aunt's mood.

Booths stretched from one end of the park to the other. "Lovely. Looks like everyone in town is here."

Aunt Lucille swung her arms like a little kid. "Isn't it wonderful? That's one thing I love about this town. It's almost picture perfect. If you come back to Macon for Christmas you'll see it. The place turns into a Currier and Ives portrait."

She'd seen the effect before, but Dana didn't anticipate visiting at Christmas. "Snow and everything." She sighed as she noticed the idyllic setting did have serenity she'd experienced few other places. But, she knew that someone in town had a big grudge against her. That took away the pleasantness that might otherwise have made her feel secure.

Yeah, Dana, the only time you felt safe in the last twenty-four hours was in Brennan Marshall's arms. A blush washed into her cheeks as she recalled the sensation of well being she'd experienced in his powerful embrace. Time to nip that particular feeling right at the root before it had a chance to grow like kudzu.

As they passed a group settled around a picnic table, she felt rather than saw their scrutiny. She glanced at her aunt. "It's probably all over town by now."

"What dear?"

"About my crash last night."

Aunt Lucille stopped swinging her arms and returned to a mature woman. "That's the way it is here. No stopping it."

Deciding that her aunt just didn't get it, Dana said, "So what does Kerrie have you doing?"

"Fortune teller."

"Ha!" Dana gave Aunt Lucille a sardonic look. "You're kidding, right?"

Her aunt's eyes sparkled like gemstones. "Crystal ball and the works."

"So that top you're wearing is for show only?"

"Of course. Do you think I'd wear this thing otherwise?"

Dana laughed. "Uh, no."

They wandered through the popcorn, hot dogs, soft drinks, and candy booths. Dana's stomach growled. Breakfast had worn off about two hours ago.

Aunt Lucille took her arm and led her toward a huge stall that sported first aid and information. "This way, dear. Kerrie said she'd be at the information booth."

"I wonder why she wouldn't tell me what kind of cage I'm minding."

"Cage?"

"A figure of speech." Dana dodged a toddler girl that ran full blast away from her scrambling-to-keep-up mother.

"Uh-huh. Why do I get the feeling you're not looking forward to this?"

"Could it be all the whining and moaning I did this morning?"

"That might have been it. But I knew you really wanted to do it. I don't know why I asked."

"Because you're a sweetie, that's why," Dana said as they reached the information stall.

Kerrie headed around the table and came toward them. "I hope all was quiet on the western front after I left last night?"

"Never fear." Dana gave her friend a reassuring pat on shoulder. "I'm as tough as boot leather. It's already been a ball of fun talking to the insurance company. Yada, yada, yada."

Kerrie's intense look transformed into determined. "This crime wave can't continue. We haven't had trouble in town like this before."

Aunt Lucille nodded emphatically. "Society going to dickens in a hand basket."

Dana smiled at the exaggeration. "Come on, ladies. It's not that bad around here." Not wanting to dwell on the accident, Dana continued. "Now, where's this booth and what do I do?"

Aunt Lucille grabbed Dana's forearm. "Now wait a minute, young lady, you're not supposed to go anywhere without Skeeter."

Dana shoved a hand through her hair and winced when hairspray kept the strands together. "I forgot. But really it doesn't matter. Skeeter can stay with you, and I'll go with Kerrie. No one is going to try anything in this huge crowd."

Her aunt didn't look convinced. When Skeeter strolled up to them with a wide grin plastered on his model perfect mouth, Dana figured the jig was up.

"Ladies, is there a problem?"

Dana started to open her mouth, but Aunt Lucille zipped in faster. "My niece needs to go to her booth."

Skeeter grinned, his eyes luminous with good humor. "No problem, Mrs. Metcalf." He nodded toward the crowd and made a hand signal that looked something like sign language. "Logan can help us out."

Logan Reece sauntered through the noisy crowd toward their group. Dana took in his tall form with appreciation. No flannel today for this knock-your-socks-off-man. Instead he wore a plain navy blue T-shirt and jeans along with athletic shoes. Several women in the surrounding area gawked at him like he was the last slice of chocolate cheesecake at a picnic.

"Who's that? I saw him dancing with you last night, Dana," Aunt Lucille asked.

"Logan Reece. A friend of Marshall's," Dana said.

Logan's lazy smile as he approached made Kerrie and Aunt Lucille blush. This man could conquer the entire female population of Macon with one hand tied behind his back.

After greeting them, Logan said, "I'll be watching you whenever Skeeter can't be around."

Dana heaved a sigh. "Okay. Let's get this show on the road."

"Don't worry, Dana." Logan started back toward the crowd. "You'll never know I'm there."

"That's comforting," Dana said as soon as he drifted out of earshot.

Kerrie cleared her throat. "Come this way."

They left Aunt Lucille to get ready for her fortune telling booth. Dana strode alongside Lucille as they headed for the outskirts of the carnival like atmosphere. They passed the Ferris wheel and a few other children's rides. Dana watched the Ferris wheel and could have sworn she saw Marshall in one of the seats with a little girl.

"Did you recognize the car that ran you off the road?" Kerrie asked.

So much for forgetting about last night. "I can't remember anything about the sedan or the person in it."

Dana meant to say more, but then she saw the booth. She stared at the banner strung across the overhang belonging to the stall.

Kerrie, why you little—

"Are you out of your mind?" Dana asked with a squeak.

The sign said: Kisses For Charity: Minimum Donation, One Dollar.

Chapter 10

Dana could tell by Kerrie's expression she knew she'd hit big time trouble.

Kerrie's sheepish look lasted all of two seconds. "Come on, you know you're going to love it."

"Love it? Are you nuts? Kissing for charity? Whose charity? The Colorado Chapter of the National Kissing Disease Foundation?"

"Now don't have a cow."

"Maybe if it was for Mad Cow Disease I wouldn't mind."

Kerrie steered her behind the booth. Of course, the table had been draped with a tablecloth that had large passion red lips on full display. "You said you wanted to help me. So you're helping."

Dana's slow burn fuse began to light. "Why me? Why not some nubile tart from town?"

Kerrie wrinkled her nose. "Tart? Does anyone really use that word anymore?"

"Smart aleck." Dana stomped from one side of the booth to the other. "It's claustrophobic. You can't leave me in here."

"Bull." Kerrie's eyes took on a mischievous gleam. "Maybe I can persuade Logan to come over here."

"Don't you dare."

Kerrie relented and showed her the money box beneath the table, and the bowl of individually wrapped mints. "The mints are for men who have…uh…"

"Unpleasant breath." Dana smacked her lips. "Oh, goody."

"You got it. There's also a jug of water down there in case you get a dry mouth."

Dana produced another long-suffering sigh and sank into the metal chair. "The things I will do for a friend."

As Kerrie smiled and started to walk away, Dana stood up. "Hey, wait. What charity am I sacrificing my lips to? You know, in case someone asks?"

"The child development center on Center Creek Boulevard. It suffered more damage than any other building during the tornado. We're planning on buying new toys and supplies."

Now I feel like a jerk. "Oh. Do you have a kissing booth every year?"

Kerrie laughed. "No. But when I found out you were coming to Macon, I added it in."

"Why me?"

"Your aunt suggested it."

Dana groaned and sank into the chair.

Tabitha, blond ringlets tossing in a riot, came to a screeching halt next to Marshall and Eric. Marshall enjoyed spending time with the little girl, who considered him an uncle. Her expressive green eyes reminded him of Eva, Tabitha's mother. And yet Tabitha's warm, giving nature seemed so different from Eva's sometimes cool, detached attitude. Marshall hoped the little girl would remain a sunny, expressive child.

She handed Marshall a court jester's hat. "This is for you, Uncle Brennan."

"Uh, thank you."

"I got it specially for you. For your hat collection."

"It's really nice, Tabitha."

Eric's expression held enough mischief for both himself and his daughter. "Try it on."

Tabitha's face lightened with glee. "Yeah, Uncle Brennan. Try it on."

Marshall gave Eric a smile that said he'd rather eat shoe leather. When he looked down at the little girl, though, he knew he couldn't refuse. He looked around and hoped no one was paying attention. He removed his baseball cap, stuffed it in his back pocket, and plopped the new hat on his head.

Eric chuckled and Tabitha clapped her hands. "Way to go, Uncle Brennan."

Two people walking by gave Marshall odd looks and he felt a blush heat his face. *Now if this doesn't cut it! I probably look like an escapee from an insane asylum.*

"I wanna go on another ride," she said.

Marshall got down on his haunches. "Which one?"

She didn't hesitate. "It's Daddy's turn to ride with me."

Marshall gave her a mock frown. "Oh, yeah? What's he got that I haven't got?"

Tabitha put her small hand on his shoulder and matched his feigned seriousness. "Later, Uncle Brennan. And only if you buy me cotton candy."

He chuckled and looked up at Eric. "This young lady drives a hard bargain."

Eric ruffled her hair. "That's my girl." He looked into the distance. "Well, would you look at that? Unbelievable."

Marshall scanned the area as he stood. His senses went on alert. Hyperaware since Dana's accident last night, he half expected something bad to happen today. "What is it?"

Eric gestured toward a booth in the distance, almost too far away to read the lettering. "Does that say kissing booth?"

"Daddy, what's a kissing booth?" Tabitha asked, her piquant face curious.

"Uh, well..." Eric's expression turned comical as he searched for words.

"Usually a place where people give money to charity for a kiss." Marshall supplied the words, hoping Eric wouldn't take offense. "I think that's the first time I've seen a kissing booth at this fair, though."

Tabitha yanked on Marshall's pants leg. "Would you kiss someone for charity?"

He blinked, looking down at her innocent eyes. "Maybe. Guess it depends on who I get to kiss."

"Why don't you check it out?" Eric asked, one of his brows twitching up. "Might be a really gorgeous woman. I heard a rumor Jenny Pizer would be here."

Marshall gave his friend a disbelieving look. "I don't think so." He shrugged. "Besides, I need to check on Logan and Skeeter. They're watching over Dana Cummings."

"Suit yourself," Eric said, smiling. "I'll see you later."

"See ya!" Tabita waved as they strolled away hand in hand.

After the two left, Marshall felt a pang of regret and need. Deep inside he knew he'd never experience the father and daughter scenario except when he spent time with Tabitha. He'd wanted kids, but his ex-wife hadn't. He'd been a fool and a half to not broach the subject with her before he'd married her.

Sighing, he took a closer look at the kissing booth. He hated indecision. Used to making moves that could mean life or death, he'd trained from an early age to choose with confidence and precision. Niggling doubts had no place in his life. *Yeah, so why did you allow Helen to push you into marriage when you had doubts about compatibility? Why?*

He looked at the kissing booth again. Might as well. Marshall trudged forward.

Gregory's accusation this morning and the stupid lie he'd told him made Marshall apprehensive. No, he hadn't kissed Dana, but he'd wanted to more than once. Where had the bastard gotten the idea he'd fallen in love with her? Sure, he wanted to protect her, but he'd do the same for anyone else he believed in danger. Aggravated that he'd allowed Gregory to get to him, Marshall moved onward until he saw something that rooted his feet into the ground.

"You've got to be kidding." Marshall's mouth dropped open.

He wondered if Dana had protested about working the stall. Yep. Probably. Then again, you never could tell with a woman.

Marshall felt that fierce protectiveness for Dana rear up inside him again. Hoping he wasn't making a horrible mistake—a big, rotten egg error—he strode toward the kissing booth.

Dana saw the clouds gathering over the mountains surrounding Macon. Another thunderstorm threatened. She tried not to get fidgety, but the idea of sheltering in this flimsy booth if rain started didn't appeal to her. If the weather turned nasty she'd abandon ship and the men of Macon would have to pucker up some other time. Within seconds, something more intriguing distracted her from the weather. Gregory was coming her way. Oh, yuck.

"Hi, Dana." His amiable expression didn't fool her. Just being within a yard of his snake oil salesman personality made her shudder. *Today he wore blue jeans and—oh, yeah—flannel.*

Give me a break. Whatever gives him the jollies, I guess.

Better to keep things to the point with him and maybe he'd get bored and go away. "What's up?"

He reached in his pocket and extracted four quarters. He slapped them on the table. "Where's my kiss?"

Drawing her hands into fists, she contemplated walloping him in the kisser. No, that would be too good for the stinking, steaming sack of—

"You know, I've heard that sex is good for straightening out writer's block." Gregory's eyes took on a salacious gleam. "Loosens up the cogs. Greases the…" His gaze speared up and down her body. "…wheel. If you're not getting any, well you know. Your imagination dries up right with the rest of your—"

"Shut up." She'd found the words, no matter how inadequate. "And get out of my sight."

His smirk increased to titanic proportions. "That's the best you can do?"

"That's all. Oh, and when you leave town, don't bother to say goodbye." Dana grabbed the coins but his hand landed over hers.

He threw her another smug look. The pig thought he'd won a few points. "No kissy, no money."

Dana inhaled slow and deep, trying to keep her temper under control. "Get your hand off me."

"Or you'll what?"

"Bite out a chunk of your sorry butt and feed it to you," she said through her teeth.

Giving her a smarmy grin, he said, "So you can give it up for Deputy Dog, but not for your dear cousin?"

"What are you talking about?"

"He told me very, very early this morning while he was unlawfully interrogating me, that he'd already kissed you."

Dana's face filled with heat and she almost drew back and slapped him. "You really are a maggot, Gregory. I never really knew how much until now."

"Pissed you off, did I? Don't worry, your little affair with Marshall is a secret with me."

She gritted her teeth together before letting each word grind out. "I am not…having an affair…with Marshall."

He waggled his eyebrows. "Sure."

If by the count of three he didn't release her, she'd do more than gnaw him, she'd scream for help. That ought to get his attention.

One beefy hand landed on his shoulder. Gregory jumped and released her.

"Hi, Metcalf." Marshall stood next to Gregory as he turned. "What's new?"

Gregory's mouth opened and closed, then fury covered his face. Dana's mouth opened and stayed parted.

Unbelievable. A smile fought its way to her lips, and she held back a laugh. Marshall's hat sat square on his head, a crazy concoction of dangling multi-colored balls. His nonchalant expression added to the hilarious picture. Never in a million years would she have pictured Mr. Serious and Stable wearing a hat like this.

"Something funny?" Marshall asked, looking at her and ignoring Gregory.

Gregory straightened to his full height, but his self-confident veneer seemed to melt a little under Marshall's attention. Amazing how a man wearing an idiotic hat could still make Gregory shrink back. He might be taller than Marshall, but her wise-ass cousin couldn't compete with the under sheriff for sheer brawn and presence. Reigned tension strummed from Marshall, and for a few seconds she wondered if the two men might argue. She tried not to stare at the lawman's ridiculous headgear, but she couldn't help it.

"So, Marshall, you come to kiss Dana again?" Gregory frowned. "Wait your turn."

Marshall tilted his head back a little, since he could look down on the man this way. The colored balls on his hat swayed.

She bet herself a candy bar the hat would slip off the back of his head. “Well, I see it like this. You made your donation. If the lady doesn’t want to kiss you, that’s her prerogative.”

Jeez. What would one of them say next? That this town wasn’t big enough for the both of them?

Dana glared at her kissin’ cousin. “You heard the Marshall, get outta here.”

Gregory’s head tilted like a confused dog. “The Marshall.”

She shrugged but didn’t let him in on the joke. Gregory glanced from Marshall to Dana, growing uncertainty showing in his eyes.

“Say goodbye, Metcalf,” Marshall said.

Without another word, Gregory left.

Dana sighed in a release of pressure. Rid of one pain-in-the-posterior, plagued by another. She turned her attention to Marshall and when she looked at his hat again she let out a small laugh.

Her chuckle gathered steam and turned into full-fledged laughter. She waggled a finger at his hat.

“Where—where did you get—” She gasped for breath between giggles. “Where did you get that?”

Frowning, Marshall snatched the hat off his head and tossed it on to the table. “Tabitha bought it for me.”

She didn’t know if she could stand his presence too long. Now that he’d removed the hat, she found his rough brand of masculinity enough to unnerve her down to the roots. She had to acknowledge how good he looked in the blue polo shirt that revealed his forearms and faded jeans that curved against his body close but not tight. He hooked his thumbs in his belt loops and she swallowed hard. Marshall looked way too good for one man. Good, hell. Try scrumptious. Try incredible. Try—enough!

Dana shoved her hand through her bangs as the increasing wind fluttered through the area.

She lifted her hands in a pleading gesture. “Is Gregory that dumb?”

"Dumb is too kind a word for him."

"He's a perfect troglodyte as far as I'm concerned. I hope he's leaving town soon."

"Just ignore him. I'm keeping a watch on his activities from now on." His gaze assessed her. "Maybe he wants you out of the way."

She hadn't considered the possibility. "I suppose. But why?"

"Your guess is as good as mine at this point, but if he drives you off, he knows Lucille will be vulnerable. And if you can ask Lucille what she really thinks without having a tantrum—"

"I wasn't planning on having a fit, thank you very much."

His expression said he didn't believe her. "That's not all. He said something else to make you angry. What was it?"

For a half second she thought she wouldn't tell him. It slipped out. "He said I was loosing my edge in my writing because I wasn't getting enough sex."

As soon as she said it her face flamed, and she wanted to take it back. *Jeez, Dana, what were you thinking? You should have blasted Marshall about saying that he'd kissed you instead of practically telling him you have no sex life.*

A gleam entered his eyes, one that said his inquisitiveness had launched into high gear. He lowered his voice, as if he didn't want anyone else to hear. "Is that true?"

"Which part?" She glared. "That I'm losing my edge or I'm not getting enough sex?"

A grin tried to take over his mouth, but she saw him fighting the urge. "Either. Both."

"Why would you want to know?"

Her harsh words didn't make him flinch. "You're a complex woman. If a man wants to survive around you he's got to understand you in and out."

A vision sprouted to mind…a wanton…forbidden picture. Marshall knowing her inside...

Every bit of spit in her mouth dried up. She fumbled under the table for the water jug and filled a paper cup. After drinking the water all in one gulp, she took a deep breath.

Marshall kept his steel-eyed gaze on her, as if she might move and he'd lose sight of her. "I'm surprised you haven't told me to mind my own business."

Instead of receding, her blush increased two-fold. "I should."

He cleared his throat. "Sounds like Gregory is full of shit…on both accounts."

Dana didn't bother to illuminate him that she hadn't had sex in what seemed like years and years. So long that she'd almost forgotten how. She scrubbed her hands over her eyes. "This is all crazy. Everything is nastier than fruitcake." She gestured at the canvas walls that served as shelter for the table. "This booth is nuts. Why would anyone want to kiss me for charity?"

Dana realized the minute she spoke she'd opened herself up big time. He didn't comment right away, his interested look coming full force.

A blast of thunder overhead made her squeak with surprise. Clouds had pushed over the park area and now obscured the sun. She'd been so engrossed in the men visiting her booth that she hadn't noticed how menacing the weather had become. Dana thought she'd dealt with the phobia a long time ago, but the fear had returned in the last few weeks. Nothing had altered her phobia of thunderstorms for eighteen years, not since she'd turned fourteen. The birthday from hell. The day Daddy died.

"I think you'd better get out of this stall and come with me," Marshall said as he looked up at the encroaching weather.

A perverseness she couldn't hold back made her lean on the table and look him dead in the eye. She made sure she kept her expression straight. "You arresting me, Marshall?"

"Not this time, but don't tempt me too much." His voice dropped to a subtle, almost hoarse tone that sent frissons of heat over her body. "You haven't seen the inside of my cell."

Marshall's insinuating tone had the effect of multiplying her twitchiness. "I imagine it's all dark and dank and foreboding. Filled with secrets."

One corner of his mouth almost attempted a smile, then schooled itself back to serious. "Secrets you don't want to know."

She wondered if he'd dropped a hint. Did he mean she shouldn't become interested in him?

A rumble from the heavens made Dana flinch, and she had about two seconds to wish she'd already left the tent before rain poured down. An expletive reached her lips before she could stifle it. He rushed around the side of tent and grabbed her hand, tugging her to her feet.

Dana dug in her heels. "What—"

"We aren't staying under these metal poles. It's not safe. Come on."

Chapter 11

Fear raced like earth tremors through her as her phobia reared its head. She cringed under the onslaught of violent nature and her own inability to fight her panic.

As they rushed toward the Grand Cherokee, Dana asked, "Are you sure Macon isn't really a Dean Koontz novel? Or maybe a Wes Craven horror movie? I can't believe this."

He tossed her a half-amused look, and then they'd reached the vehicle. He unlocked the car and she almost dove into the passenger side to find refuge from the storm. Soaked, she shivered with a combination of rattled nerves and cold. He slid into the driver's side, slammed the door, and reached into the back seat.

Dana shivered and held her arms close to her body. "I feel like a drowned dog."

When he handed her a towel and a blanket, she grinned. "Oh, heaven." She set to drying off, rubbing over her body with the towel to generate heat. "I'll bet you made a great Boy Scout."

His rain soaked shirt clung to his chest, and he pulled it away from his body. "I was never a Boy Scout."

While he spoke his gaze dropped to her breasts and she

realized that her nipples hardened from the cold. She dropped the towel to her chest and held it in front of her, self-conscious.

"I find that hard to believe," she said to cover her nervous gesture.

"Believe it." He slid the blanket around her shoulders, his warm, gentle touch sending new feelings of need through her. The close confines of the car made her ever more aware of him.

Dana's heart sped up, an overwhelming desire for him to draw her close and kiss her rocketing through her system. *You're losing control.* With effort she sucked a deep breath into her lungs. "What about you? I mean, don't you have another towel or blanket?"

He nodded. "In the back. I don't plan on crawling back there to get it right now."

She started to peel the blanket away. "Here."

Marshall clasped her hands to keep her from removing the blanket. "No. You need it more than me. Your teeth are almost chattering."

True. She couldn't recall the last time…well, okay…last night she'd almost frozen waiting for him to arrive at the scene of the crash. More lightning rammed overhead, and she flinched. Marshall gave her a curious look. As thunder rolled overhead, she shuddered like a whipped pup. She couldn't let him know about the fear still coursing through her body. He'd think her weak, no doubt about it.

What of it? He wouldn't be the first man to find her phobia too much to handle. Another clap sailed over the car, lightning illuminating the cab of the vehicle like a giant torch. She almost left her skin.

"It's all right," he said, eyeing her. "We're safe in the car."

Her heartbeat accelerated despite his assurances. "I know."

"Are you cold?"

"No."

When he brushed her face gently with his fingertips, new heat and surprise rushed through her. "Then why are you shaking?"

Before she answered he gathered her right hand in both of his big palms. She tried to tug from his grip, but he held tight. "Your hands are trembling."

"Very observant of you."

Marshall's gaze narrowed, as if he could ferret out the truth if he stared at her long enough. "That's not all. Something else is scaring you." A look of half horror came over his face. "God, it's not me, is it? You're not afraid of me?"

"Of course not." Yeah, she was afraid of him all right. But not in the way he thought. Deep growls of thunder rumbled overhead, and she jumped again. She concentrated on his touch to forget the storm outside.

"I know I told you that you should be cautious." He shifted closer. She didn't know whether to feel grateful for his body heat, or to insist he back off. Instead she allowed him to rub her hands, generating warmth. "But I'd die before I hurt you."

Sweet, trembling need tightened along her body as she almost dissolved into mush under his husky declaration. He gazed down at her until she wanted to sink straight into his arms and never leave.

"Tell me what's wrong. Is it what happened last night?" he asked.

Did she really care if he knew? She wasn't hiding her phobia well right now. "No. It's not that. I know you'll keep me safe."

Dana saw clear emotion flicker through his eyes; he liked that she trusted him with her life. The realization sent a wild zing of staggering pleasure through her. Even though his mandate as a lawman said he'd guard her, she thought she saw more than professional interest radiating from those deep-as-sin eyes. At least she thought she did. *You've deluded yourself before. Don't fall into the trap of thinking he cares for you more than he does. Frank left before you'd both do something you'd regret later.*

"Tell me what's wrong, Dana. What happened all those years ago to make you so frightened of the weather?"

She swallowed hard. She felt like she'd just taken a big bite of peanut butter and couldn't unglue her tongue from the roof of her mouth. Memories, those she tried to slam back whenever a storm arrived, threatened to burst through. *Do it. Blurt it out while you still can.*

"My father was killed by lightning when I was fourteen. Right in front of me."

Marshall's eyes darkened like the clouds outside, his brow furrowing. "Oh, God." His gaze traveled down to the ring on a chain around her neck. "You said that was your father's?"

"Yeah." She gave wry grin. "His lucky college ring. He…uh…he always wore it and said it brought him luck." Another shudder rippled through her body. "Problem is he didn't wear it the day he died."

When she stayed silent, he nodded. "So you remember him with this ring."

She nodded. "It's sort of a talisman, I guess you could say. Against bad luck. I guess if he wasn't wearing it when he was killed, then maybe the good luck wasn't with him that day."

"You really believe that?"

Shrugging, she extracted one of her hands from his and rubbed the precious metal. "I don't know. It's just something I have to do. I have to wear it. It makes me feel like part of him is always with me."

His nod said he understood, so she continued. "I was…I was outside with him. It was a partly sunny day, but this big thunderhead was rearing to the west over the mountains." Keeping her gaze riveted on their hands, she tightened her grip on his fingers, as if he could anchor her. "I'd never liked storms but I wasn't that afraid at that time. A big wind had turned our TV antenna around and he wanted to get on the roof to adjust it. The clouds weren't even directly overhead and it hadn't started thundering. Dad climbed up on the roof and had barely gotten a few feet up the side when the bolt just slammed him. It was so violent."

Dana saw it again and closed her eyes, the sheer horror of the memory jolting through her. She hung her head. His right hand slipped into her hair, and he brought her against his chest, his other arm wrapping around her back and holding tight. Warmth and comfort seemed to radiate in waves through his body to hers, giving her strength.

"I saw him." She licked her lips, whispering the words and not sure Marshall could hear her. Marshall's fingers threaded through her hair and caressed her with gentle touches. "It was like a blaze of light from the heavens, and so loud and brutal I fell backwards into the grass. I lay there, stunned, and he fell right toward me. I rolled out of the way…I remember screaming and screaming for him and he landed on the ground next to me. He was…he was…"

Another shiver wracked her body and he held her closer than ever. "Easy. It's all right. You don't have to explain it all now if you don't want to."

He whispered against her ear, and his hot breath sent warm tendrils of pleasure through her, masking the fear and bad memories.

She shrugged and sniffed. "He, um, he was literally fried to a crisp. Momma came out of the house and screamed and screamed. I passed out and woke up in the hospital a day later. They said the bolt may have hit me, but it was far enough away that I only received a secondary shock. I didn't suffer any burns, so they weren't certain."

"Dana, I'm sorry."

Dana realized that the rain had stopped and the thunder and lightning had eased back to a low grumble in the distance. Sheltered in his arms she'd forgotten the fury of the short storm. Anger rolled through her like the receding sound of thunder.

Tucked into his embrace she let him inside and he witnessed feelings she hadn't shown to any man since Frank. She knew a man could act this tender, this caring and still not love her in the end.

She stiffened in his arms and looked up. The sweet, unadulterated worry in his eyes almost threw her resentment out the door. "So now you know. I'm phobic. Satisfied?"

Her snappy tone didn't have the effect she expected. Instead of getting angry his touch became even gentler. He brushed his thumb against her face. "Dana if you don't—"

"What? Shape up?"

She knew her attitude needed major improvement, but she felt out of control. Dana took in one slow breath to try and regulate her pounding heart. His heat burned through the blanket and her clothing straight to her skin, her body flushing as he leaned in close. She gulped.

He asked, "Why are you so defensive about being phobic? Plenty of people are like this. Afraid of heights, snakes, you name it. It's nothing to be ashamed of. You had a horrible experience. Besides it appears you've got a good handle on the phobia. It doesn't bother you quite the way it used to, does it?"

She shook her head. "No. I've gotten better at hiding it. At not feeling it."

"Then you're fine. You've made progress and that's all the counts. There's nothing to be ashamed of. There never was."

Astounded, she took in his words, not certain she'd really heard him say it. "No one's ever said that to me before. Most people just give me a strange look, like I might go nuts on them at any moment."

"That's ridiculous."

"Of course it is, but that's the number one reaction I've gotten." She had to look away. His dark eyes burned with something that looked like consternation, and maybe anger that anyone would treat her that way. "I had better control of the phobia until I got here. The tornado came and just a few minutes ago I thought my heart was going to pound out of my chest." She gulped again. "People don't understand."

His arm shifted, tightening around her, but his hand had stopped caressing her hair. "People who don't deserve to know you. Why do you even care about them?"

"Because it hurts to be treated like I'm…I'm some sort of idiot, that's why." Defensiveness rose out of fear and she allowed it full power. She shifted and he got the message, releasing her. "Can we get out of here now? It looks like the rain has stopped and it's time for me to get back to the booth."

Marshall swept back his wet hair, and she saw his widow's peak and wondered how many women had slipped their fingers through those thick, wavy strands.

"I'm not finished yet. You've got a few more questions to answer."

She made a gasp of disbelief. "What? Do you find it exciting to pick a woman's brains for rotten memories?"

He blinked, amazement covering his features for a full minute before he recovered. "Don't try that with me again. I know what you're doing. You think if you can throw some acid laced bull at me I'll back off."

Incredulous, she swept a wet strand of hair off her face. Now she'd take the jump off the cliff and ask him about that so-called kiss. "Well, here's some more acid for you, Marshall. Don't ever tell lies about me again."

His brow wrinkled. "What lies?"

Her dry throat felt tight as skin stretched over a drum. "Why did you tell Gregory that you and I kissed? Were you playing some macho game with him?"

Marshall gaze eased over her, warm and searching. At the same time his fathoms deep eyes said he fought some demon she couldn't read. His mouth moved as if he might smile, then thought better of it. "I was interrogating him about your crash last night. I did the same with Neal."

Her eyebrows shot up. "You told Neal I'd kissed you?"

"No." He held a hand up. "No. Gregory taunted me about you…made some stupid statements when I told him to stay away from you."

Gratification flowed strong as a river through her. She forgot to be angry as she thought about what would motivate him to tell Gregory to stay away. "He didn't come to the house last night as far as I know. But what did he say? What did he taunt you with?"

"He said a lot of stupid things. Number one was not telling me who he was with last night."

"Where was he?"

"At a ratty hotel outside town."

Ratty suggested many things. "Who do you think was with him?"

He shrugged. "Haven't a clue, but that doesn't mean I won't find out. I had nothing to hold him on, so I let him go. I found Neal at his hotel and talked with him, then he came by later in the morning. He had nothing to add. I'm not sure who is hiding what, but you can be sure I'll find out."

She settled into the warm towel, a ripple of remaining chill rolling through her. He hadn't answered her earlier question about the fictitious kiss, and it grated on her. "What could he have said that made you lie about kissing me?"

When he didn't answer she reached for the door handle. He leaned over and put his hand over hers, and once again she found him too close for reasonable comfort. "Don't. Don't go yet."

His fingers seemed to burn hers, and yet excitement thrummed through her blood. "Why?"

"We've got some unfinished business."

Awash in a sudden heat that gathered in her face and fanned downward, she locked eyes with him. Mistake number one: not looking away. Mistake number two: she couldn't look away now that he'd captured her.

Her mouth felt dirt dry again and she licked her lips. "You didn't stop at the hospital last night."

A fire ignited in his gaze, and his nostrils flared the slightest bit. "Did that surprise you?"

Dana spoke before she could think too much about the right answer. "No."

"Disappointed you?"

Did she detect hope in his voice? Nah, that wouldn't make sense. "'Course not. Why would I be disappointed?"

He leaned forward a little farther, and she wished he'd kept on his fanatical hat so she could ignore everything mouthwatering about him and fixate on the outlandish. "You tell me."

"Are you ever not a cop?"

He inhaled and his broad chest heaved. She caught a peek of dark chest hair revealed at the collar of his shirt. Tension glided like sweet, spiced wine deep into her stomach, filling her with tingling warmth. *Not like you haven't seen his chest before, Dana. Better shove that tongue back in your mouth before you step on it.*

As Marshall's gaze cruised over her with a hot, undeniable message, Dana speculated on whether he recognized this heart-pounding need in her eyes and decided to take up her offer. He reached into his back pocket for his wallet. As he extracted a greenback, she at first didn't know what he intended. Then it hit her.

Holy mother.

"Fifty dollars?" she asked, her voice warbling. "What's that for?"

"Charity." His lips parted after the words, and her gaze affixed to his mouth. A mouth that seemed destined to touch her. Before she could make another sound, he slipped open the blanket surrounding her, and tucked the fifty dollars into the pocket on her shirt. "For taking you away from the booth and..." Marshall's attention drifted over her face in a lingering, carnal assessment. "...making you remember nightmares."

"This isn't necessary, Marshall. Really."

He leaned closer and closer and before she could blink, his lips hovered over hers. His mint-scented breath, so hot and stimulating, drove her to this side of psychosis. Maybe she'd meet him halfway. Maybe she'd give this stubborn, bossy, incredible man a kiss. It would be heaven. *Somehow I just know it would be the most erotic, most exciting kiss of my life.*

"Is fifty dollars enough?" he asked, whispering low. "I'd pay a hundred."

"I am not for sale, Marshall." She wanted her tone to sound stern, but instead it emerged breathless. Her hands reached for his shoulders, tested the strength of steel muscles. A woman could get lost in all that sinew and never come up for air.

"Then shut up."

She couldn't recall the last time a man's husky, demanding voice had made her want something so much. Her breath accelerated, a flush passing through her entire body.

The radio squawked. "Marshall this is central, what is your six?"

Marshall flinched and drew back, an expletive spewing forth as he reached for the radio.

After identifying himself he said, "This had better be good."

As the dispatcher explained what she needed, Dana ached with a mix of relief and frustration. Since it had stopped raining, she rolled down the window a crack. The scent of a recent rain filled her nose, refreshing the stuffy car. Amazing that a short time ago nature had raged. Peace filled the cool, clear air as fluffy clouds drifted away and blue sky showed among the mountaintops.

A tapping on the window made her jerk in surprise. Aunt Lucille stood outside with Skeeter. Skeeter's expression said he had a secret he'd rather not share, and it dawned on Dana that they had almost caught her and Marshall kissing.

Lovely! Rumors would have flown far and wide. Aunt Lucille didn't have a reputation for keeping her mouth shut, so the entire town would have known about it. The old adage, *saved by the bell,* fit this time.

Dana stepped out of the car. “Hey. I see you’ve survived the tempest.”

Aunt Lucille’s gaze bounced from Dana to Marshall, even though Marshall continued to talk on the radio. “Some storm. Are you all right, dear?”

Aunt Lucille knew about her phobia, and her concerned gaze said she worried. “I’m fine.” Dana shrugged off the blanket and refolded it. “I’m ready to get back to the booth. There are tons of hungry lips out there just waiting for charity.”

Marshall replaced the radio. “I’ve got to go.”

“Isn’t it your day off?” Skeeter asked.

“Yeah, but Sheriff Pizer needs a favor. He’s feeling under the weather and has some paperwork he has to get finished.”

Skeeter grinned. “Wait a minute. He was supposed to take his old mama shopping today, wasn’t he?”

Marshall’s frown should have scared away about anyone, but Skeeter’s irreverent expression didn’t fade. “Yeah.”

“Well, I guess there’s always something good about going to the Pizer’s,” Skeeter said.

Aunt Lucille winced. “Jenny Pizer. Oh, boy.”

Dana felt an instant twinge somewhere in the region of her heart. “Humph.”

Lucille tossed Dana a curious look. “I don’t think that it’s healthy she still lives with her parents, do you?”

Dana opened her mouth, but Marshall spoke first. “I don’t think it’s any of our business.”

Ignoring Lucille and Skeeter, Marshall surveyed Dana with a quick gaze that reminded her of the almost kiss. A fire seemed to blaze in her belly and made her wonder what might have happened. Logan appeared at the side of the truck.

“Don’t worry,” Logan said before Marshall could say a thing. “I’ll look after her.”

"I'm not a toddler, guys." Dana took a deep breath to steady her warring emotions. "I think I can find my way to the booth with no trouble."

Marshall's glower took on mammoth proportions. "That's not the point, and you know it."

Without another word he closed the passenger door and roared out of the park.

The next evening Dana parked her body on the long, low-slung sectional couch that lined one wall of the living area in the basement. As she turned down the lights, she caught a glimpse of herself in the gold speckled mirrors that lined the wall behind the couch. It almost gave her a heart attack. She put her hand to her chest and took a deep breath. Her red cotton pajamas, tangled hair, and startled expression would be enough to scare any ghost. Snickering, she settled onto the couch and snuggled deep under the blankets. Maybe, as Aunt Lucille had said, this was a strange idea. Frankly, she didn't care. If she could discover who or what haunted the basement, maybe she could wrap up this situation and go home.

Home.

Back to New Mexico to her cozy place filled with the books she loved, the solitude, the few friends she could depend upon. She'd negotiate with her landlord and explain to her mother that Aunt Lucille was fine. She'd finish this book and forget about Macon...someday....

Dana knew her toughest problem, writer's block, hadn't resolved. Going back to New Mexico now wouldn't mean she'd start writing again. She'd yet to spend a day sunning on the balcony and penning a few inspired words. After today's fiasco with Gregory at the kissing booth, the rain, and her confession to

Marshall, she didn't know if she could find the interest in writing. She should. After all, the last few days had filled with enough odd occurrences and intrigue to fill a novel. Not a horror novel, though. She wanted the time and the quiet to give this story another chance so the one chapter nestled in her notebook on the side table would turn into several chapters. But how could she do that? The need, the overwhelming desire to write had sprung a leak like a helium balloon, squealing for answers and receiving none. Her muse, as her Aunt Lucille said earlier in the evening, had plum tuckered out.

Looking to her left, she realized she couldn't see the heart-shaped bed from her position. The bar, pool table, stereo and ping pong table stood in the way. Still, if even a sigh erupted from that area, she'd run over there and find...what? Ghosts?

Okay, ghosties, where are ya?

Dana shivered as she looked at the fireplace. She should have started up the gas hearth. The glow and warmth would have comforted her but driven away the specters.

"Bah, humbug." She could imagine Marshall's disapproving look. She already knew what he'd think of this set up. He'd give her an indulgent look if not a disbelieving one.

The quiet atmosphere surrounded Dana, and she decided she'd try writing a little, even though the surging need to create remained dormant. She reached for her pen and her idea notebook sitting on the side table, shifted into a comfortable position and took a deep breath. She closed her eyes, drew in several deep breaths, and commanded her imagination to set to work.

A little free writing. An attempt at unleashing what imagination she had left. Let it rip.

She imagined a cool, splattering waterfall with diamond points of light scattering across the pond below the pounding liquid. Surprised at how easy the image came to her, she decided to let the fantasy go a little farther before she tried writing it down. Perhaps if she let her mind's eye tango instead of trying to hog tie herself to the outline, she'd find new directions.

Before she knew it the image increased in power. She stood at the edge of the pond, naked and trembling. Yet the trembling didn't come from cold. Instead she sensed a power and need that shook her from the inside out, a desire to break free from constraint and convention and let the whole damn world see who resided under the veneer she created after she published her first novel.

The beauty surrounding her strummed like notes from a guitar, arousing and relaxing. Bird song filled the air and she watched the winged creatures flit among the tall stand of pines around the area. Warm sun lit the area, but a fresh breezed brushed against her skin. She didn't feel self-conscious. Instead she wanted to reach for the water and the excitement she knew lay beneath the shimmering liquid. Somewhere, under the rippling blue water, she'd find answers to all her problems, doubts, and fears.

Come on in...the water's fine.

Obeying, she jumped feet first into the cool depths. Right away she discovered the water didn't reached her neck. In fact, it covered only half her breasts. Her nipples tingled with delicious and painful delight as the shock of the water startled her senses. Water lapped over her nipples, tickling them like a man's tender touch. Dana tilted her head back, spread her arms over the surface, and let the cool water turn to warmth. Ah, yes. She drifted there for eternity, enjoying relaxation and the continual stroke of the water under her breasts, around her breasts, over her nipples. This place gave her a thrill, deep down like a lover's caress. Maybe she would stay here and forget to return to the real world.

Another splash caught her attention.

In her fantasy her eyes flew open and she saw a man had entered the pond and swam with slow, measured strokes in her direction. Wild spirals of excitement darted through her body as Marshall glided in the water like a sleek, powerful animal. She didn't know whether to vault from the pond or stay rooted to the spot, excitement building as he came toward her. Dana had never seen a man swim like this before, as if he conquered the water and directed its movement. His muscles bunched and released in a counter play that mesmerized her. His wet hair gleamed, water droplets streaming down his face with each movement of his head. When he came within two feet of her he stood and the water came halfway up his chest. Rivulets of water trailed through the dark hair on his pectorals. Her temperature rose as his gaze took her in, encompassing in an assessment that spoke of undeniable needs and sensual secrets. Instead of dark chocolate, his eyes turned almost black with desire. She knew he wanted her, and wished with everything inside her he'd relent and take her in his arms.

Dana released a shiver, a sigh parting her lips. "This is good. Really good. I've got to write this down."

Instead she longed for him to come closer and reached toward him, hoping he'd accept her hand. The dare and challenge in his eyes told her if she wanted him she'd have to make another move.

Someone cleared his or her throat. Dana gasped and her heart almost jumped out of her chest.

Chapter 12

Dana's eyes popped opened and she let out another gasp. She dropped her paper and pen as she stood and her blankets fell down around her ankles.

The object of her fantasy had appeared from nowhere.

Unlike in her wild fancies, though, this man was not naked.

Marshall stood by the fireplace dressed in his head-to-toe black, secret agent man attire. Grinning like something was pretty funny. "Damn it, Marshall!"

He put his fingers to his lips. "Shhhh. No need to wake Lucille." He glanced around. "Including the ghosts."

She wanted to throttle him, but held back the urge. "She's at bingo. The ghosts won't show up if there is a whole bloody parade going through the basement. Now what the—"

He stepped forward so fast she didn't have time to say another word before his big hand covered her mouth and his other arm went around her waist. Her jerked her close.

Dana made muffled sounds under Marshall's hand, but he shook his head and glared at her in warning. "I thought I heard something."

She stiffened in his arms, as much from the heat of his proximity as from not wanting to alert Aunt Lucille if she returned from bingo early. When she heard no indication Aunt Lucille was home, Dana moved in Marshall's arms, pushing against his chest. Powerful muscle resisted her struggles. He shook his head again and kept his hand over her mouth. The feeling of his hard chest under her fingers sent a wild zing of unholy pleasure through her. She stopped moving and savored the sensation for a few seconds as it burned and tingled along her body.

He feels good against me. So hard. So male. Good, my ass. He feels sexy as hell. Her internal dialogue demanded honesty, and yet she didn't want to admit having this man's arms around her caused her to light up like a Roman candle. A perverse idea came to mind. She stuck her tongue out and touched his palm with a wet wiggle.

He cursed under his breath and stepped back like she'd slapped him.

"Brennan Marshall," she growled. "You annoying, big, nasty, lug-headed..." She sputtered. "Mangy, oversized..." She sputtered again.

"Go ahead. I think you missed at least a couple of letters in the alphabet."

"Don't get smart with me. What are you doing here? How did you get in here?"

"You really ought to curb that language of yours, you know. There are other words in the alphabet besides 'hell.' Someone might get the idea to clean your mouth out with soap."

If her blood pressure hadn't skyrocketed into the atmosphere in the last few minutes, it did now. She stalked toward him and planted her hands on her hips. "Just who do you think you are, breaking into this house? You're not above the law, just because you are the law."

He held up one hand. "Calm down. I'm seeing how easy it is to break into this house."

"Why did you break into the house? And, I might add, disrupt a pretty good fantasy?"

His eyebrows lifted at her last sentence, speculation fueling a fire in his gaze. "Fantasy?" His gaze dropped to the writing pad that had fallen to the floor. "Horror?"

"Never mind." So what if her imagination had turned toward romance rather than horror the way she'd hoped. She could dig something horrid and terrible out of the pond scene she'd created in her head. Surely.

A tiny smirk formed at the side of his mouth. It made him appear way too handsome, especially when she wanted to be annoyed with him. "Aunt Lucille needs new locks. It was too easy to get in here. I wanted to make sure that you were both safe."

She wanted to thank him for the information, at the same time she wanted to brain him with the fireplace poker. "That's all well and good, but why couldn't you have told us you were going to try and break in here? And how did you get in?"

"Through the far window at the end of the basement. Don't worry, I didn't damage anything."

Her brows pinched together. "I can't believe I didn't hear you. That's incredible. Those are practically brand new windows."

Marshall lifted his stocking cap off his head and ran a hand through his hair. "Brand new, but not invincible."

"That doesn't excuse the fact you broke in without telling anyone you were going to experiment. Aren't you worried about getting in trouble with Sheriff Pizer for pulling something like this?"

"Not at all. Sheriff Pizer knew about it and so did your aunt."

Immediate and clear, the message came through. "I see. Well, I guess I'll just have a little talk with Aunt Lucille about this. Since you still don't trust me, and apparently neither does she."

Maybe the hurt came through her voice, for his expression altered to some remorse. "Trust is important to you, isn't it?"

"Of course it is. Wouldn't it be for you?"

"Yeah." He narrowed the space between them. His gaze did a foray over her pajamas. Tweaking the collar of her top with his index finger, he asked, "Flannel, eh? And you talk about me."

Twisting her lips into a sardonic smile, she bent down to pick up her blankets, already aware of the chill in the air without them. "Wise-acre." She fought a smile. "Since when did you get a sense of humor?"

He cocked an eyebrow. "The day I met you."

Soft and low, his voice made her hot and edgy and restless. Itching, frankly, for a draught to quench this odd thirst she felt whenever he stood near and asked her ridiculous and probing questions. His gaze swept over her with disconcerting evaluation.

Dana plopped down on the couch and leaned back against the cushions. A sigh escaped her. "This is crazy. Can we wrap this up now? The ghosts will never show up with all the noise going on down here."

One corner of his mouth did turn up for about a half a second. "You really think that ghosts are just going to appear?"

She shrugged. "Why not? As I said before, I wouldn't have believed it if it hadn't been for what I heard the other night."

Marshall headed for the sliding glass door, pushing aside the drapes and unlatching the door. "I'll leave you to your ghost busting. I'll see you Sunday at the football game."

Dana stood. Disappointment flickered over her, and she hated to admit she didn't want him to leave. The feeling mingled with her confusion. "Football?"

"Lucille didn't tell you? Two teams of men against each other for the golden prize. Actually, it's an annual charity event."

She put her hands up in a gesture of surrender, then let them flop to her sides. "Of course she didn't tell me. No one tells me anything around here." When he started to speak, she held one hand up. "No, don't tell me. The golden prize is kissing a woman. Or getting a date with a woman, or—"

"No." Marshall turned away from the sliding glass door and headed toward her, each step decisive and slow.

As he strode toward her, Dana's heart flip-flopped in her chest. She stood stiff as a tree trunk. He came in close to her, so near she thought he might tumble her onto the couch. Swift and sure, before another synapse could connect, he leaned down and planted the lightest, sweetest kiss on her mouth she'd ever had. It couldn't have lasted more than two seconds, and she didn't have time to think much less respond. Before she could say a word, he turned and left. When the sliding glass door closed he dissolved into the night. Stunned, she touched her lips, expecting somehow that they would feel different. Hotter.

Her heart picked up speed, and she let the stunning, thrilling rush invigorate her blood. Curse him. Now she'd never get to sleep.

"So the bed didn't make a noise?" Kerrie asked, sinking with a sigh into the chair at the breakfast nook in Aunt Lucille's home.

Dana stood on the other side of the breakfast bar, stirring sugar into her coffee. "Not a peep. A waste of time."

Today she needed super high-test caffeine. She stayed half awake all last night, parked in the basement, waiting for the heart-shaped bed to let out a groan, moan or otherwise. She rubbed her eyes. The entire time she wondered if she'd imagined the whole episode with Marshall. In fact, she couldn't say if the tiny peck on the lips had evolved from a tired mind. It must be one big, fat illusion.

Dana watched the coffee swirling around and around. She put down the spoon, then took a sip. "Jumping holy jalopies, this is like sludge. I'm surprised it didn't eat through the spoon. Where did this recipe come from? Marshall's office?"

Chuckling, Kerrie put her mug down. "It's not that bad."

"What does Aunt Lucille call this?"

"Super-dooper java. It's Lucille's blend of beans. She grinds them herself. I'm surprised you haven't tasted it before."

Dana wrinkled her nose in distaste. "She's always trying something new. Maybe that's what I should do…start up a coffee shop. This town could use a good mocha latte, cappuccino, you name it beverage shop."

"In your spare time? When would you write?"

Since Kerrie seemed to be taking her seriously, Dana said, "I could write in the evenings."

Kerrie's skeptical expression flowed with her next words. "You don't write days or evenings now. What's it going to take to get out of this slump?"

"The mystery of the humping ghosts. Solved."

Kerrie laughed, her voice going from somewhat amused to hilarity in two seconds. "From what you described about last night, that doesn't seem likely."

Grimacing, Dana gave her friend a weary look. "Oh, well. Nothing should surprise me in this town. I swear the weirdest things have happened since I arrived."

"So are you saying it's you that's causing the weird things or that Macon stepped out of one of your novels."

"That's what I told Marshall. I mean that this town has a great Salem's Lot atmosphere. Definitely a weird twist." She took another swallow of coffee and decided the caffeine boost outweighed the hideous taste.

"You aren't afraid of the ghosts?"

"Nah. I didn't feel anything creepy about the basement. That's what makes me wonder if it's human intervention making the noises. Nothing ectoplasmic about the situation at all."

"Still…" Kerrie shifted her spoon around on a white paper napkin. She looked up with a puzzled expression.

"Still what? It's crazy I'm still here in this town trying to solve the case of bed hopping ghosts, or that someone tried to kill me?" She knew nothing would make her feel safe until whoever tried to kill her had gone to jail.

Kerrie shook her head. "None of the above. It's just that something very out of joint is going on here and I can't decipher what it is."

"You're telling me?"

Kerrie went silent for several moments, her deep thoughts evident in the concentration she poured onto the table in front of her.

Moments later she spoke. "And to think I was trapped in the bathroom yesterday while all that excitement was going on around me at the park."

"Not exactly excitement. More like terror." Dana had told her friend about the way the storm had affected her. Kerrie had known about her phobia all along.

Kerrie leaned back from the table, resting against the hard wood chair. Sunlight sent streamers through the parted curtains and across her face. "You haven't told me everything. I know when you're holding out on me. What happened in the truck while you and Marshall were sheltering in his car?"

No way, Jose, Juan, or whatever the name might be. She couldn't say that Marshall had almost paid her fifty dollars to kiss him. "He, uh…offered me a bit of money for a kiss."

The words slipped out and she slapped a hand over her own mouth.

Kerrie's conspiratorial grin broadened. "Aha! I see how it is. It's just as I thought."

A strange panic laced through Dana, and she wished she could sink into a hole and disappear.

Kerrie stared into her coffee, then pushed aside the almost empty mug. "Lucille and I knew you and Marshall would set sparks off each other."

Kerrie pushed back her chair. While she reached for the coffee pot, she nodded toward Dana's cup. Dana made a positive motion with her hand, and Kerrie poured a new steaming cup of the nasty stuff for Dana.

"What inspired you to do all this conspiring to get Marshall and I together?" Dana asked, resigned to the facts.

"We didn't conspire. We just thought if you two got within a city block of each other there'd be thunder and lightning and fireworks in general. Yesterday was good evidence."

Dana didn't know whether to scream, or give into their machinations without a whimper. What did it matter? Whether she found the man attractive or not, a simple brush of lips across lips didn't necessarily mean much. Perhaps she'd imagined every hot, needful look he'd sent her way.

"You're nuts, Kerrie. A freak thunderstorm does not a conspiracy make. There are no sparks between Marshall and I, so you can get that idea right out of your head. There can't be any special feelings."

Kerrie's brows drew down as she frowned. "Why not?"

Why not?

The words rang in her mind. For a full thirty seconds she said nothing, because she didn't know the answer. "Because I'm not staying in Macon forever. Once this whole ghost thing is finished I'll go back to New Mexico where I belong."

Kerrie appeared skeptical. "You mean you'd throw away a really wonderful opportunity with a fantastic man? You wouldn't stay and see how your relationship progresses? What are you afraid of?"

Doubt crept around the edges of Dana's lame excuses. She wanted to hate Kerrie for being so reasonable and right. Before she could speak Kerrie continued.

"Eric said that Marshall believes the same thing. That you two are not having a mutual attraction."

Dana hesitated, unsure she'd heard her friend right. "Eric? You've been talking to Eric about Marshall and me?" A new feeling emerged—pissed off. "Eric said Marshall is not interested in me?"

A flush filled Kerrie's cheeks. "It slipped out. Eric and I were talking one day and we both noticed this…this thing going on between you and Marshall and Eric said he tried talking to Marshall about his ex-wife."

"Ex wife? I didn't even know he'd been married." A stab of jealousy and annoyance toyed with Dana. The annoyance because she didn't like her personal life splattered about like gossip in a tabloid.

Kerrie put up one hand. "Wait. One situation at a time, please."

Curiosity made Dana lean forward, her hands clasped together on the table. "Go on."

"Yes, he's been married before. But he's divorced now and has been for some time." A heavy sigh ushered from Kerrie. "You're right, I shouldn't be talking about this. Marshall is going to have to explain about the divorce and what it has to do with Eric."

Too many things tangled in her mind, and Dana realized if she wanted to know what cranked Marshall's chain, she'd have to ask the man himself. "Now that sounds interesting. But I don't think I'll ever find out. I'm not about to ask Marshall personal information like that."

"I wish you wouldn't say that. Eric can't get much out of him. If Marshall had a good woman he could confide in, that might help him to heal. He's got some wounds inside that could use some serious balm."

"Yet Marshall isn't interested in me, according to Eric." Dana felt the earth sink about an inch, along with a little piece of her emotions. Okay, a big piece. "That's a fine howdy-do. And all right with me."

"What I mean is, Marshall might say he's not interested, but I've seen the way he looks at you."

A thrill raced through Dana's midsection, erasing the lump in her intestines. "Oh, yeah? How's that?"

Kerrie smiled. "Like he wants to eat you up."

Sweet shivers seemed to attack Dana from all sides. But mystification mixed with a desire to know what went on in the infuriating man's head. "I wouldn't expect Marshall to talk with anyone like that. He seems a little too hard, too internal to let anyone in."

Kerrie drained the last of her coffee, then stood and took the cup to the sink. "Are you sure? He was married once. Don't you think he had to get close to her?"

Dana closed her eyes a moment and imagined him intimate with any woman. Just the idea of him touching, maybe even kissing another woman, made the acid burn in Dana's stomach. *Rats! Now I've done it. I've started to care. Enough to be jealous of the woman he isn't married to anymore. Double crud.*

Wrestling with treacherous feelings, Dana stood and rinsed her coffee mug and they put the cups in the dishwasher. Dana mulled things over in her head before speaking again.

"You obviously have an interesting relationship with Eric Dawes if he'd confess his friend's secrets to you." The idea made Dana feel better than she had moments before.

Kerrie shrugged and an embarrassed flush covered her cheeks. "I've got several confessions to make."

"Okay, I'm the priest. Go for it, and it better be good."

Instead of smiling as Dana thought she would, Kerrie sank further down into her seat until she could prop the back of her head against the wood. "Eric and I have always been pals, and it wasn't until a few weeks back that I started to think of him a different way."

Dana sat upright, her back feeling tight as a board. Awareness prickled over her as well as mischief. "Different? The way pumpkin pie is different from lemon custard pie?"

"Uh, you could say that. Eric's handsome. But if that's all it was, I'd be able to ignore him. I never thought after my husband died I'd be interested in another man. Ever."

Tears stung Dana's eyes, and she took a heaving breath to shove back the wave of unexpected sadness for her friend. "I can only imagine."

"Anyway, I spent some time with Eric and Tabitha and discovered that I love being with them. We've uh…."

Dana's eyes widened. "You've slept together?"

"No, no." Kerrie laughed. "Nothing like that. We're in an exploratory stage."

It made sense. Kerrie and Eric had both experienced some rough times and their spouses had died in accidents. "You share something in common."

Kerrie speared her friend with a sharp glance. "I try not to think about that."

"I know. I'm sorry. I didn't mean to remind you."

"It's all right. When Eric and I have been together we haven't spoken about the way our…the way his wife died and the way Stuart died. It may be too soon. In a way the pain is too fresh."

Threads of hurting spilled through Kerrie's words. She reached across and clasped Kerrie's hand for a moment. "I'm really sorry. I've been selfish. I've been caught up in my writing problems, my landlord situation, and the bizarre stuff going on in this house. I've ignored everyone else's feelings." Guilt brought more sympathetic tears to her eyes. "I apologize."

Kerrie smiled, her warmth evident and shining from her eyes. "Oh, come now. You're the best friend a lady could have. And you can't take the world's weight on your shoulders, either. Especially when someone tried to run you off the road. That's a lot more serious than Eric and I suffering from old grief."

Dana didn't believe it. Kerrie had always tried to stay strong, and now Dana could see the way it had worn her down. "Have your tried talking with Eric about his wife, about any of it?"

"Like I said, no." She made a rueful smile. "You could say I'm a chicken."

Dana grinned. "Okay. Kerrie, you're a chicken."

Kerrie's laugh echoed around the room. "Anyone ever tell you you're a smarty pants?"

"Someone asked me that question the other day."

Kerrie put her index finger to her chin in thought. "Let me see, who could that be? Does the first name start with a B?"

"You got it." Dana tried another sip of coffee and decided she'd done Aunt Lucille a wrong. The energy boost she got from this stuff went on and on. She wrinkled her nose. "I gave him an outline of all the other people who'd called me smart-ass. Just so he'd know he wasn't the first one."

Kerrie laughed. "I see. So he wouldn't have the pleasure of thinking he was first."

"Exactly."

Kerrie sighed. "You are bad. Really bad."

The phone rang, making them both jump. Knowing that Aunt Lucille was in the attic and wouldn't hear the sound, Dana rushed to grab the phone. "Hello?"

"Dana, this is Marshall."

Her heart started stuttering and slamming. As if she wouldn't know that voice anywhere. "Speak of the devil. We were just talking about you." A long pause made her speak again. "Are you there?"

"Yeah. Listen, do you have some time to talk?"

"Sure. Fire away."

"It's private."

A strange, tingling anticipation slid like warm honey through her veins. "Kerrie's here. Is that private enough?"

"No."

Dana looked at her friend, but Kerrie seemed to have read her mind. "I get the hint. Must be Marshall."

Chuckling, Dana said into the phone, "You're driving away my friends."

He grunted.

"I see. The gorilla has spoken, Kerrie."

"Tell the furry fellow hello," Kerrie said with a wave and a smile. She left the house.

"Gorilla?" His inquiry sounded indignant.

Then she remembered that she'd vowed moments ago to give people more slack. "Sorry."

"Why were you talking about me? Did you mention last night?"

His curiosity made her wonder why he cared. She scrambled for something to say. "Uh, no. Not last night. I thought you might want to keep your nocturnal wanderings a secret. I did tell her that I was in the basement and didn't hear anything."

A sigh came over the line. "Good. Because no one else needs to know. It ties in with what I needed to talk with you about. What I propose should happen after the football game on Sunday."

"That's only a day away."

"Just listen."

Exasperation warred with her promised patience. "Okay. What is it?"

"I want to spend the night with you. Just the two of us. Alone."

Dana almost swallowed her tongue. "Stay all night with me?"

"We need to investigate further."

"Investigate?" she asked, her voice coming out as a croak. Heat crept up her neck into her face.

"The ghosts. In the basement. I figured I could stop by after the game and finally get to the bottom of what's going on with that bed."

Oh, he's talking about ghosts here and I'm thinking he means...oh, hell.

"But you said you don't believe in the ghosts," she said.

"I don't believe it's ghosts, but someone is messing around in that basement and I'm finding out who it is."

Tiny panic inched under her skin. "Okay, I'm sure Lucille will approve. You could camp out in one of the rooms upstairs."

"I'm not staying in a bedroom. I'll be downstairs. And you'll be with me."

Dana didn't like the direction the conversation turned. Carrying the cordless phone, she walked from one side of the kitchen to the other. *Honestly. Now you've taken on his annoying pacing habit?*

"A man not only of few words but even less explanation. Why just us? I'm not letting you off the hook."

"Because you obviously care about your aunt and want to solve the mystery. That's as good a reason as any."

Someone cleared their throat and Dana whirled. Aunt Lucille stood in the entryway to the kitchen, her smile broad. "Who is on the phone, dear?"

Dana handed the phone to her aunt. "Marshall."

Delight covered the older woman's face as she took the phone. As she listened to Marshall's proposal, Aunt Lucille took up the pacing Dana had started earlier. "Of course. What a fabulous idea. But I've got that Ladies Auxiliary meeting in Carter. Dana must have forgotten to tell you. You'll have the entire house to yourself for the evening."

Dana glared at her smiling aunt. Bull hockey! There was no auxiliary meeting in Carter. She'd made it up on the spot, the conniving matchmaker.

After she hung up the phone, Aunt Lucille clapped her hands once and smiled. "This is wonderful. You can make a party out of it. The catch the ghost party."

"Party?" Dana asked.

Aunt Lucille flapped her hands. "You know. Chips. Dip. Maybe even pizza."

"Uh, I don't know about that. I think all he's looking for is covert stuff. Hiding behind the couch and watching for the bogie man. Things like that."

"You're absolutely right, dear. Chips crunching would scare the ghosts away. Pizza it is."

Dana had to laugh. "Are you sure this is a good idea?"

Aunt Lucille hid behind a grin. "Of course. I can't obstruct the law, you know." She took Dana's hands in her thin, cool palms. "Dear, you know there's nothing to be afraid of."

"I'm not afraid of ghosts."

"That's not what I'm talking about." Releasing Dana she walked to the bay window that formed part of the breakfast nook and waved a hand at the panorama outside. "Why don't you go outside and lay on the hammock. Daydream a little. Find something pleasant to fantasize about so that you can let your writing mind go free."

"What does that have to do with our ghost party?"

"Release of tension. Release of that block that is keeping you from more than just writing."

"Such as?"

"Pent up frustrations. You need to have some fun, darling. I think your life is too much work and not enough play."

Dana suspected she knew what her aunt meant. "How can I play while my unfinished manuscript languishes like a half eaten sandwich? Soon my ideas will be all moldy."

"Honey, it's because you're not playing that your ideas aren't bearing any fruit."

Dana grinned. "You're saying I need the writer's version of prunes."

Aunt Lucille laughed. "Exactly right, my dear."

Logic warred with emotion. "What would you call this? I've been here a short time and all I've done is play. I've been through several adventures, gone to a dance, been run off the road. What more can I ask?"

Dana went to the window. Beyond the multi-paned glass stood a covered patio with the hammock, deck chairs, and table. She could picture herself enjoying the fall weather. Pine needles graced the ground beyond, leading into a dark forest rife with horror novel possibilities. Passed that, hiding among nature, lay the answer to her writer's block.

Dana looked at her aunt. "Maybe you're right."

Aunt Lucille patted her shoulder. "Of course I'm right. Now enjoy the Indian summer. I hear a snow storm is due next week."

With her imagination beginning to awaken, Dana envisioned a log fire and the taste of hot cocoa. Along with that she saw Marshall snuggled on the couch downstairs with her. His arm would be around her, drawing her against him as he lowered his head, his lips tasting—

Startled by the intimate picture, she jerked back to the present. Heat flooded her body.

"Pleasant thoughts, my dear?" Aunt Lucille asked with a grin.

Aunt Lucille's question made Dana grimace. "Not exactly." She headed for the kitchen door. "I'd better get on that daydreaming if I want to write a few pages today. Before that big lug Marshall arrives."

Marshall strode through the Sheriff's office after his call to Dana, wondering what the man wanted.

When he knocked on the Sheriff's closed door, he received an instant reply to enter. He slipped inside the small office. Pizer looked up from paperwork and gestured toward the chair in front of his massive desk. "Sit down, Marshall. "We've got to have a talk."

For the first time in a long time Marshall's gut clenched. He sat down. "Anything wrong?"

"Yes and no. It's about this Cummings woman."

The sheriff's tone, edged with roughness, didn't endear him to Marshall. "Dana Cummings?"

Pizer's eyes narrowed. "You know who I'm talking about."

"If it's about Skeeter watching out for her—"

"We've got a man power problem around here Marshall. You've pulled plenty of extra shifts to know that we can't pamper one person in this town to the detriment of all the others."

Marshall stiffened in his chair, letting anger wash through him and hoping it didn't show on his face. "I wasn't aware protecting Miss Cummings against further attack was pampering her, sir. It is our job to protect and serve."

Pizer shifted behind his desk, leaning back in his chair with a relaxed, 'I-could-care-less' attitude. "We can't afford to have Skeeter protecting her around the clock. That's just the way it is."

"Skeeter isn't protecting her around the clock. You know about Logan. They're spreading the work out in shifts. Besides, I've been…" He realized too late what he'd revealed.

Pizer's gaze turned hard. "You've been watching out for her?"

"On my own time."

"And what exactly motivates you to spend extra hours looking out for Miss Cummings?"

Marshall didn't think too deeply about that. "Trying to do my job is enough motivation."

Pizer didn't appear to buy it. Instead he straightened in his chair. "You're not falling in love with her, are you Marshall?"

The words hung in the air long enough that Marshall felt them like solid entities, weighing on his conscious and his beliefs. "I care what happens to her. But only in the way I care for the rest of the people in this town."

"Uh-huh." Pizer reached inside his desk and took out a box of toothpicks. He offered the box to Marshall as if it were a humidor of Cuban cigars. Marshall shook his head. "So if any other woman in this town needed the same type of assistance you'd offer her protection."

"Of course."

"Uh-huh." Pizer picked his teeth, then rolled the toothpick around in his lips. "That still doesn't solve our problem. Pull Skeeter off the detail."

Swallowing hard, Marshall took the plunge. He knew if Pizer refused his request, he'd find a way around it. "All right. But I'd like to replace him. Full time."

"What?"

Marshall knew the Sheriff had heard him. Maybe Pizer thought he'd say something different if he played deaf? "I want to be placed as her full time bodyguard."

Pizer took the toothpick out of his mouth. "What about your other cases?"

Marshall shrugged. "I'm requesting vacation as of right now. I've stored up a significant amount and I'm in to the lose it or use it category. Besides, crime isn't rampant in this town. This is the biggest thing we've got going in Macon right now."

Pizer tossed the toothpick into the trashcan and leaned his elbows on the desk. He slanted his gaze at Marshall, his expression suspicious. "You say there isn't anything amorous going on between you and that woman?"

Marshall wanted to stomp out of the office. "My personal life isn't the issue, sir. A woman's life may be at stake. If anything happens to her…if anything happened to her, I wouldn't forgive myself. And you wouldn't forgive yourself if the Sheriff's department got a black eye by way of bad publicity. Dana's got enough friends and family that you can be sure they'd have our heads on a pike if they found out we didn't provide proper protection."

Staying quiet for some time, the older man gave Marshall a long stare. Marshall had worked with this man long enough to realize you couldn't give him too much information or you'd find your head under the guillotine. Better to keep things straight and never vary too much from the topic.

"So you want to protect the department," Pizer said.

"That's right." Marshall tightened his grip on the arms of the chair.

Shrugging, Pizer said, "All right. Vacation granted. When are you going to start this observation?"

"After the football match."

Pizer frowned. "Guess she can't be too important to you if you're willing to play football over watching her…body."

Pizer's double insinuation made Marshall's stomach roll. "If Logan wasn't watching out for her, you can be sure I wouldn't be in the game."

"You ain't playing anyway, are you?" Pizer sniffed.

"Second string, sir. Like always."

Chuckling, Pizer waved his hand at the door. "Okay, then. Get outta here."

As Marshall experienced the relief of leaving the Sheriff's cramped office, he thought about everything the man had said. *Come on, Marshall. What do you feel for Dana? What is pushing you so hard on this case?*

Back in his office he tried to ignore the fact that answers wouldn't materialize. At least not ones he wanted to think about.

Chapter 13

As Dana strode through the crowd in the park with her Aunt Lucille, she felt a strange excitement. Children squealed as they tumbled around the playground under the watchful eye of parents. One kid let out a whoop as he sailed by on a skateboard. She seemed infected with the sounds of laughter around her, and the idea of watching Marshall, Gregory, Neal, Eric and most of the other men in Macon battle it out on the green.

Right. Admit it. You want to see Marshall flex those incredible muscles. Uh-huh, that's right admit it. She wanted to see Marshall in action, wanted to cheer like she was a girlfriend watching her guy play ball.

Sunlight spilled through high clouds, promising to warm an otherwise chilly morning. The air smelled of wood fires and the coming of fall. People spilled from the non-denominational church across the street, ready to watch the mêlée in their Sunday best.

Dana inhaled the fresh air, wishing she had more time this morning out on the patio. She'd taken her aunt's advice the other day and loved the results. A long session dozing in the hammock resulted in two dreams that Dana knew she could add to her novel. Something vicious. A hairy nightmare. Followed by a romantic dream filled with hazy images of a tall man drawing her into his arms and kissing the stuffing out of her.

This morning she'd sat in the hammock armed with pad and pencil. In the last two days she produced twenty pages. She felt ready to tackle the world after creating on paper. The words had flowed, refusing to leave until her hand cramped and she knew nothing more would materialize that day. Few things gave her as much pleasure as writing in flow, letting her muse spill words onto the page at a furious pace.

After the fantasy…ur…dream, she'd realized she wanted heavy duty romance added to her horror novel. *Now that'll give my agent a heart attack, by golly.* But she wanted love included in her story. It would make it richer, more intriguing. Now, if the rest of it would come together she'd leave Macon without regrets.

Dana knew she possessed a silly grin, and when she saw a man in the distance who appeared familiar, she took a closer look. He wore almost shoulder length hair, beard, mustache, and muscular body suited out in a red T-shirt and shorts. Long, strong, hairy legs. Her mouth almost watered. Yeah, it was Marshall all right.

Aunt Lucille came to a stop and squinted. "I wonder where Marshall is?"

Dana pointed to the grouping of men. "He's right there. See?"

Aunt Lucille grinned, and her smile contained a teasing slant. "Oh, yes."

Her aunt's rambling continued as they walked, her enthusiasm never waning even after two teenage boys rushed by them and almost knocked them over.

The bleachers came into view at the same time Kerrie did. A young girl, perhaps nine years old, trailed alongside. Blonde like Kerrie, the girl smiled.

"Tabitha!" Aunt Lucille waved at the girl, and the child ran to her. Kerrie followed behind, a content look on her face.

The young girl looked up at Dana with an innocent smile. "Hi. I'm Tabitha Dawes."

Dana, warmed by the child's friendliness, put her hand out. "Nice to meet you. I'm Dana Cummings."

"Daddy said you're Uncle Brennan's friend."

Deep inside she knew the little girl couldn't know what that implied, so Dana said, "Yeah, that's right."

"You're here to watch him in the football game?"

Dana flicked a look at her Aunt and Kerrie. Both carried broad smiles. "Of course. I'm here to watch your daddy, Uncle Brennan, and everyone."

Tabitha didn't quibble, and as they went to the bleachers, Dana noted the child's smile never disappeared. She tried to imagine being that age again and living without a mother. Just the thought made her heart ache for the girl's loss.

They'd settled into the bleachers when Dana spied Logan in the crowd. She should have felt secure, but the knowledge someone might wish to hurt her never left her mind. If this had been a novel, she might have enjoyed the prospect of action. Instead her insecurities tingled over her skin like the touch of an insect.

Kerrie, sitting on Dana's left side, said, "Oh, there's our heroes."

The men suited up in red shirts ran onto the field. A cheer went up from some people who'd decided they wanted the red team to win. Dana and her companions cheered as well.

"Why am I cheering?" Dana asked after the racket lulled to a muted roar.

"Because it's team spirit." Aunt Lucille continued clapping until the people around her looked at her.

Dana twisted her mouth into a sardonic smile. "Yeah, but they're all from Macon."

Kerrie nudged her with her elbow.

"Ow," Dana said. "What was that for?"

Kerrie looked skyward. Her expression said without words, don't you know anything? "The red team has our guys on it."

"Yeah!" Tabitha cheered and clapped as her daddy went up for the toss of the coin. "Daddy and Uncle Brennan!"

"Uh-huh," Dana said. "There's Neal and Gregory on the blue team. Is that Sheriff Pizer dressed as a referee?"

"Looks like it." Aunt Lucille snickered. "Now that should make for an interesting game."

Dana tried for nonchalance. "Since it's flag football it shouldn't be such a big deal. It's not like they'll be grinding their gizzards into the dirt or anything."

"Ahem." Kerrie gave Dana a lopsided grin. "Not exactly. Macon has an intriguing style of flag football. A little closer to rugby."

"You're kidding?" Dana asked.

"Nope."

Dana watched Marshall and wished they'd taken a bleacher seat closer to the field. From the middle section she could see how he ran onto the field with long, certain strides. Yep, sure enough, the man she'd seen earlier had been Marshall. Raw pleasure coursed through her as she watched him. He laughed at something one of the other men said and headed for the sideline.

Dana took a gander at the Blue Angels and saw that Neal talked with other team members. Gregory, true to form, strutted around like a rooster overseeing a hen house. To her shame, Dana let her imagination roam and she envisioned Marshall smashing Gregory's nose into the grass.

"Wow, doesn't look like Marshall's on the varsity," Kerrie said, leaning forward to peer at the men below. She grinned. "But Eric is."

Aunt Lucille nodded. "The way I hear it, that's the way it's always been. Eric always made the varsity because the coach thought he was hot stuff on a silver platter."

"So Marshall ended up junior varsity? Are we talking about college?" Dana asked.

Kerrie tossed back her thick braid. "Nope. They never went to college together. High school."

The game started with an obnoxious blast from the bullhorn speaker in the booth above the stands. "Welcome Macon! This is J.D. Crowner with KFTR country announcing today's game between the Red Devils and the Blue Angels! The captain of the Red Devils is Dr. Eric Dawes!"

Tabitha and Kerrie let out a squeal and clapped with the others.

The announcer shouted above the cheers. "Team captain for the Blue Angels is Spider Hamrick!"

A burly dude with long blonde hair and a reddish beard sauntered away from the sideline with a swagger that screamed look at me. Cheers rose from the stands again.

"Marshall. Spider. Skeeter," Dana mumbled. "What's with this town and weird names?"

Kerrie lifted one disdainful eyebrow. "My name isn't weird."

Tabitha frowned. "Mine neither."

Realizing she'd planted her foot deep into her mouth, Dana threw them a weak grin.

"Go Blue Angels!" A group of cheerleaders appeared along the sidelines behind the players. They pranced as they called out a cheer. "Go Blue Angels! Give 'em the beak, the beak, the beak. Give 'em the beak, the beak, the beak!"

The Red Devil cheerleaders, dressed in the same uniforms except with red on white, cavorted near the blue women. Their attempts to out shout the Blue Angel cheerleaders made a wild mess of noise.

Dana's mouth opened and closed. "Cheerleaders?"

Kerrie giggled. "Is that Jenny Pizer in that super short uniform for the Devils?"

"Is that Marshall and Eric ogling her?" Aunt Lucille squinted and leaned forward. "By golly, I think her pom poms have their attention."

Dana would have laughed if she hadn't seen Marshall's gaze glued to Jenny's generous pom poms. Jenny lost no time bouncing in his direction. He smiled at her as she swung her hips from side to side in a bump and grind that went with the o-la-la music issuing from the speakers. Seconds later she reached for him and gave him a hug. He hugged her back, looking mighty pleased. Then, before the heavens and everyone, Jenny laid one on him. A no-holds-barred lip lock.

Dana felt a blaze of unexpected fury slam through her. "Why that son of a—"

Kerrie's hand flew out and clamped over Dana's mouth.

"Don't say it." Kerrie glanced at Tabitha, who didn't seem to pay the least attention to adult high jinks. Instead she laughed at the Devil mascot…a red devil, of course.

Marshall pulled back from the kiss, looking a little embarrassed.

Dana swallowed her words as Kerrie removed her hand. She couldn't believe she'd almost cursed in front of the little girl. She'd about called Marshall a son of a buckster for doing what all red-blooded men did at one time or another. She gagged on the disappointment. Of course he wouldn't be different. Marshall pried Jenny's arms from around his neck, and Dana experienced a new satisfaction. At least he wasn't lingering in Jenny's arms. Kerrie nudged her with an elbow again.

Dana scowled. "Ouch! What did I do now?"

"You look like you just ate a bug. What's wrong?"

"Nothing. When is this game going to start?"

Kerrie didn't need to explain, for the referee's whistle sounded as Eric and the Angel captain went for the coin toss. The Devils won the toss.

As the game started, Dana also noted that Eric had lined up as wide receiver. She wondered if in high school he'd also played the part. With his loping stride, he ate up the sideline as he went out for a pass. He caught the quarterback's throw with grace. The crowd let out another whoop as Eric tore up the field and headed for Angel territory. Dana had enough time to notice Marshall cheered on the sidelines, his hands balled into fists as he gestured. Eric almost made the ten-yard line when a bruiser from the Angels came across the field and snatched his flag. End of play. Groans of disappointment went up from Devil fans, including Kerrie, Tabitha and Aunt Lucille.

The game went on with no one making a score, each team evenly matched. When one big dude went down with a sprained ankle, the coach put Marshall in on first string. Unexpected pride and pleasure welled within Dana when she saw him run onto the field for the first time as a defensive back.

Kerrie nudged her again with that annoying elbow. "Would you look at that?"

Shrugging, Dana decided to play it cool. "What?"

"Marshall's finally playing, you dope. Isn't that great?"

Making a disgusted noise, Dana said, "I suppose."

Tabitha let out a whoop. "Go, Uncle Brennan! Go!"

After the first quarter ended, the Devils gained ground with two forward passes that achieved twenty yards. When a touchdown and extra point gave the Devils a seven-zip lead, Kerrie, Dana, Aunt Lucille, and Tabitha cheered until they almost lost their voices. The score held until half time when the Angels moved into the Devil side of the field and stopped on the twenty-yard line.

Dana admitted to herself that she hadn't experienced this much fun in a long time. As their little group watched the cheerleaders perform some pitiful jumps and leaps, they tried to keep from chortling. When Jenny did some splits that didn't quite form all the way, Dana clapped for her anyway, determined to keep her hostility hidden.

Kerrie and Aunt Lucille eyed her, though, perhaps unconvinced.

"What are you looking at?" Dana asked them.

Kerrie patted her on the shoulder. "Good try, my friend."

Aunt Lucille patted her other shoulder, and Dana glanced at them, feigning bemusement. "What?"

"No way to hide it now," Kerrie said. "I saw your face when Jenny kissed Marshall."

Dana grunted. "He kissed her."

Aunt Lucille's brow wrinkled in concentration. She perused the cheerleaders cavorting on the field. "No, I think Jenny hugged and kissed him. Of course, he did have an interesting grin on his face...."

Dana itched to escape the speculation. She shrugged, rolling her shoulders as if to relieve tired muscles. "It doesn't matter. If Jenny and Marshall are an item, that's their business. Not mine."

Tabitha's sweet young face pinched into a frown. "No way. Uncle Brennan doesn't like her. He's just being polite."

Just being polite to lay a big kiss on a woman? I don't think so. Dana gave the little girl an indulgent smile, but said nothing. Children, as she knew by now, didn't always know when to leave well enough alone.

Tabitha measured Dana with a curious look. "I remember him saying something super nice about you, Miss Cummings. But I don't remember what it was now."

Dana's heart did a back flip. Before she could say anything else, the crowd applauded as the cheerleaders went off the field and the battling foes returned to the green.

Several plays went forward, but Dana didn't notice much of the action. Instead her attention stayed glued to Marshall. She couldn't stop looking at him, and each time her gaze snagged on his body, she wanted to scream. *No willpower. No willpower at all.* She sighed and closed her eyes. The man had the balls to look unconcerned about anything, while her gut churned with a bizarre anxiety she barely recognize. Despair? Excitement? Who knew?

His wind tossed hair, bone-melting gaze, and miraculous muscles lived up to the name Red Devil. Shoving back her emotions, she took in the scent of greasy food stand and mouth-watering popcorn. Her stomach let out a growl loud enough that Aunt Lucille, Kerrie, and Tabitha all looked at her.

Dana blushed. "Sorry. Didn't eat much breakfast."

With that explanation, she started taking food orders. She trekked to the concession stand, thankful for the distraction. The walk seemed to go for miles, giving her plenty of time to ponder.

So what if Marshall looked tough and rough? So what if he bristled, as usual, with an undeniable, palpable masculinity that made everything feminine within her react to everything male within him? Dana sniffed in contempt. She kept seeing him smile as Jenny had hooked her arms around his neck, and then imagined herself in Jenny's place. Her arms looped around his neck, her mouth pressed to his. A flush coursed through Dana. *I'm green-eyed. But he'll never know it.* She'd be pickled before she admitted that she cared about Brennan Marshall enough to be jealous.

A hand clamped on her right shoulder, and she almost squeaked. As she whirled around, Logan released her. He put his hands up in surrender.

"Logan, you scared the shit out of me."

He gave her a weak grin. "Sorry, but you're as slippery as lo mein noodles. And if I let you out of my sight, Marshall will peel my ass."

Twisting her lips into a parody of a frown, she crossed her arms and sighed. "Well, he is pretty crabby sometimes."

Logan looked heavenward as if to agree one hundred percent but afraid to vocalize the concept. "Come on. Let's get food and head back."

As she started walking again, she wondered if anyone with sinister intent watched from the stands, and the idea made her stomach roil in apprehension. As she scanned the crowd, she could have sworn a million eyes kept her in sight. A weird sense of danger made her shiver. Logan must have sensed her fear; he slipped his arm around her for a moment.

As she glanced back at the playing field, she heard a roar from the crowd and turned about at the same time Logan did. She added her own whoop and cheer as she caught sight of a Red Devil catching a ball intended for a Blue Angel wide receiver.

Marshall's got the ball! His determined expression as he sprinted down the field with the ball gave him the look of a warrior going into battle.

"All right, Marshall!" Dana clapped.

Almost as if he'd heard Dana's exclamation Marshall glanced her way. It took that minor distraction to slow him the slightest fraction.

A Blue Angel defender roared across the field, brawny legs pumping as he charged. Dana opened her mouth to shout a warning, but the sound fell victim to the screaming crowd. With a growl Gregory plowed into Marshall. Taken off balance as Gregory pushed him out of bounds, Marshall slammed into the chain link fence, his entire body shuddering from the impact. Then he fell into a crumpled heap.

Chapter 14

"Marshall!" Dana's cry rang through the area as she ran toward the fence with Logan following.

Boos and howls of indignation issued from the stands. Dana knew Gregory would be in mega trouble for adding the extra touch to the flag football. The coward didn't stick around to see what kind of damage he'd done to Marshall. Instead Gregory turned and ran back to the sideline. Dana knelt by the fence, gripping the links. Marshall lay on the ground on his right side, a cut above his left eyebrow pouring blood. His eyes remained closed and his face pale as chalk.

Unleashed fear slammed through Dana. "Marshall!"

Logan's concerned expression and voice echoed Dana. "Marshall, you okay?"

At the sound of their voices, Marshall's eyes popped open, and he struggled onto his elbows. His stunned expression sent deep worry through her.

She took a shuddering breath. "You're bleeding. Are you all right?"

A look between dazed and amused crossed his face. "Never been better."

Relief poured through her. If he had his sense of humor he might be okay.

Before anyone could say a word, Eric rushed up with the coach and several other Red Devils. Eric knelt beside his friend with the medical bag. "Hey, don't move." He quickly pressed gauze against the cut on his friend's forehead. "You hurt anywhere else?"

Marshall sat all the way up and shook his head, then winced as if the movement hurt. All the while his gaze stayed pinned on Dana, and she took him in like a starving woman. "Great. I feel just great. Remind me to kick Metcalf's butt when I get the chance."

Dana licked her dry lips. "He's bleeding, Eric."

She knew her obvious statement sounded stupid, but she didn't care. Worry continued to batter her as she saw blood drip onto Marshall's shirt.

Eric threw her a reassuring look. "It doesn't mean it's serious."

Logan pressed her shoulder. "He'll be fine. He's tougher than twenty year old jerky."

Eric began his examination, testing Marshall's vision and pupils. A quick bandage was taped to the cut on his forehead, and within a minute or two Marshall was able to stand. The crowd cheered as they saw Marshall on his feet. Dana rose at the same time, wishing she could help him.

Eric looked over at Dana and Logan. "I'm taking him to the hospital."

But Marshall shrugged off helping hands. "I'm finishing the game."

"Brennan Marshall," Dana said, her mouth opening and the words spilling before she could stop herself. She gripped the chain link fence and realized her fingers hurt from the pressure. "Don't be stupid. What if you have a concussion?"

Marshall's stern expression turned almost icy cool. He glanced at Eric. "Do I have a concussion?"

"You don't appear—"

"Okay, then. I'm playing."

Eric looked about ready to protest, and so did the coach, but Marshall gave them a solid glare. Eric shrugged. "All right, but if you fall over dead because you're too damn stubborn, don't blame me."

As Eric and the others walked away, Dana added her own glare to the implacable look on Marshall's face. "You big, dumb—"

Logan put his hand on her shoulder again. "She's right, Marshall. You could be hurt worse."

"Save it," Marshall growled, and started to walk away.

Dana's concern, churning in her gut, mixed with piss and vinegar. "Why you arrogant, unfeeling...." She sputtered for words. "You...you..."

Marshall spun around and marched back to her. Logan must have realized his presence added fuel to the conflagration, so he stepped several yards away. Marshall's continued hard-ass look puzzled Dana down to the roots. When he reached the fence, she kept her grip on the metal, using it like a lifeline.

"I'm playing," he said with deadly soft assurance.

Unexpected tears welled in her eyes, and she blinked them back with determination. "You don't care about anyone but yourself."

"What does that mean?"

"Your friends are worried about you and you want to march right out there and maybe drop over minutes or hours later because you're too freaking stubborn to admit when you're defeated?" Releasing her death grip on the fence, she started to turn away. Tears escaped and she brushed at them, hoping he wouldn't see them. She turned back a half step. "Fine. Go ahead and see if I care."

Taking a shuddering breath, she left the area without Logan, heading toward the food stand at a trot. *Good deal, Dana. You've acted like an idiot in more ways than one. First you show that you give a damn about him, then you cry. He'll get the idea that you've got a thing for him.* She couldn't, wouldn't have that.

Marshall felt pole-axed. Not by the brutal kiss of the chain link fence, but by the look in Dana's eyes as she marched away. Logan appeared pissed. It had been a long time since Logan had speared him with that contemptuous an expression. Realization came two fold. His head felt like cottage cheese and in the morning his body would ache like crazy.

Something else reared up and bit him in the butt. He'd seen more than anger in Dana's eyes. He'd seen tears.

Tears of worry? No way, he must have been mistaken.

Logan approached the fence as Marshall watched Dana march away. "I guess you really did get the sense knocked out of you, Marshall. I've never seen you act so stupid in all my life."

With that admonition, his friend followed Dana toward the food stand.

Stupid all right. Ignorant as a mule with a lobotomy. He'd let Dana distract him when he noticed Logan striding along with her, his arm looped about her shoulders. Unreasonable, blazing jealousy had rocked him enough to slow him down. Gregory had taken advantage and slammed into him. An illegal slam, but a kick butt maneuver that had taken him out of commission and prevented a touchdown for the Devils. He shook his head and regretted the movement as a dull ache penetrated his skull. With one last glance at Dana and Logan, he headed back to the gaggle of people at the bench. Jenny had stayed in the background when everyone else had run to his aid. With the way she'd hung all over him since the game started, he'd been glad she'd stayed back.

Eric came up to him as play resumed. "You all right?"

Marshall shook his head. "Nope."

"What's wrong? Do you feel dizzy or sick?"

Marshall crammed his hand through his hair. "No. I'm just mad as hell. You're right." With that he started toward the ambulance. "I need my head examined."

Eric strode alongside him as Jenny appeared from the side. The pesky woman grabbed Marshall's arm and almost brought him to a halt. "Oh, Marshall, that's going to make a scar."

Marshall wondered if she liked the idea of a scar on a man, or hated the concept. Either way, he decided to say nothing. When he gave her a bland look and kept going, she pouted and released him. As he remembered the way Dana had accepted Logan's arm around her, Marshall realized he didn't want to see another man holding Dana. *Dangerous thoughts, man. Very dangerous.*

He yanked his rampant feelings back into a safe place. So what if Logan and Dana had a thing for each other. Dana's heart would be broken when Logan went back to Atlanta, but he couldn't make that his concern.

An examination at the hospital showed Marshall didn't have a concussion, so Eric released him. Marshall ached in several places; bruises had popped up as time went forward. Most of the time he kept stone faced and displeased. When a nurse came in the cubicle and announced that the Red Devils had won by a touchdown, both men shook hands and clapped each other on the back. She then told them Gregory hadn't repented, even when the referees had slapped him with a penalty and refused to let him play for the rest of the game.

"Serves him right," Eric said. "Bastard had no right to hit you like that."

Marshall grunted. "If I hadn't been distracted, it wouldn't have mattered. I almost outran him."

"Oh, come on, you may be a fast runner, but he'd have caught you anyway."

Marshall didn't know whether to feel pleased at Eric's assessment, or hacked off. "Thanks. I think."

The nurse smiled and shook her head, muttering something about men as she left.

"Get outta here," Eric said as Marshall slipped off the examination table. "If you suffer any strange symptoms, get back here immediately or call an ambulance."

Marshall smiled and saluted. "You got it. I have work to do tonight, though."

"What?"

"A stakeout at Lucille's house."

Eric followed him into the hall. "You sure you'll be welcome there?"

Marshall frowned. "Yeah, why not?"

Turning back, Marshall waited for his friend to speak. He'd seen Eric look this uncomfortable before, but didn't understand why he'd look that way now.

"It's none of my business, but I think you owe Dana an apology."

"What for?"

Eric sighed. "Think about it. The answer will come to you."

Marshall thought about it all the way home. Could those have really been tears he'd seen swimming in Dana's eyes? He marveled that she might have worried about him that much. He couldn't remember anyone other than his mother caring about him that way. Yeah, Eric and the guys in the sheriff's department cared about him like good friends would. But a woman, no.

His ex-wife Helen had never looked at him with that dewy-eyed terror that said she feared for him in the line of duty. When a stray bullet from a hunter's rifle had taken skin off the top of his right shoulder, she'd barely acknowledged concern.

In contrast he visualized Dana crouching next to the chain

link fence as he'd opened his eyes. Metcalf had barreled into him so hard his insides had rattled, and for a full half minute he couldn't capture a breath. When he'd seen Dana's wide eyes, he didn't know if her stark worry had been real. Instead he'd let his jealousy rule his actions. *Instead I acted like an idiot and a jackass.*

Back home he took a shower, made a sandwich for dinner, and recruited his courage. He dialed Lucille's house.

Lucille answered after three rings. "Well, I'll be. How are you doing? I was about ready to call and see if your bell had stopped ringing."

He chuckled. "I'm okay. Not even a headache anymore. Eric pronounced me alive and well."

Lucille's sigh came heavy over the phone. "Dana will be so pleased to hear that."

He made a noise that sounded halfway between a grunt and a laugh. He eased his butt into a kitchen chair. "I wouldn't be too sure about that."

"By the way, what did you say to that girl? She had a look of disappointment on her for the rest of the game. After you climbed into that ambulance, she looked away and didn't say much until after we'd gone home. Then she tried this cheerful act. She's as peppy as a teenager. I don't believe it for a minute."

Marshall put his hand up in defense, though he knew she couldn't see him. "I think it's what I didn't say to her. Look, can I talk to her?"

"I don't suppose you'll still be coming over tonight?"

"Actually, it's still on…as long as Dana will have me there."

Aunt Lucille paused before heaving another dramatic sigh. "Well, you'll have to ask her. Just a moment."

He knew Lucille had repeated his words back to him on purpose. He put his elbow on the table and sat in the semi-darkness as night spilled into the room. If he wanted to catch so-called ghosts, he'd keep his resolve to hang out in the basement with Dana.

"Hello?" Dana's soft, level voice made heat stir low in his midsection.

"Hey." It was all he could get past the roughness in his throat.

"Marshall? Aunt Lucille didn't tell me it was you." Her voice sounded somewhat accusatory.

"If you'd known would you have talked to me?"

"Probably not." The reply came sharp and certain.

Okay. I deserved that. "Look, Dana—"

"I'll understand if you have to cancel tonight."

Her interruption made him sting with rebuttal. "I'm not canceling. I'll be there at eight o'clock."

"What...what about your head injury?"

"Eric sent me home. I'm fine."

"Really?"

"Really. On another topic, where are Neal and Gregory? Wallowing in their defeated dreams?"

She chuckled, and the sound gave him hope. "Apparently. They said something about heading to a party for all the beleaguered Angels."

Marshall knew the one. "Better them than me. I'll see you later."

He hung up before she could think of a reason to refuse him.

Dana's nerves pinged like rats racing in a maze, trained to perform a stress test. She rushed about the basement, cleaning. She didn't know why she cared what the place looked like. As Lucille had pointed out before she left for her meeting, 'the place is so clean you could lick the floor.' Dana looked at the thick gray carpet and thought better of the idea.

She'd had the rest of the day after the game to contemplate her feelings. And she didn't like them one bit. Embarrassment smothered her. She'd cried because of the big doofus, and she'd hated the confused, worried, unmanageable feelings she'd allowed to invade her space. She'd shown more than one person today that she cared a lot about Brennan Marshall. Aunt Lucille and Kerrie had questioned her mood the rest of the game, but she'd brushed off their queries. Unhappy with being grumpy, she couldn't seem to shake it. If she could have gotten her hands on Gregory and wrung his thick neck she would have. His call to the house not long before Marshall's had prevented retaliation because Aunt Lucille had picked up the phone.

"You should have let me talk to Gregory," Dana had said. "I would have kicked his balls from here to eternity."

Aunt Lucille had grinned. "No doubt, my dear. That's why I didn't let you talk to him. You'll need all your energy for tonight."

Her aunt's crafty smile had made Dana curious. "Oh?"

"For ghost hunting, my dear. Ghost hunting. From what I've heard it can be an exhausting business."

Dana couldn't quite tell if her aunt referred more to the beasties that rattled the bed, or if Marshall's presence would wear her out.

Attempting to write hadn't calmed her soul. She'd sat on the hammock, lolling in the fading sunlight, absorbing nature and trying to leave butterfly stomach behind. When words wouldn't come, she'd gone into the house to change into a warmer top—a burgundy waffle knit Henley tunic. Jeans and sandals would have to do. Not like she was going on a date.

When she'd found herself primping in front of the bathroom mirror for the tenth time, checking what little makeup she wore, and applying another coat of clear lip-gloss, she'd groaned in disgust.

She sank onto the sectional couch, stared into the fireplace, and fiddled with her father's ring. Today the weight of the jewelry hung heavy about her neck. Perhaps she'd put it away.

"Well, Dad, what would you advise? Run? Hide?"

She waited in the quiet, knowing she wouldn't receive an answer. One thing her dad had always done for her. He'd let her make mistakes and as a result she'd grown up fast. Sure, she'd made some big 'uns but no more than the average person. So why did she feel like running to daddy now? But Dad couldn't be here, hadn't been here for so long.

She glanced at the long bar, unable to see the heart-shaped bed from this angle. Did Marshall honestly believe the bed would make noise tonight? If it did, it would be the oddest occurrence in the annals of paranormal phenomena. She'd placed a tape recorder on the bar in hopes it would pick something up when and if the bed began to make noises.

When the doorbell rang, Dana knew the one man who could drive her crazy had arrived. She scampered up the stairs. Once she reached the front door she looked through the side curtain and saw Marshall's vehicle. Nervous flutters took up residence in her stomach. Inhaling a fortifying breath, she opened the door.

Marshall stood with his hands behind his back. His expression went from blank to a warm grin. The fluttering in her stomach accelerated and joined with her heart in a mad dash to see who could go faster. *Calm down. So what if he looks better than a hot chocolate sundae with sprinkles on top? So what if he's lost the 'I don't give a crap look' and replaced it with come hither sensuality?* His dark hair, swept back in waves, and the bandage on his forehead made for a rakish picture. He'd topped it off with a black cowboy hat. The whole get up made him look like a rustic, a man ready for the range or to croon a country-western melody. A few seconds passed before she realized she stood like a dunce, staring into his heart-stopping eyes.

"Hey," he said a little gruffly. His hands came into view and he held out a single red and white carnation wrapped in green florist paper.

Her breath left her as she reached for the flower. "Oh. Wow.

Um…thank you." Feeling dry mouthed and awkward, she moved back from the door. "Please come in."

Superb. You sound like a nervous schoolgirl on a first date.

When he slipped through the door and closed it behind him, she said, "I love carnations." Then something perverse sprang to life and she had to know more. "What's the occasion?"

Marshall took off his hat and stepped closer. She drank in the exciting scent that seemed all his…spicy and musky. A potent combination that made her dizzy and warm.

"An apology for snapping at you today."

It didn't take much to summon a smile. "And you think this makes up for it, eh?"

A tiny smile at the corner of his mouth combined with clear interest in his eyes. Was he even closer? "Is there something else you want?"

His returning question stumped her…no…stunned her for a few seconds. Heat filled her face, and she figured avoiding his question would be the best route. She looked down, unable to meet his gaze. "Thank you for the flower." The delicate scent of the carnation met her nose. "Come on downstairs. I've got our campsite set up."

As he followed Dana downstairs, he said, "I thought when I called you'd tell me to go to hell."

She decided if he would be blunt, then so would she. Once inside the basement, she headed around the bar. "I considered it. For about a half minute."

Without saying a word Marshall went to the sectional couch and looked around. She wondered what he'd think of the temporary indoor campsite. Dana had placed a cornucopia of fruits in a basket on the bar, as well as trail mix, and crackers and cheese.

Filling a small vase with water, she put the carnation inside and placed it on the wood bar. She glanced at Marshall and noted he stood in the living area, his hands on his hips.

Taking a deep breath, she realized her stomach tossed and turned. She'd better get her nerves under control or he'd become suspicious and think she hid something from him. *Well, you are hiding something from him, aren't you?*

"Blankets and pillows?" his deep voice asked from the living room. "Munchies?"

She suspected her grin would look nervous, so she didn't try to smile. Instead she went around the bar and joined him. "In case your stakeout goes late into the night."

When he trained his gaze on her, the world did a topsy turvy movement. "Good thinking. It just might."

Clearing her throat, she asked, "Would you like something to drink? Aunt Lucille has just about everything down here. Soft drinks, juice, you name it."

Marshall asked for water, and she decided her stomach couldn't handle anything else either. After locating two sparkling waters in the small fridge under the bar, Dana crossed to the sectional couch. She sat at one corner while Marshall sat at the other, and in a way it looked ridiculous. Like one of those thirty person tables in a castle great hall. She'd have to shout for him to hear her at the other end.

Silence stretched between them. Dana wondered if he kept mum to unnerve her. Yet she sensed a strumming in the air, an energy that vibrated with unspoken needs. Terrified of those needs, she continued to deny them.

Sounds invaded her; the ticking of the bar clock filled the air; outside the wind brushed the bow of a pine tree against the sliding glass window. Now that night encroached, she felt glad the drapes had been pulled over the sliding glass window. She smelled the pine-scented cleaner she'd used to wipe down the bar, and the special but indefinable scent that always reminded her of Aunt Lucille's home.

Dana looked over and realized he stared at her, his bottle of water almost empty. She swallowed hard as she saw a dark flame ignite in his eyes. Inside she ached to know the meaning of that look. That burning, intense, eat-you-alive expression made her itch and burn to understand this man in every way possible.

Grasping these facts made her do a mental squirm. His stillness added to the fever. She stood and went to the fireplace, aware that the encroaching night had turned the basement cool. Later she might wish she'd started a fire.

When she looked at him, his gaze had attached to her again. If she'd felt bolder tonight she'd have asked why he stared. Instead she took another angle. "Why are we here, Marshall?"

"Stakeout."

"Okay, so we're doing monosyllables again. No, I mean why are we really here? Do you realize that Aunt Lucille hasn't heard the noises in days, and neither have I?"

He nodded. "I suspected as much."

"Why?"

He put his drink on the coaster on the side table and leaned forward. "Because I've investigated. If I wasn't looking into this you'd still hear the noises all right."

"You think your interrogation of all of us has scared away the culprit?"

"Maybe." Another long pause started, his face a contradiction of soft and hard in the dim light. "But we've gone over this ground before."

"So you'd rather sit here and say nothing?"

"No. Tell me about your…books."

She heard his hesitation, and decided teasing him would lighten the mood. "Singular. I have one book."

He nodded. "Right. I haven't seen a copy of it, but then I don't read horror much."

"You probably get enough of that on the job."

He broke into another killer smile. "Haven't encountered many ghosts or ghouls in my line of work. Unless you count people like Gregory. But that has nothing to do with your book. Fire away. Tell me all about it."

Dana tasted her water, then plopped back onto the couch, this time a section closer. "No way. You've got to buy a copy."

He laughed. "At least tell me what it's about."

So she gave him a small synopsis, adding that her next project would feature romance. As soon as the word "romance" spilled from her mouth, she wanted it back.

His eyes narrowed. "That sounds interesting. That's a rare combination, isn't it? Horror and romance."

She shrugged and finished her water. "Depends on who you talk to. Some people have had horrible romances." Incriminating words kept spilling from her mouth and she couldn't seem to stop them. "Haven't you?"

Marshall's intent gaze caught hers and held. "I've had my share. What about you?"

She nodded. "One was enough for me, thanks."

His gaze turned curious.

Dana knew she struggled with conversation because of fear. Stark, unrelenting fright. What if he asked about Frank? She'd told few people about him, Kerrie being one. Most people didn't understand. They couldn't. Better to ask him first.

"So what horrible relationships have you had?" she asked in a rush.

He didn't say a word and mortification and disappointment started to assault her. *Take it easy. You'll drive him off with your stupid questions.*

Shifting toward her, he pinned her with a look that said he'd ease her curiosity. He looked at the fireplace. "Chilly in here. I could make a fire, then we could talk."

She couldn't argue with good, sound logic. After he'd gotten the fire roaring in the grate, she settled on the hearth to enjoy the heat and the hypnotic effect of dancing flames. Marshall did the same.

"It started when Eric and I were in high school. We were in sports together. Wrestling, football. Eric was always the better athlete."

Dana allowed her gaze to glide over his broad shoulders, powerful arms and strong legs. "You're kidding?"

"No. I wasn't bad…just not as good as him. If it had been Eric with that interception today, Metcalf never would have caught him."

She heard the self-recrimination in his tone, and wanted to smack him. "So what? I saw you run and you were incredibly fast. I saw how you played earlier in the game when they let the second string—"

"Second string." He held up two fingers. "Second string."

She sniffed. "Oh please. I never figured you for a man whose ego is so fragile that kind of thing would matter to you."

"It does matter when you're sixteen or seventeen years old. My ego was no better than most boys that age. My parents encouraged me, supported me. But you know how it is to be a teen with hormones blazing and foolish notions. Eric was my best friend, but I hated being second best."

She recognized hurt behind the power of his words. "But Eric is a wiry, almost skinny sort of man and you're so powerful and muscular."

Dana swallowed the rest of her words, wondering if she should check herself into the loony bin tomorrow. When would she learn to keep her trap shut?

Again he stared at her until her skin tingled under the force of his attention. A gentle smile flickered over his lips. "You know as well as I that muscle isn't all. He had the coordination. He still has the ability."

Nodding her answer, she wished she could disappear into a void and come back to find this conversation never happened.

"And what did this have to do with broken romances?" She held one hand up. "Wait. You're going to tell me he stole your girlfriend, aren't you?"

He chuckled. "Yeah. How did you know?"

She shrugged. "It's classic. I think every man has had the experience at least once. Everyone woman, perhaps." She sighed, well aware that if she didn't watch it, he'd have her babbling about Frank. "I'm sorry. Go on."

Marshall stood and headed for the bar. Snatching some fruit, he popped one plump green grape into his mouth and returned to the fireplace. "When I was seventeen I had this crush on a girl. Eva Steele. She was the most gorgeous thing I'd ever seen up until then." Marshall's gaze traveled across Dana and she felt her skin heat. "And Eric stole her from me."

Dana's breath almost stopped in surprise. "Oh, my."

"Yeah." His lips twisted in a sardonic smile as he ate another grape. "She was a cheerleader, and you know the old thing about cheerleaders and football players."

She recalled all too well the scene from earlier in the day. When she did nothing more than nod, he continued.

"Eva and I had dated for a couple months, since the beginning of the school year. Little did I know that she had the hots for Eric. One night, after football practice, I caught Eva kissing him behind the bleachers."

"Oh, my God."

"That's the way I felt."

"Eric betrayed you?"

Marshall shrugged. "In a way, yes. The way he tells it, Eva planted a kiss on him first. His teenage boy hormones took over before he could think about me."

Fierce memories seemed to cross his face. Anger, passion, indisputable hurt. Even after years and years, he could feel those pains as if they'd happened a day ago, and she knew it. She felt it within her, as if she'd been the one deceived.

"What did you do then?"

He didn't smile when he said, "I put his lights out for him."

"Marshall!"

"I punched him, then ran away." He chewed the last grape. "We didn't talk for almost the rest of the year. He continued to go out with Eva. On graduation day we broke down and talked. I forgave him, realizing that if Eva wanted to lock lips with him, she didn't really want me. And why would I want to be with a girl that didn't want me?"

The fireplace didn't seem warm enough to erase the chill in her heart. Somehow she knew the story didn't end there. "Very mature thinking."

He wiped his hands down the thighs of his jeans. "He went off to college with Eva in tow. They married and had a life together."

"Tabitha is their child?" she asked, understanding for the first time why Marshall might have been drawn to the little girl in a special way.

Reflection on years gone by seemed to wear him down, and he no longer sat up straight. She wanted to caress those big shoulders, massage away the hurt and kiss away the past.

"Once Eric completed residency and moved back to Macon, I knew it would be difficult to stay friends."

She frowned. "You still held a grudge against him?"

"No, because on the first day they were back in town, ten years ago, Eva came to me and wanted me to make love to her."

Chapter 15

Surprise slammed Dana again as she wondered how deep this story went. She wished she could add Eva to the 'list of people in Macon that need strangling.' Then she realized Marshall had never answered her question about whether Tabitha was Eric and Eva's child.

A startling thought hit her. "Oh, Marshall. You don't mean…you don't mean that Tabitha is your child?"

His expression went hard, filled with a deep-seated sense of irony. "No." Looking into the flames, he outlined the next piece of the story. "She wanted me to commit adultery and I refused. And I didn't want her after all that time. I could never want a woman that lied and would betray my best friend."

Adultery.

Most all her life she hadn't understood people who went against their marriage vows by having affairs. She thought she'd never do anything like that. Until Frank had come along. If Marshall had slept with Eva, she wouldn't have rebuked him. She couldn't when she had almost broken the rules, too.

"What happened then?" she asked, almost afraid to hear the whole story.

He shrugged. "I guess she and Eric did well together, because about nine months later Tabitha was born."

Dana spoke like a robot all the thoughts she should have kept to herself. "What if…what if she isn't Eric's child? What if she went to another man in town?"

"What?" His sharp question, punctuated with a deep frown, made her backtrack.

"Maybe she found solace elsewhere that night. What if Tabitha is the union of Eva and another man? It sounds like she might be that type of person. Eva might have deceived Eric with another man when you wouldn't make love to her."

Marshall nodded, his eyes glassy with what looked like fatigue or the trauma of past events. "The thought occurred to me already. A long time ago."

She wanted to fidget to release tension as her shoulder muscles became tighter and tighter. Instead she stayed silent and still. An eternity seemed to pass before he looked at her. Firelight danced over his face, turning his skin to a golden glow.

She wanted to assure him that he shared no guilt for what had happened with Eva.

"You did the right thing, Marshall. In refusing her."

"I know." His gaze stayed steady on hers.

Clearing her throat, she said, "My aunt said that you were…um…married once." Dana clasped her father's ring, looking for strength to ask the next question. "What happened?"

A sarcastic grin curved his lips. "I made the second biggest mistake of my life. The second horrible romance, as you called it. I met Helen. Helen Beecher."

Warming to the subject, despite the uneasy jumble in her stomach, she pressed onward. "When did you meet her?"

"Ten years ago at a dog show. I'd gone with Eva and Eric. I didn't really want to be around Eva, but if I wanted Eric's company she sometimes came with the package."

His pause made her nod with understanding. "Of course. But it must have been awkward. Did Eva try to come onto you again?"

He pushed his hands through his hair as he straightened. "Thankfully, no." He sighed. "Helen was an acquaintance of Lucille's, though your aunt didn't know Helen very well."

Surprised rippled through her. "Aunt Lucille didn't say anything about her being a friend."

"Not a close friend. An acquaintance. Anyway, to make a very short story even shorter, we dated for months. Within the year we got hitched."

The thought of him married to anyone made Dana's muscles tighten with a strange dissatisfaction. Silence gathered around them, and although the fire blazed hot now, she knew she couldn't move or she'd somehow break his ability to continue the story.

"You loved her. I can't see you marrying a woman just because—"

"I thought I loved her. I say thought because if I'd looked deeper I would've realized I was marrying an Eva clone."

Dawning awareness made her break into his explanation. "Trying to get the love from Helen that you could never get from Eva."

He shifted until his legs went out and he crossed them at the ankles. He rested his back against the bricks behind him. From the pensive look on his face, she saw the struggle running through him to answer her sensitive statement. Would he? Could he admit he'd repeated a losing pattern?

Instead he said, "She found a million ways to remind me every day that she looked a lot like Eva. Talked like Eva. Lied like Eva."

When he stopped, Dana waited. She didn't dare stir, the air around her thick with anticipation. He seemed to realize that she had no intention of commenting and foraged onward. "Helen knew all my vulnerabilities. There are things that are ingrained deep in me, and that includes my sense of values. I won't apologize for them, and I won't change."

"I've seen that. Stubborn, I think, is the word."

He didn't smile. He crossed his arms, and his body conveyed the caged stiffness of a man closing down. "Helen thought it would be funny to taunt me by commenting on how handsome this guy was or that the man next door looked great in a muscle shirt. That sort of stuff."

Dana cringed inside. "She wanted to make you jealous? Why?"

"She told me once I was cold. That I didn't show her enough love. Enough passion."

Deep inside her stomach shivered, rippled with hot sensation. Shocked by her reaction, she let the sensation spill through her in crazy waves. Incredulous, she waited for the sparks of need to subside, but they continued like an ocean tide, battering at her defenses. In a million years she couldn't imagine this man as cold. Somehow she knew if he kissed her, made love to her, the passion would burn her alive.

"If she made you jealous she figured you'd have more passion for her?"

He gave an ironic, sarcastic grin. "Oh, yeah. And you know, it worked. I got jealous. Flaming jealous after trying to ignore it for months. After five years of marriage I told her to keep her hands off of other men."

"She touched other men?"

"Whenever and wherever she could. I was embarrassed more than once by the way she flaunted herself. By then I realized I didn't really love her."

"Do you believe it was all her fault?" The question catapulted from her, and by the grim expression lining his eyes and mouth, she wondered if he'd retaliate with livid words.

Instead he assessed her. She couldn't decide whether to enjoy the judgment of his eyes or cringe under the accusation she saw there. "I don't think I'd realized what real love is, not with Eva. Not with Helen. I married Helen under false pretenses believing I'd found someone I could love. When she proved false and shallow I pulled back what affection I'd given her. So, yeah. I made it worse by not confronting my feelings and not being honest with Helen, by not working on the problem up front. Even if I had been upfront, I don't think our marriage would have lasted with love."

Realizing that Marshall did believe in love sent a spiral of heat straight through her body. Pleasure expanded inside her. She didn't understand her reaction entirely, but let it blossom anyway.

"How long were you married?" she asked softly.

"Five years. We've been divorced three years. She left for Montana with her cowboy lover."

A sharp knife of pain wedged deep into her heart. "What?"

He straightened, his stance once more open. "The final Chapter's a pretty scary one. Sure you want to hear it?"

Dana stood and retreated to the bar. "I always did like a good rip snortin' ending. Reading or writing it."

One corner of his mouth managed a smile. "You going to write a book about my horrific love life?"

Dana shrugged as she reached under the counter to grab a small box of tea. She needed something to warm her chilled soul. "Tea?"

"Please."

As she boiled water in the microwave, his gaze followed her movements. He stood and came to the bar, leaning on it and staring at the grains in the wood.

The microwave pinged after two minutes and she retrieved the mugs. "That's not the end of the story, I take it."

"Not by a long shot. The final straw came when she started an affair with a rodeo circuit guy. He came through town a few times a year, and that explained her sudden interest in rodeo on TV or when a rodeo was held in town."

Dana allowed two bags of tea to steep in large mugs. As she dunked the bags up and down she asked, "She was watching for lover boy?"

"Yep."

"Shit."

"You can say that again. She took up with this guy, and before long, they were going at it on weekends. Sneaking around, looking for reasons to see each other. When I came home one day and she was deep in conversation with him, she didn't realize she had the speakerphone on in the living room. She hadn't heard me come home."

Wondering if her heart could feel any more offended for this man, Dana came around the side of the bar and handed him a mug. "You got an earful, I take it?"

"Yeah. I confronted her." Following Dana, he went back to the fireplace and settled down. "She denied it, but I'd heard and seen enough. I filed divorce papers the next day."

Dana wondered if he had really healed. She'd heard of many men and women that never found a true love. She'd often thought she fell into that category. Now, with this man, she felt the beginnings and stirrings of longing become deeper. It trapped her, filled her, and stretched her beliefs.

Awkwardness seemed to rule the moment as a hush closed over the room again.

Marshall took a deep breath and let it out. "Dana, I've...I've got some apologizing to do."

She saw a strange wariness in his eyes, as she might haul off and slug him for what he might say or what he would say. When he waited, caution written all over his face, she pressed onward. "About what?"

Clasping his hands between his knees and propping his elbows on his legs, he gave her what amounted to a nervous expression. "Thanks for your concern earlier today. When you...I saw tears in your eyes. Thanks for caring."

Her mouth opened but she couldn't think how to reply. He'd gone from grizzly bear to teddy bear. Trying to predict which one he'd become in any given moment could make a woman batty. Then, because she had lost her mind along the way, she reached up and touched the side of his face near the bandage. Her fingers met silky hair and warm skin. She snatched her hand back.

"Does it hurt much?" she asked, her voice sounding raspy.

A small grin met his mouth. "Nah. Barely even know it's there." His big shoulders made a shrug and a twist. "I'm going to ache tomorrow."

"The stakeout could have waited until you felt better."

His glance strayed to the area near the bed. "No, this couldn't wait. Saying I was sorry couldn't wait. Maybe catching the jerk that is doing this couldn't wait."

Marshall's confession, his softening, sent her insides into double turmoil.

Despite the heat from the fire, she shivered. "For a little while I forgot about that. I forgot to be nervous about who or what is out there."

A look of guilt flickered over his face. "There's more."

She smacked her forehead. "Marshall, if you don't stop hitting me with these lovely surprises—"

"This one's not so lovely, Dana."

Before Dana could ask what he meant, Marshall launched into an explanation.

"Skeeter's been taken off the watch. Sheriff Pizer says we can't afford to have Skeeter on permanent assignment to watch over you."

She frowned. "Oh." She shrugged. "There's still Logan."

Swallowing hard, he shifted his gaze from his hands back to her face. "Logan isn't enough. As it was, I hoped the three of us could cover all bases. Now we're down to two."

It took several seconds for her to make sense of his cryptic undertone. "You mean…wait, you mean you were assigned officially to watch over me?"

He shook his head. "Skeeter was the only official one. Logan did this because he was coming to Macon anyway and he's a good friend."

The answer dawned. "You watched over me because you wanted to, not because you were assigned."

"Exactly. Before you were run off the road I kept a surveillance going at the house."

She nodded, recalling when he'd turned up at the front door on the night she'd seen a prowler in the woods.

He continued. "When that bastard ran Bertha into a tree, I knew something worse than little malicious mischief was going on. When I couldn't be around I felt…I knew Logan and Skeeter were top notch at what they do. But that didn't satisfy me. Pizer called me into his office and told me we couldn't have Skeeter protecting you that many hours a day. So I told him my solution."

"Solution?"

"I told him I'd take vacation. I'll protect you on my own time. Twenty-four seven."

Again she became speechless, scared witless by what he'd said. What his attention might mean.

When he stood she felt bereft at the same time she experienced relief. He made them another cup of tea, and as the microwave hummed she took a good look at this man that had rocked her world. He was tough. Unyielding. Stubborn. Critical. Strong. Opinionated.

Heart-stopping, breath-stealing, amazing.

Tender, giving, and passionate.

She decided their conversation about Eva, Helen, and her own current problems had ended too quick and simple. There had to be more lying deep beneath the brooding, smoldering exterior of this big lug. More to understand about why he wanted to protect her. More to understand why she wasn't royally upset with the prospect of having this man near day and night.

She stood again, restless. "Why did you assign yourself to

me? You could have left Logan on the case and gone about your business."

Instead of bringing her the fresh mug of tea, he came around the bar, all the time pinning her with a penetrating stare. When he stood within less than a foot of her, his heat enveloped her like the fire from the hearth. It burned her in a way physical conflagration never could. She trembled under it, feared it, and wanted it.

"Because I don't want Logan this close to you." His liquid voice, filled with a velvet and silk combination, almost unraveled her control. "He's a good man and a great friend, but I don't want him distracted. And believe me, you're distracting."

She decided to be flattered by what he'd said instead of hacked off. "Why? You're not thinking I—" She stopped dead, then restarted as she realized what his statement might tell her. "You think he's interested in me romantically?"

He tilted his head the slightest bit. "Or maybe you're interested in him."

He sounded, dare she think it...jealous. *Nah. It simply couldn't be.*

"Rest assured, Marshall, I may think he's a great looking guy, but unlike Eva or Helen I don't chase men around like a bitch in heat."

Her blunt words didn't appear to make a dent in his armor. He didn't wince or flinch or show any outward sign of belief or skepticism. Instead he returned to the bar, dunking the bags of tea like she had not long ago.

Did he imagine she could be cut from the same hair shirt as Eva and Helen? She wanted to growl and howl at the injustice. Instead she delved deep into the well of the inane, knowing that she hadn't reached his complete trust. She sensed he wouldn't talk about his horror filled romances any more that evening. No coercion would do the trick.

She cringed at the thought of enticement. Images of nubile women with beautiful blond hair and stunning smiles made Dana want to run, run now before she found herself lacking. Became entangled once again in another dead end relationship like the one she'd had with Frank.

Gazing at the man who'd made her twenty types of mad in one day, she wondered how many women in Macon had looked on him and found their temperatures hitting triple digits? Had they wanted to feel his arms around them, his lips taking, giving, exploring?

He'll never be that way with me. He'll never need me that way. Damn Eva and Helen to purgatory for ruining this man for anyone else. And damn me for giving a rat's hind end.

Words shot off her tongue before she could think. "Why did you grow that beard and mustache?"

That's it, Dana. Find something mundane and harmless to talk about, but try not to make the question so stupid next time.

Marshall's eyes darkened like a late summer storm. His denim shirt was open a couple of buttons at the neck, the tail not tucked into the waistband of his jeans. She recalled the first day she'd met him and the time he'd pulled off his wet shirt. Then she'd seen the clear definition of hard pectorals covered with a sprinkle of dark hair. A swatch of hair covered his flat stomach. Her gaze had hitched on that hard, flat stomach that was muscled but not the six-pack she'd seen on many men who exercised at the gym.

Combined with a relaxed pose, he looked exposed down to the last nerve. He seethed with a mysterious, powerful secrecy that made her ache to understand him. Something deep and primitive ached inside her, and she knew this man was to blame.

No one man should be allowed to have that much testosterone.

When his stone cool expression changed to wicked, teeth-exposing grin, Dana's heart came to a complete stop. Marshall crossed his arms and the rolled up sleeves revealed sculpted forearms and a portion of hard biceps.

Finally he said, "Covers up my ugly puss."

Lord, I almost forgot the original question.

A predatory gleam entered his gaze as he reached for his mug and took a generous swallow.

A wash of emotion flooded her. Something totally knee-buckling had happened again. Had been occurring for days. Every time she thought she had a grip on his modes operandi, this man changed directions.

"You excel at this, don't you?" She couldn't resist asking. A force deep inside would not let go. "Keeping people close, then turning them away gives you a power trip. You want complete and total control of the situation."

Lines in his broad forehead creased a little more. Was that a smidgen of regret, a paltry bow to anxiety entering his expression?

"You really think I'm a big, dumb, hard ass, don't you?" he asked, the timbre in his voice lowering.

A sensation, almost a hot flash, coasted over her body and left a trail of fire in its wake. "Well, aren't you?"

His grin came back, and she wondered if he realized the chameleon effect kept her tottering on the edge of screaming surrender. Surrender, however, to what? She knew his potent force lay in wait, ready to take her on a journey she could never return from. Once within Brennan Marshall's sphere you were never the same.

He slowly marched toward her. Her heart jumped and startled flutters flipped in her stomach.

Apparently he planned to answer her, but he couldn't be planning— What on earth was he doing?

His feet tread silent, but she could see the rise and fall of that magnificent chest. Dana refused to look away, and when he came to a stop in front of her, one corner of his mouth turned up. "I'm sorry."

She blinked. "What?"

"You were right. I haven't been too hospitable since you came into town. And I wasn't friendly at the game today. Forgive me?"

Those last two words issued as a low rumble. Her body responded to his pure masculinity. Her common sense told her to resist his appeal. Marshall's gaze, an intense alertness overlaid by Southern Comfort, compounded his magnetism.

His attention made her so hot she could have melted like chocolate. For a startling second she imagined the taste of his lips, a combination of that sweet concoction and whiskey.

No!

"Well?" He lifted his right hand and gently pushed hair away from her forehead. Under the soft brush of his fingers along her cheek, Dana shivered with panicky delight. "I always tell the truth, Dana. Even when it hurts."

His fingers left her skin. She swallowed again, trying to form words and finding it difficult. "How convenient. How can I tell that you're not lying about that?"

"When did you think I lied to you?"

"All the time."

Astonishment, or something remarkably similar, widened his eyes. "Then you haven't learned much about me in the last hour."

Dana shook her head, and as he took a last step closer, she trembled. "No, I haven't. You've got the wall up high. There's no way to get in. You're as tough as…as…"

"Dried cow shit on a hot summer's day?"

Despite her anger, she almost laughed. A small smile slipped out. "Exactly."

This time his hands cupped her shoulders and the heavy heat ignited her. Right then and there, as his fingers caressed, she realized she'd never experienced a more unforgiving wave of desire in her life. Dana felt caught in a bizarre chemical that brought her to a boiling point.

Marshall's grin faded, replaced by a haunting tenderness she couldn't have imagined on his face seconds before.

"Do you really want to know me?" he asked softly.

While logic screamed in the negative, the rampaging need inside couldn't deny him. Before she could blink his lips hovered over hers. Before Dana could reply, his mouth descended.

Chapter 16

Dana's mind scrambled for clarity and found none. This infuriating, sexy man would kiss her any second.

A moan, husky and deep with passion filled the room. Dana knew it hadn't come from her, and it hadn't issued from Marshall either. He stepped back like electrical wires had prodded him in the backside.

He glanced around and cursed. "What the—"

The sound returned, whispery soft this time. Less masculine. It rose and fell like gentle wind. A woman in the throes of some bone-melting passion. Another groan entered Dana's ears, this one a counterpoint to the feathery utterance.

"Oh, my God." Dana looked at Marshall as if he'd sprouted seven arms and fourteen legs. "It's the bed!"

She rushed toward the area, but Marshall snared her with his left arm, drawing Dana back against his body. She sucked in a breath as his powerful arm held her tight against his warmth. Instinctively she gripped his forearm. Silky hair brushed her fingers, and muscles flexed under her touch. *God, the man is like concrete…his muscles are so solid…*

"Wait," he said softly.

Despite her resolve to remain unmoved by his touch, the strength of him holding her and the feel of his body made her shudder with untamed excitement. Heat flared low in her belly. She'd never leave this basement without his potent brand of sexuality burning her to a crisp.

"But I've got to turn on the tape recorder," she said, sounding breathless.

Maintain, Dana, or he's going to think you're losing oxygen over him and not the idea of getting the weird moans and groans on tape.

Marshall nestled his mouth close to her ear and she shivered as his breath caressed her sensitive skin. "Wait."

She couldn't have moved if an earthquake had rattled the room. Each fiber within her strummed to a sinuous beat as sounds filtered through in a continuous pattern, reaching from the far corner of the room. Nerve endings tingled. She felt heat rise in her skin as awareness of the man standing behind her blended with the wild noises near the bed.

She expected to feel angry that he held her back. Yet when his right hand clasped her upper arm, her body and mind betrayed her. His arm loosened a fraction, and her breath rushed out. But when his right hand landed on her right hip, she sucked air again. Didn't he know what his touch did to her? Or did he intend to tantalize her, mangle her self-control, and make her ache with deep longing? Heat swirled low in her stomach and she wanted to tilt her head back and feel the support of his shoulder. Her clasp on his forearm never faltered.

"Ohhhhh…" the high, frantic female sound came from the bed, and Dana's eyes widened.

"There's no one there," Dana whispered.

"Might be a recording." Again his hot breath tickled her neck and ear.

She shivered, unable to hold back the reaction. "Yeah, but we'll never find out unless we investigate." She tried for humor. "Sheriff's Officers do investigate, don't they?"

His fingers spread, cupping her hip even more. "Yeah."

She knew she couldn't take being this close to him much longer. She squirmed in his hold.

Big mistake.

Instead of loosening his tenacious clasp, he slid his right arm around her as well, bringing her flush against his rock hard chest, stomach and hips. Dana almost mewled in a combination of protest and sweet agony. Her breasts tingled, the nipples hardening. *Oh, God! He'll see through my shirt and know that he's turned me into a bowl of quivering gelatin!*

"Stop wiggling or you'll regret it," he whispered. "Quiet."

"But—"

"Put a sock in it."

Blood filled her face, but not from embarrassment. "What a rude, nasty—"

"I'm giving you one more chance to be quiet, Dana," he said into her ear.

Sure, she could stomp on his toes and maybe break his hold. Maybe. She couldn't remember the last time she'd been wrapped in such strength. Perhaps if the sensation of being cradled in his arms had repulsed her she'd have tried harder to free herself. Instead she relaxed a little and enjoyed the guilty pleasure of feeling protected and wanted.

The next thing she heard blew her mind. Mad squeaking. Bed springs protested as the ghost lovers accelerated the rate of passion. Dana blushed again like a schoolgirl at her first prom and subsided back against Marshall.

"Well, I'll be a son of a bitch," Marshall said.

"You won't get any argument from me there."

The gasping and moaning from the bed reached apocalyptic proportions.

As much as she loved his arms around her, she knew they'd discover nothing standing there like two dead weeds. "Marshall, I've got to turn on the recorder and we've got to investigate."

"Yeah," he said again, this time husky and low. To her surprise he released her.

She didn't know whether to be disappointed or relieved. He started toward the bed and she followed on his heels. Dana almost passed him in her frantic charge to the tape recorder. She grabbed the micro cassette device and flipped the record switch. Excellent. She'd capture at least the grand finale. From the non-stop rattling, the screech of protesting bedsprings and the ecstasy filled sounds coming from the ghost participants, the end had to be near.

She dared to speak. "It sounds like the ghosties are about to go thermonuclear."

Marshall stood by the bed, hands on hips and gaze trained on the bed. The bed sounded as if might collapse under the strain, but to Dana's surprise the heart-shaped monstrosity didn't make a twitch.

"This doesn't make any sense," she said, sideling up next to him. "Any live beings making that much racket would have caused the bed to practically walk by itself."

Instead of scowling and telling her to shut up, his eyes sparkled with amusement. A hearty chuckle issued from his chest.

He knelt down and looked under the bed. "No bogie man under there."

He touched the walls near the bed, then searched in various other places around the room while the happy ghosts humped as vigorously as ever.

"Now I know it's got to be a recording," He mumbled as he continued to scan the room for a device. "Help me look."

Complying, she went into the small bathroom that had served as shelter during the tornado. She fumbled in the cabinet underneath the sink but found nothing but cleaning products, bath soap, and toilet paper. Her eyes widened when the female voice coming from the bed whimpered in frustration or bone-rattling delight. Dana couldn't be certain.

Giving up her quest, she returned to the bed. Marshall touched the coverlet as he had before.

"Is it warm?" She asked.

He nodded. "See for yourself."

She touched the middle of the bed, her fingers almost brushing his. "It's hot. But there's no vibration."

She looked up and caught his frustration as it spilled across his features. He sighed and straightened. Seconds later a fluting, feminine screech filled the night, startling them both.

Maybe the pesky ghost had finally—

A guttural, agonized moan echoed into the room. Dana couldn't say if satisfaction or agony fueled the sound. "I can't freaking believe this." As the noises continued, Dana's mind reeled with amazement. "When is this going to end?"

"Gives new meaning to the saying, 'can't get no satisfaction.'"

She laughed. "Brennan Marshall, I can't believe you said that."

His gaze turned unforgiving, raking over her body in a predatory assessment. "You think I'm made of cold steel, don't you? You think I can resist anything you say or do? You think I'll never reach a breaking point?"

"Yes." She fumbled for the right words. "No."

His mouth curved a fraction, as if he couldn't decide whether to be pleased or pissed. "Make up your mind."

Exasperation got the better of her. "Well, you don't seem to believe the obvious."

"Which is?"

"This is what we were talking about at your office the first day we met. My aunt has heard these ghosts on numerous occasions. She said it sounded like they couldn't…um—as you said—complete the act. They are perpetually stuck." Dana went on to tell him about the two lovers who had been killed by the girl's father. "Maybe the couple didn't get to finish making love before her father came in and shot them."

His mild grin changed from amused to amazed. Turning away from the bed, he pined her with pure disbelief. "You really think this porno movie soundtrack is honestly a couple of horny ghosts?"

"What else could it be? We haven't found any tape players or other devices that would prove deception."

Marshall shook his head and cocked his head like a confused animal. "You're incredible, you know that?"

Dana might have brushed off his comment if his voice hadn't sounded silky soft and sinful. "You're pretty extraordinary yourself, Marshall."

She couldn't tear her gaze away, and once more he approached. "I think you meant that as an insult."

In self-defense she shrugged with nonchalance. It wouldn't do to show him how his presence effected her. Despite her casual air, his relentless stalking didn't slow down. She backed up a couple of steps and bumped into the bar.

Before Dana could utter a protest or move out of his way, Marshall's hands came down on either side of her on the bar, his arms a cage. "I think this is about where I left off in my office that day. And I'm tired of waiting."

"Waiting for what?" She gulped.

"I said if you didn't stay quiet there would be hell to pay."

She couldn't resist it. The big, tough man in front of her thought he had her cowed. He thought she'd buckle under his knee-weakening gaze and intimidation. With a gentle poke she tapped her finger on his chest.

"Back off Marshall. I'm not some young sweet thing that thinks your long hair and sexy…I mean, dark eyes are sexy beyond belief. I don't know how many women this has worked on-"

"I've never done this before."

"Trapped a woman between your arms?"

"Before you. Before you came to this town, life was pretty content and maybe even a little dull. You had to arrive and shake up the whole place."

She made a face. "I hardly think my presence is enough to shake up an entire town."

He was so close less than two inches separated them. He leaned forward even more, and she could avoid his tantalizing scent or the sheer power of his presence. Dana shivered in reaction as his warm breath touched her face. "I've never felt this way before. I've never listened to ghosts having sex and finding myself so insane from the heat I can't keep my hands off you. I can't take it anymore, Dana."

It took more seconds than she liked for comprehension to dawn. Had he said the ghostly humping was turning him on? Did that explain why she felt boiling, restless, excited and about ready to scream? Or was she just annoyed into the next century?

Her mouth felt dry and she licked her lips. Every muscle tightened in her body, filled with longing. A need to be touched. Caressed. Taken in the most elemental way a man could take a woman.

Marshall's incredible mouth hovered near hers again. "I don't have fifty dollars tonight. Will you take a rain check?"

Overwhelmed by the industrial electricity jumping between them, she couldn't speak.

As it turned out, she didn't have to.

His mouth covered hers. Insistent. Startling. Astonishing.

Before she could respond, his lips parted hers and explored. Moved back. Tasted. Retreated. Marshall gave her about ten seconds, as he gazed into her eyes, to do something besides feel her insides tremble and her senses go ballistic. When she didn't stomp his foot, elbow him, or knee him in the family jewels, he moved in with the heavy artillery.

He kissed her again and again. Short tastes that touched her lower lip, then her upper lip, capturing her with sweetness. Heat rose within Dana as he sampled her, never quite plunging all the way, making each kiss long enough to torture but not striking the match. Marshall's unmistakable ardor made her move in his arms, made her utter a soft moan.

Her mind echoed what her lips wouldn't say. *Don't stop. Don't ever stop.*

His next kiss didn't ask, it made a statement. His tongue coaxed and caressed before plunging inside. A tiny noise of surprise emanated from her throat. Stunned, she absorbed the heady pleasure. Every molecule in her body seemed to rush together; her stomach tingled deep, and her breathing accelerated. The continual stroke of his tongue against hers made her senses swim and her head feel lighter than air.

She'd spent far too many hours wondering what this man's lips would feel like. That itty-bitty kiss he'd given her the other night hadn't prepared her. Now that she knew her mind turned to porridge and her limbs to noodles. Before her knees could collapse his arms slid around her and tucked her against his hot, solid body. His hand speared into her hair, cupping the back of her head as his kiss went super nova.

He didn't gentle her into the passion, he propelled her with a kiss that caressed, controlled and demanded. Yet even his command sought her favor and capitulation. Dana's senses reeled as his mouth possessed with gentle sweeps, then probing insistence. The kiss went on and on, the moaning and gasping and sighs coming from the bed a strange ballet dance to accompany their real passion.

Her arms went from being trapped against his chest to being wound around his neck. His hands caressed her back with greedy exploration, as if he wanted her so much he couldn't decide where to start first. Part of her screamed with alarm that she'd surrendered and shouldn't have. The other part didn't care. She couldn't deny that he wanted her. Hard and unmistakable, the evidence of his desire pressed against her, reminding Dana he was flesh and blood man, and of her own need steaming to the surface.

Sweet languor echoed inside her as the warm, sweet taste of his mouth lulled her into a haze of desire. Dana's fingers tested the length of his thick hair. He sampled her, small kisses that she answered. One. Two. Three. Four. He drew back, his soul deep gaze heating her with desire.

She knew nothing…and everything. With a bone-melting, staggering kiss, he'd upset everything she'd believed about her ability to resist her feelings for him.

"Marshall," she whispered as his mouth hovered over hers again.

"Yes?"

"What are we doing?"

One corner of his mouth turned up, his breath coming in deep exhalations. "Losing our ever loving minds." Rough with need, his voice showed how much their embrace affected him. "You are driving me insane."

Another crazy moan erupted from the bed near them. Again, before she could unscramble her thoughts, Marshall kissed her, his arms tightening.

Excitement strummed through Marshall's body. Every brush of her lips, caress of her tongue, sweep of her hand blew him apart. Thoughts, other than how much he wanted her, left his system. His lips found a spot near her collarbone that made her gasp. She writhed as he concentrated on that spot for maddening seconds before he moved to sensitive territory under her ear. Shameless, mindless with building need, he shivered when she explored his biceps and shoulders. His hands cupped her rib cage, exploring the delicate structure, reverent with the knowledge that underneath her shirt lay soft skin.

As Marshall feasted on her neck, he cupped her right breast in a tender hold. Dana gasped. Seconds blended into minutes where his mind took flight into dreams. Where was he taking her? How far was he taking her? He half expected her to object to the intimate touch.

Take me. He wanted to hear her say it. Shriek it while he slipped deep inside her.

He primed her with sweeps of his fingers along the underside of her breasts, never touching the nipples. He reached under her shirt and when she didn't protest he searched for the clasp of her bra. When he found it he undid it with one movement.

Oh. Oh, yeah.

Her skin, softer than anything in his imagination, lit a new fire within him. He repeated his caresses, this time circling her nipples with his fingers until a tiny gasp wrenched from her. When his thumbs passed over the tight nubs, he drew back to look at her. Eyes closed, head tilted back, her kiss-swollen lips parted on another inhalation. A sound that told him she liked what he did and wanted more.

"Dana," he whispered, lowering his mouth for another kiss.

He removed her shirt, then her bra. He palmed her shoulders and arms and back with continuous strokes, reaching down to cup her buttocks in both palms, drawing her tight against his arousal.

His tender touches removed all her inhibitions. Nothing would stop her from having this man right here, right now. Dana ached low in her belly. Beyond retreat, she yanked at his shirt until her hands touched skin over solid muscles. When he let out a low sound that almost matched a groan, she slid her hands through the hair on his taut stomach, then up to his pectorals. Sweet heaven. Rough hair under her fingertips sent a sigh of satisfaction through her lips. The texture. The springy curls. Iron hard muscle.

This is right.

When he took her mouth in another soul searing kiss, she began to slip his shirt off his shoulders.

A loud bang from upstairs vaulted them out of the kiss. The noises from the bed stopped.

Marshall's eyes went from dazed with passion to full alert. "What the—?"

"It's probably my aunt," she whispered. She wanted to kiss him again and who cared about the torpedoes.

She kept her grip around his neck, unwilling to move from the haven she'd found. Another loud clang, crash and bang sent them out of each other's arms. Reality came rolling in and Dana realized that no matter who it was, she was half dressed and so was he.

"Oh, my God," she said, releasing him and whipping into action. She grabbed her bra and shirt from the floor and dressed.

Marshall cursed and buttoned his shirt as he headed toward the door. Another thump came from above.

"That doesn't sound good," Marshall said.

"Maybe she's had an accident."

Marshall grabbed her arm again. "Stay here."

"But—"

He drew her against his side and stared down into her eyes with a fierce expression that made him warrior and lover all in one. "I want you safe, damn it. Now stay here while I check things out."

When someone had run her off the road she'd felt bone-deep terror. Now she wanted to fight alongside him if an intruder had invaded upstairs.

"I'll feel safer if I'm with you," she said. "Besides, you might need my help."

Two emotions warred in his eyes. Concern and admiration. Respect flickered into heat as he lowered his head and gave her a quick, hard kiss. "We'll finish this later. Stay behind me and if anything happens to me you get out of the house, you hear?"

She nodded. "Got it."

* * *

Marshall's heart hammered as they ascended the stairs.

He pushed away thoughts of passion slamming through his blood, knowing he'd protect Dana with his life if it came down to it. He heard grumbling and mumbling before he saw the shape at the top of the stairs. He held his weapon at the ready, leveling it on the dark form.

Though his throat felt tight, he ground out authoritative words. "Halt. Sheriff's department."

Before he could tell Dana to flip on the light switch and illuminate the intruder, the figure swayed and fell straight toward them.

Marshall uttered a curse and Dana echoed as the body took a header. Marshall didn't have time to evade airborne arms and legs as the guy tumbled straight into him. The weapon in Marshall's hand went flying.

Dana grunted as he cannoned into her, unable to stop his momentum. Grunts, cries of pain and mingled expletives ushered from them as the body that had caused the fall rolled with them down the stairs. Marshall felt an elbow in his side, then something hard kneed him in the gut. Air rushed from him in a gasp, but when they hit bottom he sprang upward, worried about Dana. Before he could ask if she'd been hurt, she scrambled to her feet.

Dana looked down at the same time Marshall did, and he saw the blood on her shirtfront and on his pants. Dana gasped as they looked at the remaining body on the floor. Gregory lay in a heap, his shirt covered in blood.

Chapter 17

Marshall and Dana dropped to their knees next to Gregory's sprawled figure.

"Oh, no," Dana whispered as Marshall checked Gregory's condition. Dana vaulted back to her feet. "I'll call 911."

While Dana scrambled to get help, Marshall discovered to his relief that Gregory didn't appear to have any broken bones. His satisfaction disappeared when he discovered the stab wound in the man's left side and a deep gash on the back of his head. After calling for help, Dana retrieved the first aid kit in the small bathroom and they set to work trying to reduce the bleeding.

"The stab wound doesn't look too deep," Marshall said, instructing Dana to apply pressure to the wound. He glanced at her, hoping she could take the sight of all that blood. His brow furrowed in concern when he realized how pale she looked. "Are you all right? You're not hurt?"

"No. You?"

"Other than being covered in his blood, I'm good."

"What happened?"

"Obviously he's been attacked."

Her frown increased. "Where is Logan? Do you think he's been assaulted, too?"

"I doubt it. No one's ever been able to get the drop on him."

Before Marshall could call the sheriff's department for backup, his cell phone rang. When he answered he discovered it was Logan. "Where are you?"

"Just coming in the back door now. Looks like Gregory left it unlocked. I saw him drive up and then stagger out of the car. I thought he was drunk."

Marshall explained that Gregory had been wounded.

Logan cursed. "I'll make a check on the house, then go out for recon."

"You didn't see anyone earlier?"

"No one."

After he finished talking to Logan, Dana said, "Gregory had to have been attacked somewhere else."

Although he no longer believed she had anything to do with the weird occurrences at the house, Marshall asked, "How do you know?"

She shook her head. "We haven't heard anyone else moving around and no one has attacked us. Someone must have stabbed him somewhere else and he drove here. But why would he come here? Why wouldn't he go to the hospital?"

A soft whistle came from the top of the stairs and Marshall knew Logan had arrived.

"No one in the house. Nothing outside," Logan said as he came down the stairs.

Marshall looked up from the injured man next to him. "Any clues in the car?"

"Nothing I could tell without opening the car door, and you know what the cops would think of that," Logan said as he dropped to one knee next to Metcalf. "How's he doing?"

"Not good." Dana's soft voice made Marshall's insides feel like jelly. He couldn't believe how close he'd come to making love with her. The thought made him ache with need and at the same time angry at his own folly.

Before he could berate himself any more, the ambulance with paramedics appeared as well as two deputies. As the emergency team worked on Metcalf, Deputies Johnson and Castone took statements. Neither of them looked eager to question the under sheriff, but Marshall wanted it all by the book. He'd have plenty of explaining to do to Pizer anyway. Soon the emergency crew loaded Gregory into the ambulance. After the deputies finished obtaining statements, Logan and Marshall huddled on what approach to take next.

Dana sat on the sectional couch looking stunned. Blood stained her shirt and Marshall felt his insides shudder with the thought she might have sustained injury because of his stupidity...because he wanted her so much he couldn't see anything beyond making love.

Dana looked up at him. "We've got to notify Neal and Aunt Lucille about Gregory."

Logan headed for the phone behind the bar. "I'm on it."

Dana's frown sent creases across her forehead. "How does he know where they are?"

Marshall sat down next to her, resisting the urge to put his arm around her. "He's kept tabs on everyone. Logan knows his work."

A faint smile came to her lips. "What is he, a secret agent man?"

Glad to see her sense of humor intact, he dared to smile back. "Something like that."

"You could tell me but then you'd have to kill me?"

"Logan would kill me."

She slumped back against the couch, looking uncomfortable in mind and body. "Now that would be a sight to see. What do we do now?"

"If you want to see Metcalf at the hospital, let's make it later when I can go with you. In the meantime, we're going to my office. Logan will see if he can get any information out of Gregory when he wakes up."

She looked amazed and pleased. "I can't believe you let up and said I could visit him. You're usually ranting and raving—"

"Yeah, yeah." He shoved his right hand through his hair, then remembered he hadn't been able to get all the blood off his hands. "Don't push it. Come on, we need to get into some new clothes and get out of here."

As he headed for the stairs Dana followed and her footsteps made muffled thumps on the carpeted stairs. "Why am I going with you?"

He sighed when he reached the top of the stairs. "I know you're an intelligent woman, Dana." He turned toward her and stopped as they entered the living room. "Which is why I'm not going to ask why you don't know."

She stopped, her hands propped on her hips. He remembered how those curved hips had shaped under his fingers, and a dart of arousal pierced his belly. Marshall noted that her hair had become mussed from the fall and maybe the way he'd pushed his fingers through it. She looked wild and ready for anything.

"I'm not helpless, Marshall."

Fire returned to his blood, the kind that always surged when she tried being contrary. Refusing to argue with her might work. When he cupped her slim shoulders, she stiffened under his touch. He almost let her go, remembering how yielding and warm she'd been earlier.

"I know that." He kept his tone low, hoping she'd lose that sandpaper look. "I'd like you to come with me because it's not safe here. And even if Logan stayed with you…" Swallowing hard, he let a corner of his feelings show. "…even if he was here, I want to keep you safe. From now on, until we figure out what the hell is going on, I'm not letting you out of my sight."

* * *

I'm not letting you out of my sight until we figure out what the hell is going on.

Dana heard the words over and over again in her head as she slumped in the chair in Marshall's office. She drifted in and out of sleep, realizing as the sun peaked through the vertical blinds in Marshall's office that morning had arrived. She wished for a warm bed and maybe a cozy book to read. *No. A warm bed and Marshall. Yeah, no use pretending I don't want him. I wanted him last night, and I want him now.* Instead the hard chair under her head and butt was all she had to keep her company.

Aunt Lucille called about an hour ago to report that Gregory hadn't wakened. The doctors said he sustained a concussion around the same time someone knifed him.

She sat up and groaned. A kink had formed deep in her back and neck and she stifled a curse. She'd had enough scares in her short time here to conjure nightmares for the next ten horror novels.

"Dana?"

She started. "Damn."

Marshall had opened the door without her hearing him. He closed the door and crouched down next to her chair. "Hey, why don't you lie down on the couch outside?"

Feeling cranky and stiff, she slumped again. "Sleeping in all that noise? I don't think so."

"All that noise? I wouldn't call this place hoppin'."

"No, but a hard plastic couch isn't my idea of comfort."

He touched her hand as she clutched the armrest, and her skin tingled as his big hand covered hers. Before she could say a word, he reached up with his other hand and brushed his fingers over her cheek. "You're exhausted. I'm sorry we're still here. It won't be much longer, I hope."

She stared at him, aware of the dawning glow in her stomach region that signaled desire.

In the silence, she gathered the heat of his stare into her where it warmed the last cold spot in her soul. She knew this man had stolen a piece of her heart and carted it off…she'd never get it back, no matter how many years passed or how far she traveled.

Oh-oh. You've got it bad, Dana. Really bad.

Could she run far enough and fast enough to escape the feelings barreling through her like a stampede? Probably not. Better to ride it out until this whole mess disappeared and she could leave Macon again.

"Anything new?" she asked. "What about Neal?"

He shook his head. "Logan is checking the hotels. He wasn't at his usual hang out."

As much anxiety as she'd had for Gregory being attacked, her worry over something dreadful befalling Neal outweighed it. "What if something's happened to him, too?"

Concern touched his eyes. "I don't give a damn about him."

A smidgen of anger tickled her. "A great attitude for a law man."

"My top priority is you. Yeah, I want to uphold the law and make sure other citizens are safe, but your well being is my biggest concern."

By the fierce expression in his eyes she realized his conviction ran deep in his bones. He'd keep her protected no matter how high the water rose. "You'd better watch out, Marshall. A woman could get real used to this kind of treatment."

Dana saw two emotions pass through his gaze…alarm and satisfaction. When he didn't speak, she took the plunge and decided to speak. "Does that expression mean that I've just scared the crap out of you?"

"Pretty much." He allowed a grin to spread over his lips. "I'm not used to you approving of my actions."

She smiled. "Don't get too used to it. When can we get out of here? I think my ass is starting to adhere to this chair."

His gaze glided over her, hot and full of unspoken, erotic messages. "Please don't start talking about your pretty butt. I don't think my heart can stand the strain."

She let out a short laugh. "God, Marshall. I never knew under all that...that..." She made a helpless motion with one hand. "Stoicism lay such a...a..."

He leaned closer, his voice dropping into a husky pitch. "Spit it out, sweetheart."

Sweetheart. The word said so many things coming from him. Teasing. Flirting. Tender. She shuddered deep inside, excitement flickering up like the beginnings of a bondfire. She licked her lips and his gaze settled on her mouth.

She could barely get the words out, her heart pounded so much. "A wild man."

His slow, gentle grin tormented her, and she wanted to crawl into his lap and show him how crazy she could be. "We'll be out of here soon. We're going to my place."

"Your place?" Dana didn't know if she liked the sound of that. It meant she'd be alone with him again. Alone and tempted.

"Just outside town. I built it about a year ago."

Her eyebrows shot up. "I didn't know you had such talents."

He grinned. "There are lots of things you don't know about me."

"There are lots of things I want to know," she said before she thought about the implications.

Again he gave her a long, hot stare that ate into her defenses and melted them down to the core. Maybe the ache of hunger in her stomach, both for food and his love making, had rattled her brains and made her vulnerable.

"I didn't really build the house myself. My father's an architect. I gave him ideas on what I wanted and he built the plans from the ground up," he said.

"I can't wait to see it."

Before she knew it she'd cupped her hand against his bearded face and caressed him. He felt so good against her she wanted to give him a big hug.

The devouring look in his eyes reduced her to quivering deep inside. "I've got a big tub you can soak in to take away the aches. Or a shower."

The rasp in his voice gave the desire in his gaze an edge. She slipped her hand free of his face. "A shower big enough for two?"

"Big enough for two. The tub is huge. You can practically do laps in it."

Erotic possibilities danced in her head. The message came clear. Once they made it to his house…well…all restraints would dissolve. The idea of pushing aside inhibitions and finishing what they'd started at Aunt Lucille's house had infinite appeal.

A knock on the door interrupted them. Skeeter walked in as Marshall shot to his feet and turned toward the door.

Marshall's frown could have melted steel, and the young deputy took a step back. His expression held regret for barging in. "Sir, it's Lucille Metcalf. She's calling for Dana."

"We'll take it in here," Marshall said.

Dana picked up the phone, her stomach doing back flips. "Aunt Lucille?"

"Hello, darling. Are you all right?"

"I'm fine." Dana sank into the chair, too tired to endure much more. "How is Gregory?"

"His vital signs are improving. But he still hasn't regained consciousness. A deputy is here to get his statement when he…if he wakes up. Logan is still here."

Dana twisted a strand of her hair around her finger. Her throat felt tight. She realized that Marshall had slipped out of the office. "Not if Gregory wakes up. When."

Aunt Lucille's sigh echoed over the phone. "My dear, I realize he hasn't treated you well. He's been boorish and insensitive, and down right ugly in his dealings with people. But you understand why I have to be with him? He has no one else, and I think Brent would like it if I looked after him."

When she explained to her aunt about the ghosts doing the nasty once again, Aunt Lucille managed a small laugh. "It doesn't surprise me, dear. It does make me wonder what is going to make the bed stop. An old woman's heart can only take so much."

Dana laughed. "An old woman's? What about mine?"

They chuckled together and Dana enjoyed the momentary respite from anxiety and fear. "I'll be at Marshall's later if you need me."

"Good. That's what I hoped to hear. Now what about Neal? Any sign of him?"

"Marshall said they haven't found him." A long silence commenced and Dana knew her aunt had to be thinking the same as she. "He'll be all right."

"You can't know that." Aunt Lucille sounded resigned. "It would break my heart if either one of these boys…"

"Don't think it. Just concentrate on staying safe. Logan will watch out for you."

"He's a sweet boy. Has a fierce look sometimes, but he's really very nice." Aunt Lucille's relief at changing the subject came through. "Now if you weren't already in love with Marshall I'd say Logan would be a nice man for you."

Dana gasped in surprise. "Aunt Lucille, you are a very naughty girl."

"Now don't try and deny it. The truth has to come out eventually. You are in love with Brennan Marshall. That's the only bright spot in the mess, I think."

How could she tell her aunt that she didn't love Marshall when the idea made the old woman so happy?

Marshall returned to the doorway, and his scrutiny made Dana watch her next words. "I'll call when I get to Marshall's house."

When she hung up he stepped into the room. His mouth held an angle she'd seen before when he wanted to strangle someone. She frowned as she wondered what she'd done now. "Okay, out with it. You look like you've eaten a lemon."

He sat on the edge of his desk and fisted his hands. Now she could see that she'd mistaken annoyance in his eyes for something far worse. "They just found Neal in the woods near his hotel. He's been shot."

Chapter 18

Dana walked through the hospital lobby toward her aunt, her steps making an urgent click on the cloud gray linoleum. Marshall stayed close behind. As Dana approached Aunt Lucille through the glare of florescent lighting, she wondered if fate had handed them both a big raspberry.

Correction. Dozens of raspberries. Overripe, no less. Life can't get any more exciting than this.

Then she saw Kerrie, Eric, and Logan in the waiting room area and felt a little better. They stayed seated while Aunt Lucille rushed forward and embraced Dana. Dana felt a shudder ripple through her aunt, then a soft sob issued from the older woman's slim body.

"Oh, Dana," Aunt Lucille whispered. She pulled back from her niece; her eyes brimmed with unshed tears. "I can't believe this is happening. What is the world coming to?"

Dana didn't have the heart to tell her the world had always been this way. "It will be all right."

Aunt Lucille sniffed and turned to Marshall. He pulled her into his arms and closed his eyes as he gave her a bear hug. Lucille looked swallowed up in his arms. "We'll catch whoever did this. Prints were taken out of Gregory and Neal's hotel rooms, though most of them are probably from the hundreds of people who've stayed there."

"Hundreds?" Kerrie asked.

Marshall nodded. "Apparently neither of the owners are exactly the cleanest people there. When they dust the rooms they do it lightly. No rubbing oil into the wood and eliminating prints. Good thing for us." After a sizable sigh, he brushed a hand through his hair. "Lucille, the nurses told us that Gregory and Neal aren't allowed any visitors for the rest of the day."

Lucille nodded. "That's right. Just me. They're letting me stay here in case one of them wakes up. And of course Logan and Skeeter will be there as long as I am."

"I'm not going to Jamaica with all this happening," Kerrie said.

Dana put up one hand. "Now wait a minute. You've got reservations and it'll cost you money if you back out now."

"But—"

"No buts. Go and enjoy yourself."

With a self-depreciating grin Kerrie slipped an arm around her stubborn friend. "I can't go without knowing you're safe and I'll worry the whole time I'm there. What kind of vacation is that?"

"A safe vacation. Away from here." Dana hadn't wanted to say it, but she did. "Macon is not a good place to be right now if you're close to me."

Marshall made a noise that sounded somewhere between disbelief and annoyance. "Wait a minute. We don't know this has anything to do with you."

Giving him a calm, steady look, she proceeded to correct him. "I think it does. Sure, the bed in Aunt Lucille's house was doing the two-step before I got here. And other weird things were happening, too. But nothing violent occurred until I got here."

No one spoke. The whisper of automatic doors opening and

closing at the entrance, the soft swish of people bustling by, and the lingering odor of pine antiseptic all made their impression on Dana's senses. She held on to that peace, unsure how long the rest of her world would remain stable.

Eric put his hand on Kerrie's shoulder and she looked at him. "Maybe Dana is right. Better to be safe."

Kerrie's lips firmed. "Friends don't leave friends alone in times of trouble."

Dana reached for her friend's arm. "Excuse us a moment everybody. Can I speak with you in private, Kerrie?"

Without waiting for an answer, Dana tugged her friend toward a refreshment alcove where a humming soda machine stood.

"Dana, what is it?"

"Do this for me, will you? Go to Jamaica and enjoy yourself as best you can. You say you won't like it there if you're worrying about me. Well it's the same here. I can't get to the bottom this if I'm concerned about you. If you're near me, bad things could happen. That seems to be a major feature of my life."

Kerrie's gentle eyes turned pensive. "How? You're not thinking what I think you're thinking?"

"Yes. That's right. Problems have always followed me wherever I go. Since my father died, as a matter of fact."

"Are you trying to say that you've got some hocus pocus curse on you or something?"

Dana snickered. "No, but it certainly feels like that sometimes."

Tilting her head slightly to the side, Kerrie assessed Dana. "Then spit it out. What are you talking about?"

"What I'm saying is that I have to go with my gut in this situation. A lot of my life I've spent going by logic rather than instincts." She gave a sarcastic laugh. "I think that's what created my writer's block. Too much logic, too much trying to go by what is reasonable and has always worked before. You remember when

I said I wanted to add romance to my horror novels, something that isn't done often?"

"Yes."

Dana rubbed her cold hands together. "I've spent a good portion of my life hiding from adventures. Hiding from things that are different, from ideas that would change my life in ways I've never dreamed. It's like this whole trip is designed to show me the error of my ways. As if someone is trying to tell me to bust lose and explore. At the same time there's danger involved."

Kerrie's eyes widened in comprehension and maybe discomfort. "Some sort of weird synchronicity?"

"I can't prove it. Logic can't answer it. But I can feel it. There are a few lessons to learn, and I'm tired of fighting against the grain of what I'm supposed to do with my life."

"What are you going to do?"

"Open myself to every possibility from now on…if my instincts tell me it's the right thing to do. I can balance the logic with the intuition and stay in the middle. I can go whatever way I'm supposed to go."

Kerrie nodded. "Get out of your own way."

"Exactly."

"But it isn't logical to apply the same thing to your life being in danger, Dana." Kerrie's eyes filled with tears, and Dana almost hugged her right then. "Your creativity, yes. But not your life."

Frustration made Dana's voice sharpen. "What would you have me do? Run to Jamaica with you? I'm through with hiding. Whoever these bastards are that want to ruin lives…well I'm going to confront them now before anyone else gets hurt."

"Dana," Kerrie rasped. "This is insane. You've got Marshall and Logan to protect you. Don't go off and do something rash. It'll get you killed."

Dana could see her friend didn't quite get it all; this surprised Dana a tad. Kerrie had always caught on to her more esoteric ramblings. Maybe stress had made Kerrie's mind feel like Dana's. Mush city. "All these adventures have been unfortunate, but they've opened my creative mind to new possibilities. I just realized that even with all the crap hitting the fan the last few days, I've started thinking up all sorts of new scenarios for my next book."

Kerrie's sincere expression of disbelief changed into anger when she said, "That's a pretty stupid way to get rid of writer's block, and as far as I'm concerned, it's a crock. This isn't some arcane billboard sign in the sky telling you to let your creative juices rip. A creep is running around out there apparently trying to destroy your family." Kerrie's pale skin turned pink with indignation. "And I think it's pretty nasty of you to think of this as opportunity to write a book." Holding her hands up as Dana started to interrupt, Kerrie continued. "If that's the way you want it…if you want to take advantage of all the pain going on here, so be it. I'll take that plane to Jamaica tomorrow and I won't look back."

Stunned, Dana watched as her best friend stomped back to Eric and whispered something in his ear. Eric's concerned frown turned deeper as he looked at Marshall and shrugged. He said something Dana couldn't hear, then looping his arm around Kerrie's waist, they came back in her direction. Maybe if she explained more, Kerrie would get the drift. Kerrie sent her a quelling glare as they went by her. Eric shrugged and gave Dana a bewildered look as he passed. Within seconds they'd left with the swish of the automatic doors closing behind them.

Nothing could have prepared Dana for the stark, unrelenting sadness slamming through her body. Did she even understand what she'd tried to say? *Maybe I do know what I mean and maybe Kerrie plain doesn't like what I have to say.*

Marshall and Aunt Lucille came her way while Logan headed toward parts unknown.

"What was that all about?" Marshall asked.

Dana sighed, feeling deep dejection. "I think she's thoroughly incensed. I want her to go to Jamaica. I guess what I said did the trick."

Looking heavenward as if for guidance, Marshall groaned. "Great. Just great."

Aunt Lucille gave him a quashing glance. He immediately looked contrite. Marveling at how her aunt could make this big guy melt like sour cream and butter on a baked potato, Dana vowed to ask her later how she did it.

"Tension is high right now." She patted Dana's shoulder. "Kerrie will be out of danger if she has nothing to do with me or Dana."

"Divide and conquer. As long as we scatter, maybe whoever is messing with us will make a mistake. Then we can kick their butts," Dana said.

Marshall folded his arms. "I hate to say it, but your plan almost makes sense."

"Almost?" Dana lifted a doubting eyebrow.

"There's a flaw. We still don't know the motivations of the culprit and we don't know how many people are involved. That leaves us pretty vulnerable. We appear to be at the mercy of some pretty sick puppies."

She agreed with silence for about a half minute. "We're not at anyone's mercy. I'm surprised you think that."

He shook his head, another disconcerted expression crossing his face. "You know what I mean."

"You should go now, my dear," Aunt Lucille said, warming her with another hug. "Go with Marshall and be safe."

Worry nudged Dana like an annoying elbow. "What about you?"

"I'll be fine here."

Soon Dana and Marshall piled into his car and headed on their way. They climbed into the mountains, going back the way she'd come that first day when a tornado had pitched her into Marshall's arms and his life. Daylight streamed through the tall trees, sparkling on the car hood. Grateful for her sunglasses, she plopped them on her nose and tried to relax. She hoped the ride would soon be over. She wanted to try out that tub, with or without Marshall.

Quiet continued to surround them as dim light played against her face through the side window. As the car ate up miles, she decided she had to speak first. Her mouth started to open.

"Tell me what you said to Kerrie to hack her off," Marshall said.

She shrugged and explained what she could. When he kept the pooh face she asked, "Have I made you mad too, or do you understand what I'm saying?"

He slid his hands over the wheel from ten o'clock and two o'clock to the nine and three position. Then his hands moved back to ten and two. She recalled the feeling of those hands on her body. On her naked breast. She wanted more. So much more.

She swallowed hard. "Marshall?"

At his spearing glance she caught her breath. Marshall's brand of intensity gave no mercy. She wondered if she'd managed to piss off the entire world.

"I understand what you're saying, Dana," he said with a rough edge to his voice.

The tense line of his mouth gave away the facts. "You're a poor liar, Brennan Marshall."

His head snapped around and he glared. Then he pinned his gaze back on road as he made a left turn that sent her swaying against the door.

He cursed—one word strong enough to convey his feelings. "So are you. You try so damned hard not to show what you feel. But it won't work. I know you well enough. You forget that I'm a cop and my instincts into human behavior aren't exactly shabby."

She made a noise of derision. "Yeah, right. If you understood me so well you'd know what you said applies to you equally well."

She realized seconds too late that she'd better shut her trap or she'd give away those feelings he claimed he could read. He couldn't know that he'd turned her world into a spiraling confusion of no return.

They continued for several miles until he turned next to a large black mailbox printed with his name and address. The long driveway twisted and turned, perhaps designed to hide the house from prying eyes.

When Dana caught site of the log cabin home at the top of the drive, she whistled.

"Hot doggie!"

She felt Marshall's stare and when he said nothing and continued to drive down the dirt driveway, she turned to watch his hard profile.

"Really. It's beautiful," she said.

"Thanks."

A rough, reluctant acknowledgment, but an acknowledgment nonetheless. She tried to see imperfections in the structure, but as the cathedral windows at the front loomed in front of her, Dana saw a rustic bounty. No doubt about it, Marshall owned a nice home.

Marshall parked in front of the detached garage. "Okay, pile out."

Without warning Dana's nerves went into overdrive. She remembered she hadn't come here to play house with the man who'd sent lust and passion ramming into her life. Someone wanted her dead, and someone had tried to kill Gregory and Neal. Shivering with an immediate and overwhelming fear, she flinched when Marshall touched her arm.

"What is it?" Soft and gentle, his voice worked at returning her calm.

"I'm fine."

"Nothing is going to happen to you with me here. Nothing and no one is going to get through me."

His strong statement told her his feelings for her went deep enough that he'd put his life on the line, and that meant a lot to her.

He reached up and cupped her face. His thumb brushed her cheek. Sparks of sweet relief started to spill through her veins and warmth began to thaw the ice that had frozen her sensations.

"Come on." He opened his door. "Let's get inside."

Like a good little soldier she did as told, reaching into the back seat for her overnight suitcase. Once on the porch she felt an excitement to see the inside of his abode. She wondered, with a wild flush and a thundering heart, if they could make the kind of impassioned love the ghosts had attempted over and over but never finished.

Maybe that's what hell is. Having sex and never being able to finish. She almost laughed. She'd brought the tape recording of the ghost's fun; she hadn't listened to it yet.

A wicked grin curved her lips. If she had anything to say about it, unlike the ghosts, their lovemaking would equal a melt down larger than Chernobyl.

He fumbled with his keys and she looked up at the sky. "What? No tornadoes?"

Her gaze caught Marshall's and he seemed to lose all movement. He stared and stared, his lips parting and his pupils dilating. *Holy macadamia nuts!* The key ring slipped from his fingers and clanked onto the porch.

Dana crossed her arms. "Don't tell me we have to kick the door down."

He reached for the keys and when he came up, he smiled and uttered a low curse. "You're a barrel of laughs, Dana."

She decided not to be offended.

Once inside the cabin he took her coat and overnight bag

and headed down a long hallway, leaving her standing in the middle of a living room with vaulted ceilings. The expanse of hard wood flooring seemed to cover all the bases. Living room, dining room, and tucked in a large niche, the kitchen. She'd never been one for totally open homes. Dana always thought she'd feel exposed living in one. As she turned around, gazing at the old West paintings gracing some of the walls, she thought maybe her attitude had changed. At least here she felt secure, her fear from earlier easing away in the cozy feeling this living space provided. Then again, perhaps this house didn't provide the safe feeling, but the man who lived here did.

With subdued western flavor, the room looked warm and homey in a way she wouldn't have expected. With big windows unencumbered by coverings, she saw the pine forest and mountains with crystal clarity.

His taste in furniture ran to dark burgundy leather, with a large couch and loveseat centered on a huge rug before a brick fireplace of cave-sized proportions. Loveseat and couch both sported a large Indian blanket draped over the back of each of them. Once again her imagination took flight. She saw a blazing fire in the hearth. She'd be curled up on the couch, covered in a warm Indian blanket…naked…his arms around her.

"Like the view?"

Dana jumped. She turned toward Marshall, a ready admonition on her lips. Instead, she stopped and gazed at his somewhat mussed hair and the extra growth of beard on his face.

"Very much. Don't you feel a bit…exposed with all these uncovered windows?" she asked.

"No." He advanced on her, and again she knew a forbidden thrill as he stalked her until she'd bumped into the back of the couch. "Besides, there are curtains in the bedroom…" His gaze lingered on her mouth, then slid downward. "Where it matters most."

His innuendo put the last nail in her coffin. Heat spiraled upward until it centered deep in her stomach and flared. She knew real desire when she felt it, and she'd tried to ignore this man for far too long. "It really is a wonderful place."

He smiled and seemed to draw back a little, as if sensing she would explode, that he would combust if he came any closer. "Thanks."

Yeah, she'd noticed that. Although life had turned rough in the long hours, he'd done a lot more grinning than he used to.

Moving away, he gestured toward for her to follow him. "I'll show you the guestroom and you can get some sleep."

As she tagged behind him, she said, "I don't think I'll ever sleep again."

He gave a male grunt. "It's okay. You can put your mind at ease. This cabin may look unsophisticated in some ways, but it's got a full security system. We are as safe as anywhere."

He opened a set of rustic double doors and led her into a sizable bedroom. She stopped and gaped.

She wouldn't have expected anything like this room in a house inhabited by Marshall. A large four-poster bed in Queen Anne style graced the center of the room and held her overnight case. Covered with a pale blue and pink comforter, the bed looked like something that belonged in 'The Princess and the Pea.' Matching curtains covered the two large windows on the far side of the room, sheers letting in enough light to warm the room, but not enough to give a clear view to anyone outside. The furniture, a small chair in one corner, a potted plant, a vanity…all of it said female touch. French flavor with white wood and gold highlights had never appealed to her personal style, yet this room held a beauty that couldn't be ignored. *And it screams woman.*

In the center of the wall, away from the bed, a huge brick fireplace rested.

She turned around and observed the sumptuous room one more time. "Wow."

"You've said that a lot lately."

"It's so cozy." She couldn't imagine this room being his idea. It didn't go with his rough and tough attitude. "Feminine."

"Surprised?"

"Frankly, yes." She wondered if the question she wanted to ask would be received well. "Did a woman help you design it? I mean, there aren't too many guys in love with pastels. Not exactly manly man stuff."

Her teasing must have come through as a smile tried to overtake his mouth. "Jealous?"

"Of your decorating abilities? Nope. I've got my place just the way I want it. If I could get rid of the landlord from purgatory it would be perfect."

"No. I mean are you jealous because a woman helped me decorate?" He said it with nonchalance.

It stung deep to realize how close to the mark he'd come. "Oh, really, Marshall."

He went to the dresser and retrieved an eight by ten pewter framed photograph and handed it to her. "She's the one who helped me decorate this entire house."

The lady in the photo had a sweet countenance, youthful and wise at the same time. She had a cloud of short brown hair, rich and thick, and her green eyes held a spark that added to her warm smile. She looked about fifty-five or sixty. Her mind raced around the idea that Marshall had an 'older' girlfriend. Then she recalled the conversation they'd shared at Aunt Lucille's last night. No way this woman could be his squeeze.

Before she could ask he took the photo and placed it back on the dresser. "It's my mom. My parents live in Casper."

Relief flowed through Dana. It's his mother. Good. Why the idea pleased her was easy to define. She didn't want another woman having a claim on him.

"Speechless, Dana?"

"For once." She'd admit it. Her feelings for him had gone way beyond casual and far over simple lust.

"Mom's an interior designer and Dad's an architect. He helped me put together a perfect plan for this house."

"Are you an only child?"

He tucked his thumps into his belt loops. "Nope. My little sister Teresa is thirty and married and lives in Casper. My little brother is in the Army. He lives everywhere, moves around a lot." He turned away, looking a tad uncomfortable. "Look, there are towels in the bathroom, so you can take a shower if you like."

"I'd rather try that tub you were talking about." The words escaped without thought. "I've been dreaming about it the whole way here."

She saw his Adam's apple go up and down. "Is that all you've been dreaming about?"

"I'm wishing this whole murder and mayhem thing were over."

"There hasn't been a murder yet."

She paused, watching Marshall once again come within close proximity. "Gregory is a bastard, but Neal doesn't deserve this."

"Maybe he knew something or saw something he shouldn't have."

She shivered at the idea that someone stalked them. She knew what it felt like now to be pursued without knowing about it. "I don't even want to think about it right now. Now what about that whirlpool tub?"

Dana gave him a half-smile, hoping he'd respond this time to her gentle query. Instead of refusing, he turned back and walked toward her again. With scarcely an inch between them he looked down at her. His nostrils flared as he took a deep breath.

"No tub. Not yet," he said with soft gravel in his voice. "Because when you're in that tub, I will be with you."

Before she could move or speak, her gaze locked with his dark eyes and all the breath went out of her. "Marshall—"

"No," he whispered, shifting a fraction closer. "Don't say anything."

"Why?"

He dipped his head lower until his lips came close to hers, not touching, but teasing, his breath the only caress. "Because if I hold you in my arms, I won't want to stop. I'll want it all. All you want to give me."

Her breath tightened. *Oh, yes. I want so much to give you everything.* She ached with needs and she didn't want to hold back her feelings any longer.

Marshall touched his mouth to hers, grazing it with a sweet, almost chaste touch that tortured. When he pulled back she thought he'd finished. Instead he caressed her lips one more time, tender and exploring. She responded, hoping, wanting so much more.

Pulling back, he took a deep breath, chest heaving as he clutched his fists. He hadn't touched her anywhere else during the excruciatingly wonderful kiss. She knew the power she had over him right then and almost took advantage of it. Almost threw herself into his arms and pushed him over the edge. Instead she watched as he gave her a last scorching look, then turned and left.

Chapter 19

Marshall stared into the flames dancing in the fireplace. Silence covered the house, except for the snap of sparks in the hearth and the insistent tick of the grandfather clock. He heard Dana moving around in the bedroom and his imagination powered into overdrive.

Dana smoothed moisturizer on her arms, on her flat stomach, and on her long-as-sin legs.

Heat rose in him at the thought of her naked, and he wanted to barge into her room and tug her into his arms.

"Marshall?"

Her soft voice made him jump. In seconds he took her in, her navy T-shirt, her relaxed fit jeans, her feet covered in white athletic socks but no shoes, her damp hair appearing dark red rather than the fiery color he was used to seeing. His gut made another helpless clutch of burning need.

"You all right?" she asked when he continued to stare at her.

He broke from the trance. "Yeah. Want something to drink? I've got some wine around here. Pop, milk, water, you name it. If you're hungry there's plenty in the fridge."

She stuffed her hands into her pockets. "No, thanks. I'm good."

A raw, primordial rhythm seemed to beat inside him. He might have kissed her before but he ached as if he'd never touched her in his life.

Dana moved toward him and he half hoped she'd sit in the leather chair, half hoped she'd sit next to him. She sat on the other end of the couch from him, and he sighed with relief and disappointment. Part of him wanted to scream. What he'd felt for Eva and Helen paled in comparison to the overwhelming, gut-wrenching protectiveness burning a hole in him right now.

She sat sideways so her leg came up on the couch part way. He wondered if she used the position of her leg as a mental or physical barrier. She stared into the fire, and he found the quiet surrounding them almost comforting.

She sighed. "This place would be good for writing. It's so tranquil here." When she smiled at him he saw the world in her eyes. As if something had broken lose and set her free. "I think I might be over the writer's block. And I owe it all to Macon."

"Why did being here help?

"I didn't think it would. You remember what I told you in the car and about what I said to Kerrie?"

He nodded. "Yeah. Look, I'm sorry. I didn't explain what I meant earlier. I do understand what you're talking about. I'm just afraid I've got a lot of things in my life that aren't settled yet. I don't have that 'break loose' feeling that you have."

She seemed to brighten, as if his acknowledgment that he understood warmed her from within. He liked that. He liked it a lot.

Clasping her hands together in her lap she asked, "What's holding you back, Marshall? What is your road block in life?" A reluctant edge crept into her voice. "What are you afraid of?"

"One question at a time." Marshall sagged and put his head back on the cold leather. He closed his eyes. Maybe he could answer her if he didn't have to watch her animated face or see her reaction to what he decided to reveal. "I'm not afraid of much."

She made a scoffing noise, but he didn't open his eyes. "I don't believe you. I'm a writer, remember? I specialize in watching people and looking at their reactions. Paying attention to what motivates them."

"So you've got me all figured out?"

"No. You're a tough nut to crack. Like a piece of granite that refuses to be carved. I'm not sure what to make of you, and I think you like that I can't figure you out."

He raised his arms above his head, then tucked his hands behind his neck, trying for a casualness he didn't feel. "Why do you care so much? Most people give up by now."

"You don't want anyone close to you. Are your parents even close to you? Your brother and sister?"

"Yeah. Family is important to me."

"What about Eric?"

Marshall shrugged, resolved to keep his eyes closed. "We're best friends and he tries to 'bring me out' but there's no point in that."

"What about Logan? You guys seem like good buds."

"We're friends, but he's got plenty of demons of his own."

"I sensed that."

He felt her shift, and he opened his eyes and lowered his arms. Instead of looking at her, he kept his gaze pinned to the hypnotic waver of flames in the fireplace. *If I look at her it might be all over. I'll cave in.* "Anything you don't sense?"

She cleared her throat. "Maybe. Like why you're determined to keep me safe."

"It's my job."

Maybe his tone kept her from asking more about that subject, and she plunged into another topic with a vengeance. "Eva and Helen really ruined you for other women, didn't they?"

He did look at her this time. She smiled with self-satisfaction and the grin of a woman who had hit the mark.

"Yeah. They did." *Okay, if you're going to play it hard, I've got something for you.* "Who ruined you?"

Dana felt his question all through her body, from the top of her head shooting straight to her toes. Oh crud. If he didn't plan on getting involved with her, emotionally involved, what did it matter? Nothing to lose at this point, she concluded.

"I…no one—"

"If that isn't a load of bull—"

"It's not. No one ruined me." She licked her lips. "I've done more damage to myself than anyone else could have done. You've got to let people do things to you. Deep inside where it hurts. If you keep people shut out, then no one can do damage, can they?"

His eyes changed from semi-hostile to curious. "Right. So who was he? Who was the bastard that hurt you?"

"I'm not telling you anything."

"Come on. Fair is fair. You know about Eva and Helen and what they did to me. Or what I allowed them to do."

He turned his body so that he mimicked her. When he lifted his leg onto the couch in that half open stance, Dana let a wave of pure need grip her body. "It's complicated."

"So?"

She waited, trying to bring on the courage. She began, as tentative as a baby attempting first steps. "Frank Chester." She took a deep breath. "It happened when I was in college. A relationship that went bad. That's all I'm going to tell you for now."

His eyes narrowed, dangerous and dark. "I could make you talk."

She uttered a nervous, thin laugh. "How? Arrest me again? Threaten to keep me here until I spill my guts? If you want to keep yourself aloof from women, Marshall, why are you asking about Frank? What do you care?"

His chest expanded as he took a breath that shuddered through his frame. "Do I have to spell it out?"

Please do. Please. I'm drowning here. "I'm not a mind reader."

Marshall leaned forward, his casual stance turned to intense, his gaze capturing hers in a breath-stealing grasp that threatened to send her out of control. If he didn't say something or do something in the next minute, she'd do…what? Run screaming from the room?

"We've kissed, Dana," he said huskily. "We've done far more. We've been pretty intimate."

Ire rose in her, and suddenly it felt like old times between them. "As you're so fond of saying…so? If it's just lust and you only want to have sex with me, then I'm not willing to tell you about Frank and about—"

"Damn it, Dana." Before she knew it he moved across the couch and stared her down like a fighter ready for fist-a-cuffs. "Tell me or I'll have to do something desperate."

Her breath came in tiny puffs, almost gasps. She thought about leaning away, but knew he'd follow. "Do what? Tie me up? Throw me in the clink?"

His gaze went from determined to startled amusement. One corner of his mouth twitched, then his eyes turned inferno hot. Not with anger, but a mingled toss of intense desire and exasperation. "Brat."

The one word did it. She giggled. "Bully."

He slid one hand behind her neck. "Apologize."

"For what?"

His mouth was so close now his warm breath touched her lips. "For being a maddening, crazy—" He swallowed hard.

"Yes?" She knew the word came out like a plea for more, but she couldn't help it. His warm fingers caressed the back of her neck and sweet tingles radiated down her spine.

"For making me care about you so much," he said, his throaty confession sounding raw and hurting.

His words made her heart beat faster and warm gratification filled her heart. Before she could think or say another word, his mouth came down on hers. Hard.

Oh, God! Yes!

This was it. No more waiting. No more insane repartee designed to keep them apart.

Without preliminaries Marshall plunged his tongue inside, tasting her like a man drinking his first cup of water after a trip across the desert.

She exploded into her need, almost ripping the buttons from the front of his shirt. Under her quick fingers his shirt parted and she sighed. Dana couldn't remember feeling this uninhibited. Desire bit her like a snake, stabbing deep with teeth that pumped heavy passion through her in great waves. She arched against him as his hot kiss tormented her with a provocative rhythm. Restraints came down, washed away by a fierce hunger. Emotions engulfed her as hard and hammering as surf driven by high winds. Up and down it tossed her, the white water closing over her head. She decided to drown. She wouldn't kick to the surface and try to escape.

Marshall groaned into her mouth, dizzy with pleasure as she traced her hands over his face. He drank in her sighs and sounds of pleasure. Cupping her back, he smoothed her shirt across her skin, teasing. He wanted to touch her soft skin so much he burned deep in his loins, the arousal turning him hard and aching.

As he stopped kissing her, his right hand came up and cupped her neck in mockery of imprisonment. He let his fingers glide with self-assured strokes along her skin. She shivered and touched his chest again. He let out a rough noise, caught between a growl and a gasp as she traced her fingers across his muscles. Like a feather she teased him.

Marshall never wanted to please a woman as much as he wished to please Dana, and he knew he'd do anything to get her to that teeth-grinding point of release. He'd love her until she screamed and begged him for it, and until he teetered on the edge of explosion.

Dana knew they'd lost control. Without a doubt this man gave her security she'd never had with another man. She trusted him with her life.

Slipping her hands over his shoulders she gripped the wide, incredible musculature and felt him move under her touch. His breath rasped, hard and eager. She welcomed the lustful, super heated need in his eyes as he looked at her.

Marshall attacked her neck with nibbling kisses that excited her even more than the touch of his fingers had moments ago. His hands cupped her hips, then reached around to delve under the waist band of her loose jeans. The flicker of his fingers above her buttocks made her arch against him in frantic jerk. She opened her mouth to speak yet nothing escaped but a whimper.

At the same time his hand found her breast and cupped it. As his thumbs flicked over her lace-covered nipples, the burning sweet pleasure made her writhe in his arms. Before she realized it he'd tilted her backwards on the couch, freeing her breasts for his view. As he leaned over her his gaze took her in, transfixed as if he'd captured an unimaginable prize. The firestorm in his eyes told her everything a second before he cupped her breast again and his tongue explored. She panted and arched, wanting to be closer.

Dana never thought, not in a trillion years, that anything could feel this good. As he taunted her nipples with lingering licks, she drove her fingers through Marshall's hair and cupped the back of his head. She anchored him, pressing him onward until he encompassed one nipple in his mouth and suckled. She shuddered again and again, loving his unremitting possession. She couldn't pretend only lust drove her headfirst into his arms. She'd fallen into an emotional roller coaster that demanded fulfillment for her mind as well as her body. This man had taken her emotions to places they'd never touched on, driven her to seek answers. Perhaps, in his arms, she'd find her Nirvana.

Dana whispered his name, desperate for a rescue from the building pressure. On and on he tongued her, lush strokes that brought her to blinding arousal. Then he sucked hard and without mercy. She cried out as an ache throbbed between her legs.

"Marshall, if you don't—oh, God!"

Marshal knew she hung on the edge. He zeroed in on the waistband of her jeans as he made short work of the snap and zipper to gain access to the soft skin beneath. His hand slipped into her pants at the same time he captured one of her nipples between his teeth and tugged. A plea slipped from her and she lifted her hips to give him better access. His fingers traced and lingered and taunted until she squirmed. Marshall slipped down, searching until...

Dana saw heaven.

"Yes," she groaned as his middle finger found her, touching the hotwire drawn tight with excitement.

Marshall started a slow journey over slick, hot softness. Her eyes popped open and she stared at him wildly. Before Dana could catch her breath, his soft, barely there touch sent her flesh into a trembling that astonished her and blew her right out of her mind.

She uttered a strangled moan as he strummed her flesh with fluttering brushes and swirls.

The warmth that poured through her earlier turned to a conflagration as he concentrated on her greatest pleasure, then slipped one finger deep inside her. She gasped as he inserted another finger and stroked, giving her no mercy. She felt herself tightening against invasion and welcoming it at the same time, incredible pleasure clasping her muscles over his fingers.

Dana twisted in his arms, her groan of rising pleasure stifled when Marshall captured her mouth with his. He circled over and around with his thumb. Sparks of light seemed to dance against the inside of her eyelids as her breathing accelerated. A deep throbbing began inside her.

He moved his thumb once. Twice. Three times.

She lost it.

Burning, breath-stealing passion consumed her and she detonated. A gasping whimper escaped her.

She opened her eyes at the crest and saw the savage male pleasure etched into his face. Another twist of his thumb sent her up higher and her body trembled against his, convulsing. A buzzing filled her ears and she felt light headed as the last tremors rippled through her. She moaned as he eased his hand away and rested his palm against her belly.

She buried her face against his throat and waited as she caught her breath.

Seconds later he looked at her, a tender, heart-melting smile curving his sexy mouth. "You're beautiful. So beautiful."

She smiled back, unable to contain the joy that bubbled up inside her. Her body had known it perhaps before the rest of her did.

I love him. I'm helplessly, irretrievably in love with him.

She loved him so much she ached to give him the same screaming pleasure she'd experienced moments ago.

Dana realized she couldn't wait any longer to be his.

"Now." The word escaped her with a shiver. "Marshall."

"Now," he agreed.

As he pulled back she saw the flush in his face and knew she affected him as much as he did her. He swung her up into his arms and carried her to the bedroom. His bedroom.

She barely had time to revel in the feel of powerful muscles holding her when he lowered her to the bed. Dana registered few things about the darkening room in her sensual haze, pin-pointing all her concentration on the man before her.

Marshall slipped out of his shirt, flinging it away. It hit something and landed on the floor with a soft swish. He yanked off his athletic shoes.

He hesitated for a moment, standing with his legs apart and his chest heaving with each breath, his fists clenched at his side. Dana sucked in her breath, a primitive thrill responding to the naked male before her. A wicked grin came to her lips.

He's male all right. So male I want to torment him and make him feel so much pleasure he'll never forget me as long as he lives.

Dan watched him disrobe and she took in the broad plains of his shoulders, the defined pectorals in his chest, the ripple of muscle in his stomach. Excitement ran through her like a rushing river. Unable to wait, she sat up and reached for his waistband, struggling with the buttons as she ripped at them. Seconds later they came undone. He took control, shoving his pants down along with briefs until they landed on the floor. Dana caught a glimpse of hard masculinity. Then she was in his arms again.

When she tried to roll him over, he whispered against her ear. "For you."

Not to be denied, she pushed her fingers through the hair on his chest, defining him, enjoying the evidence of a hard male body in the rippling muscles. She gripped his biceps, felt them shift and bunch. He quivered under her touch.

His fingers traced over her breasts with reverence, lingering over her waist and hips with a gentleness that tightened her throat. Tears stung her eyes and the ache became profound. Dana clasped his wrists and held him in place, glorying in the hardness and hairy roughness of his powerful body pressing against her.

As he slid down the bed she knew what he intended to do once he reached his destination, and the idea excited her so much she held her breath. As his tongue and lips found tender places, she twisted on the bed, maddened by staggering pleasure. He traced and patterned and molded her. Each stroke within and without arched her higher and higher. She almost reached the pinnacle, hanging by a tether, ready to snap.

He moved back, his breath rasping. Then he arrived again, this time inserting two tormenting fingers. He started a rhythm. His tongue moved.

Pleasure screamed through her, threatening an imminent flare-up.

"Marshall. I want—"

"What do you need? I'd do anything for you." His voice came hoarse and tight with desire. "Everything."

Love me. "I want you."

Her husky request was his undoing. He slid up her body, propping on his elbows as he anchored his hips between her thighs. Insistent hardness touched her heat, and she gasped in reaction. Marshall's answering groan told her he felt the same way. He cupped her face. In the same instant he pressed forward, slow and deliberate. Dana arched in trembling pleasure as hot man penetrated. He drew out the process, sliding through tight folds to reach the heart of her, pushing so tight and deep she shivered in ecstasy.

Oh, my God. He's...oh, my!

Her eyelids fluttered open in delighted shock.

Nothing could have prepared her for this. For the forceful heat and amazing power of his total possession. He kissed her as he pressed upward. She whimpered as he thrust that final inch.

Marshall heard her soft exclamation, and he looked at her through the dim light. "All right?"

A tentative smile twitched the corner of Dana's mouth. He speared his hands through her hair and sucked in a breath, as her body seemed to ripple around him, drawing him deeper. He wanted to move, his body quivering with need. Instead he waited, unable to rush this moment.

A feathery sensation tickled his spine. When her fingers clutched his backside he inhaled sharply. "Don't."

She grinned. "No?"

Dana's teasing question, so much like the taunts she'd given him in the past, fueled his need to take her hard and fast. Slow would come later. When his head didn't feel like it was about to pop off and his loins weren't screaming for fulfillment.

"Think I can't handle it?" he grated out, each word an effort.

"Show me."

He smiled and drew back. The chemical reaction that had existed between them since the first day they'd met set off a chain reaction. Marshall kissed her at the same time he slammed home.

Dana gasped. She had never felt anything remotely this wonderful.

Thick. Hot.

Heaven. This is heaven.

She shuddered under the onslaught of shattering pleasure and a love so strong she knew she'd never be free of it. A growl issued from him and he arched, as he pumped hard, grinding, moving inside her with powerful, merciless thrusts. Each time he entered she rose against him, answering the wicked torture. She felt the stirrings of climax reach for her, demanding her quick surrender.

Surely she couldn't stand much more. Bliss rose inside her like a firestorm. A frantic sound escaped her, hot on the trail of the little moans that issued from her lips.

She let him know with her whimpers that he was driving her straight out of her mind. Clutching at him, she showed him with hands and lips that she didn't want him to stop.

Her love for him grew as he gave her everything he had. His hands went under her buttocks, tilting her just right. Hammering deep and high he forced her up the hill until her passion became an inferno.

One last thrust hit the mark. Her fingers dug into his back, ripples of overwhelming pleasure radiating outward, tingling through her limbs. As she tensed around him she cried out. Pulsing delight held her suspended, quivering and panting as the climax overtook each muscle, each fiber of her being.

Marshall felt her release, and male satisfaction blasted him straight to the top. Frenzied, he loved Dana with a wild abandon. His muscles burned with effort, his heart slamming in his chest. He would claim her and no other man would have her. Ever.

Relentless, he thrust once more. Twice. Again.

Yes.

Every muscle in Marshall's body stiffened. Pure, shattering pleasure hit him.

Her name roared through his lips. As his body shivered his mind went blank and road the pinnacle until the last shudder relented and he sank upon her.

Chapter 20

"I think we gave the ghosts a run for their money, didn't we?" Dana asked, snuggling into Marshall's embrace.

He'd rolled to the side and gathered her tight in his arms some time ago. Now his hands passed over her hair, her back, and her rear as if he couldn't get enough of touching her.

He chuckled. "They're probably still back in the basement trying to finish the deed."

"You really think so? I mean it's ludicrous. Ghosts having sex?"

"Maybe we should go back to Lucille's and check out the basement again. You could play the tape you made of the ghosts and see what happens."

Her cheeks burned when she thought of the chemical reaction between her and Marshall while they'd listened to the horny ghosts do the nasty. Supernova didn't quite describe the situation. She traced a delicate pattern on Marshall's butt with one finger.

He twitched, his arms tightening around her. "You're on very dangerous ground."

She sighed and slid her hand down, exploring a rock hard

thigh muscle. "I really do feel sorry for the ghosts. I mean, at least we got to, um, you know…"

"Come?"

She smacked his gluteus maximus, and he twitched. "Ow! What was that for?"

"For being so crude."

Marshall cupped her neck and tilted her head up. She couldn't see his face well, but his dark, dangerous tone sent a shiver slipping through her belly. "Lady, if that's crude, you haven't seen nothin' yet."

"There's more where that came from?"

He grunted. "Yeah."

"I can't believe…I mean I never would have guessed that we…"

Embarrassment reddened her face. *Talk much?*

"Go on," he said, pushing his hands through her hair again and kissing her forehead. "You never would have guessed what?"

Marshall's reassurance comforted her and eased her mortification. "That you and I would have ended up like this. I thought you couldn't stand me and that you believed I had something to do with Aunt Lucille's predicament, and now here we are recreating the dancing bed."

He laughed, and the sound rumbled deep in his chest. "I never disliked you. Not really."

"But you were suspicious of me."

"At first."

"Not anymore?"

"I wouldn't be here like this if I didn't trust you."

"So what do we do now?"

His arms tightened and his hard thighs shifted against her. "What do you want to do?"

Ignoring his double entendre, she said, "I want this person who tried to run me off the road and apparently tried to kill my cousins, to get out of town. Just leave us all alone."

"They won't do that."

She sighed. "I know."

"You're safe," he whispered into her hair. "I'm not letting you out of my sight again."

Silence hung between them for several moments. "Whatever happens I want you to know something."

She couldn't say that she loved him. Not yet. Dana couldn't leave the last portion of her heart open to him in that way without knowing for sure his feelings.

"Dana?" he asked when she didn't speak.

"I want you to know I'm sorry about all the things I said. The stuff I hurled at you when we first met."

Warmth flooded her as he tilted her head up again so he could kiss her nose. "You didn't trust me."

Time to confess a little. "It felt like a hot wire connecting us and I guess I was so attracted to you I used that bull as a defense mechanism."

He nodded, his stubble-roughed jaw rubbing against her cheek. "I've never felt anything as crazy as what I feel now with you."

Despite her languor, their spicy after sex talk kept her fire lit. If he kept it up she might have to attack him here and now.

She sighed in contentment. Snuggling deep into his arms, she enjoyed the sensations of hard male against her feminine contours. His lips shaped hers, and no doubt the kiss would have led to more if the phone hadn't rung. He groaned and reached for the bedside table, snapping on the light. He grabbed the phone. She hoped the conversation wouldn't last long so they could continue where they left off.

"Mrs. Pizer," he said.

Wondering what the woman could want, Dana snuggled up behind him. A wicked idea formed, and she slipped her hand over his hip and downward.

"Well, I don't know, Mrs. Pizer, that's very nice but—" Marshall let out a gasp as Dana reached her destination. "What? No, I'm fine." His hand trapped hers, but she wiggled her fingers. His muscles—all of them—tensed. "Of course, yes. She knows about it. It isn't necessary."

Dana smiled, glorying in her power. That particular muscle hardened under her touch.

"Oh, but it is necessary," Dana whispered in his ear.

He almost dropped the phone when Dana squeezed. "Uh-yeah, all right. Okay. But I'll have to ask her. She may not be able to attend. Thank you."

When he dropped the receiver into the cradle, he rolled toward Dana and pinned her under him. His grim expression was overlaid by mischief in his eyes. "What were you trying to do?" He leaned down until their lips almost touched. "Let the whole world know I'm in bed with a beautiful woman?"

She inched her hands over his wide shoulders and wallowed in his lascivious look. "I'm shocked, Brennan Marshall. Who is the woman?"

He nipped her ear, and she let out a yelp. "The woman that better stop squirming."

When he tongued her ear she shivered in delight. "Mmm. What did Mrs. Pizer want? It sounded grim."

He sobered and loosened his hold. "She wanted to make sure you'd attend the ceremony with me tomorrow night for the award presentation."

"Of course I will. I was planning on going at least by myself. But it sounds like you want me to be your date."

He didn't smile when he said, "I only want you to be there if you're comfortable."

"Why shouldn't I be comfortable?"

"Gossip."

Well, that said it all. Sure, she hadn't thought about the gossip. If everyone in Macon knew she had jumped his bones it wouldn't bother her a bit. Another idea came to mind. "You never said if your family is going to be there."

He rolled off her and put his arm over his eyes. She sensed Marshall's reluctance to take the commendation, and recalled when he'd taken the gift from Tommy. While she admired his humble pie, she wanted to see the man she'd fallen for receive the kudos he deserved.

"No, because I didn't tell them."

Surprised, she realized he hadn't told her everything. "Why?"

He shook his head. "Because they really don't have time for it."

"You've known for a week and a half and they don't have time?" Exasperated, she made an impatient noise. "I know you love them and they'll be so disappointed. You deserve to be recognized, Marshall. You saved that boy's life."

He lifted his arm and gave her a gentle grin. "Thanks, sweetheart, but I…it's my job. I have a problem with people being rewarded extraordinarily for just doing their job." His husky endearment thrilled her at the same time his self-depreciation bothered her.

"Yes, but there's a big difference between reward for doing enough to get by and doing more than most people would. Your parents would want to be there." Somehow she knew he'd have sickeningly affectionate parents. Marshall's good upbringing was written all over him with indelible ink. "Brennan Marshall, you're such a twit! I ought to skin you alive."

Instead of looking hacked, he gave her a slow grin designed to set her on fire. When he didn't speak, she went onward. "Do you have a camera?"

"Yeah."

"Good. I'll take photos. At least your parents will have that."

The phone rang again and Dana jumped, startled. "Grand Central station around here."

Marshall reached for the phone, and Dana decided she'd leave his body alone this time, difficult as that may be. As he spoke he rolled over onto his back. "Lucille. Everything all right?"

As Marshall's brows came together in a frown, Dana's heart thumped with worry.

Seconds later he said, "That's good news." Another lengthy paused followed until he said, "What? Again? All right. We'll stop by the hospital first, then head over to the house and let you know what we find." He hung up and turned to Dana. "You're not going to believe this. Lucille and Logan stopped at the house so Lucille could freshen up and change clothes. They heard noises down in the basement, and when they investigated they discovered the bed is at it again. Full throttle."

Dana laughed lightly. "I wonder what Logan thought of that."

Marshall's smile said he couldn't wait to ask Logan. "He's so level-headed I'll bet it freaked him out. Knowing him, he probably tried looking for the source of the noise and found exactly what we did."

Dana sighed. "I feel it down deep in my stomach, Marshall. All the trouble that's happened is because I arrived in town."

His warm palm slid down over the curve of her breast and to her stomach. She sucked in a breath of excitement. "Down here?"

She smiled. "Yeah, down there."

Groaning, he rolled away from her and got to his feet. "Don't get me started. I'm having a hard enough time keeping my hands off you as it is."

She surveyed his body. Hard definitely described his situation. Raw feminine pleasure coursed through her. "I see."

"Stop looking at me like that or we'll never get out of here." As his drop-dead gorgeous body turned and headed for the bathroom, she sighed in appreciation. What a hunk. He turned around again and caught her eyeing his backside. "Last one dressed cooks dinner tonight."

She leapt from the bed. "You're on."

* * *

Marshall and Dana headed through the automatic doors, and her nose wrinkled as she inhaled the unmistakable odor of eau de hospital. Her stomach rolled, and she knew it wasn't because she hadn't eaten for some time. She didn't like the way she felt now. Uneasy. Exposed. Alert. Could danger lurk around the corner like a nasty beast in a horror movie?

"Marshall," she said, not knowing what she wanted to ask or say.

He glanced down at her, his frown drawn tight. "What's wrong?"

"I don't know. I feel like someone is watching us."

"You're safe."

As Marshall put a proprietary arm around her waist, she sank into his protection with welcome. Amazing how this man could wrap her in shelter with his mere presence. She'd always wondered if she'd feel that way around a man once in her lifetime. She'd never experienced it with Frank, and now Marshall gave her security she'd never thought she'd need.

She shivered. "I keep thinking I should be able to use this…this feeling in my horror novel."

His mouth formed a small smile, half curious, half apprehensive. He spoke softly. "Which part of your experience in Macon are you talking about? The tornado? The wreck? Or…" His voice dropped to a husky whisper. "…our lovemaking."

Lovemaking! Her heart did a triple flip and her stomach a sweet tremble. The way he said that word pushed fear straight from her mind. She cleared her throat. "The sense of fear, actually. The unwanted suspense." When his armed tightened around her, she nestled close. "And the lovemaking…that's too personal." A wicked grin touched her lips. "Maybe."

He made a sound somewhere between a laugh and a strangle. "Maybe? If I notice something mighty personal showing up in your next novel, I'll know where you got the idea."

She couldn't help the small snicker that escaped her lips.

As they reached the ward where Gregory lay, Marshall became all business. Two deputies outside the door let him in. They moved passed several beds, and Dana took a deep breath, fighting back the emotions of those around her.

Logan stood at the foot of Gregory's bed, while Lucille kept vigil at her stepson's bedside. After greeting them, Aunt Lucille said, "I think he's doing better. He's drifting in and out of consciousness. How are you two?"

Dana kissed her aunt's cheek and hugged her tight. "Good."

Aunt Lucille's cagey assessment left Dana feeling as if her aunt had to know what had happened between her and Marshall. Marshall looped his arm around Dana's waist.

Aunt Lucille grinned. "I can see that."

Dana blushed, and the look Marshall gave her made her melt into her shoes. A combination of heady love and stunning fear mixed into a soup in her mind. She had to admit. She liked that he didn't mind showing how he felt about her.

"How is he?" Marshall said, nodding toward the bed.

"The doctors aren't sure whether you'll be able to question him or not. They think he'll come out of it shortly," Logan said.

"I'm out of it now," Gregory's scratchy voice said.

Startled, the grouping turned to the man in the bed. Pale, with a minute cut on his cheek, Gregory appeared smaller somehow. As if his big stature had shrunk in a few hours. With his head bandaged, and tubes entering his nose and his arm, he seem vulnerable in a way Dana never would have expected to see.

Marshall stepped forward immediately. He pulled a pad and pen from his jacket and held them ready. "Who did this to you?"

Gregory's eyes fluttered open, and the glaze of pain and confusion clouded his gaze. "I don't know."

Marshall looked from Gregory to Dana, the grim set of his mouth giving away nothing. Dana wondered if he believed her cousin.

"Try and remember," Dana said, keeping her voice gentle. Despite her dislike for the man, she had compassion left for him. "The sooner you tell Marshall the quicker we can catch whoever is behind this."

Defiance raged in Gregory's weak smile, his body stiffening under the white sheets. "I'm telling you I don't know."

Aunt Lucille circled the bed until she could reach for Gregory's left hand. "We have to know. Neal's also in the hospital." To Dana's surprise her aunt's voice came out determined, unwilling to put up with Gregory's brand of deceitfulness. "He was shot, Gregory. Someone shot him in his hotel room and left him for dead."

Gregory's mouth sagged, falling open. "What?" Panic laced his face. "No!"

Dana never would have guessed Gregory could show worry for his brother; she'd never seen it in him.

"That's why we need your help. He's in worse shape than you are," Dana said, aware of the manipulation in what she said. For the greater good, in this case, she'd use this against him.

His fingers squeezed Aunt Lucille's hand and Dana saw her aunt flinch. "I was on my way back from a bar on Main Street and was going to stop at the house. I parked over by your SUV." He looked at Marshall, nodding and wincing. "When I started past the doorway I was attacked. Someone slashed my side. I swung back and I know I hit them. I heard them grunt and fall."

"What happened next? After you were stabbed?" Marshall asked, his words rapid fire.

"I ran to the house and got inside. I thought whoever was behind me might follow me in the house. I was going for the phone when I heard more sounds in the basement. I figured maybe the crazy-assed bastard that got me was down there somehow got in through sliding door." He moved his fingers on the sheets, as if grabbing for purchase. "I was at the top of the stairs when the basement door opened and I passed out."

"You heard Marshall and I downstairs," Dana said. "You fell."

Gregory pinned her with a skeptical gaze. "What were you doing down there, cuz? Screwing Deputy Dog?"

Amazed at the man's audacity, she sucked in a breath. Marshall started to say something, his face suffused with anger.

Marshall took Dana's arm and started for the door. "I'll be back to question you again, Metcalf, in case you're memory starts working better. I will find out the truth."

Going into Lucille's dark house made Dana nervous, even though Lucille left the porch light on. "Thank goodness she left lights on inside, too. I really don't like this."

"We won't be here long." Marshall unlocked the back door and they trailed into the house the same way they'd come the first day they'd met. When he stopped at the head of the basement stairs she almost ran into the back of him. "Do you hear anything?"

Unmistakable. The sounds of two people in the throes of passion echoed loud enough it could be heard through the closed door at the bottom of the steps.

A sliver of light showed under the door. As the gasps and moans reached a higher pitch, Dana felt heat wash over her. She didn't know whether the feeling emerged because of awkwardness or a forbidden arousal.

The female ghost's enflamed voice roared out, making Dana jump. "Uhhhhhhhhhh. Ohhhhhhhhhhhhh."

Dana gripped the back of his coat sleeve. "Boy howdy."

"Holy mother—" Marshall cut himself off. "I can't believe I'm actually hearing this again."

Without another word, he headed down the stairs. Drawing his weapon, he opened the door slow and steady. She followed, half fearing that they'd find a real couple enjoying the heart-shaped mattress. She couldn't decide if she was relieved when they found no one.

At least no one alive.

Once again the bed felt warm to the touch, and yet the sounds issuing from the bed did not make it move. Tying into an impulsive mood, she lay down on the bed and closed her eyes. From here she thought the utterance sounded louder, but she couldn't say for certain.

Marshall made a noise somewhere between a snort and a chuckle. "What are you doing? Communing with the spirits?"

She folded her hands over her stomach and kept her eyes closed. "I'm not sure what I'm doing. I just thought this might stop them. Anything is worth a try at this point."

"Anything?"

She felt a weight drop on her, and she squeaked, her eyes popping open. She flailed about as Marshall wedged his hips between her legs and braced over her on his forearms. His lips curved in an unrepentant, boyish grin.

"Brennan Marshall, what are you doing?" She allowed her hands to settle on his shoulders.

"You did say you'd try anything. Maybe we can help the ghosts rest."

Dana put her hands on the satin coverlet and experienced the odd heat under her fingers. "Feel this."

Marshall's hips moved, pressing into the cradle of her thighs in a way that made her gasp. "I am feeling it."

She pursed her lips and bucked under him. "Feel the satin, or get off."

Rising to his knees, he touched the satin. "Feels warm, like it did before."

"What else?"

His brow crinkled in concentration. "Vibration? Don't tell me this is a vibrating bed?"

"No, no. At least, not vibrating in a conventional sense."

The noises turned desperate, and Dana felt it seeping into her, making her want to close her eyes again and surrender to the raw emotions and passions the sounds generated.

"The poor ghosts are not only torturing themselves, they'll haunt Aunt Lucille forever. Can you imagine listening to this kind of stuff for eternity?" Dana asked as Marshall moved off the bed, and she followed.

One corner of his mouth turned up in a wicked smile. "Uh, yeah."

From the gleam in his eyes she realized what he was thinking. "Marshall, you're very naughty."

"So?" He stepped closer, leaning down and lowering his voice to a suggestive drawl. "What are you going to do about it?"

"You or the ghosts?"

"The ghosts."

"What makes you think I know how to get rid of them?"

"You must have some ideas."

She wished she did. "An exorcism? A ghost hunter extraordinaire? Beats the beejeebers out of me."

When he tilted her chin up and gazed down at her with sin and heat in his eyes, she trembled. "What are you thinking, Marshall?"

His finger traced over her cheek and sent wildfire through her limbs. "I've got a plan."

As Marshall's deep, probing gaze searched her face, she felt a breathless anticipation stealing over her. "Is it guaranteed to work?"

He leaned in closer, and his body heat almost sent her into heart attack mode. "No. But it might be worth a try."

He touched her chin with a soft brush of his thumb, his body touching her now from chest to knees. She slid her arms up and burrowed her hands into his open jacket. Shuddering, he released her long enough to shove the jacket off his arms. It fell to the floor. His hands cupped her face, and she quivered as he kissed her ear, then nibbled at her earlobe.

"It's worth experimenting," he said.

"Show them how it's really done?" she asked, gasping.

His tongue found her ear again and searched inside. She gripped his waist and squeezed, shuddering in delight as he made quick work of the front of her blouse and his fingers flicked open her bra.

He rasped into her ear, "Give them an example how to finish the deed."

He groaned and his lips found her neck. As Marshall sampled her she gasped again and said, "And I don't think a little nibble here and there will accomplish the task."

It was then Dana hear the feathery voice of a woman exclaim, "Oh, don't stop!"

Dana looked around. "Where did that come from?"

Marshall surveyed the area. "I don't know. All I care about is you and I together right now."

As his gaze traveled over her in hot assessment, his chest heaved and he took a deep breath. His thumbs slipped back and forth with feather light sweeps over her nipples and she almost came unglued.

Her mind wouldn't function as she slid one more step toward insane desire. When his tongue traced a circular path across one nipple she yelped.

"Marshall." The sound escaped, desperate and eager.

The ghosts seemed pleased by the turn of events as they turned up the volume, escalating their noisy and never ending pursuit toward climax.

This time a ghostly male voice groaned with excitement, "Ohhhh..."

"What on earth?" Marshall asked, his face etched with disbelief. "The ghosts are talking?"

Another seriously excited moan filled the room as the ghosts pursued their lovemaking with full vigor. Dana almost laughed. "It's like they're listening to us listening to them."

Marshall grinned. "This is kinda kinky."

She did laugh then, and plastered herself against him as she slipped her arms around his neck. When their lips came together he taunted with delicate, tender strokes that surprised her. She'd seen the passion roaring out of control in his eyes seconds ago, but he'd slowed down enough to drive her within a half inch of begging him to put them out of their misery. When he pulled back she saw a dark, dangerous, consuming sexual desire ignite in his eyes.

Dana knew she was a goner.

An animal need pounded in side her, speeding up her heart and quickening her breath.

The ethereal occupants of the bed moaned with need, and Dana felt the ghostly passion simmer inside her. Warmth flooded her entire body with a pounding urgency. Marshall picked her up in his arms, and before she knew it he dumped her on the heart-shaped bed and came down on top of her.

"I think...we...were...here...before," she said between each sweet kiss.

"I want you," he rasped. His eyes blazed with a frenzied desire. "Now. Here."

The very idea of now and here turned the last switch required to start Dana's pilot light. Her thighs tightened in reaction, arousal burning at the core.

Here. Now. Hard. Fast.

"Oh, my God, Marshall."

He moaned as she kissed his nose, his chin, his cheeks. "Exactly."

This time it seemed written in the heavens that they would make love on this bed. Perhaps the ghosts agreed because they continued their unapologetic noise.

"Sweet heavens." A breathy voice, feminine and sweet, echoed in the air. "Sweet, sweet heaven."

The ghost's voice sounded faint now, mixed in with the moans and groans of delight. Thrilled that the ghosts might find their own special enjoyment, Dana poured on the passion.

Marshall plucked at her nipples, and Dana shivered in delight. His knee wedged between her legs and she rubbed against it in frantic search to ease the ache. As he kissed her his tongue moved against hers in a relentless stroking. She ripped at his shirt and seconds later it came open. She plunged her fingers through the hair on his chest, glorying in the feeling of hard muscles beneath her touch. He shuddered, a soft moan slipping through his lips. Seconds later he unzipped her pants and pulled them down and off along with her panties. She found the zipper on his jeans and yanked. When it resisted, she tugged again.

He moaned and trapped her hand. "Sweetheart, easy on the equipment."

Slowly he pulled down the zipper and within seconds she had him in hand. Literally.

His breath hissed through his teeth as she tested the length and the width of him. "In my wallet."

She could barely think straight. "What?"

He reached into his back pocket and yanked out his wallet. Through the haze of passion she realized he'd remembered protection this time. Seconds later he sheathed himself with protection and settled between her thighs again. As he kissed her with hot hunger, she knew they couldn't wait any longer. He slid deep with one solid thrust that sent her arching against him with a gasp, glorying in the way he filled her with hard pressure. Marshall stayed immobile, gazing down at Dana with bone-melting intensity that said he knew nothing else, felt nothing else but her. Her emotions swelled under a lash of sweet love. She wanted him, needed him with more than an overwhelming physical hunger. No man could equal him in any way, shape, or form. She'd never meet a man like him again.

As the pulsing inside her threatened to go volcanic, she twisted against him. With a savage, satisfied smile, he licked her nipples, rasping over them with long strokes. She shivered in excitement.

"Marshall!" She gasped, squirming.

He uttered a muffled growl as his hips ground against her, then started to thrust, picking up to hammering speed immediately. Everything blurred as all emotions, all sensations centered on the rhythm. Dana knew without one shred of doubt she'd never love any man as much as she loved Brennan Marshall. If today ended, here and now she wouldn't regret the soul-searing love and demanding passion.

Her hands found the bunching, rippling muscles in his arms and shoulders, then her fingers plunged through his hair as if grabbing for purchase. Breathing wasn't necessary, thinking impossible as sensation piled upon sensation. Marshall's rocking motion, emphatic and relentless, brought her to within an inch of detonating. She hovered on a skull-splitting edge, whimpering and panting. Dana felt him reach something deep and high inside, and it fragmented her world.

Then she did something she'd never done before.

A scream ripped loose from her throat.

She heard Marshall's guttural exclamation of satisfaction as he continued to slam deep inside her. His last ramming thrust took her over again, bursting sweet and hot. He shuddered, his entire body rigid.

For a second she heard the ghost's voices reaching for the heavens, mingling with their human counterparts in an eerie and incredible choir.

Chapter 21

Incredible. Total heart attack sex.

Marshall's brain attempted to register what had happened as he sagged onto Dana and tried to suck in a breath. As a little consciousness crept in, he realized he'd experienced the most breath-stealing sex of his life. He knew the idea of making love to Dana on this bed had sent him over the edge.

Not to mention the horny ghosts making racket.

He hadn't been able to keep his hands of her as alarm bells shrieked inside his head that Lucille might show up any moment and find her niece in a compromising position. He grinned. Had danger made him this hot, or was it Dana alone that sent him out of control?

Dana. God, she's so beautiful. So sexy. He managed to shift, leaving her body but not her embrace. As he rolled to the side he wrapped her tight in his arms. Her soft scent and warmth threatened to arouse him again.

His gut clenched. "Dana."

"Mmm." She moved against him and kissed his neck, her

hand skimming down to clutch his butt. "Oh, my gawd. We just, we just—"

"Had mind blowing sex on a heart-shaped bed?"

Her breath feathered against his jaw as she sighed. "You can say that again."

Silence flooded the room.

Silence.

"Marshall? Do you notice anything different?"

Oh-oh. A woman question. The kind that could get a man in trouble if he didn't think fast. He noticed that since they'd made love the first time she looked at him with desire and maybe admiration. Her eyes shown with a special potency that made his heart ache with deep longing.

He cleared his throat. "Yeah. I've noticed that you're still soft and..." He slid his fingers down to the apex of her thighs and found the softness that had enclosed him. "Hot."

With a startled sound she surged against him, and he teased her until she fell into another gasping, panting release. As she lay against his chest, breathing hard, he savored the warmth of her in his arms, and his heart squeezed on an emotion he recognized and dreaded. The thought of anything happening to Dana filled him with overpowering fear. It blossomed like a malignant bloom, growing until he wanted to roar in fury.

He wouldn't feel like this if she were a stranger.

He wouldn't feel like this if she were just a friend.

Emotions this powerful meant one thing.

Panic clutched him and he reacted without thinking. He released her, rolling to his feet and hitching up his pants. He staggered into the little bathroom and gazed into the mirror. Man-oh-man, his hair looked as if it had been processed through a blender. He sighed and pushed a hand through the tangled mass. It didn't make much difference. He was still a damned mess. When Marshall surfaced a few moments later, he'd already buttoned his flannel shirt and zipped his pants. Scanning the room, he found his baseball cap lying on the floor. Dana had knocked it off—he couldn't remember when. Snatching it up, he mashed it down on his head.

Dana rearranged her clothes, put her pants back on, and buttoned her shirt. His gaze pinned her, drawn to stare, to observe everything about the woman who owned him in ways she could never know.

Her cheeks went pink and her eyes glittered with a satisfied gleam. She looked so good he wanted to sweep her away somewhere hidden, somewhere he could indulge their fantasies until they wrenched the last teeth-clenching orgasm out of their system.

Her smile faded as he looked at her. "What's wrong, Marshall?"

Unable to resist, he walked toward her, cupped the back of her head and leaned down to place a kiss on her forehead. "Not a damned thing. Now what were you going to say earlier? Before I made you forget."

Dana's soft laugh sounded throaty and sexy against his ears. When she reached up and touched his beard, sliding her fingers over his jaw in an affectionate touch, he almost pulled her into his arms again. "I might be enticed to forget again. Ghosts or no ghosts."

"Speaking of ghosts, I wonder if the exorcism worked. Did you hear them?"

"Yeah, I think so." She sounded a tad embarrassed, and he liked the way her face flushed. "I know I heard us."

As they left the house, the night sky had turned into blue velvet with a blanket of diamonds, and he wondered how many more nights he would have Dana in his arms. Soon he'd catch the bastard that terrorized her and her family. She'd return to New Mexico and her novels. If he saw her again it would be the odd visit to Lucille's home. Deep inside this realization burned like acid, making him uncomfortable as a porcupine on a pincushion.

No. If he had anything to say about it, he wanted to see her as often as possible. Maybe they did have a chance.

As he drove Marshall recalled she hadn't finished telling him about her old boyfriend. Fred? Phillip? Frank? Whatever his name was. Part of him said to forget about the guy, but the other part recognized plain old-fashioned jealousy. He wanted to know about the man who had hurt her.

"Tell me about this old boyfriend of yours," he said before he could chicken out.

In the dim light of the car he could still see her frown. "You're not going to let that go, are you?"

"Damn right I'm not. After what I told you about Eva and Helen, it's quid pro quo."

She glanced at him, a furtive sidewise movement. "Frank was a year younger than I. Nothing significant. We met in a class and sort of danced around each other like mating birds for about six months. Not quite ready to—"

She stopped, and Marshall realized with a shock that she described the same situation between her and him right now. They had engaged in a minor war since the day they'd met. When he said nothing she continued with her story, as if she wanted to spill it all right this minute. "He was intriguing, smart and funny. We had few things in common but something kept drawing us back to each other."

"Lust?"

"Yes." She sounded hesitant to admit it. "He seemed to fight his attraction for me, and I know I fought what I felt for him."

"What did you feel for him?"

"It was more than physical attraction." She shrugged and slid down in the seat a ways. "We had an affection and a common base of understanding." She passed a hand over her face. "Friends warned me to stay away from him."

Marshall frowned. "Why? Was he dangerous?"

"No. Nothing like that." When he glanced over at her she looked edgy. Sort of like a seal under the beady-eyed observation of a shark. "We went out for drinks a few times. He seemed very good at getting me to reveal things to him that I had never told another man."

When she stopped he said, "Such as?"

"I talked about old boyfriends."

"Uh-huh." Again she dropped into silence and he wondered what it would take to make her regurgitate the entire story. If she held back this much there must be something pretty bad hovering around the edges. "How did he persuade you to talk about that stuff? Most guys don't give a rat's butt about former boyfriends."

She laughed. "You're asking me about an old boyfriend. What's you're excuse?"

She's got you, Marshall. By the balls.

He added a soft growl into his voice. "All right, all right. Don't change the subject. Why did he want to know?"

"I guess he figured he'd know my vulnerabilities, or he really cared about me. Maybe both. Anyway, I coughed up the info. He spent time putting down another boyfriend I'd had. Called him a jerk. Said he'd met him and the guy was only after me to get me in bed."

"That made you angry?"

"Yeah, actually. It did. I didn't believe the other guy only wanted me for sex. Frank apologized the next day, though. We had this...thing...whatever it was. It drew us together again and again."

Something nagged at him like an old wound plagued a man on a cold night. "Why did your friends warn you away from him?"

She stayed silent for so long he thought she'd never answer. "You're getting ahead of the story, Marshall," she said wryly. "One night I broke down and asked him over to watch videos and one thing lead to another."

His gut tightened as his head filled with pictures of a faceless man holding her in his arms and kissing her. He hated it. Hated the idea beyond words.

He'd been so absorbed in her explanation he almost missed the turn off to his own house. When he pulled into the driveway, parked and turned off the engine, he didn't open the door to go inside. The truth, right now, seemed more important.

Gripping the steering wheel, he looked at that dark sky with the sparkling stars and took a deep breath. "And?"

"We stopped. Actually, he stopped before we could…make love. He didn't have to say why. I knew his reasons."

"What was his reason?" Marshall almost reached for her, turning so he could see moonlight fall across her face.

"He was married."

He sucked in a breath as the truth ate a hole in him. "Married." Though he sounded like a parrot he felt like a fool. "Did you know he was married when you and he were about to make love?"

"Yes. But he was separated and had been for several months. He never did go back to her, even after he left me. I saw their divorce notice in the paper a few months after. I never saw him again."

She didn't hesitate, and that bothered him double. If she'd been an innocent in this he would have understood, but the facts screamed out at him like a neon sign. One word stood out among all others.

Adultery.

Images of Eva and Helen merged in his mind with Dana until the picture formed a three-headed woman. Bitterness shoved past restraint and he opened the car and got out. He started for the house. He didn't think about being polite or reasonable. Right now he wanted to be alone. Think about what Dana had said and why it burned a hole in his gut the size of Montana.

He heard the other car door open, and she ran after him. He let them inside the house, set the security system, then headed for the kitchen.

"Marshall." She grabbed his sleeve. "What's wrong?"

He spun around and she lost her grip on his shirt. "I just need some time to think."

He went to the refrigerator and rummaged through it for a cold drink. When he found one he popped the can and spewed cola all over the front of his flannel. He cursed and as he set the drink on the counter, more soda spilled over.

Dana reached for a towel, and she came at him like she meant to dab at his shirt. He took the towel and ineffectually wiped at the material.

"Marshall, what's this all about?" She reached for his shoulder. "Are you angry?"

He wanted to be, but he also didn't want to act like a jerk. Confusion and old memories ran amok in his head.

He took a deep breath and kept a straight face. "No. I'm not really angry."

Worry entered her eyes. "Are you jealous of Frank?"

"Of course I'm not."

"Then what is it? What set you off?" She looped the towel around her neck and planted her hands on her hips like a football coach ready to kick butt and take names. "And don't tell me it's nothing."

He should have known she wouldn't back away. Leaning back against the counter, he folded his arms, ignoring the wet shirt. "It's like this, Dana. I have a difficult time understanding why a woman would date a married man. Been there, done that. Got the T-shirt. The idea rubs me the wrong way."

Her mouth flopped open. Then closed. Then opened again. "I didn't commit adultery. We were just friends. We didn't do anything about the way we felt. We stopped before it could get out of hand."

"If he hadn't stopped would you have slept with him?"

Uncertainty flickered across the features he'd mapped with his fingers, his lips, and his memory. "I don't…I don't know."

"You don't know." For long, agonizing seconds he stared at her and she at him. For a moment he didn't know what to say or do. He shoved one hand through his hair. "Look, I need some time to think right now, okay? We'll talk later."

He walked away, feeling her gaze boring him in the back. She didn't rush after him or argue, and he knew they needed to discuss his feelings. Right now he didn't know how he felt.

Sunlight speared through the bottom of the curtains in the guest room, and Dana rolled to her other side with a groan. Her head throbbed, her throat ached and her eyelids felt as fat as Portobello mushrooms. A cold seemed to be creeping up on her.

Falling into bed after Marshall had retreated to his bedroom had been an easy thing. She'd been tempted to toss her pillows around the room like a madwoman to relieve a little anxiety. Beyond ruining Marshall's property she knew if she made that much noise he would have burst in the room thinking she'd been attacked.

She heard the rustle of someone moving down the hall, then the clank of pots and pans in the kitchen. All night she'd tossed, unable to sleep but for short snatches of half lucid dreaming. Dreams where she'd tried to make Marshall understand she had always regretted her actions with Frank.

Marshall had made his share of mistakes with women; he'd told her all about Eva and Helen yesterday and she'd seen a vulnerable side to Marshall she'd never imagined when she'd first met him. Maybe the uncertainty she'd seen in his eyes yesterday would have cleared by the time she saw him at breakfast this morning.

Maybe she'd made one whopper of a mistake telling him about Frank and now she'd lose Marshall because of it.

Maybe she'd never had him.

No. I've seen it in his eyes. He does care for me.

Sitting up, she put her hands to her head and moaned again. She rubbed her temples. Some painkiller for breakfast and maybe hot tea and toast would mend her world.

If only it were that simple.

After dressing and showering, she made her way into the living room. She found Marshall sitting at the dining room table with a cup of coffee. She expected to see a big meal in front of him. Instead his empty plate matched the contemplative look in his eyes.

A gentle smile touched his mouth, and relief flooded through her as she grinned. Maybe he did understand about Frank.

"Morning," he said. "Coffee's fresh. What would you like for breakfast?"

As he started to stand up, she said, "Let me make breakfast. As a thanks for your hospitality."

He nodded. "Okay. Thanks."

After she'd scrambled eggs and cooked up some bacon, she sat across from him. Should she bring up Frank or let it alone for now?

"Your aunt called," he said before she could make a comment.

Dana's head snapped up. "What? I didn't hear the phone."

He pushed back from the table and took his coffee mug and plate to the dishwasher. "About an hour ago. She says Neal hasn't regained consciousness and Gregory still maintains he doesn't know who attacked him."

"I don't know if I believe Gregory. Something isn't right."

"You can say that again."

She sneezed and pulled a tissue from her jean pocket. Dabbing at her nose, she looked at him and saw concern in his eyes.

"You all right?" he asked.

She sniffed. "I think I'm getting a cold."

His brow creased as he walked toward her and gently put his hand on her forehead. "You've got a bit of a fever. Maybe you should take it easy today."

Dana shrugged. "Can't keep me down for long. Besides, I'm a horrible patient. I can assure you that you don't want to play nursemaid."

Marshall allowed his fingers to trail over her cheek in a tender caress. She reveled in the sensation. "How about playing doctor?"

His sexy suggestion made her face fill with heat. "Why, Marshall, what a naughty boy you are."

He winked. "You haven't seen anything yet."

His drawl, combined with the heat in his eyes, almost made her wish she felt up to his suggestions. "Rain check? My head feels like a watermelon."

Gathering her into his arms, he pressed her head against his shoulder. "Of course." He held her for several moments, and she enjoyed in the sweet care of his embrace. "And I'm sorry about yesterday."

"Sorry?" she asked, not wanting to assume he meant his reaction to her news about Frank.

He pushed his fingers through her hair. "I wasn't really angry yesterday when you told me about your relationship with Frank. I was confused and needed to sort out my feelings."

Relieved, she looked up at him. "I hope you know that in a committed relationship—any relationship with a man—I want complete honesty. I'd never betray the man I loved by getting involved with another man."

She knew right then she admitted something profound. Her willingness to tell him, to spit it all out right then made her feel terrified and powerful all at once. His expression, warm and tender, told her all she needed.

"I realize you're not like Eva and Helen, and last night I thought about that good and hard. I don't want my relationship with you cluttered up by old baggage." His tone, soft and reassuring, gave her new satisfaction. "Forgive me for even doubting you one moment?"

She gave him a wicked smile. "I'd kiss you but I don't want to give you my cold."

"Bank it. I'll make you pay up later. Let's find you some cold medicine."

On the way to the hospital, Dana pushed the power window button and drew in the crisp morning breeze. Thunderheads reared over the mountains in the distance, threatening to converge on Macon by afternoon. Lovely. That's all they needed. More storms. Unexpected tears backed up in her eyes. Too many things had happened since she'd come to Macon. The car wreck that destroyed Bertha, her stepcousins almost killed, her aunt's house plagued by mysterious events, and horny ghosts.

She almost smiled. At least the ghosts would make for good fodder in her next novel. She never gave it thought before, but she knew her experiences with Marshall would translate, someday, into good background for her work. She could relay on the page all the passion and love she'd discovered in his arms. Something deep inside her said it would be good stuff.

Once at the hospital they found Aunt Lucille in the waiting room along with Logan.

Logan filled them in. "Skeeter's still up there with Gregory. I think if he waits him out he'll learn something."

Dana hugged her aunt. "It'll be all right. If anyone can get him to explain what happened, Marshall can."

"Don't count on it," Marshall said. "He's not exactly the forthcoming type."

With that he marched away, Logan following behind.

Aunt Lucille put her hand on Dana's forearm and drew her down onto a hard, cold plastic chair. "What's going on dear? You two look a little...different."

Dana didn't know how to say it. Didn't know if she could. How did you tell your aunt that you were doing the hunka chunka with a man? "Par for the course for him."

"I realize he's one intense young man, but you can't fool me. I know when something is going on." Aunt Lucille's face softened, her gaze scanning Dana with compassion and understanding that belied her reputation as eccentric. "You're like a daughter to me. You can tell me anything."

"Well, last night I told him about Frank. The man I…the married man I knew a few years back."

Aunt Lucille's brow creased in confusion, then cleared. "Oh, my."

"Yeah." She elaborated, explaining Marshall's initial reaction to the news, then his apology.

"I remember you telling me about that other man. Nothing happened between you, though, did it?" Aunt Lucille asked.

"A little something happened. I'm just lucky Marshall didn't think I'm scum."

Making a scoffing noise, her aunt took her hand and pressed it between her thin, cool fingers. "Now if that isn't a load of bull hockey. I've seen the way he looks at you."

Between embarrassed and intrigued, Dana squeezed Aunt Lucille's fingers, drawing comfort from her closeness. "How does he look at me?"

Warmth filled Aunt Lucille's eyes. "Like a man seriously, deeply in love."

Unwanted tears swamped Dana, and she sniffed. Reaching for a tissue in her handbag, she dapped her eyes. "Getting a cold."

"Uh-huh." Aunt Lucille's expression said she understood all too well. "I can see that. I take it the teary eyes mean you've fallen for him, too?"

"I—" Dana choked up and two tears escaped.

With a soft, reassuring noise, Aunt Lucille slipped her arm around Dana. "It'll be all right. A man like Marshall doesn't invest his heart lightly. He loves you." She snapped her fingers. "And he won't lose that love just like that. But I think I can explain why he reacted so strongly to hearing about Frank. Everyone knows his wife Helen had affairs."

"I know. That's got to make a guy cautious about other relationships."

"Everyone makes mistakes in their past, my dear. He's made mistakes, too. He can't judge you based on what happened with Eva and Helen."

Dana gazed out the window across the room at puffy clouds rising high in the west. "It's all right. We did talk it out so there's no misunderstanding." After several moments of silence, Dana said, "We cured your bed, by the way."

"What?"

"Don't ask me how we did it, but…"

Aunt Lucille's slow grin made Dana smile. "Yes?"

"We didn't get a chance to play back the original tape of the ghosts. But I think we exorcised them anyway." Dana ran the words together fast. "At least they seemed to let us know they like the ritual."

"Ritual?"

Her aunt's wide-eyed innocent look made Dana smile and she started to laugh.

Dawning understanding slipped over Aunt Lucille's face. "You didn't?" When Dana continued to laugh, Aunt Lucille's mouth dropped open. "You did."

Aunt Lucille's smile widened and she joined in the mirth. Soon she had Dana giggling and the two of them hooted while a couple also seated in the waiting room stared at them like they'd lost their sanity.

Chapter 22

Marshall followed Logan into Gregory's room, his thoughts geared toward making Gregory spill his guts. A rumble of thunder heralded another storm, and he thought for a second about Dana and her phobia.

I hope she isn't frightened. While he knew she was strong, he found it difficult to force back his protective feelings. His thoughts lanced him, burning hot in a way he never expected, ripping him as much as if he'd been stretched on a rack.

Skeeter sat in a chair next to Gregory's bed, flipping through an entertainment magazine with an air of boredom. Skeeter rose from the chair when Marshall and Logan appeared, his expression nervous. Gregory lay in bed with his eyes closed and Marshall wondered if the man had fallen asleep.

"Now ain't that a pretty sight?" Logan asked.

"He's been out of it for awhile," Skeeter said, tossing the magazine on the small bedside table.

"I'm not asleep." Gregory opened his eyes, leftover pain evident in his tight mouth and rasping words. "And I'm not talking to any more cops."

"I'm not a cop," Logan said, crossing his arms. He turned on his don't mess with me look. His dark hair hung loose around his shoulders, giving him a feral mien that had scared more than one suspect out of their minds. "So you can talk to me."

Gregory blinked. "Then you have no authority to ask me questions. Who are you anyway? Larry, Curly, or Mo?"

Logan leaned on the railing alongside Gregory's bed. "Look, I've dealt with South American drug lords with far bigger orifices than yours, and believe me your ass isn't big enough to hide in. So don't even try it."

Skeeter laughed. Gregory blinked again, his mouth dropping open slightly.

Marshall smiled, giving Logan his due. He'd forgotten how intimidating his friend could be. "I don't know, Metcalf. You'd better listen to him."

Gregory tried to look unimpressed, but Marshall could see the uncertainty in his eyes. "So if you aren't a cop, what are you?"

"D.E.A.," Logan said, his words clipped. "Don't. Even. Ask."

Skeeter chuckled again.

Gregory's face screwed up in disgust. "Very funny."

Logan looked at Marshall and asked in a deadpan voice, "I thought it was hilarious. Didn't you think it was amusing?"

"Hysterical," Marshall said, unable to hide a slight grin. "Now that we've got that straight, we need to know several things in rapid order, Metcalf."

"No way. If you think you can intimidate me—"

"Oh, we can do more than intimidate, believe me," Marshall said.

Marshall stared him down, hoping it would work as it had before. He moved to the left side of the bed and increased his glare. "I'm not standing this close to you because I think you smell nice. I'd think a smart guy like you would realize your silence isn't buying you anything but a bad rep."

Gregory snorted. "People in this town respect me."

"I suppose they'll also understand when word gets around that you refused to assist the law with an investigation."

"It doesn't matter. As soon as I'm out of this sorry excuse for a hospital gown I'm out of Macon, too. You won't see me again."

"What are you running from? Your guilt? You can't escape it by leaving a town, Metcalf. Guilt clings to you like flies on carrion."

"You're a bastard. I don't see what my little stepcousin sees in you. She must be nuts."

Marshall bristled. "Leave her out of this."

Gregory's smile held triumph. "What did she do? Tell you to get out of her pants? Or maybe you haven't gotten there yet? How do you like rejection? Doesn't feel too good, does it?"

Marshall tried to stem his own anger at this scumbag's assertions. Struggling with his professional demeanor, he decided the best route in dealing with Gregory lay in not reacting to personal attacks. "Doesn't it seem odd to you that you get slashed and then someone shoots your brother on the very same night?"

"Yeah, I do think it's suspicious. But I don't see the Sheriff's Department doing anything but harassing me," Gregory said, his voice laced with arsenic. "For the last time, I don't know diddly about what happened to my brother. Wouldn't surprise me if some girl he'd messed with decided to off him." Gregory sniffed. "I just want out of here and away from my crazy relatives. Lucille and Dana talking about screwing ghosts. Give me a break!"

Marshall smiled. "Oh, believe me, the screwing ghosts are real."

"What?" Gregory and Logan asked at the same time.

"Never mind," Marshall said. "I will find out the truth, no matter how long it takes. And it won't matter, Metcalf, if you're out of town when I do it. I'll find you and you will be brought to justice if you have any part in what has been happening."

"Gee, so nice of you to care about me. It's not like I'm not a victim here."

Marshall shrugged and stepped back from the bed. "You're about as far from a victim as it gets." Marshall tipped his baseball cap to the man in the bed. "See you around. And as they say in the movies, don't leave town."

As they left the room and Skeeter went back inside to keep an eye on Gregory, Logan asked, "You're kidding about the ghosts, right?"

Marshall felt heat rising in his face and hoped his friend wouldn't notice. "D.E.A, Logan. D.E.A."

"Hey, what mischief are you ladies cooking up now?" a deep male voice asked Dana and Aunt Lucille. Eric strode into the waiting area, looking handsome in his white medical coat.

Dana immediately thought of Kerrie and wondered if Eric had heard from her. It still hurt that they'd parted on bad terms. Dana hoped when all the shenanigans in Macon resolved she could touch base with her old friend and mend their friendship.

Aunt Lucille stood and gave him a hug. "We were just discussing the ghosts in my house."

Eric gave her a cock-eyed grin. "I dunno. I'm a man of science. I'm not sure I believe in things like that."

Aunt Lucille patted him on the arm and smiled with conspiracy twinkling in her eyes. "Not to worry. Dana and Marshall thought of a way to get rid of the ghosts."

His eyebrows shot up. "Oh, yeah?"

Dana gritted her teeth and smiled at the same time, feeling like her face would stretch out of shape.

Aunt Lucille nodded. "Complicated process."

"Very scientific," Dana said, then realized she'd dug a deeper hole for herself. *Good going, dunce. Next you'll be confessing the whole thing. Keep your trap shut.*

Luckily Eric approached the whole thing like a man, and that meant the finer subtleties seemed to go right over his head.

Eric sat down next to Dana. "I heard from Kerrie last night. She said she'd call you, but I'm not sure when."

"Oh, good." Dana sighed with relief. Maybe, if her old pal wanted to speak with her, their friendship couldn't have been damaged too much. "Is she having a good time?"

He shrugged. "You know Kerrie. The eternally optimistic. I think she'd have a better time if she knew you were out of danger."

"When I talk to her I'll tell her not to worry," Dana said.

"Good luck." Eric smiled. "So is Marshall upstairs with Gregory?"

Dana leaned back in her chair, reaching for her tissue and dabbing at her nose. "That's why I'm here, tagging along."

Aunt Lucille pouted. "Poor dear. You should be home in bed."

Eric frowned and leaned forward. "What's wrong?"

Gazing at the ceiling in exasperation, then back at Aunt Lucille and Eric, Dana smiled. "Just a cold. I certainly don't need to crawl into bed over it."

All doctor now, Eric placed his hand on her forehead. "You've got a fever. I'd do like your aunt says. Get Marshall to take you home. Do all the usual things. Drink lots of fluids, take a pain killer. Sleep."

"Yes, doctor," Dana said, then sneezed.

"See, he knows what he's talking about," Aunt Lucille said, crossing her arms as if Dana might refute it.

A moment later Marshall and Logan appeared. Dana felt her heart stumble and do a dip at the sight of Marshall.

After greeting Eric, Marshall stood with hands on his hips. "Gregory maintains he doesn't know who stabbed him or who shot his brother."

With a disconsolate sigh Aunt Lucille sank back in her chair. "Oh, dear."

"That's an understatement," Dana said, realizing she sounded like a grumbling child. "Macon is one big barrel of fun. This place could compete with Peyton Place."

Dana sneezed. Then sneezed again.

Logan chuckled. "Hey, Marshall, you'd better get Dana home. She'd got a cold."

Aunt Lucille patted Dana's shoulder. "And with that pneumonia you had recently you shouldn't take chances."

"I'm fine," Dana said, feeling a wave of heat pass over her. Yep, she had a fever all right, and she did feel like doo doo. "Nothing a little vitamin C and a nap won't take care of."

Marshall sank down in the chair next to her. "I need to stop by the office first. Can you last that long?"

Dana nodded. "Sure. No problem."

The P.A. system squawked. "Dr. Dawes to X-Ray, please. Dr. Dawes to X-Ray."

"Gotta go," Eric said as he popped up from the chair. "Maybe when Kerrie gets back we can all have dinner together?"

Dana shook her head. "I probably won't be here. As soon as this whole mess is over, I've got to get back home and finish my book."

In that moment Dana saw several emotions swing through Marshall's face, none she could be one hundred percent sure she understood. One emotion, though, seemed to stand out.

Disappointment.

Dana wore a simple turquoise, long sleeved suede-like tunic and matching pants as she stepped into Marshall's living room. He was nowhere in sight, so she glanced out the window and marveled that the storm clouds hadn't burst. They hovered over

Macon like dark harbingers all day, making her nervous and half expecting a lightning strike to slam close to her any minute.

She couldn't recall the last time she'd felt this jumpy. As she turned away from the window and slumped on the couch, memories vaulted through her. Marshall leaning over her, his tantalizing scent, hot expression and seductive words almost causing her to self-combust.

Another surge of heat overtook her, but this time it couldn't be fever. She sneezed, then took out a fresh tissue.

When Marshall emerged from the hallway, Dana didn't know if she could take the heart palpations as he strode toward her. He'd decided to wear a dark gray suit with a power red tie. His clothes fit like tailor made, and he looked so delicious her throat almost closed up.

God, the man could make me come by just looking at me. She felt her jaw go slack and was helpless to do anything about it. A wave of love slipped through her. "Marshall, you look..."

He continued forward until he stepped close, forcing her to inhale his warm masculine scent. "Like an idiot?" One corner of his mouth twitched up. "Go ahead and say it. I know you want to."

"No. Not at all. You look so handsome it makes my heart stop," she said breathlessly.

Damn! Oh, damn, I can't believe I just said that!

His face warmed into an unexpected, sexy grin that added to her heart's mad thumping. With assured male ego, his gaze coasted over her face and the rest of her body. "And you're beautiful. So beautiful I—"

She felt the heat and the gentleness hang in a balance, teetering on precarious ground. If she moved she'd break it. If he moved, he'd break it.

Marshall moved closer, and she sucked in a breath. Man alive she wanted his kiss so much she could almost taste him. *Oh, yes. Please kiss me.*

He made a small groan, and the husky sound reminded Dana of the first time they made love. The velvet soft sound of his voice as he'd coaxed her toward implosion. He'd whispered in her ear as he'd pounded into her, gasping her name and urging her to come. The hot, erotic words had shocked and delighted her all at once. As she stared at him she knew she'd never forget those moments as long as she lived.

He ran his fingers through his hair. Disappointment surged as he gave her a look with regret written all over it. Regret for almost kissing her? Remorse for not kissing her? She wanted to scream down the house in frustration.

Marshall checked his watch. "Come on, let's get out of here."

With a sigh she followed him out the door.

When they reached the community center, the number of cars surrounding the place didn't surprise Dana. Once inside the center people swallowed Marshall in well wishes. Sheriff Pizer and Mrs. Pizer stepped up, eager to congratulate him. Dana faded into the back of the crowd. She loved watching him talk, walk, and speak. Simple as that sounded, she found pleasure seeing him praised by others.

He turned and caught her looking at him, and without warning his dark eyes transformed into pure, smoldering sexual heat. The barn burner gaze lasted for but a few seconds, but she recognized it without fail. She'd know that wicked, toe-curling assessment anywhere. He tossed that look at her often enough, even when he'd suspected her of participating in a plot against Aunt Lucille. Sighing with pleasure, she managed to avert her gaze before she went into thermonuclear meltdown.

She waited until the horde filed into the main area. Folding metal chairs lined the room facing the small stage and podium. From the size of the crowd it would soon be standing room only.

The mayor snagged Marshall. The thin, balding man with the campaign smile shook hands with Marshall and gave her a passing glance of disinterest.

"Brennan, you're finally here. Listen, we've got a seat for you right up front with me and Tommy and his parents." The mayor looked at Dana. "Of course…um…we might have room for one more."

Dana felt a twinge of anger at the mayor's brush off, but she decided she didn't want antagonism to spoil her enjoyment. She opened her purse and held up the camera. "I'll stand in the back. Easier to get photos."

Showing sure signs of relief, the Mayor slapped Marshall on the back.

After the mayor left, Marshall smiled. He leaned closer and kept his voice low. "Sorry. He can be pretentious. I'll sit back here with you."

She waved one hand in dismissal. "No, no. Go on up there and enjoy the spotlight." She nodded toward a secluded spot near the pantry area hallway. "I'll stand back there and take photos." When he still hesitated, she gave him a grin designed to melt his suit. "Maybe we could have some time alone later?"

If she thought his earlier smile had caused her heart to go into spasms, his heat-filled eyes made her long for his kiss with everything inside her. "I'd like that. We need to talk."

"Sounds serious."

"It is. Very serious."

Not knowing whether to be worried by his words or enjoy the anticipation of being alone with him once again, she took up position in the back and watched the proceedings.

Of course the mayor puffed up and added too much pageantry to the ceremony, dragging forward with all the speed of a drunken turtle. As Marshall took the podium, his big grin seemed to encompass the room. She took several pictures in rapid succession, eager to obtain as many good shots as possible.

A tap on her shoulder startled her and she swung around. Jenny stood there, a look of concern on her face. Jenny's jeans and T-shirt surprised her. She'd never seen the young woman look anything but elegant.

Jenny grabbed her arm. "I need to talk to you."

"Can't it wait? I'm taking pictures."

"This is urgent." Dana stepped forward into the narrow hallway and Jenny waved her farther down the hall. "This way so no one will hear us."

Dana frowned, annoyed at the interruption. "Look, Jenny—"

"This is important. It's about Tabitha."

Concern flashed through her. "Tabitha? Dr. Eric Dawes' girl?"

"That's why they're not here. Tabitha had an accident on her bike and she's been seriously injured."

Dana's heart constricted. "Oh, God."

Jenny kept walking, reaching an exit door. She opened it and Dana followed, eager for information. "Eric couldn't reach you guys earlier because it just happened."

The door clicked shut behind Dana as they emerged into the dimness of approaching night. Clouds filtered out most of the sun, and a cool breeze blasted through Dana's hair. Thunder rolled close, and Dana reached for her father's ring as if it could protect her from nature. Lightning flickered and thunder groaned low.

Dana didn't have time to say another word, because Jenny reached inside her jacket and pulled out an evil looking piece of metal. She leveled the gun on Dana.

"Jenny, what the—"

"Shut up." Her mouth curled into a caricature of a smile. Blond and small she might be, but the gun made her ten feet tall. "One more word and I'll just shoot now."

Dana gave one thought to resisting, using what she knew of self-defense to render Jenny helpless. She didn't have time to hesitate and wonder why Jenny had pulled a gun in the first place.

Before Dana could move, the gun came down on the side of her head.

Chapter 23

Marshall didn't think the ceremony would ever end.

Trying not to squirm in his seat, he almost winced when words of praise were heaped upon him. When the mayor asked him to come up to receive the commendation, his knees had the consistency of rubber. His mouth felt pasty dry.

The mayor handed him the plaque, reading the inscription.

For bravery beyond the call of duty.

That's all he heard; his heart seemed to be somewhere around his neck. So far he'd managed to make it through the presentation without choking. He spoke a few words of gratitude.

Tommy and his parents beamed from the first row. Tommy had come through a terrifying situation, and that mattered more than this stupid plaque and ceremony. Marshall looked for Dana in the crowd. Seconds before he'd seen her in the back, snapping photographs. When they'd first arrived at the center she'd watched him, her gaze almost hungry. It had lit a fire in him so deep he'd almost torn through the crowd, grabbed her wrist, and tugged her into the pantry for a quick, blazing display of passion she'd never forget. He'd pin her against the wall and they'd bang away at each other.

"Speech, speech!" the crowd urged.

Silence hung. Dana no longer stood at the back of the crowd. She'd disappeared.

A million thoughts launched through his head. All of them bad.

Marshall realized the crowd looked at him in anticipation, some with worried frowns. He cleared his throat. "Sorry. All this attention has made my head swell so big I can't pry my mouth open."

Laugher filled the room, but Marshall didn't feel happy. *Finish the speech, and be quick about it.*

"Thank you to everyone who put this beautiful plaque together for me, and for everything you've done. Thanks to Tommy and his parents for thinking of this commendation." His words felt valueless on his tongue. He meant what he said, but his thoughts remained on Dana. "Thank you to the mayor, and Sheriff Pizer for putting up with me."

Then it hit him. Deep in the gut like a punch. Dana would still be taking photographs unless…

She is in trouble.

His gaze scanned the crowd one more time and saw no sign of her. "Thank you very much." Without another word he left the small stage. People whispered, no doubt surprised at his abrupt speech and exit, and he heard their murmurs as he stepped into the main area and looked for Dana.

His heart slammed in a furious rhythm as he barged through, checking rooms as he went. People went by, trying to add more congratulations. He acknowledged their praise far faster and more abruptly than he would have in other circumstances.

Sheriff Pizer grabbed his arm. "Hey, what's the rush? We've got a cake and punch. My wife has it all ready."

"Have you seen Dana?"

"No."

"Damn it to hell!"

A few people looked around, and Marshall realized he'd raised his voice above the murmur of people filing out of the central room. He didn't care. He left the sheriff standing with his mouth hanging open.

Oh, God. Something is wrong.

A search of the pantry room revealed nothing. His heart seemed to jackhammer in his chest. *Hurry. Hurry.*

He burst out the back door. Then he saw the camera and Dana's purse on the ground and his knees almost folded. His heart seemed to stumble and stop. He'd failed her. He'd allowed his own stupidity to make him forget that he'd vowed to guard her. As he tore back in the building to call for backup, one thing crystallized.

He loved her more than anything. And he would get her back or die trying.

I'd give anything for an aspirin.

Dana drifted in and out of consciousness for what seemed an eternity, feeling the sway of the vehicle as it bumped over uneven roads. She wondered where Jenny planned on taking her. Her eyes refused to open, her skull pounding with a dull throb. She'd had no time to avoid Jenny's vicious blow, and it had driven her to her knees. Instinctively she'd pressed her left hand to her head to stop the pain.

She'd attempted to cry out, but Jenny had grabbed her arm and told her if she made a sound she'd shoot her. Deciding the bitch meant what she said, she had let Jenny shove her into the big SUV nearby.

"Try anything and I'll kill you," Jenny's nasty little voice had rasped. "I'll leave you by the side of the road for the buzzards."

Now Dana knew that stupidity had gotten her into this predicament. She had, like a bat with no sonar, slammed right into the cave wall. *Could I have been any denser?*

Dana's mind, fogged by pain, grasped the idea that no one had seen her with Jenny. Jenny had stayed out of sight in the hallway, coaxing her away.

Seconds later Dana felt the car come to a swift stop, the sound of gravel spitting out from under the wheels. Dana couldn't hold back a groan as dizziness swamped her. *Fine and dandy. Jenny has given me a concussion.*

"Open your eyes. We're here. Time to take our final walk."

Our final walk? Doesn't she mean my final walk?

Dana heard the reality in her captor's voice and lifted her head, unable to keep back a groan. She opened her eyes and the waning sunlight filtered by clouds hurt her eyes. She looked down and saw her clothes splattered with something reddish. Her own blood. Looking down at her hands, she realized they were smeared with crimson that slowly turned dark brown. Cold with dread, she shivered.

Dana glanced at Jenny and realized for the first time how disheveled her captor appeared. Jenny's blond hair hung in straggles about her slim shoulders. It looked as if she hadn't washed it for some time. Her face, so smooth and youthful under other circumstances, had aged. Dana thought she caught hints of dark circles under the young woman's eyes, though she couldn't say for certain in the dim light.

Jenny opened her door and slid outside. "Get out."

Dana shoved open the passenger door of the SUV and almost fell out of the seat.

Dana held onto the door, her knees trembling and threatening to give way. Stunned, she absorbed the true reality of the situation.

Jenny Pizer had smacked her with a gun, kidnapped her, and now what?

Jenny Pizer was planning her death.

Why did Jenny want her dead?

With a dark twist of humor, Dana thought about all the things that would be solved if she died. She wouldn't have to wrestle with her autocratic landlord any longer. She wouldn't have to finish her second novel and hope it sold as well as the first. And last but not least, she wouldn't have to cope with the knowledge that she'd missed her chance to tell Brennan Marshall that she loved him.

Marshall. Did he know she'd been taken? He must realize something bad had happened by now. Though uncertain of how much time passed since the abduction, Dana received the vague impression not more than twenty or thirty minutes had gone by since they left the community center.

She sucked in deep breaths of air. Night gathered at the edges like a hovering demon, waiting to cloak them in darkness. Lightning arched overhead and thunder reminded Dana of lurking danger. Her limbs suffered a fine trembling and her stomach twisted with anxiety.

Through thick pines Dana saw a narrow trail. Jenny had pulled off the road, almost into a ditch. They'd gotten this far, but from the rutted, washed out condition of the road, it didn't look safe to use the vehicle from this point.

"What are we doing?" Dana asked through lips that felt like rubber. "It's getting dark."

Jenny pulled on a backpack, dressed out for hiking with thick boots, a waterproof jacket and a determined smile. She held the weapon in her right hand and a flashlight in the other.

Jenny flicked on the flashlight. "You're going to die."

Dana sighed, unable to control her anger. "What did I do, break a church rule?"

Dana knew she'd done it then because Jenny started toward her. "Don't mouth off to me, bitch."

As Dana took an involuntary step back, Jenny halted, smirking with satisfaction. She'd managed to show her advantage by scaring Dana into retreat. "You know Marshall is never going to find you. You're never going to see him again."

"Are you doing all this because you're jealous?" Dana flapped one hand in dismissal. "I'm out of Macon shortly and then he's all yours."

At first Dana thought Jenny might whack her with the gun again. Instead, the smaller woman stayed immobile. "You're mouthy, did you know that?"

Though her words came out scathing, Dana thought she heard an element of hurt in Jenny's voice. Jenny gestured with her weapon. "Move it out. Up that trail." She pointed with her other hand. "When we get to the top you'll wish you'd never been born."

How original. Dana wanted to scream at the deranged woman that she ought to get better lines. "What is it you want?"

"Start moving or I'll shoot you where you stand. And believe me, I wouldn't miss."

Dana did as told. Better to live longer and maybe formulate a plan. She grasped her father's ring. *Please Daddy, give me strength. Give me something I can use to survive. Please, Marshall. Please find me.*

The narrow avenue between the trees started gentle and fast became steep. They weaved through the first stand of spruce and stumbled over rocks. Thunder growled like an angry god, intent on warning them of a transgression. Dana realized, to her surprise, that she didn't care about the threatening storm. More immediate danger wiped thoughts of phobia out of her mind. Still, she would rather be somewhere safe and warm when the beast lunged. She looked from side to side, hoping to see a building somewhere, but gave up that idea almost as quick as it came. Dana got the impression they'd traveled into a remote region near Macon with no homes nearby. Heavy cloud cover masked the area and she couldn't say which direction they headed.

"It's getting hard to see out here. Since I'm in the front maybe I should have the flashlight," Dana said.

"I don't think so."

Dana slipped on the sandy soil and her right ankle gave a painful wrench. She dropped to one knee with a hiss of pain and a curse. "Son of a bitch!"

Jenny jabbed the weapon into her back. "Get up!"

Dana swayed to her feet. "I'm up. I'm up."

As Dana started forward her flats slipped on rocks, unable to keep traction. At this rate she'd sprain something worse. Her ankle already throbbed.

"Walk!" Jenny poked her in the ribs with the gun.

For what seemed like miles, Dana struggled to keep balance as blisters cropped up on her feet. Her breath rasped from exertion, her head protesting with a continuous pounding.

Although Macon's altitude was about eighty-five hundred feet, Dana guessed they'd climbed much higher than that. With the higher altitude and approaching darkness came the onset of cooler temperatures. An occasional flicker of lightning and rumbling from the heavens never let her forget a tempest could settle upon them any time. Add cold temperatures to getting waterlogged, and hypothermia became a definite possibility. Dehydration could kill her right along with the weather. Maybe Jenny had no intentions of shooting her. She'd leave her out here, helpless, until she died of exposure.

No. I won't give in to defeatist thinking. I can survive if I keep my cool. I am not helpless.

As the winding trail evened out, the rain started. Dana's breath gasped out as cold water splashed onto her in a great torrent. Unlike Jenny, she wore no rain gear. Her throat felt raw and her eyes gritty. A deep cough issued from her chest.

She must survive long enough to see Marshall's face again. To kiss him and tell him that she loved him. Thinking positive seemed difficult at a time like this, but negative thoughts would mean a quick death.

Night sounds intruded, the howl of a coyote or dog, the hoot of an owl, the screech of another unknown animal.

For an eternity they walked, and when they reached a slight clearing in the trees Dana saw a small cabin. The logs looked rough-hewn but almost new, and sitting next to the structure was a sedan.

Dana came to a halt. "That's the car that ran me off the road."

Jenny grunted. "Good guess. Aren't you smart?" For the umpteenth time she prodded Dana in the ribs with the weapon and this time it hurt like hellfire.

Dana cursed, vowing she'd snatch that gun away from this fruit loop and then break her arm. "You don't have to keep doing that! I'll do whatever you want."

Jenny pursed her lips. "Oh, really? Didn't your mommy teach you right? Don't you have a mind of your own? Or are you going to follow like a little lamb? Would you jump off a cliff if I asked you?"

Dana decided not to answer.

"Open the door," Jenny snapped, shoving Dana toward the cabin so that she almost stumbled. She jammed a key into Dana's hand.

Obeying, Dana unlocked the door and opened it. She pocketed the key, hoping Jenny wouldn't notice. Jenny nudged her through the door, and once inside Jenny flipped on the light switch. A couple of lamps flooded the small room with light. From what Dana could see, the cabin consisted of a living room and dining area, kitchen, and possibly one or two small bedrooms. It appeared to be built for vacation and not for roughing it.

"Who owns this place?" Dana asked.

"My father."

Incredulous, Dana turned and glared at her captor. "Does he know you're doing this?"

Despite rain gear, Jenny's jeans looked sopping wet. She didn't seem to care. "Of course not." She pushed a strand of hair back from her face. Water dripped from her nose, but she didn't seem to care about that, either. Her face, devoid of the usual tons of makeup, had a bizarre innocence overlaid by unrepentant evil. "But then my father doesn't really care much what happens to me."

When Jenny stared at her without saying another word, Dana decided now would be the best time to extract answers from this crazy package. "You don't have to do this, you know. Marshall doesn't love me."

Jenny laughed. "I saw the way he looked at you at the ceremony. At first I thought I'd just kill you. That way when you were gone I'd comfort him and he would have come to love me. He would have seen that I'm far more woman than you've ever been. I could have given him what he needs. But now it's too late."

Dana saw then what she hadn't recognized earlier. More than anger and jealousy motivated this woman. Insanity ran unchecked through the girl's eyes, hard and glassy.

Dana slipped her hand into her pocket and gripped the key, holding it between her fingers like a short knife. "Hey, is there a first-aid kit around here? I'd like to patch up this cut on my head."

"You aren't getting any first aid, or food or water. You're going to die, remember?"

Dana swallowed hard. "How?"

Jenny laughed. "You'll find out soon enough." Jenny walked toward her, slow and methodical, a gleam of satisfaction mixed with hate.

"I don't understand why you hate me so much."

"Because you're the stupid bitch that took Marshall from me. I've always wanted him. I've wanted him since I was a girl. Then you came to town."

"All this because you're in love with him?"

"Oh, no. There's more."

A wave of dizziness assaulted Dana and she leaned against a wall. She wanted to slide down the rough surface and land on her butt for a rest, but she must remain alert and prepared to run. Her head hurt, her feet hurt, her ankle throbbed, and cold slithered up and down her body like a snake. At least in the cabin she escaped the weather. Rain drummed on the rooftop with an unrelenting beat. Thunder and lightning came closer.

"So, if I'm going to die, at least tell me what more is," Dana said.

Jenny's white, perfect smile showed how far she'd lost it. Jenny hadn't taken off her raingear or pack and she kept her flashlight and weapon. Dana estimated how she might leap forward and knock away the gun long enough to stab Jenny with the key. Nope. Jenny would blast her with a bullet before she could say mother may I.

Jenny moved around the room a little, as if observing things about the place she'd never noticed before. When she didn't speak, Dana pressed on. "Did you have something to do with the strange occurrences at my aunt's house?"

Jenny's brow furrowed. "I don't know what you're talking about."

"How about Gregory and Neal. Did you attack them for some reason?"

Jenny sneered, then burst into laughter. Her shoulders shook. "Those two clods. They never knew I was using them until it was too late." Her amusement disappeared. "Too bad they didn't die." Her laughter stopped abruptly. "Another example of my failure."

"You attacked them?" Dana asked, incredulous. "Two grown men?"

"Oh, come on. You don't think all women are as weak as you, do you? I'm in good shape."

Outstanding. I'm stranded on a mountainside with a madwoman from purgatory. Super bitch extraordinaire.

"Why did you hurt them?" A horrible thought came to Dana, one that seemed beyond belief. "Were they in on this with you?"

Jenny's curses filled the room. She waved the gun around, and Dana hoped Jenny had put on the safety. "No. I've been screwing them for the fun of it." She leaned forward and tapped her chest with the gun barrel. Dana's breath sucked in. If that thing went off all her troubles would be over. "I've been tempted to shoot you before. In front of anyone and everyone. But I'm not like my mother and father think I am. I've got control. I've been in control my whole life."

While she never would have believed Jenny capable until now, a macabre picture formed in Dana's head. "You slept with Gregory and Neal because you love Marshall?"

Jenny shrugged. "Why not? They wanted me and I wanted them." Jenny's cold, hard eyes said it all. "You're not one of those dumb bitches that believe a man loves you just because he has sex with you?"

Dana ignored her statement. "The night you attacked Gregory and Neal, what set you off?"

"While I was with Gregory I messed up and called him Marshall." Jenny pushed back the hood on her rain jacket and her hair flopped forward into her face until she looked up. "He got mad and told me that he didn't want me talking like that while we were screwing. I got pissed and told him I was also making it with Neal. That made him even madder and he left the hotel. I followed the bastard to your aunt's house and stabbed him. He didn't even see me. Then I headed to Neal's hotel room."

Jenny paced for a second, and in the lamplight Dana saw Jenny's forehead and cheeks bathed in perspiration. Though feverish and feeling like someone had run over her with a backhoe, Dana knew she must remain alert.

A cough rattled in Dana's throat, and the soreness became worse. "Gregory is a pig."

Maybe if she sympathized with the mad girl, she'd let her go in favor of finding Gregory and Neal later and cutting their nuts off.

No such luck. The squinting, nasty glare in Jenny's eyes didn't dissipate one iota. "And Neal is a weak, simpering, effeminate bastard who couldn't screw if his life depended on it."

"Why did you hurt, Neal? Did he insult you, too?"

Jenny leaned against a big leather chair, her eyes holding a vacant quality. "I told him we should be adventurous. Go out in the woods and make it like animals in the bushes. That excited him. After we finished doing it, I told him what I did to Gregory. Told him what I planned to do to you. He tried to get the gun away from me. I shot him, and he fell and hit his head. I didn't wait around to see if he was alive. I hoped he was dead."

Dana's mind froze like a glacier, slow moving and incapable of seeing an escape route. Though not a psychologist, Dana knew enough to acknowledge Jenny must have had a history of problems, psychological and otherwise. Her comment about her mother and father thinking she'd lost control gave some indication. Dana's mind turned to Marshall and if he had time to find her. Until then she would find a way to survive.

"Logan, I want answers out of Gregory now," Marshall growled into the phone at the Sheriff's Office. "We'll keep in radio contact." He took a shuddering breath. "Keep Lucille in the dark about Dana for as long as you can."

"I'll join you as quickly as I can," Logan said.

Marshall acknowledged his friend and then slammed down the receiver. When he'd realized that Dana had been kidnapped and maybe injured, he'd mobilized the off duty deputies attending the ceremony to search for Dana. All the while his heart ached and he muttered a plea. "Hang on, sweetheart. I'll find you. Just hang on." He rushed for the door and ran smack into Sheriff Pizer standing in the doorway.

Sheriff Pizer, still dressed casual, had an expression on his thin face Marshall had never seen before. "I've got something important."

"What is it?" Marshall knew he shouldn't snap at his boss, but at this point the only person in the world he cared about was in terrible danger. "I've got Skeeter, Douglas, Martin, and Griggs set to search already."

Pizer gripped Marshall's arm. This close Marshall could see the man's face had gone ghost white. "There's something you should know. I just got a call from my wife. She expected Jenny to be home but she wasn't there. She...um...said earlier that she didn't want to attend your ceremony."

"What's that got to do with anything?" Marshall asked, wrenching out of Pizer's grip and heading toward the arms room.

Sheriff Pizer followed and watched as Marshall gathered enough weapons to make an arsenal. "Jenny left a note on the fridge." Pizer's eyes went glassy with tears and his voice came harsh. "A suicide note."

Marshall froze, his instant worry for the sheriff mingling with urgency to find Dana. "Suicide."

"There's more. She said in the note she was taking Dana with her. That they were both going to die."

"What?" Marshall couldn't believe what he was hearing. Then, before Pizer could say another word, Marshall started out the door. "We've got to find them. You coming with me?"

Pizer hesitated for all of a second, then followed.

* * *

Think fast, Dana. This is spiraling into the land of no return.

Jenny became more agitated second by second. Dana couldn't guess when this woman would snap. And if that happened…she didn't want to think about the consequences.

She allowed another deep cough to shudder through her lungs. Jenny peered at her. "You going to die on me before I can kill you?"

"I just might."

As Jenny came toward her, Dana stayed immobile. Let the woman think she'd frozen to the spot with fear.

"What are you going to do?" Dana asked, her voice sounding harsh to her own ears.

"We're going to jump off that cliff I talked about earlier. You and I. Together."

Stunned, Dana didn't move, her muscles tightening with tension.

Think. Think. Make your move when she gets closer.

Jenny reached her, stood rigid and stone-faced. "You know, we could have been friends if you hadn't tried to take Marshall from me."

"I'm sorry. I'll leave town. I won't tell anyone what happened. Marshall will never see me again."

Now or never. She drew her hand from her pocket and aimed for the woman's throat, jamming it forward with a punching motion that sent the key into the side of Jenny's neck. Jenny reacted with a scream, dropping the gun and reaching for her throat. Dana sprung for the door and slammed through it.

She heard a second screech of pain and the animal quality of Jenny's howl made Dana dash headlong down the steps and veer to the left. She'd scampered maybe fifty feet into the forest when she heard the shot and felt the fire of pain.

Chapter 24

Rain slashed against the windshield of Marshall's car as he drove with Pizer into the mountainous area south of Macon. Minutes ago they received a report from Logan that Neal regained consciousness and had said that Jenny shot him. Neal reported that Jenny had whispered about leaping off a cliff to her death and that she'd stabbed Gregory.

"The big problem is knowing which cliff Jenny was talking about," Pizer said, his voice filled with an agony Marshall never expected to hear coming from this man.

Marshall nodded. "There are dozens of roads into the mountains. A virtual suicide banquet waiting to happen."

"How are we going to find them in this mess?"

Lightning illuminated the sky with an almost constant glow. The tempest reminded Marshall of the storm that had battered the area the day Dana arrived in town.

I'll find you, sweetheart, if it's the last thing I do.

Marshall kept the vow going in his head, silent and strong. The prayer gave him sanity. Marshall knew Dana would fight for her life. Strong, capable, and tougher than any woman he knew, she would live through this ordeal.

"I'm sorry Marshall," Sheriff Pizer said. "If I'd had any idea that Jenny would do this..."

"Let's worry about that later. We need to find them now."

Pizer looked defeated, as if his daughter had already committed suicide. Had Pizer been ignorant of his daughter's illness? Or had he ignored danger signals until the timer rang and rescue came too late? Maybe, just maybe, they could save Jenny at the same time they rescued Dana. Without a doubt, Marshall knew he would save Dana's life first and worry about Jenny second.

The radio crackled and Skeeter's voice came over the airwaves. Pizer picked up the handset and told Skeeter to go ahead.

"Sheriff, we have a report from a woman saying she saw an SUV heading up Gold Pan Road. She didn't think anything of it at the time. She was out walking the dog. Then she heard the report about Dana's kidnapping and the description of Jenny's vehicle and put two and two together."

"Stand by," Pizer said. He turned to Marshall. "I think I know where they're going." Pizer's voice shook, as if terror seized him by the throat.

"Where?"

"Our cabin."

Marshall's throat tightened. "That's near Jagged Point ten miles from here." He cursed and floored it, and the Grand Cherokee gripped the road with a vengeance.

Pizer's face told it all. Maybe time had already run out. "Skeeter, get up to Jagged Point and my cabin." He gave directions to the cabin. "Use extreme caution. I have reason to believe my daughter will do anything. Anything."

After Skeeter signed off the sheriff reported to the dispatcher where they'd headed.

Pizer slammed his fist onto the consol of the vehicle. "Damn it, why didn't I think of the cabin first? We haven't been up there since last fall. We're getting ready to sell the place and I just didn't think of it!"

Marshall gripped the steering wheel tightly. "Do you have any clue at all why she wants to take Dana down with her?"

Pizer didn't answer for a long time, and Marshall almost asked again. The older man cleared his throat, and when he spoke he sounded on the verge of tears. "Jenny's always been wild and sometimes totally unable to control emotions like anger. But she's smart. She managed to get that scholarship to Stanford. She's always been able to hide what she is…she always kept her grades up and volunteered at the hospital…"

"But she didn't always know right from wrong," Marshall said.

"We tried so hard, her mother and I, from the time that girl was a baby."

Marshall knew his boss struggled with the ironies of Jenny's mind. Brilliant didn't mean incapable of insanity. History was filled with cases of famous people who'd lost their minds to various mental illnesses, or had struggled on a daily basis to keep one foot in reality. Jenny Pizer might be sharp, but she'd slipped the last cog.

Pizer shifted in the seat and gazed out his side window. "Nobody knows this, but back when she was a teen, she got pregnant and decided to keep the baby. Before the word got out she miscarried and then tried to commit suicide. See, before tonight Jenny always seemed to take her anger out on herself. She could snap at her mom and I, and maybe make snide remarks when life didn't go her way, but she never hurt anyone physically. We thought about taking her to a shrink more than once. We wondered if the things she did were just anger or something more. We should have listened to our instincts."

Marshall didn't plan to psychoanalyze Jenny now, not when the woman he loved more than life could die any moment. "Do you know what set her off this time?"

"I was hoping you would know."

"Why me?"

"Because Jenny's had a crush on you for some time. Didn't you know?"

Marshall grimaced, remembering how Jenny pursued him. He recalled the football game and Jenny's lip lock. "I knew she liked me, but what's that got to do with—" He glanced at Pizer. "Wait a minute, you don't think I was having an affair with your daughter?"

Pizer shook his head. "I know you too well for that. Besides, I know you've got some deep feelings for Dana Cummings."

Seemed half the town realized that he'd fallen hard for Dana before he knew it himself. As fear raced through him, he prayed he'd get another chance to tell Dana that he loved her.

Please, God. I want to marry her and have babies with her and grow old with her in my arms.

Rain came in merciless sheets, and Marshall slowed the car.

Pizer pointed out the windshield. "There's Gold Pan now. Looks like recent tracks."

Marshall saw the rain filled tracks washing away under the torrent and turned down the road. The tires lost their grip in the mud and fishtailed, but Marshall brought them under control. Then he received a mental flash. He'd learned long ago never to second-guess a strong premonition.

He snapped up the radio and put a call out for Logan. When he located him Marshall asked, "Logan, what type of firepower do you have with you?" He glanced at Pizer a moment, then pressed onward. "Didn't you used to have a Remington .308 with a tactical night scope?"

Pizer glared at him, but Marshall ignored him.

Logan said, "You got it. But it's back in Atlanta. It's not like I expected to need it in sleepy little Macon. Besides in this weather and no ambient light, it would be hard to use."

Pizer cursed and grabbed the radio mike out of Marshall's hand. "I should have known you were some sort of spook or military man."

"I'm neither." Logan's voice crackled in the static. "I'm former D.E.A."

"D.E.A., C.I.A., F.B.I. I don't care what you are or what you were. You're not shooting my daughter. We're giving her a chance to surrender and to walk away from this so she can get the help she needs. Jenny is not a murderer."

Pizer signed off before Logan could reply.

Marshall had never experienced an easy relationship with Pizer, and now the stakes had risen about as far as they could go. As the vehicle rolled over muddy road and the wipers struggled to clear the rain, Marshall knew he'd have to use plain talk to get Pizer to understand his position.

"Jenny attacked Gregory and Neal with intent to harm or kill. Jenny said she'd kill herself. She's kidnapped Dana with the intent to hurt her. We can't ignore that," Marshall said.

"When we get to the cabin, I'll go in first. I'll talk her out of whatever she's got planned."

"Would she have access to a gun?"

"There aren't any weapons at the cabin, but we have some at the house. She might have taken one after her mother and I left for your ceremony." He sighed. "Jenny was taking so long to get ready. She said she'd come by the ceremony later. I just thought she wasn't interested. I was damned stupid thinking that. She's gone to every party she thinks you might attend. This one shouldn't have been different."

Marshall didn't offer words of comfort. As long as he'd worked with this man, Marshall never realized the secrets hidden within their family. "What if Jenny can't be reasoned with? What then?"

"I can talk her out of it."

So that was it. Marshall prayed Pizer was right. "If you can't, I will take care of this myself. You saw the stuff I took from the weapons room. I'm not underestimating your daughter, Sheriff. If she's as smart as you say, she's a bomb waiting to go off."

Pizer glared, but he seemed to be contemplating. "It's not like we're going into a situation where there are several highly trained men ready to blow our heads off."

"We don't know what we've got. We don't know what she's planned. I understand what you're thinking, sir, but you understand this. I'll do anything to bring Dana out of this alive."

If Pizer fired him after this incident, he didn't care. All he cared about now revolved around saving Dana's life. He felt he'd tested the fates. Would the woman he loved be snatched from him before he could tell her?

Pain seared through Dana's right side like a whip, and for a stunned second she wondered if she would die here and now. She grabbed her side and stumbled, veering left and right. Desire to live pushed her feet into action. Another shot zinged by, thumping into a tree trunk not far from her and spraying bark over her. She plunged into the woods as if an entire army pursued her.

Weaving side to side, she darted from one tree to another, hoping the night would cloak her. Rain soaked her again, and along with the burning in her side, she shivered deep and hard. Darkness messed with her peripheral vision and she bumped into another tree, scraping her left arm on bark. Jamming back a pained cry, she stumbled forward. Rocks, trees, fallen branches—the entire area seemed against her.

Jenny's shrieks of frustration and anger seemed to echo in her head.

Cold air rushed down her throat as her lungs labored, and over the rasping of her breath she heard her heart pounding. Or was it the sound of Jenny giving chase? Renewed terror sent her careening through the forest with no thought to direction. She didn't feel the hot burn in her side anymore; fleeing overshadowed her pain.

It seemed she'd run forever, half feeling her way through the treacherous landscape, squinting through the rain in her eyes. Lightning crashed, and she gave an involuntary shriek.

"Oh, God!"

She clammed a hand over her mouth as if she could take back the exclamation. Lightning came again and the fork of fire sent another sound to her lips. She stopped running in time to see the cliff.

Dana grabbed the tree limb next to her as her knees threatened to buckle and her side renewed it's throbbing beat. Her heart banged unmercifully, and she wondered if it would burst from her chest. A few more steps and she would have plunged off the edge.

I'll be damned. Lightning saved my life.

Weakness slid through her limbs and Dana realized her entire body was filled with a fine shivering. Her insides felt like gelatin.

No. I have to keep moving. Work my way along the cliff, back track somehow. Back to the main road. Back to Marshall.

She stepped back from the cliff edge, moving quickly until she put yards between her and certain death.

She listened. Rain pounding the earth. The howl of a canine in the far distance. Thunder rolling through the hills.

Then, before Dana could struggle against it, darkness closed around her and silenced the sounds.

* * *

The sharp teeth of icy wind battered Marshall right through his rain gear. Sticky mud sucked at his boots and rain dripped off the hat he donned before leaving the vehicle. With a pack and climbing equipment strapped to his back, Marshall carried the most paraphernalia. He hoped he wouldn't need the climbing equipment, but he wanted to be prepared.

Logan joined them at the bottom of the trail and brought along his own weapon, an assault rifle that looked as lethal as its reputation. Pizer stopped as light filtered through the tree and glowered when he saw Logan's weapon choice. Logan sent him an uncompromising expression and said nothing.

Lights shone through the cabin windows as Marshall, Logan and Pizer edge closer to the small clearing surrounding the old dwelling. They hunkered down so they'd be less visible.

Pizer inched forward, but Marshall grabbed his sleeve. "We'll go around the sides while you approach the front. Is there is a back entrance?"

Pizer nodded. "Yeah. Enters the kitchen."

"I'll take that," Marshall said.

Pizer reached into his back pocket and drew out a key. "Here, take this in case you need it. Opens the whole place."

Marshall wanted to say that he didn't plan on being that subtle if all hell broke loose. Instead he watched Pizer head for the front door. Marshall's muscles tensed tight as wire.

"You think he can do this?" Logan asked.

Shaking his head, Marshall shifted and stood. "I'm not sure. I hope he can, but I'm glad you brought the extra firepower. I've got a hunch little Miss Jenny Pizer isn't as harmless as her father would like to think."

Seconds later Logan and Marshall headed for their respective destinations. At the back door Marshall found a window with no covering and he peered into the lunch box size kitchen. No sign of anyone. Weapon at the ready, Marshall reached for the doorknob. When he tested it he found it locked.

He wondered if at any moment he would hear the sound of gunfire as Jenny took out her father. While Marshall had no driving reason to suspect that Jenny would harm him, in a situation like this, he wouldn't rule out anything.

A shadow passed over the doorway from the living room to the kitchen. Seconds later Pizer strode through the kitchen and waved at him.

Pizer unlocked the back door. "They're not here."

Marshall's gut rippled with uneasiness and a despair he refused to acknowledge. He cursed as he stepped inside the cabin. "Any sign other than the lights that they've been here?"

Logan stepped into the kitchen from the living room. "No sign of them outside."

With a sigh, Pizer said, "Nothing is moved around, but that doesn't mean they weren't here. I found blood on the floor near one wall, and a bloody handprint near the front door."

A new curse issued from Marshall's lips as he strode by them and into the living area. He looked over the bloodstains. "Dana might be hurt. I hope Jenny hasn't shot her."

Pizer's lips thinned in apparent disapproval. He shifted and his leather gun belt crackled. "I don't really think she'd do that. Like I said, she's no killer."

Marshall didn't have time for conjecture. He started for the front door. "Come on. We've got to start tracking them. There's no time to waste."

Something cold and wet ran down Dana's face. Dazed, she blinked. Where am I? She groaned as water splattered her cheek.

Shudders wracked her body, cold seeping as far into her bones as it could get. *So freaking cold. I am so cold.* Pain lanced through her right side as a cruel reminder of what had occurred. She gasped.

"Get up, bitch."

A jab in the side sent an ache radiating through her. She couldn't stifle a moan as she struggled to her feet. Mud clung to the front of her and dripped off her chin. Water ran down the back of her neck and sent a deep shiver through her body. As she struggled to focus, she saw Jenny's silhouette in the darkness.

Jenny reached up to touch her wound. "You stabbed me, you bitch. Give me one good reason why I shouldn't kill you now."

A cold, dark feeling ran over Dana; she knew without a doubt that her good luck had expired. Seconds later a strange calmness settled on her, chasing after the fear. "Because you don't want to hurt Marshall."

"What's he got to do with it?"

"You love him, don't you?"

"Yeah. So what?"

"If you kill yourself and me, it will hurt him. And that isn't what you want. He's innocent in all this. He doesn't want either of us to die."

Jenny stayed silent, for quite some time, as if she might reconsider.

Finally Jenny whispered, "I don't care. I just don't care anymore."

Ice gripped Dana's heart as Jenny grabbed her arm and marched her through the dark. *Think. Keep her talking.* "Where are we going?"

"To the cliff."

"How did…how did you find me?"

Jenny let out a derisive noise. "I spent a lot of time up here with my parents. I know these woods even in the dark."

"Jenny, if you don't care about me, think of your parents. They love you. They don't want you to die. It will hurt them so much."

Jenny marched on, her grip tightening. "They've never cared."

"I don't believe that. And even if it were true, you're the only one who can rule your life. Stop right here. Right now. You can change everything. Don't waste your life."

Jenny seemed to hesitate the slightest bit, as if she might take the bait, but the pause lasted only a millimeter before she plunged onward.

Desperate, Dana said, "Do you really want everyone else to win? Don't you see if you give up now, they win?"

Stopping, Jenny loosened her grip. "You didn't care when you stabbed me."

"I'm sorry. You understand why I tried to get away, don't you?" Dana swallowed hard, her breath rasping in her throat. "Please think about your missed opportunities. You have so much to live for, Jenny. Let me help you."

Jenny yanked Dana's arm and she almost fell. Jenny cursed. "Give me a break, bitch."

Dana tripped over a rock and pain shot through her side as she struggled to keep upright. She hissed in a breath. "Let me go now. We'll go back to the cabin and get help for both of us. I'll tell the authorities that you changed your mind. They'll go easier on you."

Dana could see the outline of the cliff not far away, and a small part of her brain screamed that now she would die. Fate had thrown her a nasty curve she couldn't escape. Her heart pumped like mad, thumping in her ears and quickening her breath. A wave of nausea curled through her. A litany ran through her head.

I love you, Marshall. No matter what happens, I love you.

They came to a stop several yards from the cliff, and Jenny kept her fingers clutched tight around Dana's arm. "It's time."

"Jenny—"

"Shut up!"

Fight now, Dana. Fight now. It's your last chance.

Dana moved, throwing all her weight against Jenny. Jenny let out a screech of rage and brought the gun up as she staggered. Dana grabbed Jenny's wrist, shoving it skyward. She brought up her knee, aiming for Jenny's gut. She connected. Jenny grunted with pain. A shot rang out, then two.

Dana thought she heard a man shouting.

Jenny recovered and leaned toward the cliff edge.

A cracking noise assaulted Dana's ears and her gut clenched in wild fear even as Jenny's grip on the gun loosened and the weapon fell to the ground. The earth beneath Dana's feet shifted as if a hole had opened in the world.

"No!" She cried out again as soaked earth broke away and Jenny took her over the cliff.

Chapter 25

"No!" A cry broke from Marshall's lips as a piece of cliff give way under the struggling women. He started running before the figures disappeared over the edge. "God, no!"

Pizer might have cried out when the women went over the edge, but Marshall didn't remember hearing him and he didn't care. Marshall sprinted, pack and all, toward the place they'd disappeared.

If Dana died...oh, God.

As they rushed to the edge of the cliff, Logan shouted, "Take it easy! We don't know how much more will give way!"

"I think it was just a few rocks at the edge," Pizer said, his voice harsh and filled with stunned disbelief. "Jenny!"

Nothing but wind answered his cry. Lightning illuminated the rocky ground before them, harsh blue and yellow light dazzling Marshall's eyes. Marshall edged toward the cliff. Logan followed behind.

Pizer's voice came out like a sob as he arrived at the edge before them. "They're dead. Oh, sweet Jesus!"

Marshall didn't have time for the man's grief. As his own heart tightened with horror, another part of him refused to give up on Dana. She was too tough. And he loved her too much to let her go.

He recalled the snowy day when he'd rappelled down to the car crash that held Eva and Tabitha. Then he remembered finding Kerrie's husband's dead body at the bottom of a cliff not far from here. Marshall's body seemed to freeze, a dread deeper than anything he'd experienced gripping his soul.

Had he fallen into a nightmare?

Logan grabbed Marshall's arm. "Don't go any closer without a rope. You don't know if the rest of the cliff is stable."

Marshall swore. "You think I give care about that?" He took his flashlight and aimed the beam downward. There he saw something that staggered him and gave him hope. "Oh, God. Oh, God."

"What is it?" Logan asked.

"I see her. She's on a ledge. Dana is on a ledge."

"Is Jenny there?" Pizer asked.

"No," Logan said softly.

With his heart careening with sudden hope that Dana might still be alive, Marshall dumped his pack and pulled out equipment. "Help me, Logan."

Logan responded without hesitation, helping Marshall put on a waist harness with a carabiner, a steel shackle with a click-on attached. Marshall retrieved steel-cored nylon rope from the pack, more than twice the length of the drop he'd need to reach Dana.

Once they had the equipment put together, they attached the rope to a sturdy pine. Marshall took the doubled rope and put it behind one shoulder, through the carabeener and then held it in front with one hand to act as a brake. He slipped on gloves.

"Be careful," Logan said grimly. "That's a damn long way to the bottom."

Within minutes Marshall jumped off, his feet bouncing on the rock face with each lurch down. And as he moved closer to his destination, he hoped with all his heart that he'd find Dana alive.

Am I dead?

At first Dana couldn't be sure. Was there pain in heaven? Her head throbbed, but it had hurt before the cliff gave way and she sailed over the edge with Jenny.

Dana's entire body felt numb. *Oh, my God. Am I paralyzed?*

She didn't know which thought terrified her more. Death or being unable to move for the rest of her life. She also couldn't remember what happened after she'd fallen off the cliff. Perhaps the panic ripping through her heart had made her pass out.

Had someone cried out her name as she'd pitched over the edge. Marshall?

Water. She felt water hitting her face. Would it never stop? Dana struggled to open her eyes and succeeded. Her vision cleared and she moved her arm, reaching up to wipe her face. Good! Not paralyzed. At least not entirely. Then she saw something moving far above her. A black shape dangled over the precipice.

Perhaps she'd hit bottom and somehow not broken every bone in her body?

It made no sense.

She shifted her limbs slowly and surely, bracing for agony that never came. Her side throbbed but it didn't feel any worse than it had earlier. When her fingers slid off the ground and dangled in air, she sucked in a terrified breath.

I'm on a ledge. I'm on a ledge!

Dana stiffened. She didn't dare lift her head, and she almost didn't breathe. New fear slashed through her body like the lightning that continued to brighten the heavens. A light shone in Dana's eyes, blinding her for a second before she saw a man rappelling down the cliff face. Marshall. As he got closer she saw his dark hair matted against his face...a face filled with desperation, determination, and fear.

Hope made her breathe. Marshall would save her.

An overjoyed smile creased his face when he looked down on her. Dana thought she'd never seen something so wonderful in all her life. She thought she heard him whisper a thank you over and over.

"Dana? Sweetheart, I'll be right there. Don't move."

She did as told, too afraid that one wrong twitch would spell disaster.

"Marshall?" she croaked the question, her throat dusty and dry as desert.

"It's all right. Are you hurt?"

"No. I mean, I don't think so." The last part slipped out as a sob. "Please get me out of here."

"I love you, Dana. I love you," he said raggedly.

Joy filled her and stifled the fear for a second out of time. Tears flooded her eyes. "I love you, too."

A smile, fleeting and filled with emotion, touched his lips.

"I'm almost there. Hang on." He hovered above the ledge. "I'm not going to put my weight on the ledge." He held out a length of rope that looked attached to him. A big loop. "You're going to have to slip this over your shoulders. Move very, very slowly."

A shudder rolled through her body, and she held her breath as she inched her arms up and caught hold of the rough rope. "Got it."

"Now slip it over your head and around your waist."

Dana heard a cracking noise and for one terrified moment thought that was it.

The ledge was breaking.

"Get the rope over you now!" Marshall's voice held a note of fright she never would have imagined hearing in his voice.

Please don't let the ledge go now. Not now when I'm almost there. Almost in Marshall's arms.

Frantic, she slipped the rope over her head and under her arms. "I'm in!"

Seconds later the rope drew tight around her waist, almost painfully. Marshall pulled upward. "I've got you."

Her feet left the ledge and she hung in mid air. A strange mingling of panic and relief surged through her. Marshall had her. She'd be all right. He began to climb and they went up, up as two figures above worked to lever them to safety.

"Dana, I need you to help me. Crawl up. Use your feet and hands so you can reach me."

She reached for the rocks. Her hands trembled and refused to take hold. "I can't."

Immediately she hated herself for uttering the words.

"You can," Marshall said.

I can.

She clawed and crawled and then he grasped her arm. "Climb onto my back."

"I'm too heavy."

"No. Trust me."

She did trust him. With her life. He helped her onto his back and they started to ascend. Dana clung to Marshall, arms around his neck, legs clutching his waist, trembling with cold and shock. The pain she'd ignored for some time came back. Dana decided she wouldn't think about it. Wouldn't care. Nothing mattered but Marshall's warm body and the security she felt now that he was here.

Their progress seemed to take forever. Inch by inch, moment by moment. Logan urged them onward; she recognized his voice. As they reached the top, Logan and Sheriff Pizer dragged them up and over. Dana fell from Marshall's back and lay on the muddy ground shaking and shuddering.

"Is she hurt?" Logan said as Marshall struggled out of his climbing gear.

Dana cleared her throat. "No."

Marshall stood and slipped his gear off, then reached for the rope around her waist. "You're bleeding."

"She shot me when I got away," Dana said, her voice warbling. "It's not that bad."

Logan fumbled in his pack and drew out a first-aid kit, and when he squatted next to her she saw Sheriff Pizer standing off to the side, his face a mask of shock and disbelief. A wave of sympathy overcame her. At the same time she realized the rain had stopped.

Marshall removed the rope from her waist and she sat up. "Sheriff Pizer?"

He turned toward her, his eyes glassy.

"I tried to stop her," Dana said, her throat so tight it ached. "I tried."

Pizer nodded, his expression never changing as he turned away.

Marshall cupped her face, and she looked into the dearest, most loving eyes she'd ever seen. Tears slid down his face. "I thought I'd lost you. I love you. I love you so damned much."

That did it. She crumpled, sobbing in earnest. He gathered her tight against him. "Marshall, I—"

"It's all right. I've got you. You're safe."

She buried her face in his soggy rain gear and let the terror of the last few hours escape in much needed release. "I…I thought I'd never see you again."

He buried his hands in her wet hair and tilted her face up. "Marry me."

Logan chuckled. "Fine time for a proposal, Marshall."

Marshall released a descriptive expletive and threw his friend a look that said 'screw you' and yet conveyed his joy at the same time. "I don't care." He gazed at her again. "Marry me."

She smiled and the tears came harder. "You just try and get away from me, Brennan Marshall."

"Is that a yes?"

"Yes. Yes. Yes." Then she kissed him.

Two weeks later

Dana grinned as she read over the last line of the chapter she'd completed in long hand. It felt good. Really excellent. Like most writers, she knew when she'd produced something that worked well.

She'd spent the last three hours writing like hounds snapped at her heels. The first draft of her new horror and romance creation was almost three fourths finished. Since the horrible night she almost lost her life, Dana hadn't taken one thing for granted. New inspiration seemed to fire her imagination in to high gear. She'd never written anything this fast before, and it felt fantastic.

Her aunt hovered over her the last two weeks, but Dana knew that Aunt Lucille needed time to get over the shock of everything that had happened. Gregory and Neal left Macon after giving evidence about their involvement with Jenny. Dana had a feeling things would never be the same between Aunt Lucille and her two stepsons.

Sheriff Pizer resigned his office. Rumor said that during the upcoming election Marshall would be voted in as the new sheriff.

Dana winced as her side let her know that not that much time had gone by since she struggled for her life on the mountain. She'd spent a couple of days in the hospital recovering from her minor injuries. The bullet wound had amounted to a small crease along her ribs. At Marshall's insistence she moved into his house once she'd left the hospital. He'd become mushy lately, and she loved it. A silly grin tugged at her mouth as she thought about how he asked her to live with him.

He'd leaned over her hospital bed and kissed her until she nearly melted into the bed frame. Then he'd looked deep into her eyes. "The second Eric says you can leave the hospital, you're moving in with me."

"Is that an order, Marshall?" she asked with a grin.

Warm and soft, his eyes had burned with a longing and passion that still stirred her heart. "Damn straight. I want you in my arms day and night. Every chance I get. Any chance I can get."

While he went to work during the day, Aunt Lucille popped over to visit and often stayed most of the day, reporting back to Dana's anxious mother. Mother wanted her to come home, but Dana didn't want to be parted from Marshall. When she'd told her to expect a wedding invitation in the mail any day, her mother almost had a heart attack. Still, she'd sounded overjoyed.

Dana experienced moments, often at night, when a nightmare reminded her of those horrifying seconds when she'd pitched over the cliff. Marshall's arms always sheltered her, giving love and comfort.

As she breathed in the cool air, she knew she'd found a home here in Macon. A sanctuary where she could write and live and love Marshall until they both turned old and gray.

"Dana, you'll never guess who is here," Aunt Lucille said as she burst onto Marshall's patio like a whirlwind. "And he's bought friends."

Dana grinned as her aunt flounced over to the hammock.

"Let me guess," Dana said, standing and putting her arm around Aunt Lucille. They headed for the sliding glass doors. "Is it the big law man?"

"The one and only. And he's brought Eric, Tabitha, and his fiancée."

Dana stopped. "His fiancée?" When her aunt just smiled, Dana stared at her like she'd lost her mind. "Who, you don't mean—?"

"She means me," Kerrie said as she walked in with Eric, Tabitha, and Marshall not far behind. "You didn't think I would let you get one up on me, did you?"

Dana squealed...all the females screeched and rushed toward each other for a group hug.

Marshall and Eric gave a collective groan.

When the ladies parted, and congratulations filled the air, Aunt Lucille rushed into the kitchen to make drinks for them.

Marshall walked toward Dana, a tender smile on his mouth. A rush of love and lust hit her right in the stomach. He slipped his arm around her and kissed her forehead. Marshall looked so handsome with his baseball cap and flannel, all topped by a satisfied smile. She wanted to eat him up, right there and then.

"Excuse us a moment. I've got to talk to Dana," Marshall said.

Eric snagged Tabitha and Kerrie and headed toward the kitchen. "Come on ladies. Let's leave them alone."

Tabitha protested, but she grinned. Kerrie winked.

Dana slipped her arms around Marshall's neck, and before she could say a word, he kissed her in a no-nonsense fashion that made her knees weaken. The embrace went on until she thought she'd drown. When he released her she let out a gasp. Somewhere during the kiss his hat had slipped off his head.

"Oh, boy," she whispered, dazed. "Think the ghosts in Aunt Lucille's basement would mind if we visited them?"

He laughed and kissed her nose. "I think they've finally got satisfaction."

She giggled. The horny ghosts hadn't been heard from since the night she and Marshall had shown them how it was done. Dana had played back the tape recording of the ghosts and discovered it was blank. Nada. Nothing. So they had no evidence the horny ghosts ever existed.

Lightning brightened the room. She flinched. Marshall tightened his hold on her and she reached up to grasp her father's ring.

He looked at the jewelry. "All right?"

She nodded and smiled. “I still find it ironic that lightning saved my skin.”

Darkness moved through his gaze. “I still can’t think of that night without being thankful you’re here with me.”

“Me, too.” She gazed at this strong, wonderful man and knew he’d be with her, be by her side all her life.

He kissed her forehead and brushed his fingers over her cheek. “I love you.”

When she managed to pull away from another bone-melting kiss, Marshall held her tight with one arm. With the other hand he reached in his front pocket and brought out a red velvet box. “Its ready, sweetheart. The jeweler called this morning at the office.”

Dana let out a yelp as she released him and latched onto the box. “Oh, Marshall.”

She sighed as she looked at the princess cut diamond solitaire sparkling with a thousand prisms of light. Marshall took it from her and slipped it on her ring finger, then he kissed her hand. His dark gaze spoke of sweet love and forbidden pleasure.

“I love you,” he whispered. “Marry me.”

She laughed. “You’ve asked me that how many times now?”

He flashed her a boyish grin. “I’m going to ask you every day until we’re in that church and we’ve signed on the dotted line. I’m going to ask once a day for the rest of our lives.”

Slipping into his arms, she whispered against his lips, “Yes, Brennan Marshall. I’ll marry you. Every day of our lives.”

Dana savored the thought that in less than a month she’d be Marshall’s wife. Life didn’t get any better than this. She also knew she’d learned many lessons from what had happened on the cliff. She wondered more than once how fate, destiny, and her own determination had brought her to this happy point.

Thunder rolled over the mountains. Although Dana would always be cautious about storms, she had found a new peace.

~END~

About the Author

Suspenseful, edgy, thrilling, romantic, adventurous. All these words are used to describe award-winning, best-selling novelist Denise A. Agnew's novels. Romantic Times Magazine called her romantic suspense novels DANGEROUS INTENTIONS and TREACHEROUS WISHES "top-notch romantic suspense." Denise's record proves that with paranormal, time travel, romantic comedy, contemporary, historical and romantic suspense novels under her belt, she enjoys writing about a diverse range of subjects. Writing tales that scare the reader is her ultimate thrill. Snappy banter is her favorite dialogue, and she not only likes reading it, she loves writing it.

Denise's inspiration for her novels comes from innumerable sources, but the fact she has lived in Colorado, Hawaii, and the United Kingdom has given her a lifetime of ideas. Her experiences with archaeology have crept into her work, as well as numerous travels through England, Ireland, Scotland, and Wales.

Denise lives in Arizona with her real life hero, her husband. She has just finished writing a romantic suspense featuring a firefighter hero, due to be released in the Fall of 2003.

Note: Dangerous Intentions by Denise A. Agnew is the winner of the Treble Heart Books award for Best Romantic Suspense 2001-2002!